A Heart Divided

Books by Kathleen Morgan

BRIDES OF CULDEE CREEK SERIES
Daughter of Joy
Woman of Grace
Lady of Light
Child of Promise

THESE HIGHLAND HILLS SERIES
Child of the Mist
Wings of Morning
A Fire Within

HEART OF THE ROCKIES SERIES
A Heart Divided

A CULDEE CREEK CHRISTMAS
All Good Gifts
The Christkindl's Gift
One Perfect Gift

Giver of Roses
As High as the Heavens

A Heart Divided

A NOVEL

KATHLEEN MORGAN

Revell

a division of Baker Publishing Group
Grand Rapids, Michigan

Published by Revell
a division of Baker Publishing Group
P.O. Box 6287, Grand Rapids, MI 49516-6287
www.revellbooks.com

Printed in the United States of America

Library of Congress Cataloging-in-Publication Data
Morgan, Kathleen, 1950–
     A heart divided : a novel / Kathleen Morgan.
        p.   cm. — (Heart of the Rockies)
     ISBN 978-0-8007-1884-8 (pbk.)
     1. Ranchers—Fiction. 2. Vendetta—Fiction. 3. Ranch life—Colorado—Fiction. I. Title.
     PS3563.O8647H4 2011
     813'.54—dc22   2010051486

This book is a work of fiction. Names, characters, places, and incidents are the product of the author's imagination or are used fictitiously. Any resemblance to actual events, locales, or persons, living or dead, is coincidental.

11   12   13   14   15   16   17   7   6   5   4   3   2   1

No man, having put his hand to the plough, and looking back, is fit for the kingdom of God.

Luke 9:62

Prologue

Colorado Rockies, late July 1851

A giant, blood red moon rose in the blackened sky. The air lay still, warm, and heavy with moisture from an impending storm. Cattle in the stock pen bawled loudly, milling about until dust blanketed them in churning, choking clouds. Yet, as sweltering as the eve was, the hand clasping the revolver shook with an apprehensive chill.

Swathed in shadow, the man dropped the empty liquor bottle and dug into his trouser pocket, extracting a rumpled handkerchief. "It's time for that reckoning, Wainwright!" he snarled as he mopped his sweaty brow. "Time to settle up, you lowlife, lying varmint. Whatever comes of this night, you've only got yourself to blame."

He stuffed the handkerchief back into his pocket, checked his revolver one more time, then stepped from the shelter of the barn. Staggering toward the small cabin, he fumbled as he tried once, then twice, before successfully cocking the gun.

"Wainwright!" the man croaked out the word, his voice

raw and whiskey belligerent. "Get your sorry hide out here. You're not getting my ranch without a fight."

For a long moment, all was quiet. Then an oil lamp flared brightly within the dwelling and the sound of muffled voices spilled from the open windows. Footsteps echoed on the pine plank floors.

The front door swung open. Light streamed out onto the hard-packed dirt to puddle before the little house.

A man's tall frame filled the doorway. One hand gripped a rifle. Behind him the form of a woman, heavy with child, moved.

"Who is it, Edmund?" she murmured anxiously. "What does he mean? Was this his ranch?"

"Not now, Mary," her husband growled, never taking his gaze off the disheveled man standing but fifteen feet away. Gently, he pushed her back inside. "Let me handle this."

"It's over, Caldwell!" Edmund Wainwright then cried. "I won your place fair and square. Now, it's mine. Get on with your life, and let me and my family get on with ours."

"It'll never be over!" Jacob Caldwell bellowed back. "We're ruined, me and my wife, and you tell me to get on with my life? Why, you blackhearted, cheating card shark! It won't be over until one of us is dead. Now, come on out. Fight me like a man."

"You're drunk. I won't fight a drunk."

Caldwell's trigger finger jerked convulsively. A shot cracked through the air, the sound echoing down the valley and out to the mountains as the bullet spent itself just shy of the porch.

"Come on out, you lily-livered coward, or I'm coming in to get you!"

"Have it your way, then, you whiskey-besotted fool," Edmund Wainwright roared. "If you're so set—"

A movement at the far edge of the cabin caught Caldwell's

eye. He swung toward it, stumbling. Inadvertently, his finger once more squeezed the trigger.

Again, the sound of gunfire exploded in the air. This time, though, it was followed quickly by a child's scream.

"Nicholas!"

Wainwright lunged from the doorway, his rifle clattering onto the porch as it fell from his grasp. "He's shot you," he cried as he ran to where his son now lay crumpled on the ground. "That crazy fool's gone and shot you!"

In stunned disbelief, Jacob Caldwell lurched back. He stared at the sight of his enemy kneeling now to gather up the bleeding child into his arms. Unbidden, a crazy impulse to fire pierced his drunken fog.

Do it. You've got nothing to lose. If the boy dies . . .

Lightning slashed across the sky. A woman's scream tore through the air, the onrushing crack of thunder adding its own spine-chilling emphasis. Caldwell's hand froze in its upward swing.

He stood there for what seemed a lifetime, then shoved the revolver into the back of his trousers. "As I said before, Wainwright," he muttered as he staggered into the blackness from which he'd first appeared. "Whatever comes of this night, you've only got yourself to blame."

Rain began to fall in loud, splattering plops. Caldwell paid them no heed. As he hurried away, though, another cry rose on the wind that had swiftly followed in the wake of the storm.

A woman's cry . . . one that suddenly changed from agonized sorrow to a keening, physical anguish.

1

Colorado Rockies, early September 1878

"I can't, Papa. I just can't!"

Sarah Caldwell turned a pleading gaze to the unkempt man squatting beside her, hiding in the shadow of the Wainwright bunkhouse. For an instant, their glances locked.

He stared back, a hard, implacable look in his eyes. The faint ember of hope that her father might relent, even at this late a moment in their unlawful plan, died.

She looked to where her two older brothers stood behind them. Caleb's and Noah's features mirrored the same ruthless determination. Sarah inwardly sighed.

They'll follow Papa in this, just as they go along with most every other fool scheme he cooks up.

"Please, Papa," she said, trying one more time. "I-I've changed my mind. Stealing's wrong no matter how much we need the money. And now you want me to do . . . do this? I can't. I just can't."

His gnarled hand jerked her to him. "Oh yes you can, girl!" His lips hovered inches from her, and his low-pitched voice grated against Sarah's ears like gravel over a washboard. "It couldn't get any better than this. Wainwright and most of his men are gone on the fall roundup, and there can't be more than a servant or two in the main house. And the only able-bodied man left on the ranch is that hand over yonder. I didn't bargain on him being so close by, but what's done is done. Besides, we'll be back in no time."

"But Papa, that wasn't the plan—"

Her father's grip tightened. "Sarah, no more, do you hear me? We've all got to play our part. And there's nothing so hard in doing what comes natural. Do you want Danny to die, just because you won't dirty your purty little hands?"

At the reminder of her seven-year-old brother, Sarah's gut clenched. With a strength that surprised even her, she twisted free of her father's grasp.

A grudge, twenty-seven years of soul-rotting enmity, had brought them to this. Though she and her brothers hadn't even been born when it had all begun, the consequences dogged their lives as relentlessly as they did her father's. It didn't matter that she wanted no part of it. They were family. And family stuck together through thick and thin.

She expelled a rueful breath. "Have it your way then, Papa. I'll do it, but *only* because of Danny. I'll do it this once, but never, *ever*, again."

"Don't make such a fuss, little sister," Caleb hissed over her shoulder. "If you play your cards right, all that hand'll have time for is a few kisses before we're back. That's *all* we expect of you."

Noah laid a hand on her shoulder. "It'll work out just fine, Sarah. You'll see."

As her father stood, she shot her oldest brother a grateful look. Twenty-one-year-old Noah had always been her best friend and confidante. He'd also never been all that enamored of their sire's often harebrained schemes. In this particular case, though, like Sarah, Noah felt compelled to carry out the robbery for their youngest brother's sake.

The three men pulled out flour sacks with makeshift eye

hole openings and tugged them over their heads. Then, though well aware the ranch was minimally staffed, they checked their revolvers one last time before making their stealthy way toward the large white-frame house. Once her father and brothers were safely around the back, Sarah stepped from the protection of the bunkhouse and strode toward the barn. As she walked, she licked her lips—a nervous gesture that never failed to soothe her jangled nerves. Never failed, that is, until today.

How am I going to charm that man? she wondered, fixing her sun-squinted gaze on the back of the tall, shirtless figure standing in the back of a wagon unloading hay. He was powerfully built, the play of muscle and sinew along his arms and shoulders moving in rippling, effortless precision. The hot Indian summer sun beat down on him, and sweat gleamed on his body.

Sarah swallowed in distaste. *What if he does try to kiss me?* At the consideration, her gut churned unpleasantly. *I've only kissed a boy for the first time last month, and that just because it was my eighteenth birthday. How am I ever going to make a grown man think I know what I'm doing?*

She toyed with the top button of her white cotton blouse. Heat flared to her cheeks. Bosoms. She was going to have to show her bosoms.

But all men liked bosoms. That much was evident from watching the town's crib girls whenever she thought Papa wasn't looking. Yet would bosoms be enough in this case? She wouldn't know unless she tried.

With a small sigh, Sarah loosened the first three buttons. A trickle of perspiration slid between her still modestly exposed cleavage. She bit back a tormented groan.

Mama, forgive me, she thought, her face flaming fire hot. *I know you raised me better than this, but you're not here anymore to talk sense into Papa, and what else can I do?*

13

She halted, jerking her embarrassed gaze down to her long skirt. The coarse brown cloth stirred in the weak breeze. *Maybe a show of limbs might help too. The crib girls certainly seem to think it does.*

After a passing hesitation, Sarah grabbed the skirt's front hem and tucked it into her waistband. A shabby petticoat and hint of slim legs appeared.

A movement just then caught her eye. The ranch hand jumped down from the wagon and disappeared from view. Her pulse quickened. *What if he's gone up to the main house? Papa and my brothers are sure to be inside by now.*

She had no choice; she had to stop him. Sarah broke into a run, the movement of her bare feet on the drought-parched earth stirring little eddies of dust.

Do it for Danny . . . for Danny . . .

The man was standing beside a horse trough on the side of the barn, pouring water over himself, his strong, brown hands gripping a bucket high over his head. His face and upper body glistened as the water slid down his naked chest and long, sinewy arms. Sarah stopped in her tracks.

A dark brow arched as he caught sight of her. "And what can I do for you, little lady?" the cowboy asked, lowering the bucket back to the ground.

His voice, deep and resonant, rasped across the sensitive ends of Sarah's tightly strung nerves. She choked back an inane giggle, forcing a slow—and what she fervently hoped was an enticing—smile to her lips.

"A better question is, what can I do for you?" Sarah purred, using a phrase she'd heard the crib girls use.

He stared at her as she once more moved toward him, his jet black eyes never missing a thing from the seductive sway of her hips to the unbuttoned blouse and revealing display of petticoat. And, as his appreciative gaze raked her, it was the hardest thing Sarah had ever done not only to endure his avid perusal but to keep on walking forward.

Finally, she halted a few steps from him. With what she fancied was a provocative toss of her long, pale hair, Sarah settled her hands on her hips. "Want to get to know me better, cowboy?"

He moved toward her until they stood but a hairsbreadth apart. Sarah's eyes widened. Despite the day's heat, a chill swept through her.

What do I do now?

He was tall, towering over her small form. At the realization of his inherent size and strength, a primitive, feminine fear washed over her. How would she hold his interest long enough to draw attention from Papa and her brothers?

An impulse to lift a prayer to God filled her. Mama had always taught her to turn to the Lord in times of need. But Mama had been dead five years now, and Sarah hadn't prayed, much less set foot in a church, ever since. Besides, asking advice on how to tempt a man didn't seem a particularly appropriate request of the Almighty.

Do what comes natural . . .

With trembling hands, she touched the bronzed form before her, sliding her fingers up a hard, muscled arm to trail consideringly across the water-damp hair on his chest. "Well, cowboy?"

A low chuckle rumbling in his throat, he pulled her to him. "Who are you, anyway? And is this just some game, one girl daring the other to try out her feminine wiles?"

For an instant, Sarah's mind went blank. *Whatever is he talking about? Think. Think fast or all will be lost.*

"And what if it *is* a dare?" she asked, sudden inspiration striking her. Her arms lifted to encircle his neck. "Either way, I win."

His eyes narrowed. *How old is she? Seventeen? Eighteen?* And where had she come from? Was she some new hire to help with the household chores? If so, it was strange that he hadn't noticed her arrival.

She had pretty green eyes, delectable lips, and a pert, charming nose in a face framed by a thick mass of corn-silk-colored hair. Far too attractive to be playing games with grown men.

A girl with her kind of looks was a powder keg on a ranch like this, lacking only a fool cowboy or two to set off an explosion. Better he nipped her fledgling seductress role in the bud. She needed a lesson—and badly—before someone less scrupulous took advantage.

With a wicked grin, his hands settled on the girl's waist, and he pulled her even more tightly to him.

"Well, if that's what you think, there's a lot you can do for me, little lady," he growled, his voice deep velvet and suggestive. "What exactly did you have in mind?"

The color faded from the girl's face. For a long moment, he thought he had finally frightened her into backing off. Then thick, brown lashes fluttered prettily against her cheeks.

"Anything you like, cowboy. I only want to make you happy."

Just as I thought. The man's mouth quirked in amusement. *She's an innocent playing the woman.*

He pulled the girl into his arms and lowered his head toward her. "Then, for starters, how about a kiss?"

Before Sarah could protest, his mouth slanted over hers. The shock of his warm, firm lips, so sure, so knowing, took her breath away. She gasped, her hands slipping from his neck to wedge between them. Jerking back against the solid, stubborn barrier of his arms, her hands balled into fists and she began to pound at the flesh so close to hers.

Compared to this bold assault, her birthday kiss had been little more than a chaste if awkward brushing of lips. Alarm filled her, the knowledge she had achieved her goal paling beneath the startlingly tantalizing onslaught of his mouth. Both repelled and strangely attracted by the conflicting emotions his kiss stirred within her, Sarah gradually ceased her pointless flailing. A moan, female and entreating, rose in her throat.

At her response, the man hesitated, then pulled back.

Sarah stared up at him, startled. *Why did he stop? Has he guessed my inexperience and found me lacking?*

Shame flooded her, a confused mix of humiliation for the passion she'd felt and for the ignominious failure of her quest. Caught up in the chaotic swell of emotions, she could do little more than stand there and watch as the cowboy's fingers found the buttons of her blouse and began to fasten them.

"It's time to end this lesson," he said, his voice gone low and hoarse, "before I forget why I started it."

A jumble of responses sprang to Sarah's lips, then died as she looked up and saw his frowning features. Panic filled her.

I need to keep him distracted. But what else can I do? Oh, hurry, Papa! Hurry—

Almost as if in response to her silent plea, swift, stealthy footsteps, then a movement over the cowboy's shoulder, caught Sarah's attention. She froze.

Not so the tall man standing before her. He reacted instantly, shoving her aside then whirling around. As swiftly as he moved, though, he was still too late.

The wooden water bucket met him, slamming into the side of his head with enough force to knock most men out. He sank to his knees.

Immediately, Sarah's two brothers were on him, striking

at his head and shoulders as the cowboy struggled to rise. He half-turned, throwing off Noah, but Caleb grabbed a handful of dirt and tossed it into his face. Choking, his fists desperately rubbing at his eyes, the cowboy stumbled back to his knees.

Once more, Noah was on him, pinning the cowboy's arms behind him then jerking him to his feet. Caleb, now joined by their father, lost not a moment. They began to pummel him.

In helpless horror, Sarah watched as the blows struck the cowboy's face and sank deep into his belly. She heard the tormented grunts with each well-placed fist, shuddering at the sight of the blood-smeared mouth that had so lately caressed hers. Watched, heard, and stood there . . . until finally even the ties of family loyalty could no longer silence her protests.

"Stop it, Papa!" she screamed, flinging herself between the cowboy's battered form and her father's upraised arm. "You're killing him!"

Chest heaving, he hesitated, his fist halting in midair. "Do you know who this is? It's Cord Wainwright. Get out of the way, girl!"

She held her ground. "It doesn't matter, Papa." Her voice quavered as she fought the sickening churning in her gut. "Y-you've beaten him enough. We came here to rob the Wainwrights, not commit murder. Let him go."

"She's right, Papa," Noah interjected just then. "We got what we came for. Let's head on out."

The seconds ticked by as Jacob Caldwell battled his mindless rage. Finally, the red haze seemed to clear. "Just as well," he said. "Tie him up, boys."

Sarah's brothers roughly bound then dragged the limp form over to lie beside the hay wagon. The limp form of a man she now realized was not a common ranch hand but the Wainwright son born the very night her father had come

18

to this ranch and demanded it back from the man he hated above all others.

Talk was, though, that Cord Wainwright had been gone from these parts for a long while, and that was why, Sarah suddenly realized, she hadn't recognized him. But that really didn't matter just now. What mattered was the uneasy premonition that, as much as she might wish it otherwise, this encounter wouldn't be their last. And that, next time, she might not come out of it half as well.

Jacob coughed hard, the sound deep and wet, then turned to his daughter. "Are you all right, girl?" he asked, pulling off his flour sack disguise. "He didn't hurt you, did he?"

"N-no, Papa." Sarah wrenched her gaze from Cord Wainwright to her pale, sweaty-faced father. "I-I'm fine."

"Well, then, good. You did a good job. I'm proud of you." He gestured toward a bulging flour sack lying by the barn door. "Like Noah said. We got what we came for, and more. Now it's time to hightail it out of here. Come on."

Reluctantly, Sarah allowed herself to be led away. She couldn't help, though, but shoot a last glance over her shoulder. At the sight, her heart twisted and she immediately regretted her action.

The handsome younger son of Edmund Wainwright lay there in the dirt, bound and bleeding, an errant breeze stirring bits of hay about his motionless form.

Two weeks later, Cord Wainwright slammed his black Stetson onto his head and strode from Ashton's Bank and Trust. He'd had about all he could take of the family business! Not only had Spencer Womack, their ranch foreman, been on his back for the past week about his suspicions that roaming bands of Utes were responsible for the occasional rustling of their cattle, but the bank president had just presented Cord with an ultimatum to pay off the loan for the prize bull his father had insisted they buy three months ago. An ultimatum that now, thanks to the recent robbery, the Wainwrights had no money with which to comply.

Long, ground-eating strides carried Cord to where his horse was tethered. In one lithe motion he mounted—and quickly remembered his bruised side when a sharp pain shot through him. He settled into the saddle with a wince, then gingerly reined the animal around and down Main Street.

He had argued with his father until he was blue in the face not to buy that bull. The demand to put the money Cord had given him in the bank had also fallen on deaf ears. Edmund Wainwright was as stubbornly old-fashioned as they came, and trusted no one's judgment but his own. Unfortunately, that overpriced bull had yet to prove himself. And an old tin box hidden behind a bookcase in the study had, in retrospect, served as a poor substitute for an ironclad bank vault.

The bright green-and-blue-painted sign of McPherson's Mercantile came into view up ahead on the corner of Main and River Street. Cord halted his horse there and dismounted, flinging the reins around the hitching post. As he stepped onto the boardwalk fronting the big building, a man, his arms loaded with packages, barreled from the general store and straight into Cord.

Shoved backward into the hitching post, he bounced hard off the wooden rail. Cord straightened and staggered up onto the boardwalk, clutching his side. Barely controlling the impulse to hit the man, he instead shot him a furious look.

"I-I'm sorry, mister," the fellow stammered, quickly sidling away. "By golly, it was an accident, after all. You don't have to look at me like you want to beat in my face."

Cord stared long and hard at the man's rapidly retreating

form. Gradually, his anger cooled, and remorse filled him. He *had* overreacted, been on the verge of striking out over something as inconsequential as a careless blunder.

He shook his head. What was the matter with him? He'd long ago learned the importance of maintaining rigid control over his temper, respecting the fearsome power he had come to possess in his fists. Maybe the robbery—*and* the events surrounding it—was eating at him more than he cared to admit. This definitely didn't seem to be his day.

The coolness of McPherson's interior was a welcome relief from the unseasonable heat of early autumn. He removed his Stetson and, still rubbing his side, scanned the high-ceilinged room. The store's tall shelves were packed with household wares, a fine selection of foodstuffs, and bolts of colorful cloth, its floor space jammed with large pickle, molasses, vinegar, and cracker barrels, bushel baskets of dried beans, and other various and sundry items. The proprietor and sole employee, Dougal McPherson, however, was nowhere to be found.

Cord walked over and laid his Stetson on the merchandise counter. "Dougal, you old coot, where in the blazes are you?" he shouted, irritation tingeing his voice.

Rustling sounds emanated from the back room. The slight, spry form of an elderly man hurried out. A thatch of snow-white hair and ruddy features set off a large nose in a kindly face. Bright blue eyes, touched with humor, met his.

"So, is this what 'tis come to, when a lad such as ye starts bawling at his elders? Well, I won't have it!" the old Scotsman roared in mock indignation. He shook his bony fist at Cord. "Hie yerself from my store afore there's fisticuffs, and ye come out the loser."

"Hold on now." Immediately, all the pent-up tension drained from Cord. He laughed, raising his hands as if to defend himself from the irate little storekeeper. "You're not tricking me into a rematch. That last trouncing was enough to last me for a lifetime."

"Och, and 'tis good to see all that fancy law schooling hasn't dimmed yer memory," Dougal muttered. "Ye might be a tad brawnier than ye were at sixteen, but the years haven't dimmed my boxing skills a wit."

He paused, a reluctant grin tugging at one corner of his mouth. "Now, tell me. What brought ye here? I haven't seen ye in over two weeks."

Cord sighed. "Bad news, I'm afraid. I need to start a credit account for any supplies we might need. And it'll likely take a while to pay it off too."

"I figured it'd come to that, once word got around ye'd been robbed. 'Tis not a problem. Pay me when ye can."

Cord strode over to stare out the front window, shoving his hands deep into his denim pockets. "Actually, it is a problem. *My* problem. The longer it takes to pay off the debts my father has run up," he muttered, "the longer I have to put my life on hold. With my two stepsisters gone now from the ranch, you know as well as I the only reason I even bothered to come home. And it was never solely to help out my father."

"Yer father's made a fine mess of things, and no mistake," Dougal said. "There's no easy way to make money, and those poor investments of his prove the truth of that. But dinna go so hard on him, lad. Meet him halfway, and 'tis sure ye'll come to an understanding."

"Oh, I understand him just fine," Cord replied with a bitter laugh. "He's hated me since the day I was born. All I want is to get the ranch squared away, then head back to New York where I belong. I can't put my life or the law practice on hold forever. My partners have already been more than patient."

"Ye won't reconsider hanging up yer shingle in Ashton then?"

"There's nothing here for me anymore. You know that. I just need to get that money back." Cord ran a hand through his hair in frustration. "There's no more where that came from. I've sunk everything I had into trying to save the ranch."

"Och, dinna fear, lad. Sheriff Cooper will find those robbers. Everyone knows 'twas the Caldwell clan."

"Maybe. But Gabe hasn't had much luck so far. Seems the Caldwells, when they put their minds to it, can be a mite hard to track down. And it's not like I got a good look at any of the men. They were all wearing flour sacks over their heads. The girl's the only one I'd know if I saw her. She's the key to the mystery."

As he scanned the scene outside, he rubbed the still-tender spot on the side of his head where the bucket had slammed into it. What had she said when they'd been beating him, just before he passed out?

"Stop it, Papa . . . you're killing him . . ."

Papa . . .

The girl had never been a new employee. And her accomplices had been her family. Dougal was likely right. Who had greater reason to hate them than the Caldwells?

Though he'd been gone for nearly eleven years, the animosity between the two families was just as evident upon his return as when he'd left. Too many unexplained things had been happening—cut barbed-wire fencing, burned line shacks, not to mention missing cattle. Occasional bands of Utes notwithstanding, odds were some of the problems also had to be the Caldwells' doing.

Yes, Cord resolved, *it has to be the Caldwells who robbed the ranch. But I need proof. And, if I'm ever to get back to New York, what with my father and most of the hands gone*

23

on the roundup for another week, it's up to me to take matters into my own hands.

"Well, I dinna know any other lass in town with hair like ye described," Dougal was saying. "'Tis the bonny Sarah Caldwell, or I'm—"

"Dougal, come here!"

At the urgency in Cord's voice, the old Scot hurried quickly to his side. "What is it? What do ye see?"

"That boy over there." Cord pointed toward a shabbily dressed lad crossing the street. "Who is he?"

Dougal studied him briefly, then shrugged. "Seems a mite familiar, but I can't be certain from this angle. Some miner's bairn, no doubt. New folk arrive every day. 'Tis hard keeping track of all the—"

Cord wheeled about and strode back to the counter. Grabbing up his Stetson, he shoved it on his head as he headed for the door.

"I don't care what you say, McPherson," he said, excitement threading his voice. "I'd know that face and form anywhere. It's that girl—the one who helped rob us!"

2

Clutching the small cloth bag tightly to her, Sarah hurried from the pharmacist's shop and back down the street to Doc Saunders's office. Well aware her family would be implicated in the recent Wainwright robbery, she was apprehensive about venturing into town. Unfortunately, they'd had no choice. Danny was sick again and had to see the doctor. The last asthma attack had been bad, *real* bad, and now they were out of medicine.

She squelched a small twinge of guilt. The money, however illicitly gained, had come at a good time. Besides, everyone said the Wainwrights had more than they knew what to do with. It was past time she swallow some of that stubborn pride of hers. Past time she accept the fact the Wainwrights owed the Caldwells for all they'd taken from them.

Four unfair years in the penitentiary for the accidental shooting of the Wainwright boy had physically broken her father, making him unfit for any kind of hard labor. As a result, the major burden of keeping the family together had fallen on her mother's shoulders. Eventually, that strain had sickened and killed her.

Sarah and her brothers had tried to carry on in her stead. But money was difficult to come by when you were forced to scrabble out an existence on a few meager acres of land that no one, not even the local Indians, wanted. No, she struggled to convince herself, the Wainwrights were just being forced to share a little of what they'd stolen from the Caldwells all those years ago. And now, thanks to them, they had enough to take care of Danny for a long, long time.

Her gaze cautiously scanned the crowd filling Main Street. Noah and Danny were waiting at Doc's office. All she had to do was make it back. Then they'd just slip out of town as quietly as they came, no one the wiser.

Doc wouldn't talk. He understood how hard it had been to scrape up money for Danny all these years. How often they'd had to skimp on everything, accept every menial job that came around, just to afford the medical bills.

Besides, Sarah reminded herself for the tenth time as she stepped off the boardwalk fronting the many shops and businesses, *in my boy's disguise and with my face smudged and my hair tucked under this old hat of Caleb's, no one's paid me any attention. Even if Cord Wainwright were around, he'd never recognize me.*

Weaving through the throngs of idly strolling townspeople, Sarah thought she'd go mad with the agonizingly slow progress. Ever since gold and then silver had been discovered in the surrounding mountains, prospectors passing through Ashton had dramatically increased the day-to-day population. Still, each minute she tarried only increased her chances of discovery. When she neared the sheriff's office, she ducked her head and quickly began to cross to the other side of the street.

No sense tempting fate. Gabe Cooper had been well aware of her in the past year or so, ever since her girlish curves had "ripened," as Papa liked to put it. Yes, she had to be careful. Disguise or no, Gabe just might pick her out.

"Git out of the way, you fool kid!"

Sarah glanced up. A freight wagon was bearing down full tilt upon her. Two lathered bays, their nostrils flaring red, dashed by as she leapt out of the way. A whiff of sweat-damp coats mixed with the pungent scent of horse drifted past. She glared after the wagon, then determinedly resumed her trek across the now dusty street.

There's no time to spare on that callous lout. A few minutes more is all I need to reach Noah and Danny. Just a few minutes more and we'll be headed from town and safe—

A hand grasped her arm, jerking her backward. Sarah whirled around, slamming into a hard, masculine body. Her hat tipped askew and fell. Her hair tumbled down around her shoulders.

The cloth bag plummeted from her hand and slammed onto the ground. At the sound of breaking glass, horror filled her.

The medicine. Danny's medicine.

As she stared down at the now crumpled bag lying at her captor's feet, rage flared. The stupid, thoughtless man had ruined Danny's medicine!

"Why you . . . you clumsy oaf!" she said in a sputter. "Do you realize how expensive this medicine—"

As she spoke, Sarah looked up past boots, blue denim pants, and a brown and green plaid cotton shirt to meet the flinty gaze of a pair of jet black eyes. Eyes that rested in an uncomfortably familiar face topped by a black Stetson. A face that smiled triumphantly, almost cruelly, down at her.

"So, we meet again, little lady," Cord Wainwright said silkily. "And this time, you're not getting away so easily."

Long, strong fingers captured her other arm. She froze, mesmerized like that day at his ranch, her mind frantically searching for some way out of her predicament.

The black Stetson. For some inexplicable reason, her gaze riveted on his hat. It lent his already intimidating presence a foreboding air. And, seeing it, something within her snapped.

The full implication of her situation hit Sarah with the force of a blow.

She kicked wildly at him. "Let me go!"

Her hard, leather-clad toe made lucky contact where the top of his own boot met flesh. He grunted in pain but, instead of releasing her, only gripped Sarah the tighter. She felt herself rise from the ground until their faces were on an equal level, the sheer strength of his arms suspending her in midair.

"Why is it that every time we meet, I end up getting hurt?" he asked through gritted teeth. "Well, no matter. The tables have finally turned." He gave her a small shake. "Now, tell me. Where's the money?"

"I-I don't know what you're talking about!" She squirmed in his grasp until he finally lowered her back to the ground. "Release me this instant, or I'll call for the sheriff."

A contemptuous sneer curled Cord Wainwright's lips. "I'm not thinking the sheriff is going to protect the likes of you." He glanced over his shoulder. "In fact, let's pay him a visit right now."

Sarah dug in her heels as he began to drag her back across the street, but her stubborn resistance did little to impede their progress. "Let me go!" Her voice rose to an indignant shriek, and she struck out at him. "Take your filthy hands off me!"

"In a pig's eye!" He stopped to capture a wildly flailing arm. "You're going to jail where you belong!"

She glanced around at the crowd beginning to form. "Help me! Please, won't anyone help me?"

At her impassioned plea, two burly miners stepped out to block their way.

"Is this fella hurting you, ma'am?" the younger of the two men asked, tipping his sweat-stained cap.

Sarah shot Cord Wainwright a quick look, and saw his eyes narrow and his jaw clench. *He isn't going to let me go without a fight. On the other hand,* she thought, *he can't very well take on two men at once and still hold on to me. And, with the crowd gathering around us, it might just be my only chance to make a quick getaway.*

"Yes." She nodded emphatically, gracing the two miners with what she hoped was an imploring smile. "Yes, he is. I hardly know him, and he's trying to drag me off—"

"She robbed me and I'm taking her to the sheriff's office," Cord cut in just then. "Do either of you have a problem with that?"

The older of the two miners scowled. "Yeah, I've got a problem with it, mister. Dragging her around like that is no way to treat a lady."

Cord Wainwright gave a harsh laugh. "Well, if she *were* a lady, I might have to agree with you. Considering the family she comes from, though, I heartily doubt that's a concern." Pulling Sarah along with him, he took a step forward. "So, do yourselves a favor and get out of my way."

"I'd do as the lad suggests," a voice, thick with a brogue, interjected just then.

Relief flooded Sarah. "Mr. McPherson!"

The little Scotsman elbowed his way to the front of the crowd. After barely acknowledging her, he drew up beside Cord and riveted his fierce gaze on the two miners.

"Stay out of this, laddies," he said. "Cord here is the son of the owner of Castle Mountain Ranch, the biggest spread in these parts. And he means the lass no harm. Ye two, though, if ye keep pushing on him, will rue the day ye ever tried to interfere. Not only did I teach him everything I know about boxing, but he used to fight professionally to pay for all his fancy schooling. Trust me when I tell ye he's not one ye wish to trifle with."

The two miners looked to each other, then back at Cord.

"Well, if he really *is* just going to take her to the sheriff's office . . ." the older man began.

"Beggin' yore pardon, mister," the younger miner added, stepping aside.

Exasperation filled Sarah. *Fine. Real fine. Isn't anyone going to come to my aid?*

Evidently not, she realized, as Cord Wainwright's grip tightened once more around her arm. The crowd parted before them, and he again began to drag her forward. Again and again, she threw her full weight against the iron clasp of his hand, until her futile efforts finally left her weak and panting. To add to her humiliation, sporadic bursts of laughter now reached her ears.

Her face burning, knowing how ludicrous she must appear being pulled along like some recalcitrant child, it was all she could do to blink back the tears. She *had* to get away and warn Noah, but how?

Blessedly, her opportunity arrived when her captor paused in front of the sheriff's office. Momentarily, his grip loosened as he shifted his hands in preparation for lifting her onto the boardwalk. In that split second, Sarah spun around and jabbed her elbow hard into his side.

Even to her surprise, he inhaled a sharp, shuddering breath, doubled over, and released her.

She didn't look back, and sprinted through the crowded street. The dark shadows of an alleyway caught her eye. Sarah wheeled off in a new direction, running toward what she saw as her only chance of freedom.

The clapboard buildings loomed to engulf her. Anticipation of escape grew, burgeoning with each beat of her wildly pounding heart.

If only I can get out of sight, hide until he gives up searching for me . . .

The sound of heavy footsteps intruded into her frantic thoughts. Sarah quickened her pace, her legs pumping furiously. Light at the alley's end beckoned to her like the gateway to heaven.

If only I can reach it, then dash into some door or around the corner . . .

Just ahead, she heard an upstairs window slide open. Out of nowhere a torrent of water cascaded down on her head. Startled, she stumbled, lost her footing, and fell as the ground beneath and before her turned slippery with the muck of soapsudsy water.

Wash water. The town laundry . . .

Sarah scrambled to her feet.

A hard body slammed into her, the force of the impact momentarily propelling them both forward. Then they fell, facedown in the mud, dirty, scummy water spraying around them to drench them head to toe.

A familiar, iron-thewed grip tightened around her waist. Sarah groaned. *It's no use. I can't get away from him no matter how hard I try.*

She twisted to look at Cord Wainwright, only to meet bits of black onyx glittering back at her. Muddy water dripped from his dark hair, coursing in rivulets down the taut, angry planes of his face. Struck by the realization of how ludicrous she must also look, Sarah swallowed hard against the inane giggle that rose in her throat. In any other instance, this would almost seem funny. In any instance, that was, but now.

"Are you through with your games?" Cord Wainwright ground out. "I've had just about all I can take from you, so I suggest you think long and hard before trying anything else."

Sarah's lips tightened and she glanced away. *What's the point in arguing?* she thought, fiercely tamping down a swell of despair. *There'll be other chances. No matter what he may think, he's only won the first skirmish, not the war.*

Cord took her silence as surrender. Deciding it was past time he turn Sarah Caldwell in to Gabe Cooper's custody and some well-earned jail time, he tried to climb to his feet with her in his arms. Try, however, was as far as he got.

Encumbered with the petite form, Cord slipped and fell again. Dirty water splattered them as he once more tumbled down atop her. Beneath him Cord heard her grunt, the force of his body slamming onto hers apparently driving the air from her lungs.

He cursed and immediately rolled off. This time, dragging her up by the arm, Cord struggled to stand. Though a bit more sodden than before, Sarah looked no worse for the wear. He shot her a warning glare, tightened his hold on her arm, and with a precarious grip on his temper, turned and strode back down the alley.

From his spot on the boardwalk outside the sheriff's office, Dougal's eyes widened as soon as he caught sight of them. Mud-coated and dripping wet, not to mention he was dragging an equally grimy bundle of irate femininity along behind him, Cord could just imagine how ludicrous he must look. And his old friend's strenuous attempts to keep from laughing only confirmed his suspicions.

"Will ye be needin' some help, lad?" the old Scotsman inquired loudly when they finally came within earshot.

Cord glanced up from his struggles trying to contain his endlessly wiggling captive. "Yes. Get Gabe out here."

Dougal grinned. "Now, sure and that'd be a mite hard, lad. The sheriff's no' here."

"Then for pity's sake, go and get him for me!"

"All the way from Denver?"

His rapidly fraying temper exploded. "Blast it all!"

Cord pulled the girl to him, his arm encircling her waist. "*Now* what am I supposed to do with her?"

Bright blue eyes leisurely scanned Sarah's grimy form. "Well, myself, I'd be for givin' the lassie a bath."

As Sarah sputtered indignantly, Cord wearily shook his head. "As much as I usually appreciate your Scottish wit, this is neither the time nor place. I hurt. I'm soaking wet, and I need her locked up until Gabe gets back and he can question her."

"Aye, that ye do, lad." Dougal paused to scratch his chin. "Well, there's always Gabe's young deputy, Sam Hayden. He could keep an eye on her in jail. But he *is* still pretty wet behind the ears, and I fear Jacob Caldwell and his boys would have her out in no time."

Cord turned to stare down at his prisoner. "So, she *is* Sarah Caldwell."

"Of course I am, you big lummox!" she snapped. "And, with the sheriff gone, you've no right to continue to hold me, so I suggest you let me go before I press charges."

He smirked. "Oh, really. And exactly what would those charges be, little miss know-it-all?"

Hesitation flickered in her eyes. "Well, for starters, assault and battery. And, for another," she added, apparently gaining inspiration as she went, "kidnapping."

"Nice try." Cord smiled coldly. "However, in the absence of the sheriff or an experienced deputy, and with the need to detain you for probable cause that you committed a felony in helping your family rob our ranch, a citizen's arrest is more what I had in mind."

"A *what*?"

"A citizen's arrest. In case your education's a bit lacking,

33

it's a practice that can be traced all the way back to English common law during the Middle Ages. It grants a private citizen the right to detain suspected criminals until proper law enforcement personnel can assume custody." Cord looked to the old Scotsman. "Isn't that correct, McPherson?"

As Sarah turned her imploring gaze up to the man standing before them on the boardwalk, Dougal nodded. "Aye, I'm afraid that's true, lass. And Cord, of all people, would know, him being a lawyer and all." He paused, his thick white brows arching in query as he stepped down to join them. "So, citizen's arrest and all, what have ye planned for the lassie?"

Cord sighed. *Why is everything getting so dad-blamed complicated?*

"What choice do I have? I'll have to take her home with me until Gabe gets back. I'm not going to let the only suspect we've caught so far get away." He glanced over his shoulder at his buckskin tied across the street in front of Dougal's store. "Bring over my horse, will you?"

The little Scotsman quickly complied. Once his mount was standing beside them, Cord gave Sarah to Dougal. Then he loosened one of the long rawhide thongs that usually secured his bedroll to the saddle and pulled it free. As the old man held her hands behind her back, Cord deftly tied them.

When the unpleasant task was finally completed, Dougal turned to Sarah. "I'm verra sorry, lassie," he said. "It near to breaks my heart to see it come to this."

Green eyes, bright with unshed tears, stared back at him. "I-I thought you were my friend," she whispered. "How can you let him do this to me? You know Danny needs me. What will he do if you let this man take me away?"

"Then tell me where the money is!" Cord angrily interrupted before his friend could reply. "Tell me the names of the other thieves and where to find them. It's not too much to ask, if you really care about this Danny like you say you do."

She rounded on him, a defiant light in her eyes. "On the contrary. It *is* too much to ask. You Wainwrights deserve what you got!" Sarah gave a disparaging sniff. "Deserve that and more!"

For a fleeting moment, Cord studied her impassively, then expelled an exasperated breath. *I'm going to regret this. I just know it.*

"Here, hold Miss Caldwell while I mount up," he growled, turning back to Dougal. "Obviously, it's going to take more than a reasonable request to get the information I need out of her. And I don't intend to begin in the middle of Main Street."

Taking care not to injure his side any further, Cord swung up onto his horse. "Hand her to me," he then said, bending toward Sarah.

"No!" She turned beseeching eyes to Dougal. "If you're really the friend you always said you were, don't let him take me. Please, Mr. McPherson. Please!"

The old man hesitated, and Cord knew he was torn between Sarah's evident fear and the loyalty he felt toward him. Finally, sadly, he shook his head.

"'Tis the best choice, lassie. But dinna fear. Ye're in no danger from the lad. Besides," he added, smiling lamely, "surely 'tis only for a week or so, until the sheriff returns."

"A week?" The horror in her voice was unmistakable. "A lot can happen in a week. Why, I could be dead!"

"Yes, you could," Cord interjected dryly. "At the rate things are going, though, my death seems a far greater probability than yours." He motioned to his friend. "Hand me up the girl."

She must have been too stunned to respond, because Dougal was able to lift her up to sit in front of Cord without any struggle. Then, catching her eye, the little Scotsman gave her a reassuring wink before turning and heading back to his store.

Sarah gazed forlornly after him until he disappeared inside, then glanced back to rivet her white-hot glare onto Cord. "You'll regret this to your dying day, Cord Wainwright," she cried. "Just you wait and see!"

He reined in his horse and nudged it in the direction that led out of town. "Believe me, I already do," he said with a rueful sigh. "Just remember one thing, you little wildcat. Whatever path my suffering leads me down, I fully intend to take *you* along for the ride."

"Mama! Emma!" Pedro shouted. "Come quick! Come quick!" The lanky Mexican boy dashed through the front door of the main house, nearly skidding into Emma as she hurried from the library, feather duster in hand.

"Sakes alive, young man," the older woman exclaimed. "Whatever is the matter?"

"*Madre de Dios!*" Manuela, flour smeared on her face and hands, ran from the kitchen. "Is it Indians? Hurry, Pedro! *Las pistolas!*"

Her son ran over and engulfed her in a big hug. "Calm yourself, Mama. It is no Indians. It is Mister Cord. He is back, and he brings someone with him." His youthful face broke into a wide grin. "And they are both *very* dirty."

The two women exchanged a puzzled glance. Then, with a shrug, they hurriedly removed their work aprons and bustled out to the front porch. Even then, Cord was pulling up to the house.

"Let me go! You've got no right. No right at all!" his sodden, mud-covered passenger was saying, all the while squirming wildly before him.

With his free arm about her waist, Cord jerked her back. "And I said, sit still," he growled, "before you end up in even worse trouble than you're already in."

The trio of servants stood there, momentarily stunned. Then lips began to twitch as they all fought to keep a straight face.

The barely suppressed amusement wasn't lost on Cord. He glanced down at the girl he held before him. At the sight of her ramrod straight form and recalcitrant tilt of her mud-caked, blonde head now resolutely turned away, fresh irritation surged through him.

The little vixen. She has the most infuriating talent for making me appear the fool.

He looked up at the assemblage on the porch, visually challenging any to speak. The servants wisely withheld comment. He motioned to them.

"Manuela, come hold my horse. Pedro, get over here and help steady her when I lower her down." His request was clipped and cold, brooking no discussion. The two hurried to do his bidding.

Though she was handed down and accepted with the greatest of care, Sarah's legs crumpled beneath her when she touched ground. Luckily, the boy quickly grabbed her. She shot him a grateful smile.

"Thank you . . . Pedro, isn't it?"

Atop his horse, Cord watched the boy flush, then nod in agreement. *Great. Just great,* he thought. *She hasn't been here five minutes, and already she's plying her feminine wiles on a hapless, twelve-year-old boy.*

As his gaze roamed over her, amusement slowly replaced his irritation. In her bedraggled state, Sarah's attempts at charming anyone were more comical than provoking. Indeed, it was all Cord could do not to laugh, noting her piquant, dirt-smudged face and mud-coated hanks of hair, not to mention how ludicrously dressed she was in clothes many sizes too large for the slender form he knew lay beneath them.

But then, I can hardly talk, he reminded himself as he glanced down at his own clothing. A humorless smile touched his lips. *We're both in dire need of a bath.* With a wince, Cord swung off his horse.

Taking Sarah from Pedro's hands, he nodded his dismissal. "Put up Scout," he said to the boy before turning to Manuela. "I'd like a bath. Could you get some water boiling for one?"

Manuela arched a dark eyebrow, her glance speculatively moving from Cord to Sarah, then back again to Cord. Then, drawing an inscrutable mask across her features, she nodded. "*Sí, Señor* Wainwright."

He watched as the Mexican woman gathered her skirts and hurried off. Manuela wasn't much on words, but sooner or later he knew he'd hear more than he might care to from her. Fortunately, it wouldn't be in the next few minutes, which suited him just fine.

The housekeeper, however, was another matter. He turned to where she stood, hands resting on her matronly hips, upon the porch.

"Okay, Emma," he said with a weary sigh. "Why don't you just speak your mind and get it over with? Then I can get on with what I'm going to do anyway."

Emma's lips pursed, and she shook her gray-streaked auburn head in exasperation. "Land sakes, Cord Wainwright. Aren't you suddenly an ill-tempered young bull? What am I supposed to think when you ride up covered in mud, with a young lady equally as muddy in tow? Did you expect me to hide in the house and peek through the curtains?"

Cord shifted uncomfortably. *Here it comes now.*

"I'm not in the mood for long explanations," he said, "but this is the girl involved in the robbery, Sarah Caldwell to be exact. And, thanks to her, I've been through an aggravating past few hours. So all I want is to deposit her in the cellar and get cleaned up. Which is, starting now, exactly what I plan to do."

As he began to pull Sarah along with him toward the front door, Emma swiftly moved to bar his way. "You're going to put that child in that cold, damp cellar? For shame, Cord Wainwright! That's no way to treat—"

"She's no lady, and she's surely no guest," he quickly cut her off. "She's a prisoner."

At Emma's look of skepticism, Cord held up his free hand to silence further protest. "No more, Emma. We'll talk about this later."

She eyed him for a moment longer, then gave him a curt nod. "Yes, we most certainly will talk about this later. You can bet your bottom dollar on that."

By the time Cord Wainwright grabbed Sarah, tossed her over his shoulder, and proceeded up the steps and through the huge double doors of the gingerbread-trimmed, white frame dwelling, she was almost beyond caring. The wild swing of emotions combined with her fruitless, frustrating attempts to escape had drained her of strength. Besides, what was the point of further struggle? She was flat-out caught, and she wasn't going anywhere anytime soon.

As Cord's long legs swiftly propelled them into the house, Sarah lifted her head and scanned the spacious entrance hall dominated by a commanding white oak staircase and three brightly colored stained glass windows. And, before he whisked her across to a short hall and down a flight of stairs, she caught a glimpse of a room off the main hall that was graced with a woman's portrait over a massive stone fireplace, and another room across from it that appeared to be the dining room.

All of this could've been ours, she thought, *if Papa hadn't been cheated in that card game . . .*

The musty smell of the cellar soon distracted her from the painful, impotent musings. Cord halted when he'd reached the bottom of the steps, and lowered Sarah to stand against the solid support of his body. After a brief fumbling in the darkness, a light flared as he struck a match and lit the wick of an old miner's lantern, then quickly closed the door of its square glass chimney.

She blinked in the sudden brightness. As her vision cleared, Sarah realized he was staring at her. There was no anger in his expression, only a bold appraisal reminiscent of that day at the barn when she'd offered herself to him.

Sarah's heart commenced an erratic beat, and she nervously licked her lips. *What's he thinking? The cellar's well-insulated from earshot from above. How far will he go to avenge himself, especially after making it plain he views me as not much better than one of Ashton's crib girls?*

"Don't do that!"

At the sharp command, Sarah jumped. "Wh-what? Don't do what?"

"Lick your lips like that. Look at me like that!" Once more, glacial anger hardened his features. "Didn't you learn your lesson last time about teasing me?" He paused of a sudden, his gaze turning speculative. "Or did you instead decide you liked it and want more?"

"*Liked* it?" Sarah nearly choked on the words. "Want more? From you? Well, let me set that crazy idea to rest once and for all, Cord Wainwright. I want nothing—absolutely nothing—from you except to get as fast and far away from you as possible!"

"Talk about crazy ideas," he replied with a derisive snort. "Despite your desires to the contrary, the farthest you're getting from me is this cellar."

He led her toward a door and, with a swift kick, forced it open. It was a small room, its darkness broken only by a high, small, slatted window.

Sarah sighed. Far too high and small to escape through.

The odor of rotting potatoes wafted to her. Her nostrils flared. *Someone needs to get down here and do a serious sorting of produce,* she thought, her housekeeping instincts fleetingly slipping past her realization of the gravity of the moment.

With a gentle shove, Cord assisted her into the room. Sarah stumbled in to stand beside a large oak barrel filled with something that smelled like cider. He held the lantern high and, as it swung to and fro, grotesque, agitated shadows danced across the small enclosure.

"I hope the accommodations are to your liking." His deep voice was curiously devoid of emotion. "They're all yours until I get the information I want."

At the reminder of her family and what they'd done, a fierce sense of protectiveness flooded Sarah. "If you think I'll *ever* tell you where they are, you've got another think coming!"

The bravado in her voice and posture was a sham. Even as she spoke, the cellar's chill was already beginning to seep through her damp clothes and into her bones, leaching away her courage. What she really wanted to do was scream, to beg him not to leave her in here. But how could he know that she had a terror of small, dark places?

To hide the fear she knew must burn in her eyes, Sarah

lowered her head. She bit back a moan of pain. Her hands hurt so badly from the bonds, but she'd rather die than beg him for anything.

"Get out," she whispered. "Just go. Leave me alone."

"Have it your way."

The door slammed shut, and a bolt slid into place. Silence, heavy and suffocating, settled over her. Sarah choked back a shriek of pure panic. *Where's my papa? Surely, by now, he must know what's happened.*

Be reasonable, Sarah lectured herself even as a rising hysteria clawed at the thin veneer of control that was holding her together. *Papa knows where you've been taken. He'll come when the time's right. And what more can Cord Wainwright do to you anyway? Even the Wainwrights aren't above the law.*

She chuckled softly, the realization flowing over her like a soothing balm. Whether he knew it or not, Cord Wainwright had already played his best hand and lost. All she had to do was wait. She'd be out of here in no time.

Sarah shifted her position in an effort to stir the circulation in her arms. The action proved fruitless. She sighed. *Yes, all I've got to do is wait. If only my hands weren't turning numb . . .*

3

Cord sat at the window seat, savoring a glass of the tart cider he loved so well. Fresh from his bath, his black hair still damp and glistening, he thoughtfully gazed through the lace curtains and beveled glass panes. The burnished gold grasslands of the Wainwright ranch undulated in the gentle breeze, moving in endless, inexorable waves toward the distant peaks.

His glance moved out across the wide valley and upward, caressing the spruce- and pine-studded mountains and craggy, rock-strewn summits. One peak, as always, caught his gaze. Crowned with a rock formation that looked like the ruins of some ancient fortress, it had long ago inspired his father to name the ranch Castle Mountain after it.

The scene, as pleasing as it was to the eye, was nonetheless marred by a bittersweet pain. He didn't belong here anymore, no matter how poignantly the land called to him. Indeed, had *always* called to him.

The past six months since he'd arrived from New York City had been some of the most miserable of his life. His father, true to form, had bungled everything, from his bad investments and ill-conceived plans to the relationship he'd always had with his youngest son. It was no different now, after all these years. After all Cord had sacrificed in coming home just to save the ranch.

Cord's gut twisted in pain and, with an angry growl, he rose and headed to his bureau. There, he set down the cider and stared at his image in the silvered glass. The reflection glared back at him, burning black eyes in a face set and hard.

He didn't like the strained, tense expression he saw, an expression he seemed to wear constantly these days. How he yearned to return to New York! There he'd been content . . . fulfilled. Well, as content and fulfilled as an aloof, unloving God would allow anyone in this life.

But no matter. That time's fast drawing near, he reminded himself as he fastened closed the buttons of his crisply ironed white shirt. *Now that I've finally got the Caldwell girl, regaining the stolen money once again is a viable option.* He grimaced. *A viable option indeed, if only I can get the information I need from her.*

Why did she have to be so stubborn? So infuriating? Before he'd left her in the cellar, he'd planned on untying her, getting her cleaned up a bit, and even giving her a blanket against the cold of that underground room. But maybe a little neglect would hasten her cooperation. Cord smiled grimly. Yes, let Sarah Caldwell stew a bit.

Sarah . . .

What a beautiful, gentle name for such a calculating little minx. Yet, she certainly hadn't seemed wicked or selfish that day at the barn. All he remembered was an ethereally lovely girl. That, and the surprisingly intense reaction she had stirred in him. What *was* it about her that made a mockery of his common sense?

His feelings for her had to be totally physical. There was no other explanation for his response to Sarah. It wasn't, after all, as if they had anything in common—he an educated lawyer and she a girl from an impoverished, low-class family who wasn't above robbing folk blind.

His physical reaction to her was the least of his problems, however. The most pressing matter was what to do with her.

A frown wrinkled Cord's brow. She couldn't stay in the cellar indefinitely, yet there was no other room in the house secure enough to prevent her escape. It wasn't as if his father would tolerate him putting bars on all the windows. All the same, it just might come to that.

Maybe he should just hobble Sarah like some horse. A fleeting image of her limping about the house, trying all the while to maintain some semblance of that ridiculous hauteur of hers, filled him with amusement. Wouldn't she be mad!

Cord chuckled, grabbed up his glass, and drained its contents. An interesting consideration at the very least, if she didn't come around to his way of things. First, though, there were a few other matters to be dealt with. Like at least untying her and providing a few blankets against the cold. Cleaning Sarah up could wait a day or so, until some time in the cellar took the edge off her stubbornness.

He set down his now empty glass and reluctantly headed out the door. His thoughts had already flitted ahead—down to a cellar wherein lay a beautiful little wildcat.

The cold. Why is it so cold? Is this where it ends, then, with me doomed to die here in this awful cellar, forgotten and alone?

Sarah rolled onto her side. Her arms were little more than leaden, insensitive lumps, aching with a strange, almost intolerable pain. But how could it hurt when they were so numb?

A tear trickled down her face. It was hard to be brave when all she wanted to do was scream, call for help, beg—anything—if only to relieve the horrible quiet.

It didn't matter that she'd been against the robbery from

the start. That she'd gone along only because Danny was so sick with his asthma and needed frequent medical help and medications. Medical help and medications that, no matter how little Doc and the pharmacist asked in payment, they couldn't afford.

In the end, though, she'd involved herself just as deeply as the rest of her family, and bore the same burden of guilt. As the one sent to distract and trick him, she may seem even guiltier in Cord Wainwright's eyes. How else *could* he see her but as a mean, treacherous little tramp?

She wanted to tell him their need had been great or they'd never, ever, have stolen. She wanted to ask him to understand, but even before the faint hope of forgiveness flickered to life beneath her breast, she quashed it.

What good would it do? He was a Wainwright to the bone. He'd only laugh at her. And she couldn't tell him what he wanted to know, no matter what. If she did, they'd all end up in jail, and then who'd take care of Danny?

It had all been for her little brother, she reminded herself yet again. Even if she alone must accept the punishment for their deed, Danny's health was all that mattered. If he survived long enough to outgrow his terrible attacks of asthma, then it would've been worth it. It *had* to be worth it. Yet why was it so hard, even knowing that?

Because you might never see him again, or be there for him, a small voice replied. The anguished admission seared her heart.

Hot tears coursed down Sarah's cheeks. What would Danny do without her—she who'd been both sister and mother to him? She was the only one who could soothe his tortured breathing when the asthma wracked his thin little body. Despite all of Papa's and her older brothers' efforts, she was the one Danny always turned to. And now she was lost to him, perhaps forever.

Failing Danny was just one more in a series of failures, all stemming from that deathbed promise she'd made her mother. "It's up . . . to you now, Sarah," Eliza Caldwell had whispered that fateful day, now five years past, her breaths halting and ragged as the consumption inexorably ate through the last of her lungs. "Up to you . . . to be the mother . . . take care of the family . . . protect them . . ."

Even now, Sarah could see her poor mother, face ashen, the fragile skin beneath her eyes smudged with exhaustion, her thin, delicate hands picking aimlessly at her threadbare coverlet. "I'll take care of them, Mama," she'd replied, choking back the tears. "You know I will."

"P-promise me!" The words escaped on a shuddering sigh. "Promise me . . . you'll always be there . . . for your father. He needs you . . . more than all the rest. Help him . . . to find a new heart . . . to find God."

With that, Eliza began to cough, bringing up foamy blood. Sarah gathered her mother into her arms, held a cloth to her lips. She didn't want to make that promise, fought against doing so with every fiber of her being. She was only thirteen. How was she supposed to know how to help her father find a new heart, after all those years of soul-rotting enmity and back-breaking failure? And what did she really know of God, despite all her mother's efforts to teach her, if God now chose to take away the only person in her life she could always count on? What kind of a God would do a thing like that?

Yet the look in her mother's eyes brooked no protest or refusal, so Sarah nodded her acquiescence. "I promise, Mama," she said. "I promise."

With that admission, something seemed to let go within her mother. She smiled softly, then closed her eyes. The coughing dissipated on a deep sigh. Her mother went slack in her arms.

Terror swamped Sarah and she screamed, crying out her

mother's name. Screamed and screamed until her father and older brothers rushed into the room. Until her father pried her arms away and handed her over to Noah, who cradled her against him, stroking her hair and crooning soft words of comfort. But there was no comfort to be found, not then, and little enough in the days, weeks, and months to come. No comfort, for her mother was gone, and with her passing, Sarah's trust and hope in God had also fled.

Sobs wrenched her from her anguished memories. Sarah opened her eyes to the cellar's darkness and became aware, once again, of the cold seeping into her very bones. Still, her recent thoughts had left her with a lingering sense of comfort. Whatever happened, though she might ultimately fail in everything she tried to do, she had done her best. And she would continue, because of her promise, to do all that was possible to protect her father, her family, whatever the cost.

A door scraped open overhead. The heavy tread of footsteps descended into the cellar. Sarah waited, half dreading, half anticipating the approaching visitor. Then, as the cellar door swung open, the tall, broad-shouldered form of a man stepped forward, backlit by the faint light streaming down behind him.

Cord paused at the bottom of the stairs to light the lantern. As the flame flared and he held the lamp high, Sarah gasped and turned away from him. He frowned. Were those tears glistening on her cheeks, or was it the flickering light playing tricks on him?

He walked over, knelt beside her, and set down the lantern. The wetness on her face confirmed his suspicions. She'd been crying. Guilt lanced through him. Some instinct told him

Sarah wasn't one to cry easily. Maybe he *had* been a little too harsh with her.

"Sarah? Are you all right?"

"Y-yes," she choked out the word. "Just go away. L-leave me alone."

"I'll do that soon enough." Cord withdrew a pocketknife. "For now, though, just roll over and let me cut your hands free."

She shot him an uncertain glance, then turned her back to him. He slid the knife blade beneath her bonds and began sawing at them. As he worked, he heard her moan.

"What's wrong?" he asked, pausing in the task of cutting through the last thong.

"My . . . hands!" she said on a shuddering breath. "I can't feel them, yet they hurt so bad! Oh, I can't stand it!"

Cord sliced through the last rawhide strip, then gently brought her arms around to her sides. The lamp's glow illuminated Sarah's wrists, bathing them in an eerie red light. Cord sucked in a horrified breath.

For the first time, he noted the deep gouges the cords had made in Sarah's flesh. How had it happened? He thought he'd tied them loosely enough. Had he, in his anger, bound her tighter than he'd intended, unconsciously venting some of his frustration at the robbery on her? The possibility sickened him.

She was weeping now, softly, lightly, in an apparent effort to keep him from noticing. Even so, the sound reached his keen ears. Something twisted deep in his gut. Cord took her abraded wrists and began gently to massage them.

"S-stop!" she cried. "Don't . . . touch . . . me. It hurts too much!"

"I have to." There was the merest catch in the dark register of his voice. "I've got to get some circulation back into your hands."

Eyes that were little more than gleaming emerald pools stared up at him, and then she sighed. "Do what you must."

Do what you must . . .

As the minutes passed, the words echoed endlessly in Cord's head. Every sharp catch in her breath, every silent tear that spilled from her eyes, sent the phrase reverberating through his mind. Was this what he'd sunk to? Torturing some hapless girl?

"Ahhh . . ." Sarah finally said, her voice shaking. "My hands are starting to tingle."

Relief surged through Cord. "Good."

He studied her. She needed her wrists tended, and though a bath and clean clothes had originally been planned as a reward for her eventual cooperation, that plan had died an ignominious death at the first sight of her tears. But that was all, he hastily cautioned himself. She was still a prisoner and would be treated as one.

Moving closer, Cord gathered her into his arms, then rose to his feet.

Sarah turned to him, startled. "What are you doing?"

"I'm taking you to the kitchen. Emma's heating water for laundry, and we might as well use it instead for your bath."

She studied him for a moment, then sighed and rested her head on the hard-muscled expanse of his chest. "That'd be nice."

A smile tugged at the corner of his mouth. "No sooner said than done."

The kitchen was a large, cheery room. The windows were dressed in a bright blue checkerboard print. A solid oak, well-scarred worktable graced the room's center, and three of the walls not lined with shelves or glass-fronted cupboards were strewn with hanging metal molds, cooking utensils, and colorful pictures. Along the fourth wall stood a cabinet with a sink and a highly ornamented cookstove, richly gilded with nickel plating, a pot of something savory simmering upon its cast-iron top. Nearby, a small door opened onto a large, well-stocked pantry, and directly catty-corner to it, a tall, wooden folding screen stood guard in one corner.

The woman named Emma walked in from the back door. Noting their arrival, she paused expectantly. Warm brown eyes in an apple-cheeked face curiously examined Sarah. There was kindness there, and after the terror of the past few hours, Sarah felt strangely safe in her presence. A shy, hesitant smile slowly spread across Sarah's face.

"Well, young man," the older woman began, bustling toward them, "are you going to complete the introductions, or have you forgotten all the manners you were ever taught?"

Cord rolled his eyes, then lowered Sarah to her feet. "No, I haven't forgotten. Sarah, please meet Emma Duncan." He glanced down at her. "Emma's the family housekeeper. She's been with us since the dawn of time. If you're her friend, she'll move heaven and earth for you, but don't ever cross her. Even my father knows better than to get in Emma's way."

"Land sakes, Cord Wainwright," Emma chided, moving to take Sarah's arm. "Don't go and frighten this child with your tall tales." She intently surveyed Sarah. "So, you're the Caldwell girl. You've certainly blossomed into a lovely young lady." Emma glanced at Cord. "Is it safe to assume you changed your mind and brought her here for a bath?"

He nodded.

"Good." She turned her attention back to Sarah. "Looks to me like you're in sore need of some cleaning up and a good, hot meal. For starters, though, let's get those filthy clothes off." With her free hand, she made a shooing motion toward Cord. "Get out of here. Scat."

Cord gave a wry laugh and walked to the work table, where he pulled up a chair and sat. "Sorry to disappoint the two of you," he said as he poured himself a glass of cider from the crockery pitcher in the middle of the table, "but I'm not going anywhere."

He took a long swallow of the drink. "One way or another, Sarah's not leaving my presence. That screen will adequately preserve her 'modesty,' though considering her decided lack of it the last time we met, I'm not sure why it's suddenly so important. But I promise not to peek around it, though that's the limit of my concessions."

Sarah drew herself up to her full height, fresh indignation sending a surge of energy through her. Her fists balled at her sides. "Why, you ill-bred, lecherous—"

"Hold on, now," Cord interrupted with a laugh. "Call me what you will, but don't malign one of the women who helped raise me." As he indicated Emma, his features slowly turned serious. "Now, make your choice and make it quickly. I'm not going to sit here all day."

Emma's hand tightened on Sarah's arm. "Come, come, child. It'd be a shame to waste a nice bath, and Cord can't see a thing behind the screen."

For a brief moment more, Sarah glared at him. Then, with a disdainful sniff, she turned on her heel. "If you think you've won anything with this, Cord Wainwright, you've got another think coming!" she said as she disappeared behind the tall, paneled barrier.

"Seems like I've heard that threat somewhere before. And I'm still waiting to see what comes of it."

Sarah ground her teeth in frustration as she sat on a stool and proceeded to pull off her boots. Emma made several trips from the stove to the metal bathtub, emptying four pots of boiling water. In the background, she could hear Cord at the hand pump near the sink, filling each emptied pot with cool water, which Emma next retrieved. Sarah's bath was soon ready.

As Sarah removed her shirt and tossed it atop her jeans, socks, and boots, Emma's eyes widened and she sucked in her breath. "Land sakes!"

She peeked around the screen. "Cord Wainwright, what in the world did you do to this girl? Have you seen her wrists? How could you be so cruel?"

He sighed. "It was an unfortunate oversight, Emma. I never meant—"

"Well-meant intentions never did hold much water with me," she snapped, cutting him off. "Her wrists are bleeding, for goodness sake!"

She ducked back behind the screen. "Here, child. Let me help you. There, that's it," she crooned as she took Sarah by one elbow to assist her. "Just slide down into that nice warm bath and soak yourself. And keep those wrists out of the water until I get back. I need to fetch my salve, bandages, and a set of clean clothes."

In a flurry of calico skirts, Emma hurried from behind the screen and across the kitchen. Sarah heard her chidingly cluck her tongue, most likely as she passed Cord, before exiting the room. Then, save for an occasional splash of water as Sarah moved about in the tub, the kitchen was silent.

"Sarah?"

She flinched, far preferring to imagine she was alone rather than admit there was a man on the other side of the screen, with her naked in a tub of water. Still, the only hope of keeping him exactly where he was until Emma returned was to answer him.

"Yes?"

"Your hands. How do they feel?"

Now, what kind of question is that? she thought in exasperation. *They burn like fire, you big knot head!*

Common sense, however, prevented her from telling him that, so Sarah swallowed hard before replying. "They're fine, thank you."

She could hear him set down his glass.

"I'm sorry that happened. I never intended to hurt you, only scare you a little. I need to get back that money."

Here we go again. "I-I don't know what you're talking about. What money?"

The creak of a chair signaled he was now probably leaning back in it.

"Can't you ever stop the games?" Cord's voice dripped with irritation. "There's no one around to hear your lies, and we both know the truth, don't we?"

For a long moment, Sarah didn't reply. Honesty warred with continuing the deception, and honesty finally won out. "I'm sorry, but I can't help you without hurting my family. And I'll never do that. They're all I have . . ."

"Family loyalty." Cord snorted in derision. "An admirable quality that's placed us both in untenable positions."

A strange sentiment, she thought. *Leastwise, coming from his side of it anyway.*

"It doesn't matter, Sarah. I won't let you go until I get what I want. And I've *got* to have the money."

What am I supposed to say to that? She moved uncomfortably in the tub, the water sloshing about. *Where's Emma?* Sarah wished the kindly housekeeper had never left.

"It's not going to matter in the long run," Cord said. "Either you'll eventually tell me or we'll catch your family. Who knows? Maybe they'll even try to rescue you from my evil clutches. I'd like that. There's a matter of a beating that needs repaying, and I'm just the man for it."

Yes, I'll bet you are. "What will you do with me in the meantime?"

He gave a harsh laugh. "What do you think? A bath and some clean clothes don't constitute forgiveness. As I said before, you'll stay in the cellar until I get the information I want."

The next few days passed uneventfully in a stalemated battle of two equally stubborn wills. In that time, Cord was careful never to visit Sarah, sending one of the servants to bring her meals or attend to her needs. His decision to let her stew, however, was one of the most difficult he'd ever made. Though he stayed close to home in case her family attempted a rescue, burying himself in ranch paperwork to keep busy, Cord's thoughts frequently drifted to the blonde beauty in the cellar.

She deserved her prison, he reminded himself over and over. She deserved that and worse for her part in the robbery. His father wouldn't go half as easy on her when he returned and found out what had happened.

Father . . . Cord's musings suddenly took another, even more unpleasant path.

The uneasy truce between them had stretched thin in the past month. Increasingly critical of everything Cord did, Edmund Wainwright seemed oblivious to how close his son was to his breaking point. And the robbery could well be the last straw. Justified anger or not, if his father made one more disparaging remark . . .

Cord rose from his desk and strode from the library. It didn't matter how hard he tried! Every time the thought of Sarah Caldwell entered his mind, he ended up angry.

Well, he'd had all he could take. Something had to be done about her. He needed his money back—and fast! Today, one way or another, he'd show her who was boss.

Sarah paced the small cellar, the tension of being cooped up for the past three days rubbing her finely strung nerves raw. *I have to get out of here. I just have to!*

The overlarge pants kept flapping in time to the jerky beat of her steps. Pausing, she fretfully shoved the sleeves of her shirt back above her elbows for the hundredth time, ruing the stiff-necked pride that had made her return the simple dress of Emma's once her own clothes had been clean again. The baggy outfit was just one more irritant in the endless hours that plodded by.

Her rapid strides once more carried her past the shelves neatly lined against the walls, filled with jars of jams and jellies with their screw-on caps, stoneware crocks of pickles, sauerkraut, and pickled beets, and preserving jars of stewed fruits sealed with wax and covered with cheesecloth. She halted, her nose wrinkling at the layers of dust that coated everything, not to mention the spiderwebs that festooned portions of the ceiling and upper shelves. Emma was busy, and Sarah felt a need to repay her for the kindness the older woman had shown her in the past days. She might as well dust and straighten up a bit. There certainly wasn't anything else to do.

If there was one thing she had always been known for, it was keeping a spotless house, Sarah mused as she found some rags and began to dust the shelves and various containers. True, their simple cabin high in a rarely traveled canyon that pierced the mountains several miles from Ashton wasn't much to speak of. The main floor consisted of a stone hearth and

TRANSIT SLIP

Transit date:
2/3/2015,14:58
Transit to: HRP
Transit library:
TIF
Item ID:
33591000515436
Title: A heart
divided

a combined kitchen and living area in one room, and Papa's bedroom in the other. A sleeping loft reached by a ladder, with a portion sectioned off for her privacy by hanging blankets, was shared by Sarah and her three brothers. The furnishings were sparse—only threadbare, flour-sack curtains hung at the few windows, and the floors were of unvarnished pine. They had no well or fancy indoor plumbing, and had to haul water from a nearby stream.

Still, for as far back as Sarah could recall, no one had ever gone hungry or lacked for warmth in the winter. And, at least when Mama was still alive, there'd been laughter and fun times, not to mention clean if oft-mended clothes and tasty if simple meals. Sarah had done her best to keep up the clean clothes and tasty meals, but since her mother died the laughter and fun times had come few and far between. Not that it wasn't for lack of trying. Nevertheless, at her mother's passing, it was as if the last shred of hope and life had drained from her father.

Fiercely, she shook her head to dispel the sad memories, forcing her concentration back to the task at hand. It didn't take long before Sarah had everything neat and tidy, and an hour passed with relative speed. Eventually, though, she found herself faced with the same problem. Boredom—ponderous, mindless boredom!

With a sigh, Sarah pulled over the cellar's single chair and sat. Immediately, a torrent of questions bombarded her.

Has it really been only three days? Only three dark, miserable days shut off from the outside world without news of my family, or how Danny's doing? Is he all right? Has he recovered from his most recent bout of asthma? And when will I ever see him again?

She leaned down, rested her elbows on her knees, and buried her face in her hands. *Escape. I* have *to escape*, she thought, choking back a swell of panic. *Papa hasn't come, and all the Wainwright hands will soon be back from the cattle drive. Once they're here, it'll be impossible for Papa to rescue me.*

It's got to be today, she decided, her resolve growing with each passing second. *After three days of my meek behavior, surely they're all lulled into thinking I've given up any thought of getting away. Easier said than done, though. For starters, how am I to take my next visitor by surprise?*

Her glance strayed to the jars and crocks stacked so neatly now on their shelves. Nearby, several cider barrels stood, their plump, rounded shapes almost begging her to turn them on their sides and send them rolling. They'd be heavy and hard to move, but she was also far stronger than her size might imply. A smile curved Sarah's lips, then died.

Guilt lanced through her at the thought of repaying Emma's generous care with such a violent act. But what choice had she? Her family had to come first. Maybe later, once she was safely home, she could get a note to the kindly housekeeper, apologizing and thanking her for all she'd done.

As if her newfound plans had been the catalyst, the upstairs door creaked open. Footsteps sounded on the cellar stairs. Sarah ran to the cider barrel and, throwing all her weight against it, managed to tip it onto its side. Then she scrambled to the shelf holding a basket of the last of the summer tomatoes, reaching it just as a hand drew back the door bolt.

Grabbing two tomatoes in each fist, Sarah whirled around. The door swung open. For an instant, the sudden glare of the lantern blinded her. All she saw was a shadowy form.

Emma, forgive me, she thought, launching the first tomato, then the next.

Out of the corner of his eye as he turned to hang the lantern on a hook by the door, Cord saw something move through the air. Instinctively, he jumped aside. The first object missed him, but the rest followed in such quick succession he was unable to avoid them. Mushy, overripe tomatoes smashed into him, one hitting the side of his face, the other two splattering onto his white cotton shirt.

As he wiped the sticky juice off his face, Cord angrily scanned the room. *Sarah. The little minx. Where is she?*

A movement in the far corner caught his eye. He heard a rumble, then saw a large object rolling toward him. Cord stared hard at it as it lumbered forward, finally realizing it was something large, round, and wooden. With a curse, he nimbly eluded the cider barrel just before it hit him.

"Blast it, Sarah!" he roared. "Stop this childish nonsense. It'll do you no good—"

Two more tomatoes sailed past his head. "Sarah," Cord rasped warningly. A tomato exploded on his left thigh.

From the darkness came a giggle. No similar sense of amusement filled Cord.

"That does it!" He lunged across the room at the small figure he could now make out hiding in the shadows. He'd had about all he could take of this silliness, and she was going to pay!

With a squeak of alarm, Sarah attempted to evade his outstretched arms. A hand clutched at her as she passed, slipped, then grasped at her again. This time it caught in her hair. She was painfully wrenched to a halt, then slowly, inexorably pulled back to him.

"Come here."

The words, spoken with deadly calm, sent a premonitory

shiver down her spine. She'd never heard him use that tone of voice before. Her mouth went dry. Reluctantly, Sarah backed toward him.

His grip on her hair never loosened, even when she moved close enough for his other hand to capture her arm and jerk her tightly to him. For a long moment, Cord didn't speak, and the only audible sounds in the cellar were the loud hammering of her heart and his ragged breathing wafting warmly, smotheringly, over the back of her neck. Agonizing seconds ticked by, the tension growing until Sarah thought she'd scream.

"You never let up, do you?" he finally growled. "Well, I've had it, do you hear me? You're nothing more than a spoiled, ungrateful little brat and—"

She'd had just about all she could take of him too, and at his derogatory words, something snapped inside Sarah. "Spoiled, ungrateful little brat, am I?" Ignoring the pain, she twisted in his grip to slam full up against him, face to face. "Well, let me tell you something, Mr. High-and-Mighty Wainwright—"

"Land sakes. Isn't this a cozy little scene?" Emma took down the lantern and held it high. "I'm sorry to intrude when you two seem to be becoming such fast friends, but we've got visitors."

"Visitors?" Cord released his grip on Sarah's hair and stepped back as if she were on fire. "Who's here now?"

"That old Ute Indian."

"Buckskin Joe?" His expression brightened and he quickly straightened his rumpled shirt. Then he glanced down, paused, and grimaced at the red splotches that marred its formerly snowy whiteness.

He shot Emma a quelling look. "Don't say a word. Not one word."

60

Her lips twitched. "Not one word," Emma obediently repeated. Her glance moved to a disheveled, red-faced Sarah.

"You might like to come along, child. Joe's brought someone who claims he knows you."

Sarah's heart skipped a beat. "Knows me? Who could that be?" A wild hope assailed her. "Is it Gabe Cooper? Has he finally come for me?"

Emma shook her head. "No, child. It's not Sheriff Cooper. Seems your visitor's a mite younger. He's a little boy, about six or seven, I'd guess. His name's Danny," she added, her glance rising to Cord's, "and he claims he's here to rescue you."

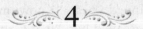

4

An elderly Indian dressed in a bright blue Mexican shirt, leather leggings, and moccasins turned his calm gaze to the three people who emerged from the house. His wrinkled, red-bronze face broke into a wide grin when he saw Cord. His hand lifted briefly in greeting.

"Found boy riding burro. He much small for big trip, so I bring him."

Cord returned the greeting. "My thanks, Joe. He's this young lady's brother," he said, turning to Sarah.

Sarah, however, saw nothing but the small child in the Indian's arms. "Danny," she whispered.

Twisting from Cord's grasp, she ran to her brother. Danny's eyes were closed, his face pale, and his little chest labored with each breath.

Hesitantly, Sarah reached up and touched his arm. "Danny. Wake up, honey. It's Sarah."

"S-Sarah?" Over-bright blue eyes opened, and a weak smile curved his lips. "I found you, I did. I told old Joe . . . I would."

Listening to her brother, it was all Sarah could do to keep from wincing. He wheezed when he spoke, and his chest moved in a slow, erratic fashion. She'd seen the signs too many times not to know it for what it was—another asthma attack.

Her fingers lightly stroked his face. "You look tired from

this big trip of yours. Wouldn't you like to have a nice cool drink and rest a while?"

"Sure would." He sighed, and his head fell back to rest on the Indian's chest. "I'm . . . tired."

"Here, Joe. Let me have the boy." Cord stepped up beside Sarah and took Danny from the old Indian. "Go on inside with Emma. She'll see to your needs."

His gaze riveted on Sarah. "What's wrong with your brother? Asthma?"

She nodded.

"Pedro." Cord looked to the Mexican boy who'd walked over just then from the barn. "Ride to town and bring back Doc Saunders pronto. Tell him it's the Caldwell boy." He turned to Sarah. "Let's get Danny upstairs and in bed. He looks worn out."

Before she could even concur, Cord set off for the house. She shot Emma a bewildered glance before hurriedly following in his wake.

Danny looked so small cradled in Cord's strong arms, Sarah thought as she ran across the foyer behind them and up the stairs. So frail, and yet so safe and protected. The rapidity with which Cord Wainwright had stepped in and taken charge took her breath away, but in some strange way it was almost a relief to let him assume control.

Though her father and older brothers helped when they could, most of their time was spent trying to eke out a living for them all. Danny's care, therefore, had mainly been her responsibility. To now share the burden of his terrible illness with a Wainwright, though, was irony of the strangest kind.

Cord paused before one of the upstairs doors. "Open it, will you, Sarah?"

She quickly complied. Hurrying over to the large brass bed that commanded the small room, she turned back the brightly flowered print quilt. Cord lifted him onto the bed, and Sarah stripped Danny down to his undershirt and drawers. Then she plumped up an extra pillow and assisted him in leaning forward against it. At her action, Cord quirked a brow.

"When Danny has an attack," she said by way of explanation, "he's much more comfortable sitting up like this. If you've got a few more pillows available, that'd help even more to support him."

"I'll get you some. Is there anything else we can do for him until the doctor gets here?"

"A pot of steaming water in the room, set close to him, helps him breathe easier." Sarah hesitantly smiled. "Also, something to sip on. Drinking liquids, something with sugar in it, keeps up his strength."

"How about cider?"

"C-cider?" Danny straightened, his wan little face brightening with sudden interest. "Could . . . could I, mister?"

Cord gently tousled the boy's hair. "Sure can, and as much as you want too." He turned to Sarah. "I'll be back with everything as soon as it's all ready."

A small cough drew Sarah's attention from the tall man's smiling countenance. She scooted onto the bed, gathering her brother into her arms. Tenderly, lovingly, she began to rub his back, a soothing ritual Danny always seemed to need during his attacks. With a ragged moan, he crept closer, his little arms encircling her.

"Danny, Danny," Sarah said with a sigh as, behind her, she heard Cord slip from the room and quietly shut the door behind him. "Whatever possessed you to come here all by yourself? You know how too much dust affects you. I don't like to see you sick like this."

"I-I had to," he explained between fitful, rasping breaths. "Papa didn't know what to do . . . and he wouldn't let Caleb or Noah come. I knew if I rode . . . with the tallest mountains on my right . . . I'd find the ranch. I-I missed you so!"

"And I missed you too, honey." She kissed his clammy forehead.

"You aren't . . . mad at me, are you? I didn't mean . . . to make you mad."

"No, honey." Sarah struggled to hold back the tears. "I'd never, ever be mad at you. Now, just be quiet and rest. It'll help you more than anything."

And please, God, let him get through this, she prayed in an uncharacteristic surge of need for help beyond the powers of man, noting her brother's blue lips, the labored rise and fall of his chest, and dark smudges of exhaustion beneath his eyes. She knew Danny had been worried about her and wondered if he'd even slept much these past days. That, coupled with the fact he hadn't even had a chance to get over the last attack necessitating that fateful trip to town, sent a shiver of foreboding down her spine.

Sarah firmly quashed the feeling. They'd always gotten through this before, and would once again. Danny needed her. She wouldn't fail him. Now, if only Doc Saunders would get here soon . . .

Danny's condition failed to improve. Cord maintained a steady journey between the boy's bedside and the kitchen as the pot of steaming water needed replenishing, until Sarah marveled at his patience and persistent dedication. His calm, steady assistance and the concern that burned in his eyes and spilled over into his deep, resonant voice seemed at times to be all that sustained her. Indeed, as Sarah went about her ministrations, Cord's transformation from harsh jailer to warm, supportive ally was a constant source of wonder.

They were enemies. Yet, as she covertly observed him helping with Danny, it became increasingly difficult to stir the
ashes of her animosity back to any semblance of its former
intensity. The sight of his dark head bent close to hear her
brother's whispered words, the aura of strength in his tall
frame that buoyed her flagging hopes, only served to build
the confusing disparity between what she'd imagined him to
be and what she now observed.

The earlier enmity died. In its place, a tender gratitude
flared to life.

By the time Doc Saunders arrived, Sarah was near exhaustion. Danny's attempts to clear the choking fluids from
his lungs had faded with his waning strength, and each
breath seemed to require a superhuman effort from his thin
little body. Doc took one look at him and opened his bag.
After administering a dose of medicine, he spent the next
few hours hovering at Danny's bedside. Not until the day
had grayed to twilight did he finally draw Sarah and Cord
aside.

"What in the blazes is going on here?" he demanded, riveting his irate gaze on Sarah. "Why isn't Danny home where
he belongs?"

She flushed. "He came to find me and take me back."

Doc Saunders rounded next on Cord. "I heard how you
dragged Sarah off the day they came to town. This high-
handed abduction is starting to get a little out of control,
isn't it? Danny's now deathly ill, and there's no telling what
would happen if the rest of their family decided now to rescue
them. Hasn't this feud gone far enough? Or are you singlehandedly trying to start it all up again?"

A tight look shuttered Cord's face. "This isn't the time
or place to discuss this. Not that I owe you or anyone an
explanation."

The older man shook his head. "And you're a young fool. If any harm comes to Danny or Sarah, you'll rue the day—"

"I already rue the day," Cord wearily interjected. He ran a hand through his hair in exasperation, and turned to Sarah. "I need a cup of coffee."

She forced a wooden smile to her lips. "It has been a long—"

"Go with him, Sarah," Doc Saunders ordered. "You're dead on your feet. The medicine looks like it's finally working, and you've done all you can for the time being."

"No." Sarah adamantly shook her head. "Danny needs me here. I-I'll be all right."

"And I said go, girl." Doc gave her a small shove forward. "You're no good to the boy if you break down. A half hour or so isn't going to make much difference to anyone but you. Send Emma up with more hot water. If Danny calls for you in the meantime, I promise to have her fetch you."

Cord took her arm. "Doc's right. Come downstairs for a bit. You haven't eaten since breakfast, and it's past supper. A cup of coffee and a slice of Manuela's peach pie will do you a world of good."

The concern she saw reflected in his black eyes mirrored that of the doctor's. With a small sigh, Sarah relented. "I suppose it'd be okay, but only for a half hour and no more."

"That's a good girl." Doc waved her toward the door. "Now, get along with you."

Sarah allowed Cord to lead her downstairs. Several lamps had been lit, bathing the kitchen in a warm, cheery light. Emma was busy at the sink, and turned at the sound of their entry.

"A slice of that peach pie for the both of us, Emma," Cord said over his shoulder as he guided Sarah to the table and pulled out her chair. "And, if you don't mind, would you take that next pot upstairs and stay with Doc and Danny until we return?"

Sarah sat down. "No pie for me, please. I'm not hungry."

"*Two* pieces of pie," Cord firmly reiterated as he poured out two mugs of coffee. He shoved one under Sarah's nose. "Cream or sugar?"

"Wh-what?" Sarah lifted a bewildered gaze to him. "What did you say?"

Cord's expression softened. "I said, do you want cream or sugar in your coffee?"

"B-both please. Two spoonfuls of sugar."

He smiled. "Coffee as sweet as your disposition, eh?"

The teasing lilt in his voice eased a little of Sarah's tension. She watched him prepare her coffee then return it to her. "Not lately, I'm afraid."

She inhaled a long, ragged breath, then paused as Emma laid a huge piece of pie before her and folded her fingers around a fork. A small, grateful smile brightened Sarah's face as she glanced up at the older woman. "Thank you."

"A clean plate when I return is all the thanks I need," Emma whispered before hurrying from the kitchen with another pot of steaming water.

Sarah watched the door swing closed in Emma's wake, then turned back to the man sitting opposite her. "The medicine. Doc's visit. I'll find some way to pay you back."

His dark, hooded gaze rose from his mug of coffee. "Returning my money would more than repay what you owe."

"No." She firmly shook her head. "It wouldn't. Some of it's already been spent. But I'll do my best to return what's left, if you give your word to leave my family out of it. And then I'll pay you back for Danny, even if I have to work it off cleaning your house and washing your clothes for the next year."

Cord's lips twitched as he set down his mug. "I appreciate your offer, but I'd rather just look upon what I'm doing for Danny as something one good neighbor does for another."

"Except that the Caldwells and Wainwrights aren't good neighbors, and probably never will be." The bone-weary slump to Sarah's shoulders straightened, and a proud light flared in her eyes. "No, it'll be as I said. I *will* pay you back, and I don't want to hear another word about it."

"Suit yourself." He paused. "You and your family really needed that money, didn't you?"

"Yes, we did." Sarah eyed him cautiously, not certain where he was going with this potentially inflammatory topic. "Danny's been sick so much these past years. Every time we managed to scrape up some money, it had to go for his medicines and doctor bills. It got to the point we were buying even necessities on credit, and finally the shops began refusing us any more. I tried everything, doing laundry, ironing, mending other people's clothes, and Papa and my older brothers started taking odd jobs in between their mining, just to bring in extra money. But instead of getting better, things only seemed to get worse."

Her hand touched his. "But it was still wrong, no matter how desperate we were when we robbed you. I knew better. Sometimes, though, it's easier to give in than keep on fighting to do what you know is right. And I'm ashamed to admit this was one time that I—"

Suddenly realizing she was about to heap the blame on her father, Sarah clamped her mouth shut. Though it seemed she was always waging one battle or another with her sire over what was right and wrong, that was family business and not to be shared with others. As was her admission of finally caving in to her father's demands that she assist them with the robbery.

"What, Sarah?" Cord supplied when she hesitated. "That this was one time when your father finally browbeat you into helping him with yet another of his plots to avenge himself on us? Is that what you were going to say?"

Anger swelled at his harsh if accurate appraisal, and she almost snapped back some cutting reply. Then the memory of all Cord had done today for Danny returned.

"It doesn't matter why I helped," she softly replied. "What matters is I'm sorry for it, and I give you my word it'll never happen again."

A dark brow arched. "So, what are you getting at here? That I just forget a crime was ever committed if you return the money?"

She felt like a fool. Her face flushed as hot blood filled her cheeks. "I'm sorry. I shouldn't have—"

He held up his hand to silence her. "Get a message to your father. Tell him I won't press charges if he returns the money *and* agrees to stop his vendetta against us. My father won't like it, but it *is* my money."

Relief flooded her. A hesitant smile touched her lips. "Yes. Yes, I can send a note with Doc Saunders. He'll see that Papa gets it." She gave Cord's hand a quick squeeze then, realizing how forward such an action was, quickly pulled away. "Thank you," she said, embarrassed all over again. "You won't regret it."

"Regret it?" He chuckled and rubbed his side. "Why, I wouldn't have missed it for the world."

Her cheeks pinked once again to a most becoming shade, and then she hung her head. "Now you're teasing me."

Teasing you? Cord thought. *Yes, in one sense I guess I am, but in another . . .*

An impulse to stroke the pale, silken head shot through him. An urge to stand up, walk around the table, and gather her into his arms grew until he thought the very desire would physically move him to action. Curious feelings—a fierce protectiveness and something more—ignited a fire in his blood, drawing him toward the slim, delicate girl who sat across the table.

Sarah wasn't to blame for any of this. That surprising revelation had been gradual in the coming, but seeing her in the past hours with her little brother had finally driven the point home. Or rather, finally driven it through his thick, stubborn skull, he added with a grimace.

She was an innocent pawn in the twisted, hopeless lives of two men who'd take their mutual hatred to the grave, dragging down all who were close to them in the process. Anger boiled through Cord. He at least had a chance, had left while there was still hope of rebuilding his life. Sarah, however, might not ever have that opportunity. An intense if misguided loyalty to her family would eventually destroy the beautiful woman-child, grinding down her fierce pride and boundless determination into an anguished despair.

Cord recognized the fate that awaited her, and it sickened him. She—and her little brother—deserved better. Somehow, some way, he would see that they got it. Money in itself had never meant all that much to him. It was just a means to an end. In time, when he returned to New York, he would send her some. That he could and would give her but, he cautioned himself, nothing more.

He wasn't fool enough to deny the growing attraction he felt for Sarah Caldwell, even as he forced himself to slam shut the portals of his heart. Yes, he'd help her when the opportunity arose, but no good could ever come of anything else.

The words of comfort he'd intended to offer her, however, died on his lips. The moment wasn't right. There was little between them but a wary truce born from Danny's need. In time, though, maybe some kind of friendship would grow and she'd learn to trust him. Then he'd offer his help . . .

"There's one more matter we need to discuss." Emotion deepened Cord's voice until it rumbled as he turned his increasingly disturbing thoughts to a topic even more upsetting.

Sarah lifted her head, her green eyes once more wary. "Yes?"

"Danny's presence here complicates things. I guess now he's also my prisoner. Unfortunately, until I hear from your father, the only secure place to keep the both of you is still the cellar." At the expression of horror that swept over Sarah's face, he paused. "I don't want Danny in the cellar any more than you do. For that matter, I'd rather not have to put you back in there, either. But for that to happen, you'll have to meet me halfway."

She studied him carefully, and Cord could tell exactly when comprehension struck. "What do you want from me?" she asked.

"Your word that you won't try to escape." He cut her off before she could put voice to the look of protest that flared in her eyes. "Be sensible, Sarah. Think about it. I know you wouldn't leave without Danny, and he'll be too weak to go anywhere for at least a few days. By then we'll have either heard from your father or Gabe will be back. Can't you give me your word until then?"

"You'd take the word of a Caldwell?"

His gaze locked with hers. "Yes, if that Caldwell is you."

He was right, Sarah thought as she sat there staring at Cord Wainwright. The only thing that mattered was Danny, and she didn't dare take him anywhere for a good many days. Besides, her brother would get excellent care here, not to mention food far more nourishing than they could ever hope to provide at home.

No, with Danny now in the middle of this increasingly

sticky mess, her choice was made. She'd agree to almost anything for her little brother. Sarah sucked in a deep, fortifying breath and nodded.

"You have my word."

"Good." A relieved grin lightened the tense lines of Cord's ruggedly handsome face. He shoved her piece of pie toward her. "Now, eat. You need your strength. It could be a long night."

The door swung open just then, and Emma walked in. Her glance met Sarah's.

"Danny's doing a lot better. He's breathing easy now, and Doc says he thinks the crisis is over. He said you could stay down here longer if you'd like—"

Before the housekeeper could finish, Sarah sprung from her chair and dashed across the kitchen. Behind her, she heard Cord chuckle.

"Leave her pie, Emma. As soon as she reassures herself that Danny's all right, I'll go up and fetch her to finish it—even if I have to carry her back here slung over my shoulder."

Sarah glanced up from the dough she was kneading, her gaze scanning the bright, sunlit kitchen. Beside her at the big work table, Manuela was carefully pressing a large circle of piecrust into a tin. Over on the cookstove a large pot of potatoes boiled. Next to it simmered snap beans seasoned with bacon.

The aroma of roast chicken wafted from the oven, setting Sarah's mouth to watering. She raised a flour-dusted arm to brush back a damp tendril of hair. The kitchen was hot with the cookstove going full blast, and only a freshened breeze blowing through the open window made the morning's work bearable.

Through it she watched Danny playing with a litter of kittens while their mother, the resident barn cat, lolled nearby in the sun. A soft, tender smile curved Sarah's lips. It was hard to believe that just the day before yesterday he'd been so violently ill. The good food and loving attention were already working their healing magic. If she looked closely, Sarah could almost imagine a faint glow to her brother's cheeks.

He already fit in as if he were part of the household. But then, who wouldn't like Danny? Merry, irrepressible, yet so dear and loving, the boy could wind his way around the hardest of hearts. She marveled at how close Cord and he had become in the past two days. Danny, after only a brief hesitation in which he'd quickly discerned Cord wasn't really mistreating his sister or that she truly needed "rescuing," had given his full trust and affection to the tall, grim man. And Cord seemed equally as taken with her little brother.

Danny glanced up just then and caught her eye. A grimy little hand waved in greeting, and his freckled face widened into a broad grin. Sarah waved back, then, shooing away a maddeningly persistent fly, returned to her kneading.

It was already midmorning and there was still so much to do. There would be guests today, and, according to Emma, dinner would be a more elaborate affair than usual. The housekeeper had requested her help when she'd brought up their breakfast this morning. Sarah, heartily sick of being cooped up in the bedroom for two days with her brother, was delighted to offer her assistance.

"Mama, Mama!" Pedro burst into the kitchen, startling both women from their tasks. "Come quick! The lady. The one with the cold eyes. She's already here to see Mr. Cord!"

Manuela sighed loudly and put down the can of cherries she'd been scooping into the crust-lined pie tin. "*Madre de Dios!*" she grumbled as she hurried after her son. "Am *I* the only one in this house? Must *I* drop everything to wait on the likes of her?"

Smiling as the exasperated mutterings faded, Sarah returned to her kneading. The day, up to now, had been far from unpleasant. The small, close-knit group of house staff treated her kindly, buffering the rare but jarring interactions with their master.

For that, above all, Sarah was grateful. Cord Wainwright was far too disturbing, too attractive, too . . . too intimidating with his dark good looks and pantherlike grace. And, adding insult to injury, there were times when she found she very much liked him.

Yes, Sarah thought with a small shiver, *Cord Wainwright is a very compelling man.* Even her fledgling woman's instincts warned her to stay clear of him. They hadn't anything in common. She was so far beneath him in everything that would matter to a man like him. Nothing good could come of getting to know him better. Nothing good at all . . .

And it doesn't matter anyway, she quickly reminded herself. *Danny and I will be leaving soon. Any day now, Papa's bound to send some message. Any day now, Gabe Cooper will return.*

And any day now the ranch hands, including Cord's father, would arrive. In the hustle and bustle of their return, Cord would quickly forget about her. Until then, however, life was peaceful and pleasant. She could dream, pretend all this was hers and Danny's, tasting for a fleeting time the kind of existence that, in reality, she knew could never be.

Emma bustled in just as Sarah was setting the loaves aside to rise, a laundry basket full of fresh-smelling sheets in her arms. The older woman glanced around the kitchen. "Where did Manuela wander off to? I'd hoped she'd have a spare moment to put these away."

"She left with Pedro to see to one of Mr. Wainwright's guests." Sarah removed her apron. "I'd be glad to do it for you, Emma. All my chores in here are done until time to bake the bread."

"Oh, would you, dear? I've still got a hundred things to do before dinner." Emma handed her the basket. "Just put them in the linen closet at the end of the hall off the cellar stairs."

Sarah took hold of the basket, but the housekeeper's hands stayed her. "You like it here, don't you, child?"

"It's a beautiful place," Sarah replied, feeling a pang of guilt at the admission. "And everyone is so kind, even Mr. Wainwright."

Emma's brows lifted in amusement. "Is that such a surprise? Cord's hardly a monster just because he's a Wainwright."

"Oh, I didn't mean that I think of him as some ogre anymore," Sarah said, flushing. "It's just that after all the problems I've caused . . ."

"He understands why you did what you did, even if he's still upset about the loss of the money. Give him time, Sarah. He's a good man." She chuckled. "And, if I haven't missed my guess, I'd say he very much likes you."

Sarah gaped at her in shock, clamping down hard on the urge to ask Emma to explain herself. "I . . . I think I'd better get these sheets put away," she stammered instead, deciding in this case flight was definitely the better part of valor.

Emma smiled. "Then off with you, child. It's time I saw to the rest of my chores too."

Sarah hurried from the kitchen, relieved at the ease with which they'd both managed to terminate what had promised to become a most uncomfortable conversation. Cord Wainwright liked her? Why, it was too ridiculous even to contemplate. She clasped the basket of sheets to her, glad for something to do to distract her suddenly chaotic thoughts.

She didn't mind the chores—actually, she was thankful for them. All Sarah had ever known was work, and lots of it. Besides, in some small way, the work here seemed to lighten a bit of the burden of debt she now owed Cord Wainwright.

As Sarah passed through the entrance hall, a commotion outside caught her attention. The huge double doors were thrown open in an attempt to cool the house and, through their opening, she saw Cord walk toward it with a trim, stylishly dressed woman.

Even from the distance of the foyer, Sarah could tell the woman was young. Her hair, topped by a green, curved brim hat adorned with ribbons and feathers, was a glorious mass of rich chestnut brown, contrasting dramatically with her delicate, alabaster features. The emerald-green-and-white-striped cotton dress with a boned seamed bodice and long skirt, looped up at the sides and back, lovingly hugged her slender form.

The woman smiled up at Cord, the action intimate and possessive. In that instant, Sarah recognized her. Allis! Daughter of wealthy merchant Maurice Findley, Allis was the reigning queen of Ashton's society.

Distaste surged through Sarah, bitter as gall. She didn't like the woman, never had, ever since that frustrating time spent trying to befriend Allis after her family had first moved to town. In those days shortly before her mother's untimely death, Sarah and her family had still lived close to Ashton. Thirteen-year-old Sarah and her two older brothers had, at their mother's insistence, faithfully attended the town school.

Though Allis had been two years older, Sarah had made every attempt to make her feel welcome. Yet, from the start, the other girl had rejected all overtures of friendship, turning up her nose at Sarah's plain, oft-mended clothes and lower social status. Sarah's consistent place at the top of the class hadn't helped, either. Allis had been the oldest girl in school and didn't deal well with coming in second to anyone.

And now, grown into a woman as spoiled as the girl Sarah had once known, Allis had apparently set her sights on Cord Wainwright. The realization sent a strange pain lancing through Sarah, a feeling she swiftly, fiercely, swept away. What did she care who Cord Wainwright chose to court? In actuality, they probably deserved each other!

At the memory of his kindness to Danny, remorse quickly rushed in to replace the uncharitable thought. Cord had been more than generous with them. He deserved better, much better, than Allis Findley.

The couple headed toward the front steps. With a small gasp, Sarah fled across the foyer. If Allis saw her here she'd die of shame. Once safe in the hallway, Sarah paused to catch her breath. As she did, a passing sound reached her ears.

She listened intently. There it was again. Though faint, it sounded like a cry for help. But from where was it coming?

Laying aside the basket, Sarah carefully inched her way down the hall, her head cocked in an effort to discern the cry's origin.

"H-help!" a deep voice groaned.

Sarah's pace quickened. It was coming from the room at the far end of the hall. She reached the door to the room and heard scrabbling movements on the other side, then a crash as some heavy object fell to the floor. She grasped the doorknob. Dare she open it? Maybe it was better if she fetched Cord or Emma.

"Please, someone . . . anyone. Help me!"

The entreaty was pain-wracked and made Sarah's decision. She opened the door and walked in. An overturned wicker wheelchair and a man sprawled on the floor several

78

feet beyond it greeted her. He lay there, unmoving. For an instant, Sarah thought him unconscious. Then he groaned.

She moved to his side and knelt. "Are you all right? Shall I fetch help?"

With a mighty effort, the man rolled over. Legs, limp and useless, followed without any volition of their own. He stared up at her, his handsome, pain-twisted face vaguely familiar.

"The laudanum," he gasped, gesturing toward a table upon which sat a small glass bottle. "Bring it here. I need it!"

Sarah rose and retrieved the bottle, along with the spoon that lay beside it. "How much? How much do you need?"

"Th-the whole bottle would be nice right about now," he said, even as his teeth clenched with yet another spasm of pain, "but two teaspoons will suffice."

Sitting down beside him, she lifted his head to lie on her lap, then carefully doled out the precious fluid. From the years spent nursing her family through their various injuries and illnesses, Sarah knew the laudanum must be allowed to get into this man's system before any thought could be given to moving him. Lightly, soothingly, she began to stroke his brow.

"Ah, that feels good," the man murmured, his taut form already beginning to relax. "You're an angel sent straight from heaven." He glanced up at her. "Sarah's the name, isn't it?"

She started, surprised that he knew her. He looked to be in his mid-thirties, with deep blue eyes and wavy brown hair lightly streaked at the temples with gray. Though his brow was lined and the flesh about his mouth furrowed, his gaze was serene. She was instantly drawn to him, unconsciously returning his warm smile.

"Yes, it is. I can't say that I've made your acquaintance,

though you do look familiar." As sudden recognition struck her, Sarah's voice faded and the blood drained from her face.

"It probably has something to do with the strong family resemblance," he replied with a chuckle as he extended his hand. "Allow me to introduce myself. I'm Nicholas Wainwright, Cord's older brother."

5

Sarah inhaled sharply.

"What's wrong?" Nick asked. "You look like you've just seen a ghost."

She gave an unsteady laugh. "In a sense, I guess I have. After all that . . . happened, I just never thought I'd meet you. Or, more to the point, that you'd ever want anything to do with me. Papa never talked much about . . . that night . . . except to say he'd have to live with what he'd done to you to his dying day. He was drunk, you know. And he never meant to shoot you or anyone, for that matter. He just thought the gun would convince your father to give him back his ranch."

"I never imagined for a moment your father was the kind to shoot an eight-year-old boy in cold blood, Sarah." His grip tightened on her hand as Sarah pulled back, suddenly realizing they were in an uncomfortable and potentially compromising position on the floor. "Hey, hold on, little angel," he exclaimed in mock alarm. "Where do you think you're going?"

Her lashes lowered in embarrassment. "I . . . I thought I'd fetch someone to help you."

"Well, I don't need anyone else just yet. Let's give the laudanum another ten or so minutes to work. Then you can find someone to help put me back in bed. Meanwhile," he added with a most engaging smile, "I'd like very much to spend the time with you. That is, unless being alone with a strange man in his bedroom disturbs you."

An unwelcome blush crept into her cheeks. "Oh, I wasn't thinking that at all," she lied. "I know you're a gentleman. It's just . . . just that I thought, knowing who I am, you might feel better if I left. After all, I am a Caldwell."

"Nice try, Angel," Nick said with a chuckle, "but I know a sweet, innocent, and well-bred girl when I see one. Besides, I don't hate you, if that's what you're implying." His smile faded. "Not only does the Lord ask us to forgive those who wrong us, but you weren't even born when all the trouble began. So what's there to forgive?"

She shook her head, confused. "I know I'm probably not making much sense. It's just that there's been such hatred and bitterness on both sides for such a long time. It has to spill over onto everyone a little."

"On the contrary, Angel." He crooked his head to look at her better. "It's a choice, whether you allow hatred to gain control of your heart or not. A choice *everyone* makes whether they admit to it or not."

Sarah eyed him warily. *What is this man about? Is he really all he seems to be on the surface? Well, there's only one way to find out.*

"True enough, I guess," she replied with a shrug. "Problem is, how to convince everyone there's a better way to handle things."

His mouth quirked at one corner. "Maybe it's time we join forces and help everyone learn exactly how to do that. Maybe you're the answer to my prayers."

"Your prayers? I don't understand."

"It's simple really. I've been asking the Lord for a long time now to put an end to this feud, to heal everyone's hearts." Nick sighed. "Believe it or not, there's a lot of pain on both sides."

She stared down at the Wainwright eldest son. *He wants to put an end to the feud? He wants to heal everyone's hearts?*

The realization filled her with wonder. Here he lay, lifeless from the waist down, a man in his prime who'd likely never experience the joy of marriage much less fatherhood. Yet he'd already forgiven when others, far less damaged by the events of a tragic night long ago, stubbornly refused to let go of their anger or consider another course. A tender regard for Nicholas Wainwright welled within her.

Sarah smiled down at him. "I'd be honored to 'join forces,' Mr. Wainwright."

"Nick," he corrected her. "Please, call me Nick."

"Then Nick it is." He was so open, she thought, so approachable and friendly. Nick wasn't at all like his younger brother . . .

"Why the frown, little angel?"

"Oh, it's nothing." With a nonchalant wave of one hand, Sarah tried to cover her discomfiture at being caught. "I was just thinking how different you are from your brother."

A wry grin twisted Nick's mouth. "Well, yes. He can walk and I can't, not to mention he's much more good looking and—"

"I didn't mean that at all," she quickly interjected. "I was speaking more of the difference in your personalities."

"Oh? And how so?"

Sarah rolled her eyes. *Here I go again, putting not only my foot but my entire leg into my mouth.* "It's really not important. Cord's very kind. It's just that his moods are so changeable and . . . and sometimes he can be so cold and forbidding. Though it's understandable, considering what I did to him. I don't think he likes me very much." She sighed. "I'm afraid your brother sides with your father in his feelings for my family."

"Well, Cord definitely has some forgiveness issues, but they're not with you or your family. Sure, he was hopping mad when the money was stolen, and his ego was bruised that he wasn't able to defend himself, considering his outstanding boxing skills, but he's never held a grudge against your family." A deep blue gaze calmly met hers. "And I don't think he dislikes you, either. Rather, far from it. You'll have to be patient with him, though. He guards his heart more closely than most."

There was a puzzling look of sadness in Nick's eyes as he spoke of his brother. Though she wasn't sure why he felt that way, thinking of her own siblings, Sarah could well understand such emotions. "You must love him very much."

"No more than he loves me." Nick shoved to a sitting position. "The library. Have you seen it yet?"

She shook her head. "Can't say as I have."

"Well, Cord singlehandedly filled half those shelves by sending books back for me. Do you realize what that must have cost, with him struggling at the same time to pay his way through college and law school? Despite my protests he kept sending them, knowing how important they were to me as my one escape from a reality sometimes almost too much to bear. Or," Nick added with a smile, "almost too much to bear until I found the Lord."

"There's so much I don't know about Cord," Sarah murmured. *How well he's kept that softer side of himself hidden*, she thought. Yet, even as she mused over the enigma of Cord Wainwright, a desire to crack open that shell, once and for all, and discover everything she could about this puzzling, attractive man filled her.

Such an undertaking, though, would require a deep trust and commitment on his part, as much as on hers. She wondered if she'd ever gain such a treasure. Or if she should even try. After all, she'd be leaving here soon and likely wouldn't see much of him after that.

"You'd be good for him, Sarah."

Startled by the unexpected pronouncement, for a moment or two all Sarah could do was stare. "What do you mean?"

"Cord likes and respects you. And the fact that you're delightfully lovely," Nick added with a mischievous twinkle, "certainly hasn't hurt your cause. How do you feel about him, all the clash of personalities and wills notwithstanding?"

"I . . . I . . ." Sarah flushed crimson. "Why are you asking me this? I've only been here a few days. Assisting others to beat up and then rob a man is hardly the foundation for even a friendship, much less anything deeper." She pushed away from Nick, then climbed to her feet. "I was beginning to think you were a good, kind man, but now I'm not so sure. You've been toying with me, haven't you?"

His expression turned solemn. "No. Never. I wasn't toying with you. Maybe I was pushing too hard, but I'd never do anything to hurt you. It's just that Cord's been paying me a lot of visits since your arrival, and we've talked a lot about you. So much so, that I felt I knew you before I even met you. But please," he said offering his hand, "accept my apologies for my lack of tact and thoughtfulness. I am so sorry, Sarah."

Unsure if she could believe him or not, Sarah stared down at Nick for a long moment. Regret, tinged with hope, gleamed in his dark blue eyes. Maybe she had been too quick to accuse him of duplicity. But with both Emma and now Nick intimating things best left unexamined, Sarah was getting very uncomfortable.

"Fine." With an exasperated toss of her head, she took his hand, gave it a brief squeeze, then released it. "Apology accepted. Let's just not talk about Cord anymore, shall we?

Besides, we've absolutely nothing in common, and I've even heard him mention he plans to go back to New York just as soon as he can."

Nick arched a skeptical brow. "Hmm, you don't say?"

"Here." Sarah walked to his bed and retrieved two pillows, which she then proceeded to place behind his head. "Enough talk, Nick Wainwright. I'll fetch some help now in getting you into bed."

"Will you come back again?"

"Of course. You might need a woman's touch in seeing you comfortably settled."

"No." He shook his head. "I meant will you come back and visit me every day for as long as you're here?"

More pleased than she cared to show, Sarah busied herself smoothing the wrinkles from one of Emma's old dresses. "Yes, I'd like that very much—if Cord will let me."

Nick laughed. "Go ahead. Ask his permission. But if he tells you no, tell him that I want you to. He won't refuse me. I've got too much on him from our boyhood days. He wouldn't dare say no."

She stared down at him in bemusement. "Whatever you say." Sarah turned toward the door.

"One thing more, Angel."

"Yes?" She glanced back over her shoulder. "What is it, Nick?"

"That statement of yours about Cord going back to New York. It's not written in stone, you know. There are a lot of things that could make him stay. The right woman, for one, just might change his mind."

Cord was reading in the library when Sarah rushed into the room. He moved the ribbon to mark his place, then closed the book. "Your brother," she said without preamble. "He's fallen and I need help getting him back to bed."

"Is he all right? What happened?" Cord flung aside his book and leaped to his feet.

"Nick fell from his wheelchair."

Not awaiting a reply, Sarah turned and hurried back down the hall. Cord hesitated, puzzlement wrinkling his brow.

"Nick?" he muttered. "When did she get the chance to meet, much less be on a first name basis with my brother?" He motioned for Pedro, who had just walked in, to follow as he set out after Sarah. By the time they entered the bedroom, he found her already kneeling on the floor beside Nick.

Nick grinned when he saw Cord. "Your tales about Sarah don't do her justice, little brother." He cocked a speculative brow. "But then again, maybe that was your intent."

"I don't know what you're talking about," Cord growled as he squatted beside his brother's shoulders. He shot Pedro a quick glance. "Pick up Nick's feet."

Nick was soon back in bed. Sarah turned to go.

"Angel?"

She halted and glanced back at him. "Yes, Nick?"

"Wait a minute, will you? I've got something to ask my brother." He turned to Cord. "Do you have any problem with her paying me a visit each day?"

For an instant, Cord was taken aback. Myriad emotions swirled within him, and most of them weren't particularly pleasant. "And why are you so suddenly interested in Sarah's company?"

"Why?" The merest hint of a smile glimmered on Nick's lips. "Well, because I like human interaction, and you and the household staff are frequently too busy to visit. And I certainly can't get my wheelchair down to the cellar or upstairs to the bedroom you've now put her in. What other reason would there be?"

Cord shrugged, not at all convinced there wasn't something more going on here. "None, I guess. You've my permission."

"Thank you, little brother." Nick's rich voice, tinged with amusement, interrupted the steady glance between Cord and Sarah. "You're a generous soul to share your little angel with me. I'm in your debt."

Cord wrenched his gaze from Sarah. "You've got it all wrong, *big* brother. First, she's not my 'little angel.' Second, she's not mine to share," he added with a touch of irritation. "As long as Sarah keeps to her promise, she's free to visit whomever she wants, anytime she wants."

Nick's grin widened. "Good. That suits me fine." He looked to Sarah. "Did you hear that? Anytime you want."

"Y-yes, Nick." Sarah began edging toward the door. "Anytime. Now, I really must be going. I'm sure Emma needs me in the kitchen."

Cord watched Sarah all but flee the room, then turned on his brother. "What's your game?"

"Game?" Nick's blue eyes widened in feigned innocence. "Whatever do you mean? Surely you're not angry that Sarah wishes to visit me? You never mentioned any claim on her."

"My feelings for Sarah aren't the topic of this conversation." Cord's eyes narrowed, remembering Pedro's presence. "We'll talk about this later. Right now, I've guests."

"Oh, and who might they be?"

"Allis and one of her friends. Would you like to have lunch with us?"

Nick shook his head. "And suffer with the splitting headache her self-centered conversation is sure to give me? Not on your life. Allis is *your* friend, not mine."

"She's a *family* friend," Cord was quick to correct him. "Calculating females have never been my cup of tea."

"Oh, well, that's a relief to us all." Nick laughed. "They've never been one of my favorites, either. Personally, I prefer little angels."

His brother exhaled an exasperated breath. "Yes, I'd imagine you would. A perfect balance to your devilish nature." He headed toward the door. "But that's a subject we'll discuss later."

Nick's parting comment followed him down the hall. "You can be sure of that, little brother," he said, laughter rumbling in his chest. "And in ways you haven't yet begun to imagine . . ."

"It won't work, you know, whatever your little scheme is. Cord's far too astute for the likes of you, not to mention all the trouble you'll be in when Edmund returns from the cattle drive."

The feminine voice, dripping with hostility, halted Sarah. She glanced up from the china plate she'd just placed on the dining room table, meeting the woman's gaze head on.

"Hello, Allis. So nice to see you again too." She turned back to her setting of the table.

Allis stepped farther into the room. "I'm warning you. Get out while you still have that greedy little hide of yours."

Sarah shot her a disgusted look. "Thank you, Allis. Your advice has been noted and filed away with all your other kind and gracious remarks. Now, if you don't mind, I've work to do."

"And who do you think you are to dismiss me?" the brunette demanded, ire rising in her voice. "You and your family are nothing but trash, a shameful, sordid blight on our fair town. You rob the Wainwrights of their hard-earned money and then have the gall to prance around the house like you belong here. Why, I've never—"

"That's enough, Allis." Sarah strode over to confront the

other woman. "I'm not going to stand here and listen to that vile tongue of yours a moment longer. I've got better ways to spend my time."

Allis grasped Sarah's arm as she turned to walk away. "I'm not through with you."

"There's more?"

"Stay away from Cord Wainwright."

"Oh, so that's what this is really about." Sarah laughed, then twisted free of Allis's grip. "Afraid I'll steal Cord from you? Really, Allis, you've got to stop being so insecure. It doesn't become a lady."

"I mean it, Sarah Caldwell." A cruel smile touched her lips. "If you try anything, I'll personally see to it that you and your entire family are destroyed. And don't think for a minute I can't do it. I always get what I want."

The malevolent gleam in Allis's eyes momentarily caught Sarah off guard. She'd always known the woman was capable of cruel and thoughtless behavior, but the vicious determination burning in her eyes just now was new. New and very disturbing.

"You don't frighten me," Sarah shot back, equally determined not to let Allis intimidate her. "I thought I'd taught you that back in school." She walked away, tossing the other woman one last, challenging glare—and stumbled right into a hard, masculine body.

Startled, Sarah looked up into Cord's dark eyes. A bemused, questioning light danced in their depths. His arms loosely clasped hers.

"And what exactly did you teach Allis back in school, Sarah?"

How much of our conversation had he heard?

She wiggled free of his grasp. "Not how to be a lady, and that's for sure," Sarah replied, glaring at Allis.

"How dare you speak to me in that manner, you . . . you little tramp!"

"That's enough, Allis." Though Cord's request was mildly couched, there was a warning vibrating deep within it. "I won't allow that kind of talk in my house."

The woman's face reddened. "You . . . you can defend her after what she's done?" she railed, turning the full brunt of her indignation upon Cord. "She all but set you up for the robbery, and now you give her free rein of the house like she's some honored guest? Well, I suppose then you won't be satisfied until she's finished the job by stealing the silver and other family heirlooms!"

"How I treat Sarah is none of your business." A muscle twitched furiously in his jaw. "First Doc Saunders telling me what to do, and now you. Is all of Ashton going to meddle in my affairs? Well, I won't have it, do you hear me?"

Allis blanched. "Cord. Darling," she cooed, reaching out to him. "I didn't mean to dictate to you. Please forgive me."

Cord took her by the arm. "It's already forgotten," he said with a grim smile. "Now, let's permit Sarah to finish her work in here, or we won't be eating our lunch before suppertime."

He began to guide her from the room. "A short walk outside will do us both good."

A simpering smile spread across Allis's face, and she eagerly followed him from the dining room. Watching them walk away, frustration at Cord's bland acceptance of the other woman's tactless behavior filled Sarah. Allis, it seemed, could get away with murder and Cord hardly blinked an eye, while she . . .

"Maybe you both really *do* deserve each other," she muttered sourly, and went back to setting the table.

Sarah gently slipped the last egg from beneath the clucking broody hen and placed it in her basket. Then, her thoughts still far away, she left the chicken coop and headed back toward the house. Lunch had ended over four hours ago, and still Allis Findley and her friend lingered. All afternoon, as Sarah worked outside in the garden, the women's lilting laughter, interspersed with the low, deep tones of Cord's voice, had carried through the parlor window.

The sounds of their mutual enjoyment only served to increase the unpleasant churning in Sarah's stomach. She shouldn't care, but it was so hard after the past days spent with Cord. He'd been so gentle, and the expression that sometimes burned in his eyes when he looked at her . . .

And you're a fool, Sarah Caldwell, she mentally berated herself. *You hardly know him, and yet you already place too much stock in his treatment of you and Danny. It's nothing more than his innate kindness coming through.*

"The two Caldwell children" was probably how Cord viewed them, yet the painful truth was that, even as short a time as they'd been together, she hardly shared such platonic feelings for him. He stirred emotions that set her heart to fluttering, and had since the first time she'd met him. Yet the admission also confused and frightened her. She'd never felt this way before.

The pounding of hooves and joyous shouts of an approaching group of riders intruded on Sarah's tortured thoughts. Her gaze sought out the road leading down from the mountains. Already breaching the hill just a quarter mile away was a band of cowboys. The Wainwright hands, most likely, she glumly realized, and led by Edmund Wainwright himself.

She stifled an impulse to hurry across the large expanse separating the barn from the main house. At that moment, Cord and his two guests walked outside. Their presence only strengthened Sarah's resolve. She wouldn't give any of them the satisfaction of thinking she was afraid to finally confront the Wainwright patriarch.

Pretending concern with her basket of delicate eggs, Sarah purposely slowed her pace. The cowboys caught her halfway to the house. With wild whoops and admiring whistles, they circled her on their horses like she was some prize heifer about to be roped.

Sarah halted, waiting patiently for their youthful high spirits to subside. Instead, they milled around her, stirring the dust as they continued their revolutions. Finally, between fitful coughs, she tried to dart between the excited horses.

"Whoa, there, little filly," one dark-haired cowboy laughed as he skillfully blocked her way. "Where do you think yore goin'? Gals like you don't come around too often. I've a hankerin' to get to know you better."

He leaned over and scooped Sarah up in a sinewy arm. It was all she could do to clutch the egg basket to her before she rose in the air.

"Put me down this instant!" she gasped, gazing into a dirt-streaked, grinning face.

"And what if I don't, little filly?" the man asked with a chuckle. "Who's to care if I have some good-hearted fun with a purty gal?"

"*I'll* care." Cord's voice, edged with anger and something more, cut through the bedlam. "Put her down, Cal, while you're still able."

Cal's smile faded. With a quick tug on the reins, he wheeled his horse toward the house. "I didn't mean no harm, Mr. Wainwright. Honest I didn't. I-I reckon I'm just a little riled after all the celebratin' in town."

"I know that, Cal," Cord replied, his voice calmer. "But it's no way to treat a lady. Now, put her down."

Ever so carefully, the cowboy lowered Sarah to the ground, then tipped his hat. "Sorry, ma'am. No offense intended."

She managed a smile. "No offense taken, Cal."

From across the dusty stretch separating them, her gaze met Cord's. His eyes glittered like blackest onyx, but even as their glances lengthened Sarah saw the tension drain from him. For a fleeting instant, a smile quirked one corner of his mouth. Then Allis was tugging on his arm and gesturing to a big, solidly built man riding toward them.

Cord dragged his gaze from her, and once more Sarah found herself alone. She tried to take advantage of the diversion to slip past the milling pack of men and horses, but the big man on horseback cut her off. Once more, Sarah halted, lifting her glance to meet eyes of the deepest blue. *The same shade as Nick's*, she thought before scanning the rest of his face.

His hair was heavily shot with gray, but the lines that furrowed his brow and fanned from his careworn eyes did little to hide the strong features Sarah had come to know well in his two sons. It was Edmund Wainwright, her father's enemy. Her chin lifted in defiance.

"And who are you, little lady? If my sons hired a new housemaid in my absence, I'll have to commend them for their good taste."

The voice was but a harsher version of Cord's, and Sarah had to fight hard against the impulse to lower her guard. Her mind swam with possible replies, all designed to hide her true identity, but she chose none. Let the chips fall where they may. She wasn't ashamed of who she was.

She opened her mouth to reply when Allis Findley silkily intruded. "Before you start drooling over that tart, Edmund, let me save you further embarrassment. She's Jacob Caldwell's daughter and is *supposed* to be a prisoner on this ranch."

Allis gave Sarah a sweetly malicious smile. "But, as you can see, she's managed to charm her way out of that predicament rather quickly."

"That'll be enough, Allis," Cord said for the second time

94

today as he came up beside her. "And I'll thank you to keep your nose out of my business from now on."

"Wainwright business, I'd say." His father swung down from his horse and strode over to stand eye-to-eye with his son. "What in the blazes is going on here? Is what Allis said true? Is this girl really a Caldwell?"

Cord held his ground. "This isn't a topic for public discussion. Let's go inside."

"Wait just a dad-blasted minute!" Edmund grabbed his arm. "No one's ordering me around on my own ranch, and especially not some fool son of mine. Answer my question!"

"And I said, this is something best discussed inside," Cord replied, his gaze going dark and hard.

Edmund's face purpled. "Why, you arrogant pup," he snarled, his fists rising. "How dare—"

Sarah stepped between them. She could care less if Edmund Wainwright made a fool of himself in front of everyone, but she refused to be a pawn in Allis Findley's attempt to humiliate her and Cord.

"You asked who I was, Mr. Wainwright," she said, mustering all her courage to confront him, "and I'm not ashamed to tell you. It's just as Allis said. I'm Sarah—Jacob Caldwell's daughter."

6

A light rap on the door interrupted Sarah. She turned from her seat near the window and quickly looked to the bed to see if the sound had woken Danny. The little boy slept on. Expelling a small sigh, she rose from the rocking chair. Whoever it was, she'd best see to the visitor before the knocking woke her brother. He at least could have a calm, uneventful day.

And what a day it had been, she thought as she made her way to the door, from snobbish Allis Findley to Edmund Wainwright's crazed ravings. Though she'd stayed in her room the rest of the day with Danny, Sarah knew Cord and his father had spent the next several hours locked in the library, deep in what had frequently been a very heated discussion. Emma had wasted no time filling her in about that when she'd brought up their supper tray several hours ago.

Sarah reached the door, then hesitated. Whatever the outcome of the two men's dialogue, she knew this was probably her last night under the Wainwright roof. The realization stirred anew the dull ache in her chest. With a force that mirrored her pain, she jerked open the door.

Cord stood there, the dim hallway light throwing his face into shadow. Nonetheless, it was evident from the slight droop to his broad shoulders and rumpled clothes that he was exhausted. An impulse to smooth the tousled hair from his forehead filled her. Only the strongest effort controlled it. There was nothing between them and never had been, she fiercely reminded herself.

"I need to talk with you, Sarah."

His rich, resonant voice reverberated in the quiet hallway, finding its answering chord in the depths of her heart. Sarah swallowed hard. "I . . . I can't. Danny's asleep."

He shook his head. "No, I meant come down with me to the library."

She didn't move.

"Please, Sarah."

Stepping from her bedroom, she pulled the door closed behind her. For a breathless instant they stood so close his nearness was a tangible, heart-stopping experience. Sarah's senses began to spin. Then he moved aside, motioning her ahead of him.

Though she'd passed the library several times today, Sarah had never taken the opportunity to examine the room. Now, as she walked in for the first time, her gaze hungrily scanned the enclosure, moving first to the ceiling-high shelves lining three of the room's four walls. There were hundreds of books, all bound in rich, beautifully hand-tooled leather.

The recollection that many had been bought by Cord for his invalid brother filled her with a warm glow. This room, of all the rooms in the house, emanated his presence the most strongly, the books he'd chosen an eloquent statement of his innermost self. An urge to take one down and read it, to learn more of the man, swelled within her.

Sarah glanced across the room to its only window. The velvet curtains were drawn against the evening's cool mountain air. The only light that stayed the encroaching darkness was that of two oil lamps set on opposite ends of a massive oak desk. It was a cozy, intimate room, and suddenly, as Sarah heard the door close behind her, the outside world melted away. The only reality was the moment—and a darkly attractive man named Cord.

"Please sit down, Sarah."

He indicated the overstuffed green velvet couch that graced a corner in front of the bookshelves. As she silently complied, words solidified in her throat. Rather than meet his piercing gaze, once she was seated she busied herself with smoothing the folds of her dress and felt, rather than heard, him settle himself in a wing chair across from her.

Reluctantly, Sarah looked up. For the briefest moment, she almost imagined she saw a tender light gleam in Cord's eyes. If she had, the light was quickly extinguished. He leaned forward.

"I want to apologize for my father's outburst this afternoon," he began, his voice soft yet vibrant in the silent room. "I hadn't planned on him finding out about you and Danny quite that way."

A smile touched her lips. "Allis seemed to have a different view of how things should be handled."

Cord sighed. "She certainly doesn't care much for you. I can't recall ever seeing her so cruel or vindictive."

"I'm afraid that goes back a long while. Don't concern yourself. Her feelings for me are nothing I can't handle."

"No, I imagine not." Grudging respect shone in his eyes. "Still, I'm sorry for what happened today. I hope you can find it in your heart to forgive my father. He too has been terribly scarred by what happened in the past. Today's events change nothing, however." He ran a weary hand through his hair. "You and Danny will stay until the money's returned or Gabe gets back and takes you into custody."

"B-but your father said he refused to let us remain under his roof."

"Once he calms down, my father is still capable of reason. He finally agreed my plan was the best of all alternatives."

Sarah didn't know whether to be happy or sad. On one hand, she didn't want to leave Cord. On the other, he was keeping her and Danny from their family. And then, on the other, *other* hand, he likely was wishing he could be rid of them as soon as possible.

"Thanks for all your efforts on our part," she replied, focusing on the likelihood Cord wanted them gone just as much as did his father.

He must have taken her tone of voice as sarcasm, for he grinned. "And just when I thought you were beginning to enjoy it here."

Her cheeks warmed. "I appreciate your kindness, especially considering the circumstances, but we both know you're keeping us all but prisoners."

His smile faded. "No, Sarah. Your father's the one keeping you prisoners. You've been with us six days now, and Danny almost three. Yet, in all that time, there's not been one word from him."

"I'm sure Doc hasn't even had a chance to get a message to him yet," she said, rising to her father's defense.

Cord shook his head. "On the contrary. Doc said he met one of your brothers in town the very next day and told him to tell your father. He's had the message for two days now."

Confusion filled her. "I don't understand. When did Doc tell you this? I haven't seen him—"

"He showed up today, a short while after my father arrived. His visit, in retrospect, was instrumental in swaying my father to my view of things."

"But I don't . . ." She cut off further protest, deciding to deal with the reality of the situation. "I'm sure Papa will get a message through to you any time now. He just has to be careful. What reason should he have to trust any of you?"

Cord shrugged. "None at all, Sarah. But then, the feeling's

mutual, isn't it? I just think the welfare of one's children should be one's first consideration, don't you?"

"I don't like what you're implying." Sarah angrily punctuated the statement by jumping to her feet. "And I've had about all I can take of insults about my papa."

Her fists clenched white as she stood there. "Let me tell you one thing, Mr. High and Mighty Wainwright. We may have fallen on hard times, but we're not trash! Despite our misfortunes, we've done the best we could. And we're still a family, loving and devoted, which is more than your family apparently has ever been!"

He leaned back in his chair, his fingers moving to temple beneath his chin. "Striking a little below the belt, aren't you, Sarah?" he asked, his voice low and controlled. "And all of this is my family's fault, is it?"

"Of course it's your family's fault!" she snapped, all the day's pent-up emotions bursting forth. "This ranch was ours until your father cheated mine. What chance did my papa have against a professional gambler? Your father knew his weakness for the cards, and pushed him until all he had left was the ranch. My papa never had a chance, and it broke him heart and soul."

Cord rose. "Come on. Be reasonable. No one's a victim unless he chooses to be. Neither of our fathers has made wise decisions, even if mine has more wealth to show for it. Yet have you or I fallen prey to self-pity or inaction? Put the blame where it belongs—on your father's back."

"No." She stubbornly shook her head. "Say what you will about your own father, Cord Wainwright, but don't you dare include my papa with yours! He may lose his way at times, but at heart he's a good man. I won't have you speaking ill of him."

Tears filled her eyes and, in spite of her efforts to stifle them, spilled down her cheeks. "Please," she choked out as she brushed them away. "I-I don't want to talk about this anymore."

It was all Cord could do to keep from taking Sarah into his arms. The reality of her situation was finally beginning to make inroads into her blind faith for her father, and he knew it hurt. Still, she needed to face it if she were ever to be free of the bonds of her father's vengeance-laden life. He just hated causing her pain.

His gaze swept her slim form. No, hurting Sarah was the furthest thing from his mind.

Her sweet presence filled the room, whirling around him in heady waves that blotted out all thought but Sarah. Sarah . . . whose moods possessed the inconstancy of the mountain weather. Sarah . . . who, like the ever-changing climate, was just as unsettling, beguiling him with her complexity, drawing him ever toward her . . .

With a jerk, Cord stepped back. What was the matter with him? It was almost more than he could bear to keep a safe distance. Yet there she stood, proud and defiant, ready to do battle for her family's honor, as dishonorable as that family was. Would they ever span that chasm of hostilities?

"Look," Cord said, trying one more time. "It hasn't been a pleasant day for either of us. We're both tired. I didn't mean to start a fight over your father. All I meant was that you've got to stop taking responsibility for him. Start thinking about you and Danny. People over whose lives you *do* have a little control."

She shook her head in denial, but Cord could tell by the sudden muting of anger in her eyes that his point had driven home.

"He's my papa. I owe him my love and devotion."

"Yes, you do." His voice gentled. "But not to the sacrifice of your own life and happiness. Neither of us owe *that* much to our fathers."

Perplexed by the fleeting thread of pain she heard in his voice, Sarah lifted her gaze to his. The fire that always burned in his dark eyes had faded, extinguished by some tightly guarded memory. He stood before her as an enemy, but also as a man. A man who felt deeply, gave of what he possessed generously, while always holding back the far greater treasure of his heart. A tempting treasure she felt compelled to mine, even as common sense told her to run as fast and far away as she could.

Cord's right, Sarah thought. *We've both had a trying day and are tired. Neither of us are thinking straight, and that could get us both into trouble.*

"I'd like to go to my room."

He motioned toward the door. "As you wish."

They made their way upstairs in silence. As she reached her door, he softly spoke her name. Sarah turned. "Yes?"

"I don't want to fight with you anymore," he said. "Can we at least finally have some peace between us?"

His eyes glowed bright and warm in the hallway's lamplight. Her breath caught in her throat. In an instant, all the anger and indignation she'd felt in the library faded. She could only remember how gentle, how kind he'd been when Danny was sick.

"Thank you for all you've done for us," she said, the emotions spilling from her heart to form words. "I know I'm short with you at times, and blame you for things you've never had any part of, but I also see you for the man you are. A good man. And, for the remainder of the time that Danny and I are here, I promise not to cause you any more trouble." She smiled wanly. "It may not be quite the 'peace' between us you'd like, but it's the least I can do."

He stared down at her, his gaze inscrutable and, for an instant, she thought he might kiss her. The memory of the touch of his lips that first time flooded her, and she wanted, oh, how she wanted, to feel his mouth on hers again! She lifted her face to him, her lashes lowering, and waited.

"Fair enough," he said and, reaching around her, opened her bedroom door. "Good night, Sarah."

Her lids snapped open and she stared up into unfathomable black eyes. Shame flooded her at what she saw as her wanton behavior in again encouraging a kiss, an act Cord evidently no longer wished any part of. With a toss of her head, Sarah gathered her skirts and flounced into her room, shutting the door behind her.

Cord stared at the oaken door, then turned, walked down the hall, and entered his own bedroom. In all the distraction and conflict of the past days, he'd forgotten how potent an effect Sarah's closeness had upon him. It was bad enough when she'd said that he was a good man. The words were sweet to his ears, but what really unmanned him was the look in her eyes as she'd said them. It was as if she'd seen clear down into his soul, and knew him.

Then the scent of her—fresh mown hay and wildflowers—wafted up to him, and her hair . . . How he'd wanted to sink his fingers into her hair and feel it tumble down about his hands! Ah, to take her into his arms and kiss her!

Muttering in frustration, Cord shrugged out of his shirt. His boots quickly joined it. Without bothering to pull down the coverlet, he threw himself onto the bed.

He cursed the day he'd ever met Sarah Caldwell. He hadn't even known her a week, and already she was driving him mad. Barely out of girlhood, she played a woman's game with consummate skill. But the way he craved her had nothing to do with admiration for her fine manner. No, far, far from it.

Well, it had to stop, this gut-twisting manipulation of hers. He had no other choice. To continue on this path with her would surely be his undoing.

Thank goodness Gabe would be back any day now. Gabe was the sheriff. Let him deal with the robbery and her family. The sooner he was free of Sarah, the better.

She was getting too close on many levels. And that frightened him more than he cared to admit.

"Emma, would you pack me a lunch basket?" Nick asked two weeks later. "I've a mind to take Sarah and Danny on a picnic."

The housekeeper glanced up from her bed making. "Why, of course, Nicholas. It's a fine fall day for an outing."

Nick nodded. "I'm hoping this might cheer up Sarah. Can you have the basket ready by eleven? I'd like to show them that aspen grove out near Ohio Creek. This time in October, their turning leaves should be glorious."

Emma smiled. "You're a kind one to think of that sweet girl. It's a sight more than Cord's been doing these past couple of weeks. If I didn't know better, I'd wager those two have had a falling-out."

"More likely the opposite." Nick chuckled. "But have no fear, Emma, my dear. That'll be remedied soon enough. My brother just needs a little help recognizing what's best for him."

"Well, all I know is Sarah's hurting real bad, with her father never sending word or money in all this time. What could possess a man to desert his family like that?"

He shrugged. "I truly don't know. But then, there are many ways to turn your back on others, aren't there?"

"Yes, I suppose there are. Still, it's a shame and that's all there is to it." Emma straightened. "Your bed's done. If you've nothing else for me right now, I'll get started on that picnic lunch."

"I'm fine, Emma. Please, go on."

She turned to leave, then stopped. "Cord's holed up in the library again with that infernal account ledger. How about I see if he'd like to go along? He could use some fresh air. Couldn't help but sweeten his ill-temper of late."

"No, I think not, at least not this time." Nick stared out the window, a slight smile playing about his lips. "I've got other plans for my brother."

Cord stared at the ranch ledger, reading the same line for the twentieth time. He'd made little progress in the past half hour. With a disgusted sound, he finally tossed the book aside. Leaning back in his chair, he propped his long legs on the desk.

He was royally sick of trying to find some way to squeeze money from the increasingly skeletal ranch budget. He closed his eyes to ease their burning.

A week ago, the prize bull had broken its leg and had to be put down, and already his father was making noises about buying another one. Problem was, none of the local ranchers were willing to sell him one on credit. News of the robbery and subsequent financial straits had gotten around the valley. It seemed only a matter of time now before they'd have to start selling off some of their herd just to make ends meet.

A heavy weariness settled over Cord. There were just too

many concerns hammering at him of late. The ranch, his father, and, of course, the problem of Sarah. She seemed, sooner or later, to insinuate herself into all his thoughts until he was almost constantly thinking of her. Thinking of her while avoiding her at all costs.

Ever since that night in the library, he'd found himself increasingly unwilling to face the dilemma of what to do with her. How much longer could he continue to keep her and Danny prisoner? Yet, some of his earlier comments to the contrary, he knew he didn't want to even contemplate the thought of her leaving.

The news that Gabe Cooper would be unavoidably detained in Denver, helping his mother set to rest all of his recently deceased father's affairs, had bought Cord a little more time to come to terms with what he must do with Sarah. In the ensuing two weeks, however, he'd found himself no closer to a solution. He should've known there'd be no easy answers . . .

Try as he might, Cord couldn't get Sarah out of his mind. He wondered how she'd been dealing with the realization that her father wouldn't be returning the money or coming for her and Danny. He despised Jacob Caldwell most of all for that—choosing his ill-gotten gains over his own children. All Castle Mountain's problems notwithstanding, could they possibly compare to the pain she was surely experiencing?

Rejection . . . Cord knew she must, at the very least, be feeling rejection at her father's betrayal. That was an emotion he understood all too well. Did she feel a similar betrayal in his own actions of late, in his overt attempts to avoid her whenever possible?

At the consideration, guilt surged through him. Though he didn't, in truth, owe her anything, Cord suddenly felt little better than Sarah's own father.

Angrily, Cord swung his legs down from the desk. The ranch and its problems could go to blazes! He'd had all he could take of them. What really mattered, in this instant of white-hot clarity, was that he was a coward and had treated Sarah cruelly. He'd left her alone to bear her pain when he, of all people, should have understood what she was going through.

Further avoidance wasn't fair to either of them. But what could he say? What did he really want? He didn't want her to leave, that much he knew. But he also knew she'd been wrong when she said he was a good man. Most times, he didn't feel all that good. But then, maybe he viewed life—and himself— too much through his father's disapproving point of view.

Cord rose and strode from the library. This wasn't about him or his perhaps overly critical self image right now, but about Sarah. Though his overtures might be rebuffed, he was going to at least try to talk with her about making some alternative plans for her and Danny's future. It was long past time she see the reality of her situation, and do something about it.

"Emma," Cord called to the older woman when he finally gave up trying to find Sarah in the house, and walked outside to where Emma worked at the clothesline, hanging wash out to dry. "Do you know where Sarah is?"

The housekeeper slowly turned, an auburn brow arching as she pulled two clothespins from between her teeth. "Sarah? And why on earth would you suddenly care? You've all but ignored that poor child of late."

"Now, Emma," he said, trying his most engaging smile on her, "it's not as bad as all that. I've just been very busy—"

"That's a bunch of hogwash, and you know it!" She advanced on him, her finger wagging in the air. "Save that for someone who doesn't know you. Admit it. You've been selfish and thoughtless. At the very least, you owe Sarah an apology, and even then I'm not so sure she should accept it."

Cord rolled his eyes and sighed. "Okay. Okay. I plead guilty. But I can't beg her forgiveness if I can't find her, can I? So, where is she?"

"Gone with Nicholas to the aspen meadow down by Ohio Creek. They're having a picnic there."

That bit of news stopped Cord in his tracks. *Sarah's with Nicholas?*

"Well, it seems my brother hasn't broken stride in my absence," he muttered, a flush creeping up his neck and face.

"And why should he?" Emma settled her hands on her hips and glared up at him. "Nick's kind to that sweet girl, and if she hadn't had him to visit these past two weeks, I don't know what she'd have done. They've gotten very close. And it's done the both of them a world of good."

"Yes, I imagine it has," Cord said dryly. He opened his mouth to make a snide comment about his brother's way with the ladies, then snapped it shut. He frowned.

"What is it? What's the matter, Cord?"

"Did you say the aspen meadow down by the creek?"

Emma nodded. "Yes. What's wrong with that?"

"Cal Jenkins and Hank Spivey spotted a rogue grizzly roaming that area a few days back. Didn't anyone tell Nick?"

Her eyes grew wide. "Well, I don't know. I hadn't even heard myself."

"Blast!" Cord turned and ran off toward the barn. "That's all I need—Nick and Sarah out there with some killer grizzly!"

"Boy, what a great picnic, Mr. Nick." Danny wiped his berry-stained mouth on the back of his shirtsleeve. "Miss Emma sure makes the best raspberry cobbler this side of the Rockies. I think I just might marry her when I grow up."

Nick laughed. "And I think she just might wait around for a boy as fine as you." His glance scanned the grassy slopes that slid into the mountains. "You know, we really should bring Emma back a present for all the work she did for our picnic. Would you do me a big favor and pick her some flowers? Take Pedro with you."

Danny jumped to his feet. "Sure thing, Mr. Nick." He ran over to where Pedro lay leaning against one of the carriage wheels. "Hey, Pedro, come help me get some flowers for Miss Emma!"

Pedro sighed loudly, then slowly climbed to his feet. Sarah had to laugh at the pair as they headed toward the nearest hill, Danny running and leaping while his older companion plodded along far behind.

"I don't think a walk right after such a big lunch is what Pedro had in mind, Nick," she said, turning to her companion on the blanket. "Not to mention any wildflowers they'd find this time of year are sure to be dried and spent."

He propped himself up on his elbows, a sheepish grin on his face. "I guess I've been caught red-handed, ma'am. It was the only way I could think of to have a few minutes of privacy with you."

"Oh?" Sarah cocked her head. "And what's the big secret you've been saving for my ears alone?"

Nick shrugged. "Nothing much, except to thank you for all you've done for us."

Puzzlement filled her. "But I haven't done anything. On the contrary. All Danny and I have done is take from you and your family since the very first day."

"Oh, but you're wrong, Sarah." Nick's hand briefly touched hers. "Our house hasn't been so bright and happy since . . . well, for a long while now. Even Father seems more at ease."

"I can't take credit for that." Sarah laughed. "Your father hardly gives me the time of day. Danny's responsible for any of your father's thawing toward us."

"He's really not such a bad person, once you get to know

him." Nick hesitated, then, as if deciding it was time to say more, gave a slight nod. "Father was never the same since our mother died bearing Cord, the day after I was shot. It almost destroyed him. He was so mad with grief, he didn't know who to blame for Mother's premature labor. And even though he finally remarried, to a kind and loving widow woman with two daughters, I suspect it was mainly to provide Cord and me with a mother, and her two daughters with a father. There wasn't much else between them but simple courtesy and respect. A true marriage of convenience for the both of them, I reckon."

"So time and another wife didn't heal your father's heart."

Nick shook his head sadly. "Far from it. And Cord ended up bearing the brunt of our father's irrational sorrow. It didn't change much, either, as Cord grew up. Father got to the point where he couldn't bear to have Cord around him. Both Emma and Father's second wife, Martha, were given orders to take over Cord's care and, in the doing, keep him as far away from Father as possible."

"But how could that be?" Sarah asked, compassion for the boy Cord had been softening her voice. "They lived under the same roof. How could they not help but run into each other, even in a house this big?"

"Well, for one thing, we didn't build this house for about the first five years, until the ranch started making good money. And Father was gone a lot in those early years, riding the range with his ranch hands, herding cattle, laying barbed wire, and all the other things needed to set up a successful cattle operation." Nick levered to one elbow. "And when he was home, Father did his level best to ignore Cord. When that didn't work, he turned on Cord, finding any and every excuse to criticize and humiliate him.

"Unfortunately, Cord seemed just as determined to win Father's love. He tried everything he could to please him, but the harder he tried, the worse it became. It was so sad, and near to broke the hearts of all of us, my stepmother and sisters included. We all tried to make it up to him. After a while, though, Cord took to pretending it didn't matter. Yet, to this day, the hurt's still there. I see it even now, beneath that cold, indifferent mask he always wears around Father."

Nick glanced down. "I almost wish I hadn't begged Cord to come back. Ultimately, the ranch may be saved, but what will it have cost Cord in the bargain? He's already suffered enough to last a lifetime."

Impulsively, Sarah took his hand. "I'd say you both, in your own ways, have suffered. It helps me understand your brother a little better, though. I'll try to be more patient with him. If anyone deserves some understanding for his moods, he does!"

Nick chuckled. "Now don't you go pitying him. That'd sting his pride more than anything I know of. Cord's one of the strongest, most resilient men I've ever met. His leaving here years ago was the best thing he could've done. It gave him the chance to rebuild the self-esteem our father tried to destroy. And Cord succeeded. He has a successful law practice in New York City, and I hear he packs a pretty powerful wallop as a former boxer. No, don't ever pity my brother. Save that for someone who really needs it."

Sarah laughed. "Oh, I'd never dare pity the likes of Cord Wainwright! If anyone's gotten more than her fill of his bullheaded pride, I sure have." She paused, then sighed. "Hearing all that, about how Mr. Wainwright treated Cord as a boy . . . well, I have to admit I like your father even less now than I did before."

Nick cocked his head. "You really care for my brother, don't you, Angel?"

Her cheeks warmed. "He's a good man, that's all."

"Well, I've always been rather partial to him."

111

The memory of Nick's story of how Cord had sent back all those books flooded Sarah. And that recollection led to yet another.

"That day we first met," she began, drawn in spite of herself to mention it, "you said that books were your one escape from a reality you could barely endure. Until you found the Lord, I mean."

"Yes, that's true. Cord didn't just buy me tales of history, travel, and high adventure, you know. He also, from time to time, sent me books of a more spiritual nature." Nick chuckled. "That nearly shocked the socks off me, coming from *my* brother. He was never one to go to church, or even say his bedtime prayers.

"That said, though, I figured he had his reasons for sending me every book he did, so I read them all. And, after a while, I began to find my greatest comfort in the books he sent me about God. In fact, there was one particular book, about a certain holy man, which finally set me on the road back to the Lord. In it, this man said our life's true work was to keep to the way of Jesus Christ—the way of love. That we must strive to advance in that journey each and every day, and persevere until the end."

He smiled. "That's what I endeavored—and still endeavor—to do. To take each day as a gift from God, as an opportunity to grow in love and service to others. Just one day at a time, and no more. And you know something? It worked. Every time I started to look back and mourn all that I could never do, or think of a future that will never be that of a normal man, I'd remind myself that I couldn't do anything about what was over and done. And I sure couldn't do anything about what hasn't even happened. All I had control of was today and, even more importantly, the present moment. And God was in that present moment."

Nick laughed. "When you think about it like that, you've got everything you need, don't you? God and the wonderful awareness of Him and all He created. And that you're loved, truly, deeply, and eternally loved."

Listening to him, Sarah felt a crazy mix of elation and unease. How she wanted to experience what Nick described! Unconditional love, contentment with her life, and happiness to be just where she was and doing what she did at any given moment.

True, there were times when she could put the pain of the past behind her and block out her worries and fears. Hanging up freshly washed laundry on a breezy, sun-kissed day, or savoring a cup of tea while the fragrance of bread baking in the oven filled their small kitchen, was right up there with the soul-stirring sight of a beautiful sunset. All of them swelled her heart so chock-full of joy there wasn't room for thought of what was to come or what had passed. In moments like those, all you could do was be right where you were, soaking it all in.

But to accept those times as gifts from God? No, Sarah fiercely thought. That wasn't the God she had come to know.

Since her mother had died, God had been Someone who just took and never gave. He'd taken Danny's health. He'd taken her father's happiness, inexorably chipping away at everything, even his sanity. He'd taken Sarah's peace of mind, leaving her with nearly constant worry over her family and how to take care of them, how to protect them, all the while forcing her into compromises that both confused her and tore at her heart.

The God she knew made life harder and more painful, not easier.

"You don't believe any of this, do you, Angel?"

Nick's words, tinged with compassion and a disturbing

insight, wrenched Sarah from her troubled thoughts. "What?" She shook her head. "No, it's not that. It's just . . . It doesn't matter. I'm happy to hear you've found a way to live your life that gives you peace. It's a rare gift. A gift most people search for their whole lives and never find."

"True enough." He nodded sadly. "And yet that gift is there all the while, right in front of our noses, just waiting to be invited into our hearts and lives."

He reached over and took her hand. "That's all you have to do, Sarah. Just invite the Lord back into your heart and life. He wants that, you know. Wants it more than you can ever imagine."

She pulled her hand free. She'd never meant for this conversation to turn to her. She just wanted to know more about Nick.

Or did she?

"Well, these days, I can't really say what I want," she said. "So much has happened of late to turn my world topsy-turvy, it's all I can muster just to keep my head on straight. But I'm glad for you, Nick. Glad that you turned out the way you are, and that I finally got a chance to know you."

"Just another one of God's gifts, wouldn't you say? A gift to the both of us."

He looked up at her so earnestly she didn't have the heart to contradict him. "Maybe," Sarah replied instead, and glanced away.

They lapsed into a companionable silence then, each content with the other and the moment. A soft breeze caressed their faces before rising beyond them to swirl among the aspens. The bright autumn sunlight glinted off the leaves, sending shivering bursts of yellow-gold color along the meadow and high up into the dark green timberline. It was a peaceful, glorious time, but as with all things of wonder, the moment eventually passed.

"Help me to my wheelchair, would you?" Nick asked, shifting restlessly. "I've been lying down long enough. It's time for a change of position."

Sarah climbed to her knees to see if she could catch sight of the boys. "Shouldn't we wait until Pedro gets back? I don't know if I can manage you by myself."

He took her hand and pulled himself upright. "Sure you can. It's not all that hard. Just bring over the wheelchair. Then, if you hold it steady, I can pull myself up into it."

"Now, that's a feat I'd like to see."

"Madam, you've no faith in me." Nick sighed melodramatically. "I'll have you know I can arm wrestle any man on the ranch, Cord included, and win every time."

Sarah laughed. "Then I beg pardon for doubting you. Can you find it in your heart to forgive me?"

"We'll see." He motioned toward the wheelchair. "Time's a-wastin'. Let's get this sideshow on the road, or we'll still be here at—"

A harsh growl from a nearby stand of aspens cut Nick short. Sarah glanced in the direction he was gazing. A huge bear stood about a hundred feet behind them. Without taking his gaze off the grizzly, Nick reached over and grabbed her hand.

"Listen to me carefully," he said, his voice low. "There's a rifle beneath the carriage's front seat. Can you use one?"

"Y-yes."

He smiled. "Good, then head on over there—*very* slowly and carefully, before the horse spooks. That grizzly's not going to wait on us much longer."

Sarah climbed to her feet and, without a backward glance, started toward the carriage. As sedately as she moved, her action must have angered the bear. She heard him growl again, followed by a loud crashing of shrubbery. A swift glance over her shoulder confirmed what she feared.

He's going after Nick! The realization added wings to her feet, yet the distance to the carriage seemed barely to lessen.

She fixed her gaze firmly on the vehicle and didn't see the protruding root of a long-dead tree. It caught the trailing edge of her skirt, ensnared it, and jerked her to the ground. With a gasp of dismay, Sarah turned to tear the fabric free—and beheld the horrifying scene behind her.

The grizzly was charging Nick, his slavering jaws wide open, his long, deadly fangs gleaming. Nick lay there, defying him with only the small knife from their meal clasped in his hand.

"N-Nick," Sarah whispered. She scrambled back to her feet and raced toward the carriage.

The rifle. I've got to get the rifle.

Yet, even as she reached the carriage, Sarah knew it was too late. She'd never be able to kill the bear before it reached Nick.

7

The horse, its head tied to a nearby tree, lurched wildly, throwing the carriage about in a crazed attempt to escape the bear. Sarah leaped into the front seat, groping beneath it for the rifle. For a horrible instant she thought it wasn't there. Then her fingers touched cold metal.

Even as she flung herself from the carriage, Sarah cocked the rifle. It was still too late. The grizzly was already lowering himself toward Nick. She took aim but before she could pull the trigger, a shot rang out.

The bear jerked convulsively, then jerked again as Sarah's bullet ripped through him. The animal fell, burying Nick beneath it.

"Nick!"

The rifle still clasped in her hand, she ran to the bear. It lay there, its massive body completely hiding Nick from view. She threw the weapon aside and began frantically to tug at the grizzly.

The animal was fearsomely heavy, but Sarah's determination fueled her strength. She'd managed to pull the bear half off the unconscious man when the sound of an approaching horse made her pause. She threw a quick glance over her shoulder.

It was Cord, his buckskin sliding to a halt even as he shoved his rifle into its scabbard. He leapt down and ran to her.

"Are you all right?"

"Y-yes," she managed to stammer, then renewed her tugging at the bear. "H-help me. Nick's hurt."

He moved her aside and quickly had his brother free. Nick lay there, his face and shirt bloodied. Cord knelt beside him, but Sarah was swifter.

"Oh, Nick," she cried as she sank down across from Cord and tenderly stroked his brother's cheek. "Nick . . ."

The tears, held in abeyance until now, flowed freely. She kept her head, however, and motioned to the canteen lying nearby.

"Give me some water on a napkin so I can sponge his face," she said, looking up at Cord. "We can't know the extent of his injuries until he wakens, and we dare not move him until then."

He was watching her with a scowl, and Sarah momentarily faltered. *Whatever's the matter with him?* She took the napkin he had dampened with the canteen water and forced herself to gently wipe Nick's forehead.

"Here," Cord growled of a sudden. "Let me pour this canteen on him. Your dabbing at his face isn't going to wake him."

Before she could protest, the full contents splashed over Nick's head. It had its desired effect. With a groan, Nick moved. He opened his eyes and looked straight up into hers.

"S-Sarah? A-are you all right?"

She smiled through her tears. "Yes. I'm fine. How are you?"

He moved, then grimaced. "My right arm. I think it's broken."

Sarah quickly examined it and found the deformity. "Lie still. We'll have it splinted in no time." She turned to Cord. "I need two straight sticks a little longer than his lower arm."

"I'll get them."

He rose and strode off toward the trees, while Sarah busied herself tearing strips from her petticoat.

"Are you sure you're all right, Angel?"

"I'm fine, Nick." She managed a wan smile. "Really, I am. I only wish I could've gotten to that rifle a little sooner."

His blue eyes clouded in confusion. "Didn't you kill the bear?"

"No, Cord shot it first. I think the bear was dead before I could even fire."

Nick smiled. "That's my little brother for you. Always shows up when you need him most."

"Yes, I suppose so . . ." Sarah's words faded as she noted Cord's approach. Nick was okay, so why was he so tense and angry looking?

He squatted beside her. "Will these sticks do?"

Sarah nodded. With his help, Nick's arm was soon splinted. Almost as if the completion of the task released the pent-up tension, Cord turned on Sarah. "What were you two doing out here with a grizzly running wild? Of all the lamebrained—"

"Hey, hold on now," Nick interjected. "Why are you getting on Sarah like that? It was my idea for a picnic, not hers."

"Then why did *you* drag everyone all the way out here?" Cord snarled, now riveting his fury on his brother. "This cozy little get-together almost cost you your life. From here on out, I suggest keeping your romantic interludes closer to home."

"R-romantic interludes!" Sarah sputtered. "Talk about lamebrained—"

Nick held up his hand to silence her, a devilish glint burning in his eyes as he locked gazes with Cord. "But how could I be romantic with all the people around at the ranch? You know as well as I how difficult that can be, and with an angel like Sarah, I knew I had to move fast."

Sarah glanced from Nick to Cord, then back to Nick. "Whatever are you two talking about? This was a picnic, pure and simple, and that's all it was!"

"Nick, you're a dad-blasted fool," Cord said, ignoring her as he slid his hands beneath his brother's shoulders, "and that's all I have to say on the subject. Your little picnic's over. It's time to get you home."

As she watched Cord drag his brother back to his wheelchair, confusion warred with righteous indignation. She wanted to tell him he was being completely unfair, but caution warned her not to interfere just now between the two men. The extent of Cord's anger was inappropriate but, as Sarah thought more on it, whenever she was concerned he always seemed to react this way.

Her glance scanned him as he helped Nick up into the wheelchair. To accuse her and Nick of a 'romantic interlude'! Would she ever begin to understand him?

"Sarah! Mr. Nick!" From the top of the hill, Danny's voice carried down to them. "What happened?"

Cord frowned when he saw the two boys.

"Sorry to spoil your illusion about our romantic interlude," Sarah said, unable to resist the small dig. "As you see, we've been well chaperoned almost the entire time."

He shot her a frigid look. "I really don't care what you do, just as long as you don't endanger my brother in the process. Do I make myself clear?"

At the stinging slap of his words, Sarah stiffened. She climbed to her feet. "Quite clear, *Mr.* Wainwright."

"That was uncalled for," Nick mildly observed as Cord turned the wheelchair around and began pushing it toward the carriage. "As I said before, this picnic was entirely my idea."

"I don't want to talk about it!"

"Have it your way then," Nick said with a shrug, even as a smile tugged at one corner of his mouth. "Have it your way, because it's not going to last for long."

Cord watched as Sarah placed Nick's lunch tray on the table beside him, then moved to uncover his food and carefully cut his meat into bite-sized pieces. From his vantage standing beside the window, he had an unobstructed view as she concentrated on his brother sitting calmly in his wheelchair, his right arm swathed in a sling. It was a rare opportunity, and Cord took advantage of it with the hunger of a man long-starved.

She wore a green and white gingham dress, another altered castoff of Emma's. The checkered print, combined with the long braid of pale gold hair hanging down her back, gave her a fresh, girlish appearance. The cotton cloth clung to her slim form, accentuating every delightful, feminine curve.

How he wanted Sarah! That realization he'd long since ceased to deny. Yet in spite of the admission, she seemed further from him now than ever before. Seeing the tender smile she gave Nick as she answered some question of his only stirred anew the possessive surge of anger—and pain.

He knew Nick wanted her as well. That certainty had hit him square between the eyes ever since that disastrous picnic a week ago. Knew that he'd lost her before the fight had even begun. And yet, if it'd been any man but his brother . . .

Sarah straightened just then. "Is there anything else I can do for you, Nick?"

"No, Angel." He patted her hand. "I'm fine for now. But will you come back and visit later?"

Her glance strayed to Cord. "Yes . . . of course I will."

He met her gaze, hiding his seething emotions behind a flat, inscrutable expression.

She pulled her hand from Nick's. "I-I must be going."

Nick's glance followed her as she hurried from the room. Then he turned back to Cord.

"I think it's time we had a little talk about Sarah."

Cord straightened. "Oh, and why's that?"

"Well, for starters, you've been treating her abysmally this past week. And, secondly, why were you so angry at us for going on a picnic?" As Cord opened his mouth to reply, Nick raised a hand. "And don't tell me it was just because of the bear. I know you better than that, little brother."

As he struggled with his surging frustration, Cord could feel hot blood suffuse his face. He desperately wanted to talk to someone about his confused feelings for Sarah, but if he told Nick, he feared his brother might step aside from his own quest for her hand. And Cord would never stand in the way of Nick's happiness, even if it cost him someone as wonderful as Sarah.

He shook his head. "You've got this all wrong. The issue here isn't me, but you and Sarah." He paused, then forced the words past a strangely dry throat. "I think she's in love with you."

Nick stared at him for a long moment, then burst out laughing. "Talk about love not only making you blind but stupid too!" At the dark look Cord sent him, he finally managed to control his mirth. "Now, tell me, how in the world did you come up with that crazy idea?"

"Anyone with eyes can see how upset she was when you got hurt," Cord replied, barely containing his rising irritation. "Not to mention all the time she spends visiting you every day. What else would you call it?"

"Sisterly affection?"

"Ha! Fat chance!"

"Come on." Nick motioned to a nearby chair. "Sit down. We need to talk."

He waited until Cord had settled into the chair. "Listen, I know Sarah cares for me, but only as a sister for a brother. Her feelings for you, however, are an entirely different matter."

At the incredulous look his brother sent him, Nick expelled a big sigh. "You'd have seen it by now, if you hadn't gone so far out of your way to keep her at arm's length the past few weeks. And you'd also, by now, have recognized your feelings for her."

Vehemently, Cord shook his head. "No. You're wrong. She barely tolerates my presence."

"Well, if you didn't always act like such a boor . . ."

Cord ran a hand raggedly through his hair. "I have my reasons."

"Yes," Nick agreed, "and we both know they stem from a fear of opening yourself to further pain and rejection. When are you going to unlock that iron cage around your heart, Cord? Father may have helped you build it, but only you can tear it down."

You make it sound so simple, Cord thought. *Like all I have to do is surrender to my feelings, trust my heart, and everything will be better. But it isn't that simple, or easy. Life isn't that simple or easy.*

"It wouldn't work, Nick," he replied instead, glancing out the window. "Be realistic. Sarah and I have nothing in common. Our personalities clash at every turn. And, atop everything else, there's no place in my life right now for a woman or commitments. You know better than anyone how determined I am to head back to New York just as soon as I get our money problems solved."

"What a bunch of hogwash!" Nick leaned forward in his wheelchair, his expression intense. "You know something? In your own way, you're more crippled than I am. But at least my handicap is only of the body. Yours is of the soul, and that's a far greater tragedy than I'll *ever* have to endure. Your insides are so twisted with all the years of cruelty Father heaped on you that it's made you afraid to embrace life. And if you let

123

it go on much longer, all the progress you made when you went away will be for nothing."

A fierce light gleamed in Nick's eyes. "You think you've beaten Father, but if you can never allow yourself to love, what have you won? Your life will turn out just as empty as his."

A dry smile touched Cord's mouth. "Calm down, big brother. Aren't you overdramatizing this a bit? It's not as if I've never had a relationship with a woman all these years I've been away."

"No more than you're being intentionally thickheaded. We're not talking about the casual relationships, a beautiful woman on your arm when you attended the opera or went to an elegant, high society party. But just tell me. Did any of them really matter to you? Did you let any of them get close?"

Cord's jaw tightened. Even if Nick was his brother and closest confidante, this was starting to get too personal.

"Look, I don't need a lecture. I get enough of those from Father to last me a lifetime."

His brother leaned back in his wheelchair. "I'm sorry. It's just I get so frustrated seeing you and Sarah always going in opposite directions, when you're so right for each other. She'd be good for you, Cord."

"No, Nick," he choked out the words. "She'd be good for *you*."

"Always ready to sacrifice for your poor, crippled brother, is that it?" The query was uttered in a voice of bitter calm. "Well, let me tell you one thing. I don't want or need your charity. You've spent your whole life trying to make up for what happened that night. And do you know how that makes me feel? Not only do I have to deal with my own problems, but I've got to bear the guilt of ruining your life too. When are you going to let go, live your own life, and let me get on with living mine?"

Cord rose and walked to the window, his emotions chaotic, agonized. "I can't help it, Nick," he finally said, his voice husky. "It breaks my heart to see you like this, to know you'll never be able to experience even half the things I have. At least with Sarah you'd be able to have a little of what any man should have. Don't you want that?"

"Yes . . . I do. And, the Lord willing, maybe someday I shall. But not with Sarah. She's already given her heart to you."

His brother's assurance plucked at Cord's heart. Sarah . . . in love with him? With a supreme effort, he rejected such a possibility.

"I don't know if I believe that."

"Then why don't you find out, instead of putting up walls? What do you have to lose? Don't be a fool like Father and throw away a chance for happiness. His life didn't have to end when Mother died. Martha was a good woman, and I think in time she actually fell in love with Father." Nick expelled a sorrowful breath. "For all the good it did her."

"He didn't deserve her," Cord muttered. "And to think she went to the grave never receiving what she wanted most from him."

"I wonder if any man truly deserves the woman who loves him. A good wife is a blessing from God."

"Maybe so." Just then, Sarah walked toward the clothes-line with a basket of laundry on her hip. Longing swelled in Cord's chest.

He turned from the window. "I just don't know, Nick. I'm not sure I'm capable of giving my heart to a woman. Father's love for Mother has nearly destroyed him. I don't know if I've got the courage to risk that. I want Sarah, but . . ."

Nick gripped the chair with his good hand, his voice softening as he spoke. "Do you really want to go through life lonely and miserable? Isn't that a far greater tragedy? It helps to join hearts, to share the journey. Hatred and mistrust can only darken your life, Cord. Why not let someone bring a little light into it? Someone like . . . Sarah."

"Nick?"

The voice was hesitant but belovedly familiar. He turned, a soft smile on his face. "Yes, Emma?"

She stood there in his doorway, uncertain and flushed. Nick instantly knew she'd been party to his and Cord's conversation. He calmly returned her gaze. "How much did you hear?"

"Most all of it, I reckon. I passed Sarah in the hall." She extended the sugar bowl. "I . . . I forgot to put this on your lunch tray, and I know how you love sugar in your tea."

Nick shrugged. "No matter. You're aware of everything that goes on in the house anyway, and I've never known you to gossip."

"Well, I do try hard to keep gossiping to a minimum." Emma walked in and shut the door. "I don't know if you did the right thing, Nicholas."

"Oh, and how so?"

"You accused Cord of always sacrificing for you, but you're just as bad." She eyed him briefly, then forged on. "Don't deny it. You're in love with her too."

His eyes narrowed. "It doesn't matter how I feel. When it comes to the heart, to that special bond between a man and a woman, Sarah doesn't know I exist. She's in love with Cord as much as he is with her. And their marriage could set into motion a lot of healing between the two families."

She shook her head. "Well, I don't know about that. Edmund and Jacob's hatred still runs pretty deep."

"All the same," Nick firmly persisted, "it doesn't change

what's between Cord and Sarah. I'm not going to muck that up. I'm just trying to move things in the right direction."

Emma sighed. "I suppose that's for the best." She walked over and placed the sugar bowl on his tray. "Eat your lunch before it gets cold."

She turned toward the door, only to be halted by Nick's deep voice. "Emma, one thing more."

A questioning gaze met his. "Yes?"

"My feelings for Sarah. Neither of them is ever to know."

"Yes, Nicholas." Emma blinked back tears. "If that's what you want. Neither of them will ever know."

A cool wind blew down from the mountains, ruffling the bright yellow aspens clinging to the foothills, driving the fall-dried meadow grasses before it. As Sarah finished pinning the last of the laundry on the line, the clean sheets snapped in the breeze. She stepped back, releasing a contented sigh.

What a glorious day, she thought as her glance scanned the intensely bright blue sky. Overhead, fluffy clouds scudded along. The first frost was imminent any day now, yet Sarah welcomed it as the frigid herald of a pleasant Indian summer so typical in this part of the Rockies. Yes, if they were lucky, winter might still be a good two months away.

As she slowly made her way to the back porch, an impulse to go for a walk swept through her. And why not? All the day's chores were done, Danny was occupied in lassoing lessons with Cal, and preparations for supper weren't necessary for at least another hour.

Sarah deposited the basket inside the door and hurried back down the steps. The small brook that ran through the far pasture would be a beautiful spot to visit.

From his bedroom, Cord watched her go. He raised the window to call to Sarah, then thought better of it. What he had to say would be better said in the more remote isolation of the brook. There was no doubt in his mind she was headed there. Emma had mentioned more than once that it was Sarah's favorite retreat.

His long strides quickly carried him from the house and across the pasture. Nick's words echoed in his head in rhythm to his steps.

She's already given her heart to you . . . Do you really want to go through life lonely and miserable? . . . You think you've beaten Father, but what have you won?

Is that what it came down to then—the possibility of a life as soul-rotting as his father's? The thought sickened him. Yet to steal Nick's chance of happiness with Sarah . . .

Nick's wrong, dead wrong, Cord stubbornly told himself. *Sarah doesn't care for me. How could she after the way I've treated her?*

Yes, how could she, yet even the possibility sent a shiver of longing through him. If there were even a flicker of feeling for him in her heart, he'd not stop until he'd fanned it into a raging—

With an angry shake of his head, Cord flung the thought aside. He was a selfish fool to think only of himself. Nick was what mattered. And today he'd make certain Sarah knew of his brother's feelings for her. There'd be another woman for him . . . maybe . . . someday.

He topped the small hill that hid the tree-lined brook from view. His gaze found Sarah seated on a large, flat stone that jutted out over the flowing waters, the wind gently playing with her pale gold hair. The clamor of the rushing waters hid the sound of his approach. Not until his tall form threw a shadow across her did she appear to realize she wasn't alone.

With a jerk, she wheeled around and glanced up.

Sucking in a startled breath, Sarah's gaze met Cord's. The unexpected sight of him turned her bones to jelly. She quickly looked away.

Had her thoughts, so fraught with memories of their recent, heated encounter in Nick's room, summoned him here? If so, what was she to do? Right about now she couldn't bear to speak to him, much less be with him.

His arrival, however, had effectively taken the choice from her. And good manners precluded her just ignoring him. With a sigh, Sarah climbed to her feet.

"What do you want?" she demanded, an edge of defiance in her voice.

If he'd noted the lack of welcome, Cord didn't show it. "I'd think that was pretty obvious," he said, apparently feeling the need to get right to business. "We have to talk."

"Oh, really?" Sarah's hands rose to her hips. "What about? Are you here to now warn me off Nick? Am I not allowed *any* friends at the Wainwright ranch?"

"I'd never come between your and Nick's friendship." Some dark, anguished emotion flitted through his eyes. "On the contrary, I'd like to see it deepen."

"Deepen?" Sarah's expression mirrored her puzzlement. "What in the world are you talking about?"

"Nick cares for you. Surely you can see that."

"He's become a dear friend," she began slowly, not at all happy with the direction the conversation seemed to be taking. "I'm honored that he cares."

"In time, he could be much more than that."

Heat flooded her face. "What are you trying to say, Cord?"

He swallowed hard, the struggle now evident on his face. "I believe . . . I *know* he'd marry you if you'd have him."

Her mouth dropped open.

"Think about it, Sarah," Cord hurried on. "Your father isn't able to afford the kind of care Danny needs and we can give him. And you've seen how your brother's flourished in just the short time he's been here. We can give both of you the kind of life you'll otherwise never have. Not to mention the happiness you'll bring Nick, with the added possibility your marriage to him might bring an end to the feud. A lot of good can come of this for everyone."

Maybe it's time we join forces . . . Maybe you're the answer to my prayers . . .

Nick's words that first day they'd met trickled through Sarah's mind. And suddenly, with Cord's startling proposal, they seemed to take on an almost prophetic cast.

I've been asking the Lord for a long time now to put an end to this feud, to heal everyone's hearts . . .

Heal everyone's hearts . . . What a beautiful, noble aspiration and one, even from that first day, Sarah immediately knew she shared with Nick. But marriage? Marriage to Nick, when her heart whispered she loved his brother?

As she stared up at Cord's granite features, his face blurred. Dizziness engulfed her. It was too much to comprehend. Cord wanted her to marry Nick. The man she wanted was trying to give her to his brother.

Sarah swayed and would have fallen if not for the sudden support of Cord's strong arms.

"Sarah, are you all right?"

She shook her head to clear the sparkling lights spinning before her eyes. She couldn't faint; she just couldn't. Mama had always said fainting was the refuge of the weak and cowardly, and she'd never shame her mother's memory. Not for Cord Wainwright or any man!

"And since when has Nick needed you to speak for him?"

she demanded, shrugging out of Cord's grasp. "Let *him* ask me, if marriage is what he really wants."

"It's not that simple. He doesn't believe you love him."

Her mouth twisted in exasperation. "And when did love suddenly become a prerequisite? I don't recall that ever being mentioned."

Cord sighed. "I'm not any good at matchmaking. I-I'm sure he loves you, though."

Her gaze narrowed. "And how do you know that? Has he told you?"

His glance couldn't quite meet hers anymore. "Not in so many words."

"Then in what words?"

Sarah moved closer, noting the tinge of anger in his voice and the muscle that now convulsed in his jaw. At last she'd begun to get under that cool layer of indifference. It was about time he felt some of the same pain and anger he evoked in her.

"In exactly *what* words?" she prodded.

With a low growl, Cord pulled her to him. "Don't goad me, Sarah. You might not like what you get."

She faced him, chin held high. "I'm not afraid of you or anything you can do to me. You can't hurt me any more than you already have."

"Hurt you?" His clasp tightened. "I swear I never meant to hurt you. I know I haven't always treated you kindly. I regret that. But you confuse me every way I turn, and I don't know what to do about it. Ever since that first day I brought you here, I haven't had the heart . . ."

He stopped, drew in a deep breath, then released her and stepped back. "It doesn't matter. All that's important is that you and Nick are happy together."

"And what about you?" She forced the question past her painfully constricted throat. "Will that make *you* happy?"

An undisguised look of yearning flashed across his face before he managed to jerk a mask of indifference over it. "Yes! Of course it'll make me happy. I love my brother."

But not me. Never me.

The words thrummed in her head and pounded so loudly in her heart Sarah thought Cord must surely hear them. She bit her lip until it throbbed like her pulse, the despair wrapping about her chest like steel bands. She looked down, her eyes filling with tears.

What's the use of fighting it anymore? Thanks to the feud, everything's become so twisted, so hopeless. Nick's a cripple, Cord's soul-tortured and blind to his own needs and emotions, Mama's dead after years of futile, back-breaking labor, and Caleb and Noah verge on becoming vengeful replicas of Papa. As for me . . . well, it doesn't matter.

Danny was the only one still unscathed, and she meant to keep him that way. She couldn't depend on Papa anymore. The past weeks at the Wainwrights' ranch had driven home the reality of his abandonment. He refused to admit his mistake and return the money, his hatred of the Wainwrights more powerful than his love for his children. It was up to her to take care of Danny now. For his sake, and his sake alone, she'd do anything.

Yes, for Danny's sake, I'll even marry Nick rather than Cord. Then, as wife of the Wainwright heir, I'll hold in my hands the potential for doing a lot of good. And it's not as if I don't care for Nick. I do. In time, maybe that affection could flower into something deeper, like true love.

But only if Cord isn't here, Sarah added as the anguish of that admission threatened to sweep over and drown her. *Only if I never have to see him again. If he stayed, I'd die a little bit each day, living in the same house, seeing him. And that wouldn't be fair to Nick. Of us all, he deserves better, far better, than that.*

Sarah lifted her gaze. "If that's what you want, I'll marry Nick. But on one condition."

"Name it."

The swiftness of his response made her wince, but she stood firm in her resolve. Better to be like him. Be cold; be direct. Get it over with.

She inhaled a steadying breath. "You may not like it, but it's the only way I'll consider becoming a Wainwright." She paused then resolutely forged on. "If I marry Nick, you must promise to leave here—and never come back."

8

For a long, painful moment Cord just stared at her. Then he laughed, the sound harsh and hollow.

"Never come back, you say? Well, that suits me fine. I only wish I could oblige you right now."

"Th-that's fine with me too." Sarah glared up at him. The hard glitter in his eyes made her so furious she wanted to reach up and smack him. He didn't care, in fact he was glad he'd finally be rid of her! Hot tears warred with her anger. Before either could gain mastery, Sarah turned on her heel and stomped away.

Across the pasture she went, her seething emotions fueling her legs until she found herself running. *He doesn't care . . . he's glad . . . he wants to be rid of me . . .*

The words, his words, mocked her in rhythm to her stride, pounding home the awful truth. What a fool she'd been. What a stupid, gullible fool!

Male voices drifting toward her from the front porch intruded on her impotent ragings. She could just make out Nick and his father sitting in the shade, and someone else standing behind them. In an effort to regain her composure, Sarah slowed to a walk. The hectic flush to her cheeks, overbright eyes, and ragged breathing, however, weren't lost on the first man who caught her gaze.

"What's wrong, Angel? You look like you've been chased home by another rogue grizzly."

Sarah's fury boiled over once again. "The only rogue around here is your brother! If I never share another word with him in my life, it'll be too soon. He's the most despicable, heartless—"

"Whoa, there. Hold on, " Nick laughingly interrupted. "He can't be that bad."

"Oh, I wouldn't be so quick to defend him," another male voice chuckled from the shadows behind Nick. "I've known Cord over half my life, and I'd say Sarah's hit the nail square on the head."

Sarah froze, her glance narrowing in an attempt to make out the face of the man who'd just spoken. There was something familiar . . .

"Gabe? Gabe Cooper? Is that you?"

A tall, dark-blond man stepped into the sunlight, a silver star glinting on his broad chest. "Yes, Sarah. It's me."

He grinned, his strong white teeth a striking contrast to his sun-bronzed, ruggedly hewn face. "Sorry to be so long in getting back from Denver. Seems you and your family have been stirring up a mess of trouble since I've been gone."

"Nothing more than you'd expect from the Caldwells." Edmund Wainwright shifted in his chair. "But now that you're back, Gabe, I expect things will finally settle down around here. At least we've got one of that thieving clan dead to rights."

"Now, hold on." Nick wheeled his chair—rather skillfully for using only one hand—to the edge of the porch. His glance riveted on something behind Sarah. "Cord's heading back this way. Let's wait until he gets here to discuss this."

At the mention of Cord's approach, Sarah tensed. There was nothing in the world she wanted more at that moment

135

than to run away. Even more than facing Edmund Wainwright, she dreaded the prospect of dealing with his youngest son. Only her stubborn Caldwell pride kept her legs firmly planted, but the wide-eyed look of apprehension apparently wasn't lost on Nick.

He motioned her up onto the porch. "Come, sit with me, Angel. No sense standing out in the sun when we've all got some talking to do."

She quickly complied and settled herself in a wicker chair near the railing, shooting Nick a heartfelt look of gratitude. He leaned over and gave her hand a comforting pat.

"Buck up. It'll be all right."

A small, tentative smile touched her lips, then faded as Cord stepped onto the porch. His glance briefly met hers, then swung over the rest of the gathering until it came to rest on the sheriff. A slow grin lit his handsome features.

Sarah's heart twisted. Even his smile, so beautiful, so devastating, could cause her pain, knowing it'd never be meant for her.

"I see you finally made it back." Cord strode over and offered Gabe his hand. "Sorry to hear about your father, but I'm glad you're home."

Grasping the proffered hand, Gabe grinned in return. "I couldn't agree more. From what I hear, you've been having all the fun."

Cord's glance skittered to Sarah and back. "Fun isn't quite the word I would've used."

"Why don't we just forego the small talk and get down to business," Edmund irritably demanded. "Are you going to arrest the girl or not, Gabe?"

The blond sheriff shrugged. "I don't know. It's Cord's money. Do you still want to press charges, Cord?"

All eyes riveted on the dark-haired man. For a fleeting

instant, a gamut of emotions played across his face. Then the familiar blank stoniness hardened his features.

He shook his head. "No. It isn't necessary. Things have changed."

"What do you mean 'things have changed'?" His father rose to his feet. "The money's still gone and she was involved in the robbery. *I* want to press charges."

Cord studied his sire with cool regard. "Nevertheless, as Gabe said, it's my money. And I'm the only one who can identify the woman who helped in the robbery, not you. So, if I don't say it was Sarah, it wasn't Sarah."

"And you're a softhearted fool," Edmund muttered, anger in his eyes. "Just like you to let a pretty girl turn your head."

"On the contrary, I think I see the reality of things quite clearly." Cord looked to his brother. "Sarah's agreed to marry you."

It was Nick's turn now to have the attention directed at him. He stared back at his brother, surprise, then growing exasperation flaring in his deep blue eyes.

He exhaled slowly, then glanced to Sarah. "Is that true, Angel? Do you want to marry me?"

She took a moment to compose herself. "Yes, if you'll have me."

"Blasted strangest proposal I've ever heard," Edmund Wainwright groused. "And I don't care what either of you say. *I* won't have it, and that's that!"

Nick calmly regarded his father. "And since when were you consulted? I'm a grown man and make my own decisions. I'll marry who I want."

"The girl's nothing but a thieving little opportunist, Nicholas!" Edmund stomped over to confront his son. "She may be part of Caldwell's plan, sent to insinuate herself into the family and destroy us from within. Why, I'm surprised she hasn't already managed to come between you and Cord, turn brother against brother. Open your eyes, son, before it's too late."

"I'm not the one who needs his eyes opened."

Cord grimaced as his brother's glance swung back to him. He refused to acknowledge his words and, instead, turned the full force of his frustration on his father.

"It's none of your business who Nick chooses to marry. He deserves his chance at happiness, and he's chosen a fine woman. If you'd ever allow yourself to get past your mindless hatred for the Caldwells, you might see that. Give Sarah a chance. She's not Jacob Caldwell. She's not your enemy."

"Don't start on me, Cord," Edmund rasped, his fists clenching at his sides. "I'll not stand here and be lectured to by some arrogant young pup. You've never understood, never suffered the pain . . ."

He paused, as if suddenly realizing the presence of others around him. "We'll talk about this later." Edmund stalked into the house.

Gabe cleared his throat to break the silence that had descended in the wake of Edmund's departure. He offered Nick his hand.

"Congratulations. Just my luck. I go away for a few measly weeks, and you snatch the prettiest girl in Ashton right out from under my nose. I hate to admit it, though, but I reckon the better man won."

Nick's gaze slammed into his brother's. "Maybe so," he softly replied, "but only by default."

Cord's reply was to stride off in the direction of the barn, leaving Gabe there with a totally mystified expression on his face. "Was it something I said?" He turned back to Nick. "What in the Sam Hill's the matter with everyone today?"

"Just people dealing with their own demons." Nick grinned up at the sheriff. "Don't let it upset you. It'll all eventually settle out."

"I reckon so."

Gabe glanced at Sarah, who'd been silently sitting there the whole time. Concern wrinkled his brow.

"Why the sad face, little lady? Don't let Cord and Edmund's personal feud get to you. Give them a chance. You're sure to win both of them over, just like you have Nick."

He moved to her side and, bending low, kissed her lightly on the forehead. "My congratulations to you too. I hope you'll be very happy."

"I-I'm sure I will," she whispered.

Gabe eyed her curiously, then shoved his Stetson on his head. "Well, it's time I was on my way. Nick, tell Cord I'll keep a lookout for Jacob and his boys." He headed for his horse.

They watched him mount and ride away before Nick broke the leaden silence. "This wasn't the way it was supposed to turn out."

Sarah turned tear-filled eyes to him.

"I appreciate your willingness to marry me, but I'm not fool enough to think I'm the one you really love."

She fiercely shook her head. "It's not like that at all. I-I care deeply for you, Nick. If you want me, I-I'd be proud to be your wife."

It took everything in Sarah to manage a smile. Then, without warning, she burst into tears. Within a matter of seconds, she regained control and hastily swiped the moisture from her cheeks.

"I'm sorry," she choked out. "I-I'm so s-sorry!"

The tears welled anew. She turned and ran into the house.

"Come here, girl. I want a word with you."

At the harsh command, Sarah's head jerked up. Edmund

Wainwright stood in the library doorway, a frigid look on his face.

He motioned for her to come in. "Now, girl."

She halted, her hand clasping the oak banister. He must have been waiting there in the library for her to finish in the kitchen and head up to bed, she realized wearily. But why now, on top of everything else that had happened today?

Her chin lifted a defiant notch. "My name's Sarah, or Miss Caldwell, whichever you choose, but it's not 'girl,'" she said, struggling to control the surge of anger at his rudeness. He was, after all, Nick's father. For his sake, she'd make every effort to keep the peace. But she'd not, not for anyone, allow herself to be treated in a demeaning manner.

Anger darkened Edmund's features. For a moment, Sarah thought he'd fly into one of his rages. Then he relaxed.

"Sarah it is then. Now, would you please come into the library? I need to speak with you."

She nodded and followed him into the room. He indicated the sofa.

"Please, sit down."

Edmund settled himself in the wing chair. "We need to talk about you and Nicholas."

Sarah arched a brow. "Oh?"

"You may have pulled the wool over everyone else's eyes with that air of sweet innocence, but you've met your match in me, my dear. Your father put you up to this, didn't he? What better way to win the ranch from the inside than by sending his beautiful daughter to seduce one of my sons? And, of course, Nicholas was your most likely target—crippled, emotionally vulnerable, and convinced no woman would ever have him."

He rose to tower over her, a sudden chill hanging on the edge of his words. "Well, I won't have it, do you hear me?

140

You're a heartless little tramp to play my Nicholas like this! And don't think I haven't guessed what you'll do after you're married, either. I know your kind. Sooner or later we'll find you sneaking out to the barn for a passionate liaison with one or another of the hands."

So, it's finally all out in the open, Sarah thought. *Edmund's played his cards. Now I know exactly what I face and can deal with it.* A strange, detached calmness settled over her.

"You've gotten it all figured out, haven't you?" she asked. "Now, what do you plan to do about it? Obviously this little get-together wasn't for the purpose of welcoming me into the family."

"Darn right," he growled. "You'll never get this ranch. What will it take to buy you off, get you to break your engagement to Nicholas?"

"More money than you have, for it'll never buy the kind of home Danny and I have right here." Her voice grew taut with emotion, with the heat of battle, for, in a sense she *was* fighting for her and her little brother's future. "As hard as it may be for you to believe, I don't want your ranch. If anything should ever happen to Nick, it's Cord's birthright. All I want is a good home for my brother to grow up in. He'll have that here, with Emma, Nick, and me, with the good food and healthy surroundings. Is that too high a price for you?"

"So, all you want is a home for your brother?" Edmund gave a disgusted snort. "And what about Nicholas? I don't know how 'experienced' you are, but surely you realize that he can never be a husband to you in any physical sense, can never give you children. You're only eighteen. I can't believe you'd willingly tie yourself down to half a man for the rest of your life. Sooner or later you'd be unfaithful—it can't be helped."

An aching sadness washed over Sarah. *Why do you think*

I'm sending Cord away? How could I hurt Nick by loving his brother more than I love him? She bit her lip to distract her from the spiraling pain.

Sarah rose and walked over to gaze out the darkened window. "You know, I don't expect you to have much confidence in me, but you underestimate your son. In many ways, he's more a man than most men."

A sudden insight struck her. She turned, a wondering look in her eyes.

"You really don't know *either* of your sons, do you? You discount Nick's strength and depth of character, and Cord, well, you've never given him a chance."

"My family and our relationships aren't part of this discussion. And it's also none of your business!"

A sad smile curved Sarah's lips. "But I'm soon to be part of the family, aren't I, Mr. Wainwright? So, it *is* my business. And one thing you'd better learn quickly about me is that I speak my mind."

"Then let's get it out in the open between us, so we won't have to dredge up this disagreeable subject again." His tall frame grew rigid. "Why do you care about my relationship with Cord? He's nothing to you . . ." Edmund's voice faded, and a considering look sparked in his eyes. "Or is he?"

For an instant, Sarah faltered. Were her feelings for Cord that transparent? It was a weapon she dared not lay at Edmund Wainwright's feet.

She shook her head in denial. "Cord's a good man, has been kind to Danny and me, especially in light of what I did to him. Nick told me how you treated him as a boy, still do for that matter. Anything that hurts Nick hurts me. Why shouldn't I care?"

"You don't understand."

"Understand?" Sarah gave a disbelieving laugh. "What's

there to understand about a father's deliberate cruelty to his son? What has Cord ever done to you but try to win your love? To grow up to be a fine, intelligent man so he could return and help save a ranch you've all but driven him from?"

"Sorry to say, this is one time I have to agree with my father," a deep voice intruded into the highly charged atmosphere. "It's none of your business."

Both swung around to confront the owner of the voice, his tall, broad-shouldered form filling the doorway.

"Cord," Sarah began, then words failed her. His dark eyes burned into hers, searing her heart to a small, smoldering lump in her chest. Would the sight of him never fail to cause her such a chaotic mix of joy and inexpressible pain?

His glittering gaze swung next to his father. "What are you doing in here with Sarah? Trying to browbeat her into renouncing her engagement to Nick?"

"That's already a lost cause." His father laughed. "She's a determined little minx, that much I'll give her. And, as you just overheard, she's now set her sights on clearing up all our family problems."

"What's between us long ago ceased to be a problem," Cord replied grimly. "You have to care for it to be a problem."

Edmund steadily returned his son's gaze. "Then perhaps that's the saddest part of all." He sighed and turned to Sarah. "There's one thing more I need to discuss with you, and it worked out quite conveniently that Cord's here."

Sarah's guard instantly went up. "What might that be, Mr. Wainwright?"

"You told me before that you didn't want the ranch, that it was Cord's birthright if anything should ever happen to Nicholas. Would you care to put that in writing?"

"You mean a legal document?"

The older man nodded. "Precisely. Cord's a lawyer. He

can draw it up right now. That is, if you really meant what you said."

She smiled, returning the implicit challenge. "I meant *everything* I said, Mr. Wainwright." Sarah glanced at his son. "Write it, please, Cord."

Cord's eyes narrowed to black slits. "It seems you've a need to make deals with all of us. Have you made one with Nick too?"

"No." The word was exhaled on a soft sigh. "He's the only one of you who seems to trust me. Why would I need to make deals with him?"

"Then why this little charade? You know I don't want the ranch."

"Who knows?" She shrugged. "Maybe I want peace between you and your father." A sudden anger flared. "What does it matter anyway? You're getting what you want."

"Yes, and it's almost more than I bargained for."

Striding to the desk, Cord pulled out a piece of writing paper and pen from the drawer. Dipping the pen into the crystal glass inkstand, he wrote for several minutes, then walked over and handed the paper to Sarah.

She silently read the contract before looking back up at him.

"Is there anything you'd like added?" he asked.

"Only that, in the case of Nick's death, I'll be allowed to stay here until Danny's of an age to set out on his own."

"That's understood, Sarah. We wouldn't cast out Nick's widow."

"Write it in then." She handed the paper back to Cord. "My word wasn't good enough to stand alone before. Let's keep it all nice and legal."

"As you wish."

He took the contract and returned to the desk. With

jerky, agitated strokes, Cord's hand flew across the page. Finally, he threw down the pen and gestured for Sarah to come over.

Once again, her gaze scanned the paper and she nodded. "Yes, it all seems in order now." Without a moment's hesitation she signed the contract, then walked over and offered it to Edmund Wainwright.

The older man quickly read the paper. As he finished and met her gaze, a strange light flared in his eyes.

"Thank you."

Sarah shook her head. "Don't thank me. I did it for Nick. If it'll keep the peace, it's more than worth it." She indicated the door. "Now, if you've nothing further to say to me, I'd like to go up to bed."

Edmund grasped her arm as she turned to go. "Just one thing more. Nicholas doesn't need to know about this. It can be our little secret, can't it?"

Her gaze briefly met his before flitting to his son, then back again. "Why not?" Sarah replied, her heart so full and heavy she thought it might burst. "These days, it's only one more among so many."

"And it's a fine mess you've made of things, Nicholas Wainwright!" Emma said with a disgusted huff as she served him his lunch in the kitchen the next day. "I've been stewing about it since yesterday. I can't hold it in a moment longer!"

Nick's mouth twisted in a lopsided grin. "Then, by all means, Emma, let it out. I daresay I'm man enough to take it."

She set down his bowl with enough force to slosh the navy bean soup over its rim. Then she put her hands on her hips.

"Land sakes! What did you have in mind, to think you could maneuver Cord into admitting he loved Sarah by backing him into a corner like that? Now *you're* going to marry her and Cord's all but given up. I've never heard of such a lamebrained stunt in all my years!"

"I'll admit it hasn't turned out quite the way I'd planned," he replied. "Cord's just a harder nut to crack than I'd imagined. The fall dance is coming up in another couple of weeks, though. Maybe there's still a way—"

"And *I* say, leave it be. Let things take their natural course. All this plotting and planning of yours have only made things worse. Let Cord and Sarah work it out for themselves."

"What, and admit defeat? I haven't yet begun to fight!" His face brightened with a sudden inspiration. "I've just gotten the most brilliant idea. Find Sarah, would you? I need to talk with her."

Emma threw up her hands. "Sakes alive, I give up! You're as hopeless as the rest of them."

Grumbling to herself, she stomped from the kitchen, leaving Nick to his thoughts. Thoughts that slowly transformed his smile into one of somber contemplation.

A light rap on the door interrupted Nick from his meal. Laying aside his spoon, he turned his chair toward the door. "Come in."

Sarah peeked around the door. "Did you want me for something? Emma said to come to the kitchen."

He gestured to the chair cattycorner to him at the table. "There are a few things we need to discuss."

"And what might they be?" she asked as she settled herself into the seat.

"Well, for one, there's the matter of our wedding date. I think it's time we settle on a day and make the formal announcement."

Sarah felt the blood drain from her face. "If that's what you want, Nick. How soon would you like to be married?"

He took up his cup of tea and sipped it before answering. "I suppose you'd like a formal wedding. Most young ladies do. Is a month enough time?"

"A-a month?" Sarah couldn't quite stifle a gasp.

"Too soon?" Nick asked with a quirk of his head. "Well, how about six weeks then? That's my best offer. I must confess to a case of the overeager groom."

"Six weeks would be fine, Nick."

"Good. What kind of engagement ring would you like then? Something with emeralds to match your eyes?"

She swallowed hard. "That won't be necessary. I know there's not a lot of extra money right now. A plain wedding band will do."

His mouth tightened. "Then what about the guest list? Obviously, it wouldn't be appropriate to invite your family, other than Danny, but if you've any special friends . . ."

This was beginning to feel like torture. The last thing she wanted to do right now was discuss wedding plans.

Sarah shook her head. "No. No one special. Whoever you decide upon will be fine with me, Nick."

"And that's all a bunch of hogwash, and you know it, Sarah!" He set down his cup and leaned toward her. "What about you?" he demanded hoarsely. "So far, all you've done is accede to my wishes. What do you *really* want?"

She had never seen Nick so angry. "I-I don't know what you mean. Wh-whatever makes you happy makes me happy."

"Then work it out with Cord. That would make me happy."

"Work what out?" She struggled to comprehend what he was saying. "What do Cord and I have to work out?"

"The love between you, of course." Nick sighed in exasperation. "Do you know you're the only two people in this house who haven't seemed to notice it yet?"

147

"I'm marrying you, Nick, not Cord."

"But it's Cord you really love, really want to marry, isn't it?"

Her eyes filled with tears and trickled down her cheeks. "N-Nick . . ."

"Oh, it's okay, Angel." He took her hand. "I've known it all along."

"Th-then why did you agree to marry me?"

"Because I was just as lamebrained as you and Cord. I was bound and determined to force that bullheaded brother of mine to think of himself just this once and admit that he loves you. Emma claims I really made a mess of things, though."

"L-loves me?" Sarah swiped away the tears with the back of her hand. "C-Cord loves me?"

"Of course he does. Ask Emma if you don't believe me."

Her eyes narrowed in disbelief. "Then why hasn't he told me? Why did he all but push me into your arms? It doesn't make sense!"

"Love frequently does that to people. Makes them senseless, I mean." Nick squeezed her hand. "Look, I just thought I'd play the matchmaker and help things along a bit. You know, try to make Cord jealous. Unfortunately, it backfired. Cord thought I was in love with you and gallantly stepped aside. Now we're all in a fine pickle. I'm so sorry, Sarah." He shifted uncomfortably in his wheelchair and hung his head. "I didn't mean for it to turn out this way."

At his downcast expression and utter remorse in his voice, Sarah couldn't help a smile. "I know you meant well, but there's no sense pretending to a sham engagement just to force Cord to declare his love for me. He and I have to work this out ourselves. If we can't, well, it isn't meant to be. I don't want a man who's afraid to let himself love."

Nick glanced up. "So what will you do?"

"I don't know. I haven't a lot of experience at this sort of thing."

"I'll help in any way I can. Just don't give up on Cord."

His eagerness was disarming, but Sarah knew better than to accept further assistance from Nick. "Thank you, but no thanks. On the offer of help, I mean. And, after what you've told me about Cord, I'm far from ready to give up on him." She rose, then paused. "Our engagement. On second thought, if you don't mind, I'd like to let everyone think it's still on for a little while longer. Until I decide what to do . . ."

"Take your time. I'm rather enjoying watching my brother stew in his own juices."

Sarah shook her head, then grinned. "You're incorrigible, you know."

"Yes," Nick replied with unrepentant glee. "So I've been told."

A week later, the carriage pulled up in front of McPherson's Mercantile, but the two women inside remained seated.

"I don't feel right about this," Sarah finally said. "Spending money on a new dress at a time like this . . ."

"Don't you worry your pretty head about that, child," Emma was quick to reassure her. "Some fabric for a gown for the fall dance isn't going to make or break the Wainwrights. Besides, as Nicholas's fiancée, you're going to have to have some new clothes sooner or later. This is as good a time as any to start."

Sarah frowned. "I still don't feel good about this."

Emma briskly climbed down from the carriage and tied up the horse. "No more of this, child. Come on. There's work to do. We've got less than two weeks to make you a ball dress."

Dougal McPherson was busy with several customers, so

Emma quickly pulled Sarah behind the counter to where the bolts of fabric were shelved. The selection was limited, especially of the finer cloths, as Dougal couldn't afford to keep a large inventory, and most people with the time to do so made use of the mail order catalogs. After much discussion, however, Sarah finally settled on an indigo blue velvet with an intricately woven black silk braid to trim it.

"I've got a beautiful black shawl you can wear with the gown," Emma said, warming to her self-appointed task as she led Sarah next to the shoes.

A pair of black kid slippers, the only dress shoes in the store, were easily decided upon, and Sarah was soon standing before a table that contained ladies' undergarments. With a sinking feeling, she watched Emma hold up a narrow-waisted corset, stiff with bone stays.

"I don't wear those things," she began in protest.

"Nonsense." Emma waved her silent. "These are the height of fashion and a must under an evening dress. We don't want Ashton's society maids and matrons looking down on Nick's future bride, do we?"

The image of Allis's simpering face smiling up at Cord filled Sarah's mind. If she could garner even half the interest he seemed to shower on Allis, she'd shackle herself hand and foot. Suddenly, in light of her determination to win over Cord, the corset looked pretty innocuous.

"Whatever you say, Emma," she said, resolutely nodding her acceptance.

An acquaintance of Emma's entered the store just then. The housekeeper left Sarah to decide upon a new chemise, underwear, and stiff taffeta petticoat. Sarah idly sorted through the various unmentionables, her glance straying to where Emma stood talking animatedly with a rotund, gray-haired woman. As she casually continued to look around the mercantile, a light tapping gradually intruded into her consciousness.

Sarah turned to the source of the noise. It came from the window directly behind the undergarment table. For an instant she just stared, startled by the face she saw grinning back at her.

It was her brother Caleb.

9

Sarah glanced around the store. Dougal was ensconced behind the counter, settling a customer's account. Emma was
still busily engaged with her friend. Sarah relaxed. No one
else had heard the tapping. She looked back out the window.

Caleb was pointing down the building, motioning for her
to come. Her gaze followed the direction of his hand and
noted a door. With a last, furtive glance to see if anyone
was looking her way, she slipped down the narrow hallway
to the back door.

"What are you doing in town?" she whispered as she shut
the door behind her. "Gabe Cooper's back. If you're not
careful, you're sure to get caught!"

Caleb's answer was a broad grin and outstretched arms.
"Now, is that any way to greet a brother you haven't seen in
over a month? Come here, little sister."

With a low cry, Sarah went to him, her misgivings fading in
her joy at seeing her brother again. "Oh, Caleb, I've missed
you so!" She leaned back to stare up into warm green eyes.
"How're Noah and Papa?"

He frowned. "Noah's okay, but Papa, well, he hasn't been
doing so good since you and Danny left. It was bad enough
when you got caught, and then when Danny joined you . . ."

Caleb shook his head. "Papa's health seems to be getting
worse and worse. And then there are the rages he goes into

these days with hardly any cause. When he's really mad, he starts yelling about how you ran out on him, turned coat to side with the Wainwrights."

"Did he get my note?"

"The one asking us to return the money? Yes. That set off his worst attack of all. How could you have asked him to do that? How could you hurt him like that?"

Stung by the reproach in her brother's words, Sarah pulled back. *He really believes it's all my fault.*

For a moment a frustrated anger washed over her; then reason returned. Trying to right an injustice was the real issue here, not her father's misguided feelings or her righteous indignation.

"He's wrong about this, Caleb. Surely you can see that." She grasped her brother's arms to emphasize her point. "And we all know he's not been thinking right for a long while. I mean, how is this suddenly my fault? *I'm* the one who he's abandoned rather than give up that money. And of all of you, only Danny so far has tried to come to my aid. Yet I've still managed to find a way to get Papa and you and Noah out of the trouble over the robbery. Cord Wainwright has agreed to drop charges if Papa returns the money. He'll let Danny and me go. What more can Papa want?"

Anger darkened her brother's features. "What's happened to you, Sarah? Has that fancy life at the Wainwrights' addled your brain? Papa's got his pride. To return the money would be to admit he's beaten, that he's wrong. He did it for us, you know? To make us all proud, so we could hold up our heads again."

"And since when is stealing something to be proud of?"

At her worst fears come to life, nausea churned in Sarah's gut. Caleb, her beloved brother, was becoming as stubbornly blind about things as was Papa. The truth behind their father's

153

silence regarding the money's return, an unpleasant reality she'd fought against over the past month, slammed home this time with sickening clarity. His pride mattered more to him than his children.

"You're a Caldwell, Sarah," Caleb said. "You know the answer as well as I." He turned to go, tugging on her arm as he did. "No more talk. It's not safe here."

She dug in her heels. "Where are you taking me?"

"Home. At least Papa will have one of his children back."

"No!" Sarah twisted free of his grip. "I-I can't."

He halted. "And why not? Sooner or later, we'll find a way to get Danny free."

"Because . . . because I've already made my decision." She forced out the words before they strangled her. "Danny and I are staying with the Wainwrights."

Caleb took a step toward her, his voice gone taut with rage. "You're doing what?"

"Danny needs a place where he can get good food, good care." She gazed up at him with pleading eyes. "Be honest, Caleb. You know we can't give him what he needs, never have. At the Wainwrights' he has a chance. Try to understand."

"Oh, I understand all right," he spat out furiously. "You got a taste of the good life and now we're not fine enough for you. You sold yourself to them, didn't you—you little tramp!"

He slapped her. Sarah reeled back from the stinging blow, her hand moving to her cheek. Tears filled her eyes, but she blinked them away.

She wouldn't cry; she just wouldn't. Caleb would see it as an admission of guilt. And she wasn't at fault here. She wasn't!

"Get out of here," she cried. "Get away from me!"

"Is that your answer then? Is that what I tell Papa?"

"I don't care what you tell Papa. He can't see the truth anymore, and neither can you. Just . . . just go away, Caleb."

He stared at her in disbelief, then shook his head in disgust. "Have it your way, little sister."

As she watched him walk away, an impulse to call him back rose to her lips. An impulse she fought with each retreating step, for her choice had already been made. There was no hope for Danny and her if they went back home. As hard as it was to accept, any hope of a future now lay with the Wainwrights.

The Wainwrights . . . their lifelong enemy. Sarah turned and walked back into the mercantile.

Twelve days later, Sarah drew up short, the low rumble of male voices emanating from the parlor the night of Ashton's fall dance shattering her barely contained resolve. "I-I don't know if I can do this," she whispered.

"And why not, child?" Emma brushed a stray curl back into place on Sarah's forehead. "You look lovely. Cord and Nicholas's eyes will pop out of their heads when they see you. And Edmund, well, maybe it'll finally make him realize what a fine lady you really are.

"Get on with you," she then urged, giving Sarah a small push forward. "We'll never get to Ashton if you hide out here in the hall. I, for one, am ready to do some dancing."

But you don't understand, Sarah thought. *Tonight's the night I've decided to confront Cord and make him admit he loves me—or forever give it up as a lost cause. And I don't know how to do it or what to say. Oh, Emma, I'm so scared!*

The words never found voice, however, for Sarah instead gathered up her courage with her skirts and walked into the parlor. Three pair of eyes turned to greet them. In the resultant appreciative hush, the men's conversation died an ignominious death.

Blessedly, in the embarrassment of the moment, Sarah barely noticed their reaction. Her nervous gaze instead skittered across the room until it found Cord.

Like his father and brother, he was dressed in a loose-fitting suit, single-breasted style, unbuttoned with a black jacquard vest and four-in-hand tie beneath it. The black wool suit cloth only enhanced his dark good looks.

For an instant, Sarah could only stare. Standing there, tall and foreboding, as unapproachable as some stranger, Cord presented a dangerously attractive but daunting appearance.

She wrenched her glance from his, but not before noting the flare of something intense as his gaze boldly raked her. A heavy warmth flooded her. It was all she could do to turn to where Nick sat.

He, too, looked devastatingly handsome in his dark brown suit. A smile of affection touched her lips as she walked over to him, the rustle of her taffeta petticoat beneath the velvet overskirt the only sound in the silent room. She halted before him.

"Please, say something, Nick," Sarah pleaded, her voice gone husky with her nervousness. "I feel like I've grown horns out of the top of my head or something."

Nick reached up to take her hand. "Forgive my poor manners, Angel. I didn't mean to make you uncomfortable, but I was momentarily struck speechless by your beauty." He turned to his brother. "Don't you agree, Cord?"

At the sound of his name, Cord jerked himself from his unabashed perusal. His gaze moved to his brother. "Yes. Sarah looks quite lovely," he managed to choke out.

The dress was elegant, the deep, shimmering blue of the velvet setting off Sarah's pale coloring to perfection. The off-the-shoulder ruffles and full sleeves only emphasized the warm, shapely throat and slender arms, the trim bodice accented with the ornate black braid and softly flaring skirt drawing his gaze downward in an inexorably sensual flow. Cord knew he was staring far past the point of good taste, but he couldn't help himself.

Did this woman standing before them have yet another tantalizing aspect to her? Youthful beauty, just embarking on the path to womanhood, he'd thought he could deal with, as well as boyish little wildcat and gently devoted sister and friend. But this . . . this sophisticated, exquisitely bewitching creature . . .

With the greatest of efforts, Cord throttled the dizzying current racing through him. He glanced around to find all eyes riveted in his direction. At the realization of how ludicrous he must appear, standing there gaping at Sarah like some . . . some love-besotted schoolboy, anger swelled. He set down his brandy snifter with a loud clink.

"It's time we were on our way."

The brusqueness of his voice seemed to galvanize everyone to action. Emma brought over her and Sarah's shawls. Cord proceeded to wheel Nick out to the front porch, Sarah following. Behind them, Cord heard his father's bemused voice.

"What in tarnation's the matter with Cord? If I didn't know better, I'd think he's mad because the girl looks so good."

"Hush, Edmund," Emma whispered. "Just let those two work it out among themselves."

"Work what out?" came the peevish reply. "What's going on here anyway? I thought Sarah and Nick—"

"Edmund!"

His voice faded to a gruff rumble.

The lilting strains of a waltz drifted to their ears as the carriage drew up before the new town hall. Cord quickly jumped down and assisted Emma and Sarah from the conveyance. Then, together with his father, he helped Nick from the carriage and into his wheelchair.

The entourage entered the hall. It was all Sarah could do to keep from halting in her tracks, a sudden rush of shyness again overwhelming her. Never in her wildest dreams had she ever imagined she'd be part of such a gala affair.

The women, for all their distance from the fashion centers of the East, were arrayed in the most elegant gowns in every color of the rainbow, and all the men looked dapper and proud in their fine suits. The large hall was decorated in autumn-hued ribbons and paper lanterns. A small band of fiddlers played quite competently upon the makeshift stage.

As she followed her companions into the room and over to a spot near the punch table, Sarah felt like an actress playing a part. Like an actress who didn't really belong and would soon be discovered in her role . . .

"Cord, do your brotherly duty and ask Sarah to dance."

Nick's request wrenched Sarah from her wide-eyed staring. She looked down at him. He smiled up at her, taking her hand to offer it to Cord.

Her glance reluctantly rose to meet that of the man whose hand now accepted hers. A dark, unfathomable gaze stabbed into Sarah, sending an apprehensive tremor through her. *Oh my*, she thought, then steeled herself to return his stare.

"Shall we dance?"

The deep voice, soft but so richly timbred, sent a pang of longing through her. *Dance? Oh yes, Cord. And may it go on forever and ever.*

The words, though, never passed her lips. Sarah's only reply was to nod and follow him onto the dance floor.

They moved together stiffly at first, their eyes never quite seeming to meet. Yet even as they whirled about the crowded room, the world existed only within the space of the few feet surrounding them. Though he maintained a most proper distance, Sarah could still feel the heat emanating from Cord's big, strong body, smell the scent of the bay rum he wore. The very touch of his hands sent tingling bursts of fire rippling through her. And she wanted, oh, how she wanted, to draw closer, to bury herself in the haven of his arms!

But it was impossible, here, in front of the whole town, knowing how rigidly Cord kept himself from her. Somehow, she must find a way to get him to relax. She forced a merry smile to her lips.

"My, but aren't you awfully formal tonight?"

He arched a wary brow. "Oh? And how so?"

"Well, for one," Sarah forged on, a teasing light dancing in her eyes, "you've got the most forbidding scowl on your face. And, for another, you're holding me like I'm made of glass. After sharing a rough-and-tumble mud bath, not to mention a vegetable fight in the cellar, I'd hardly have expected that of you."

A small grin of remembrance twisted Cord's mouth. He chuckled.

"So, you think I'm too formal, do you? And how would you have me act with you all dressed up like this? Throw you over my shoulder and twirl madly about the room?"

Sarah laughed, warming to their now lighthearted banter. "What a novel idea! I only wonder if Ashton society could survive such a scandalous display."

"Shall we find out?"

She immediately rose to the dare. "Why not? I hardly think—"

A hand clapped down on Cord's shoulder. "Time's up, boss. No fair hoarding the most beautiful belle at the ball."

159

They stopped and turned to face the owner of the voice. A brown-haired man of medium height, his thin mouth curved into a cynical smile, stared back at them. Sarah immediately recognized him as the foreman of the Wainwright ranch.

"Well, Spence, it didn't take you long to set your sights on her, did it?" Cord asked as he handed over Sarah. "Better not let Allis see you dancing with her, though. Your courting days will be over if she does."

Spencer Womack laughed. "Oh, I'm no fool. She hasn't arrived yet. Fashionably late as always, you know. Be a pal and keep a lookout for me, will you? Allis has quite a temper when she wants to, though as much as she flirts with every eligible bachelor, you'd hardly think I'm even in the running."

Cord chuckled and stepped away, leaving Sarah to face the ranch foreman. Spence grinned down at her.

"Shall we dance, little lady?"

Before she could reply, he swept her into his arms, pulling her much closer than she cared to be. She leaned back against the encircling strength of his arm, but it did little good. Womack apparently noticed the action. His grin widened.

Irritation surged through Sarah. She hardly knew the man, yet there had always been something about him she didn't like. His possessive clasp right now only fueled her distaste.

She glared up at him. "Kindly loosen your hold on me. I don't care for the familiarity of it."

"And why is that? Does my name have to be Wainwright for you to like it? Well, believe it or not, I've got a little money of my own, and plan to have a lot more soon. So," he said, pulling her even nearer, "be careful who you turn up your nose at. Women like you can't afford to be so choosy."

Sarah jerked away from him but couldn't escape his iron grasp. She glanced around for signs of Cord or Nick, but the dance floor was so crowded it blocked them from view. There was no escape from Spencer Womack unless she decided to make a scene. She turned back to face him.

"You're an obnoxious boor, Mr. Womack. I see no reason to continue this dance. Let me go."

"But we're not done, little lady." His flat gray eyes roved over her face before sliding down to the creamy expanse of her bosom. "For all your upbringing, you're a fine-looking woman. Still, the Wainwrights are eventually bound to tire of you. When they do, you'll need a 'friend.' If you play your cards right . . ."

"No, thank you, Mr. Womack. Now, let me go or I'll—"

"You'll do what? Make a fuss? Slap my face and accuse me of improper behavior? But the whole town knows you and knows what you've been doing at the Wainwrights'. Do you really want to draw even more attention to yourself?"

High color tinged her cheeks. "I don't care what you or any of this town thinks! And if you don't let me go this instant, I'll do more than slap your face. I'll—"

"I believe this is my dance, Spence."

Spencer Womack wheeled around, his face paling at the steely edge to Gabe Cooper's voice. His arms fell from Sarah and she quickly moved away. Gabe smiled down at her, then looked back at the other man.

"You know, Spence, I don't much care for your conduct. But we'll keep it between you and me if you promise to stay away from Sarah the rest of the evening. If not, maybe Cord will have to hear about it."

"I-I didn't mean any harm, Gabe." Womack began to back away. "I was just flirting a little with a beautiful woman. That's all."

Disgust darkened Gabe's rugged features. "Yeah, sure you were. Just get out of here, will you?"

He turned his back on the retreating man and smiled down

at Sarah. "Cord and Nick are fools to turn you loose in here, looking like you do." He took her into his arms as the music began again. "I guess I'm just going to have to take you into protective custody."

Sarah giggled. "Whatever you say, Sheriff."

"I'm sorry about Spence's behavior just now. I don't know what's gotten into him of late."

She shook her head and sighed. "I gather there are a lot of rumors floating around about me and what I'm doing at the Wainwright ranch. He must have chosen to believe some of the more filthy ones. Not that I can blame anyone, I guess. No matter how good a life I tried to live before the robbery, being accused of such a crime must make it hard for people to think kindly of me anymore."

"Not everyone thinks poorly of you, Sarah. Actually, from what I hear, it's only one person spreading these rumors, and only her friends who are believing it."

Sarah instantly knew who he was talking about. "Allis, of course."

Gabe nodded. "Of course. Well, don't let Spence's tales ruin your evening. He's so busy panting after Allis he can't see straight most of the time anyhow. Not that he has a snowball's chance with her, leastwise not as long as Cord's still a free man. So, consider the source and let it go at that."

"No sooner said than done," she replied with a smile, though a dubious tone lingered.

"So," he said, obviously deciding it best to change the subject, "when's the wedding going to be?"

Sarah's smile faded. "Uh, we're still trying to work that out."

"And does this delay have anything to do with Cord?"

A slow flush stained her cheeks. "Is . . . is it that apparent?"

"Well, take a look at Cord over there," he said, cocking

his head in the direction of the punch table. "He hasn't taken his eyes off you since we began dancing, and if I don't miss my guess, he looks pretty annoyed."

Sarah's glance swung to where Cord stood beside his brother. Their gazes briefly met, just long enough for her to note the glowering look he sent her way. Then Gabe whirled her by and out of Cord's view.

Wild hope swelled in her breast. *Is . . . is he jealous? Oh, let it be so!*

She turned back to the sheriff. "I don't know what to think anymore. The way he acts toward me is so confusing."

"I'd say he's pretty confused himself." Gabe hesitated. "This may be none of my business, but if you love Cord, why are you marrying Nick?"

"Because I thought Cord didn't want me . . . He even pushed me to marry Nick. And . . . and I care very much for Nick." Sarah searched his face. "I know I must sound like a calculating opportunist, but it's not really that way. I . . . I need a good home for Danny. Besides, Nick and I aren't actually engaged anymore, though no one knows that yet but you—"

He cocked his head, then nodded. "Well, your secret's safe with me. And you don't have to explain a thing, Sarah. It's your business. I only want you to be happy. God only knows you deserve a better life than you've had up to now. You and Danny both." Now, since this might be my last chance to dance with you as an unmarried woman, *whomever* you end up married to," he added with a twinkle in his eye, "I intend to savor the experience."

He then proceeded to guide her about the dance floor for two exhilarating waltzes, and Sarah enjoyed herself immensely. Gabe Cooper was a dashingly handsome man in his own right, and she couldn't help but revel in the warmth of his quite evident admiration. Like a flower opening itself to the rays of the sun, Sarah bloomed, her eyes sparkling, her face glowing, her laughter tinkling across the room. Finally, though, she pulled back from the circle of his arms.

"I need to get back to Nick," she said. "It's not proper to ignore him all evening."

Gabe nodded and offered her his arm. "Something cool and wet would taste right nice about now."

He escorted Sarah to the table for a glass of punch. Sarah couldn't help but notice, however, as they approached Cord standing beside Nick, that Cord's fists were clenched at his sides. He shot the sheriff a seething look.

Nick glanced at his brother, a smile of quiet satisfaction on his lips. "Having fun, Angel?" he asked, turning back to Sarah.

"Oh yes, Nick," she replied a little breathlessly. "It's all so delightful. I'm having a *wonderful* time."

"Well," Cord muttered under his breath, "then you're the only one doing so."

Sarah looked to him. "And why do you say that, Cord?"

He glared at her. "You came with Nick, and you've all but ignored him from the minute you walked in the door. I find that rather rude, not to mention thoughtless. He is your fiancé, after all."

Nick cut in before Sarah could respond. "Now, little brother, don't go getting riled over nothing. I don't mind at all. I want Sarah to have a good time. She looks beautiful, and I want everyone in this room to notice. This is her night to shine. I won't have anyone taking that from her."

"But you're engaged, Nick! I just want her to respect that, rather than act like some—"

"Cord! Cord, darling!"

Allis Findley's melodious voice carried across the room. The quartet's eyes reluctantly turned toward her. Dressed in a puffy-sleeved pink confection, she paused quite dramatically

164

at her father's side as she made her grand entrance—until her glance fell on Sarah. Then her eyes narrowed and, with no more than a word of farewell to her sire, she made a beeline straight across the hall toward them.

At her approach, Nick groaned and Gabe breathed an "Oh no." Cord shot them an enigmatic glance, then turned his attention back to the pink bit of fluff determinedly heading toward them.

Allis flounced up, bestowing her prettiest smile on him. "I do believe you're the handsomest man at this party, Cord Wainwright." She paused to lay her small, beringed hand on his arm. "I know I've just arrived, but I'm *so* thirsty, darling. Would you please fetch me a cup of punch?"

"I'd be honored," he replied before heading off toward the punch bowl.

"I see you managed to worm your way into the dance," Allis then purred, her gaze critically raking Sarah's slender form. "Where *did* you get that dress?"

"Why, imported straight from Paris, of course," Sarah smoothly shot back. She scanned the other woman's gown. "Yours too, I assume?"

Allis's mouth tightened in anger. "I hardly think we share the same couturier . . ."

She halted, apparently realizing how ludicrous arguing about dressmakers must sound to the two men standing there. Obviously deciding a snub was a more effective ploy, she turned her attention to Nick, and Gabe, completely ignoring Sarah until Cord finally returned.

"Oh, darling, I've changed my mind." Allis accepted the cup of punch from Cord and immediately shoved it at Sarah. "Sarah looks so damp and mussed from dancing. She needs this much more than I. What *I* need," she continued, taking his arm, "is a romantic waltz in your strong arms."

Cord quirked a dark brow. "Is that a fact?" He turned toward the others. "If you'll excuse me, it appears I owe Allis a dance."

Sarah watched him lead the woman out onto the dance floor, then turned from the scene. The pain of seeing Cord hold another woman was suddenly too much to bear. To hide her misery, she forced herself to take a sip of her punch. The trembling of her hands as she raised the cup to her lips, however, wasn't lost on the two men with her.

They exchanged a concerned glance, then Gabe firmly removed the cup from her hands. "Come on, Sarah," the sheriff said. "We can't have you whiling the night away standing on the sidelines. That music's calling us."

Before she could protest that she wasn't in the mood, Gabe whisked her back onto the dance floor. Surprisingly, the next few hours passed with whirlwind speed. Sarah could hardly complete a set with one partner before another was stepping forward to claim the next one. Cord soon surrendered Allis into Spencer Womack's waiting arms, and once more took up his position beside his brother. Yet the more he glared at her, the happier and more lighthearted Sarah's actions became.

It was hopeless, she morosely told herself even as she kept up the happy façade. Cord would never declare his love, if that was even what he truly felt. His actions tonight had hardly been that of the besotted swain.

Well, let him get angry, she thought as she twirled about the floor in the arms of yet another man. *He's bound and determined to think the worst of me no matter what I do, and I'm not letting him ruin this evening for me. I'm tired of trying to please him. Nick's not upset and he's the only one whose feelings I need worry about. Let Cord stand there and fume until he explodes. It serves him right!*

Almost as if her thoughts had drawn him toward her, Cord suddenly headed across the dance floor. The hard glitter in his eyes made Sarah momentarily quail before she turned her attention back to her partner. Cord wouldn't dare cause a scene. Would he?

"This is my dance," Cord cut in just then, firmly tapping the town pharmacist on the shoulder.

One glance at his smoldering look was enough for the other man. He released Sarah and backed away.

She glared up at the dark-haired man towering over her. "That was rude. And this isn't your dance."

An iron grip settled on her arm as she turned to walk away. "Oh yes it is."

Something in the tone of his voice warned her not to argue. Sarah relented, going stiffly into the circle of his arms. "Have it your way, but *only* for one dance."

"We'll just see about that," he growled before leading her off in time to the music.

They danced silently for a while, the tension arcing between them with crackling force. Finally Cord spoke, his words harsh and brutal.

"What in the blazes do you think you're doing, flaunting your flirtations here tonight in front of Nick? Don't you have any feelings for him, to embarrass him like this? I swear, Sarah, if you don't start acting like a lady, I'll see to it that—"

"That what, Cord?" All the frustration of the evening watching him from the sidelines, glowering at her, was suddenly too much to contain. "That I don't marry Nick? But I thought you wanted me to marry Nick."

"Don't play games with me," he growled. "The issue here isn't your marriage to Nick. It's your behavior."

She laughed unsteadily. "And who are you to dictate my behavior? You have no claims on me."

As she spoke, reality finally broke through the fragile hopes and dreams for the evening, shattering her brave composure. Sarah jerked back, tears flooding her eyes.

"Why do you persist in constantly picking at me? Oh, I don't care what the rest of them say! You hate me, don't you? You hate me, and it's never been anything more than that."

Cord stared down at her, apparently oblivious to the fact they were now standing in the middle of the floor, the other dancers circling around them in time to the music. "I don't hate you, Sarah. I . . . I only want for Nick to be happy. And I don't want you to hurt him."

For a tear-blinded instant, she stared up at him, her whole world crumbling around her. Then she took a step back. "Go to blazes, Cord Wainwright!"

Before he could respond, Sarah fled the hall, running out into the dark anonymity of the night. She stumbled once, a sharp stone ripping a hole in her gown, but she was past caring. All she wanted was to run away—far from the now false gaiety of the town hall, far from the man who once again had so cruelly dashed all her hopes onto the hard, unforgiving rocks of reality.

Silver moonlight illuminated the path out of town. Sarah ran on, seeking shelter from its prying light in the shaggy firs that clung to the hillside. All she wanted was to hide and cry her heart out once and for all, to rid herself of the last vestiges of her dreams—and bury forever her love. Then she'd return to the hall and face her future with no looking back, no regrets.

A sound—her name—whisked by on the vestiges of a breeze. Sarah froze.

"Sarah," the low voice called again, and she knew it was Cord. She halted and turned to face him.

He drew up to her, his dark eyes glinting shards of onyx in the moonlight. Before she could say anything, he pulled her to him.

"When we first met in town I called you a little wildcat," he said, his voice barely more than a throaty rasp. "But I was wrong. You're a little witch, and you've put every man here tonight under your spell. Every man . . . including me."

"Well, don't let it worry you," she retorted with cold sarcasm. "The spell fades at sunrise. It'll have no lasting effect."

"You think so, eh?" Cord pulled her closer, his gaze hungrily scanning her, his words rough with unbridled desire. "Well, I'm not so sure anymore."

At the husky timbre of his voice, Sarah's pulse quickened, her skin tingling with the awareness of his perusal. Warmth flooded her. With it came a strange surety in what she must do.

Standing on tiptoe, she molded her slim frame to his hard-muscled one. With both hands, she cupped his face and pulled his mouth down to hers.

"Then let me end the uncertainty," Sarah murmured. "For the both of us . . . once and for all."

10

She kissed him softly, tentatively and, for a moment, feared his response as he stood so stiffly before her. Something inside her quailed, but Sarah forced herself to go on.

Her lips traced the firm contours of his mouth, then moved to the strong line of his jaw and down the side of his neck. Burying her face in the corded hollows, she breathed a kiss there. Only then did she feel him tremble, know at last with any certainty that she'd pierced his defenses.

"Curse you, Sarah," Cord groaned, whispering the words into her hair as he lowered his head in defeat. "This isn't right . . . You're not mine . . ."

"Hush, my love." She looked up, silencing him with a gentle finger. "It *is* right. I've always been yours."

He stared down at her, the battle of wild hope over disbelief playing out in his dark eyes. "Then why . . ." Cord paused. "It was me all along, wasn't it? I was too blind to see what was right there in front of me."

She angled her head back and smiled. "Well, I guess you could say that. Being too blind to recognize the truth, I mean. Guess that was why Nick felt compelled to stage our sham engagement."

"A sham engagement?" Understanding slowly dawned, and Cord's mouth twisted ruefully. "Guess I should've listened to him to begin with. Instead, I was so intent on forcing you on

Nick, that I never . . ." He sighed, his hands slowly moving up her arms. "So, what do we do now?"

An impish grin played about her mouth. "Oh, I don't know. Want to get to know me better, cowboy?"

The light of remembrance flared in Cord's eyes. "And what exactly did you have in mind, little lady?" he replied, repeating the words of that first hot September day.

Sarah chuckled softly. "Anything you like, cowboy. I only want to make you happy."

"Well, then how about a kiss?" His ebony head lowered to her.

She came to him willingly, eagerly this time, melting into the hard contours of his body. "I thought you'd never ask," Sarah whispered, her lips a warm breath from his.

This time there was no doubt of his desire. Cord's mouth slanted over hers with demanding mastery. A shock of delight coursed through her.

Sarah responded, returning his ardor with equal ardor of her own. Her hands moved to the sinewy strength of his upper arms, reveling in their taut power, before rising to entwine about his neck.

Cord's kiss deepened, taking on a savage intensity. His breath rasped hard and heavy now.

"Oh, Sarah, Sarah," he breathed on a sigh. Gently, he disengaged her arms from him and pushed her away.

She stared up at him, all the old doubts rushing back to coil their clammy tendrils about her heart. She knew it wasn't right to take this any further but feared he was also telling her he still intended to step aside in deference to Nick.

He must have seen the uncertainty in her eyes. "Calm your fears. I'm not fool enough to think I could ever deny my feelings for you again. I just think a proposal of marriage might be the next step, don't you? If you'll have me, of course."

Pure, sweet bliss surged through Sarah. *A proposal? Cord wants to marry me?*

Sudden doubt followed quickly on the heels of her happiness. Cord had yet to speak of love. But surely he loved her. His actions hadn't been those of a man not in love. Or had they?

Everything paled in light of that last, lingering doubt. Passion she knew he felt, but that could never be enough for her. A comfortable life, better than she'd ever known or hoped to know, he could offer her. But so could Nick, and at least the absence of that love wouldn't hurt as much as it would with Cord. No, she had to know, and know now, or there was little hope for a life together.

Sarah stepped back. "Do you love me?"

For an instant Cord stared down at her, taken aback by the unexpected bluntness of the question. She never ceased to amaze him with her sharp changes in mood. One minute she was a warm, passionate woman and the next, somber and strangely withdrawn. But then, he hadn't mentioned anything about love, had he? The realization sent a small twinge of unease spiraling through him.

Gazing down at Sarah, so luminous, so lovely in the silver moonlight, he knew he loved her. Yet why the lingering hesitation to say the words, to make that final commitment? The pain, buried deep in his soul until now, rose with gut-wrenching intensity to his consciousness.

He feared the rejection of reaching out to another, of sharing the warmth of his heart and finding only coldness in return. It was amazing how just one shattering experience when he was young could cast its shadow upon the rest of his life. He had his father to thank for twisting his soul into such knots, knots that now seemed hopeless to untie.

Yet maybe there was still a way. Like the Gordian knot of old, said to be impossible to unravel, was it instead feasible to slice through it all with one sharp blow—with the piercingly keen edge of love?

She was the first woman who understood him and what he wanted most in the world. How he wanted, how he loved and needed her!

But would her love and devotion be enough to heal all those years of painful betrayal? And was he man enough to take the risk?

He couldn't waste a lifetime not knowing, a lifetime without her.

Cord inhaled a long, shuddering breath. "Yes, Sarah. I love you."

"And I, you, my love."

She came to him then, a joyful cry on her lips. They clung to each other, almost desperate in their need, each battling the last remnants of their doubts and fears. And, bit by bit, the gnawing uncertainties faded. A warm contentment engulfed them.

They stood there a long while, basking in each other's love and the silken splendor of the night. A gentle breeze, pungent with the scent of pine, caressed them. The low, mournful hoot of an owl soothed their souls. Moonlight bathed the land in velvet silence, as if time suddenly ceased to exist. It was a night made for lovers. Only after what seemed an eternity did they finally, reluctantly part.

Cord grinned, a rueful light in his eyes. "We'd better get back to the dance before tongues begin to wag. Neither of us made a very surreptitious exit, if you recall."

Sarah chuckled. "So you think they noticed our departure, do you? And do you really care?"

"For my reputation, no. But I'll not have people making

snide remarks about my future wife." He took her by the arm. "Come along, my dear. You know as well as I there's another, more pressing reason to leave while we still can."

"I suppose you're right." Sarah giggled at a sudden thought. "I've already got some explaining to do to Emma about the sorry state of my gown. And that, I think, is quite enough for one night."

"That it is." Cord led her back down the path toward town. "That it is, indeed."

As they neared the town hall, a sudden commotion caught their attention. Several riders had pulled up before the building. As Cord and Sarah watched, they hurriedly dismounted and ran into the hall. The music abruptly died. Agitated voices could be heard from within.

Cord's grip on Sarah's arm tightened. "Come on. There's trouble."

Edmund Wainwright nearly collided with his son as they entered the hall. "Blast it all, Cord!" his father cried. "Where have you been? We need to get back to the ranch pronto!"

"Why? What's happened?" Cord released Sarah's arm. He stepped forward to confront his father.

The action wasn't lost on the older man. His glance raked Sarah, and a knowing look flared in his eyes. Then he turned his gaze back to his son.

"While you two were dallying outside," he replied, "her family was busy rustling over fifty head of our cattle."

No sooner had they returned to the ranch that evening than Cord and Edmund, along with most of the hands, saddled up and rode back to town to join Gabe Cooper and his deputy in pursuit of the stolen cattle. Sarah, left behind at the ranch, was beside herself with worry, not only for the possible involvement of her father and brothers in the cattle thieving but also for Cord's safety. Chasing down cattle rustlers didn't always turn out well—for the rustlers *or* their pursuers.

After shedding her ball gown and dressing in plainer clothes, she first tried to soothe her jangled nerves by reading one of the books she'd chosen from the library. Lighting the oil lamp on the little table beside the rocking chair in her bedroom, she took her seat, opened the book, and then spent the good part of the next half hour staring at the page, her thoughts winging their way out into the night, mentally riding along with Cord and the others.

Finally, with a disgusted sigh, Sarah closed the book and laid it on the table. Her glance moved to the bed, where Danny slept on, totally oblivious to the drama being enacted this night. She preferred to keep it that way. Her brother's asthma was easily triggered by stress or too much excitement. Better he not be privy to the danger his father and brothers might well be in this night.

She closed her eyes, trying to shut out the memory of the moments before the men had ridden out. Edmund's face had been livid with anger and an unsettling look of revenge. Cord's had just appeared weary, as if he was mightily tired of the unending trouble the Caldwell family seemed to cause. He couldn't spare much time to say his farewells to her, but after some brief words with his brother on the front porch, he managed to steal a few minutes with her before his father came downstairs.

"It may not be your family," he said, taking her by the arms and pulling her close. "Spence seems to think it might be some renegade Utes who've been causing all the problems. So I don't want you to worry. We really won't know who rustled our cattle until we catch up with them."

"I know." Gazing at Cord, Sarah couldn't help but drink in

the sight of him, still overwhelmed with the heady knowledge that he loved her. Just being close to Cord helped assuage some of her fears. "I . . . I just don't know what my father is capable of these days. And I don't want anything to happen to anyone."

He crooked a finger beneath her chin. "Especially me, I hope."

She smiled. "Especially you, of course."

Then Edmund was hurrying down the stairs and out onto the front porch. His glance was unreadable as he took in Cord and Sarah standing there.

"This isn't the time for tender farewells," he said. "Especially with your brother's fiancée. Or has she changed her mind about which brother she really wants now?"

"Actually, she has," Cord said, releasing Sarah and heading over to join his father. "But that's a story best discussed at some other time. First things first. Let's go catch us some cattle thieves."

Edmund's brows lifted in surprise, then he nodded. "You're right about that. First things first."

He shoved his Stetson on his head and motioned toward the two saddled horses Spencer Womack had brought up for them. "Let's go catch us some cattle thieves."

In her mind's eye, Sarah yet again watched them ride out into the night, her heart so full of conflicting emotions she didn't know what to do. Watched them go, not knowing what to wish for, save that all would survive the night. And now, six hours later, she felt just as conflicted, just as terrified, as she had then.

Frustrated almost beyond bearing, she rose from the rocker and began to pace the room. At her agitated walking back and forth, Danny stirred, and she was forced to quit or risk waking him.

Maybe a cup of warm milk and honey might soothe my upset stomach, she thought, *and help ease me to sleep. It's worth a try.*

Silently slipping from the bedroom, Sarah headed down the hall to the stairs. Just as she reached the first floor, the clock in the parlor chimed four in the morning.

It'll be dawn in another few hours, she thought. *Might as well forego the milk and just make a fresh pot of coffee. I'm not getting any sleep tonight, and that's for sure.*

As she neared the kitchen, surprisingly, light shone from beneath the door. Curious now, Sarah pushed open the door and walked in. There, at the kitchen table, was Nick.

At her entrance, he half turned in his wheelchair. "Have some coffee," he said, holding up his mug. "I made a pot about an hour ago."

"So you couldn't sleep either," she observed as she went to the cupboard and took down a clean mug.

"A lot happened tonight to keep a man awake. And I've always kept vigil anytime Pa headed out on some dirty business like this."

Sarah poured herself a mug of coffee at the big, cast-iron cookstove then ambled over to the table. She took a seat, paused to add a couple of spoonfuls of sugar from the sugar bowl, then thoroughly stirred them in.

"So, what do you want to talk about first?" Nick finally asked. "You and Cord, or what might happen if it *is* your father who stole our cattle?"

She met his glance. "After he followed me from the dance, Cord proposed to me. So, you're off the hook. No more pretend engagement."

Nick reached over and laid a hand atop hers. "Believe me when I say, Angel, that I never saw our engagement as unpleasant or a burden. Still, I'm happy for the both of you."

"I am too." Sarah sighed. "I just feel so . . . so confused. Here I am, bit by bit tying my life and loyalty to your family and, in the doing, being forced bit by bit to sever my bonds with my own family. And it shouldn't be that way. It just shouldn't!"

"No, it shouldn't." He gave her hand a squeeze, then released it and leaned back in his wheelchair.

"They'll never forgive me for this—Papa and my brothers. Marrying Cord, I mean."

"Indeed, they might not."

With both hands she grasped her mug of coffee, savoring its comforting warmth. Myriad thoughts assailed her, until her mind reeled with the jumble of emotions they elicited. Anger at the feud that had brought her to this impasse. Frustration at her father for his stubborn refusal to see anyone's way but his own, and his unwillingness to accept compromise in any form. Pain at her family's apparent desertion of her and Danny.

And then there was the memory of Cord, not all that many hours ago, admitting to his love for her and his desire that she become his wife. Just the passing recollection of him holding her in his arms, kissing her, filled Sarah with such sweet joy and oh, so much love! The feelings he stirred in her almost overshadowed all the others. Almost . . .

"Why does it have to be so hard?" she cried, closing her eyes and shaking her head. "It's not fair, Nick. It's just not fair!"

"No, life's not always fair, is it? But remember what we talked about that first day we met? About putting an end to the feud? Maybe this is just part and parcel of God's larger plan, you and Cord becoming man and wife. Maybe this next step, as hard as it'll be for you, is what's needed to finally begin the healing of both our families."

Her mouth quirked. "So far, I'm not seeing how God's had much of a hand in any of this."

"That's where faith has to come in. But if you believe, you'll also accept the fact He can bring good even out of things that, at first glance, seem bad." Nick grinned. "I mean, think about it. As bad as the act was, if you hadn't helped out in the robbery, maybe you and Cord would've never met. And then he likely wouldn't have recognized you that day you went to town, and caught you, and brought you back here. And if Gabe had happened to be in town that day, then you and Cord would've never had the chance to get to know each other better. And then if Danny hadn't decided to try and rescue you . . ."

She exhaled a deep breath and held up her hand. "Okay, okay. I get the picture. A lot of things *did* eventually work out for the best, didn't they? But even if this is all part of God's bigger plan, He sure hasn't had much of an impact on my father yet."

"No, maybe He hasn't, but the time away from your father has helped *you* see things about him—and your old life—a little more clearly, hasn't it? That maybe you and Danny deserve something better than you've always had. And maybe, just maybe, God's hand is in that as well."

"But why Danny and me, and not the rest of my brothers? And even my papa? They all deserve better too."

Nick shrugged. "Only the Lord knows, Angel. Maybe He chose to use you and Danny because, as the two youngest, you're the least tainted by your father's anger and need for revenge. Because you're the most open to change. Because you're the most open to forgiveness."

They were true, Nick's words. All of them. As hard as it was to admit, she and Danny had come to a crossroads in their lives, and a better path spread out now before them. But to turn her back on her father, on Caleb and Noah, and walk away from them . . .

"The Lord isn't asking you to renounce your family, Angel," Nick said just then, as if he were reading her mind. "He asks us all to honor our parents. But God also expects us to follow Him and not look back, to do what is right, no matter how painful the consequences. He asks us to love, not hate. To forgive, not hold grudges. To turn from the darkness to the true Light."

As she listened to Nick, Sarah's jumbled thoughts gradually righted themselves. Insight filled her. No matter what she had promised her mother, she could do nothing for her father unless he chose to change. Indeed, she was just as likely to sacrifice her own life and happiness—and that of her little brother's—and still not get her father to give up his hopeless quest. In the doing, she'd also sacrifice Cord's happiness.

"Ask yourself this, for I think the answer to it is the true will of God," Nick said. "Ask yourself, where can I accomplish the most good? Not that doing the most good might not be the hardest thing of all to do. God never promises to make the road easy just because He asks some particular thing of you. On the contrary, oftentimes what He asks is the hardest road of all. But on what other road will you fulfill your life's true mission and find the deepest, most lasting peace?"

Gazing over at him, Sarah couldn't help but think the very same choice had once been offered to Nick. Surely he had wondered what possible value he had to offer others, paralyzed as he was. And surely, in those moments of greatest doubt, living had seemed the far more difficult thing to do than giving up, than dying. Yet where would any of them—and she especially—be without him and his gentle companionship and deep wisdom?

Of late, she'd also had some difficult choices to make. In many ways, the most straightforward path was to return home to her family. If she didn't, at the very least, she'd live with guilt for a long time to come. It was far easier to resume the life she'd always known than to stay with the Wainwrights and strike out on an entirely new road. A new and sometimes frightening road, and one so very foreign from what she'd heretofore experienced.

But this road also held *such* promise. There'd be Cord, Emma, and Nick to walk beside her. Danny would have a much better life. Her own existence would be richer, full of opportunities she'd never had before.

There was also the hope that sooner or later Edmund Wainwright would accept her as his daughter and, with her and Danny's help, maybe even reconcile with Cord. There was always the hope, until the day her father finally died, that he, too, might find acceptance and be glad that she had become a Wainwright.

Yes, this choice, leastwise in terms of her family, might cost her dearly. But maybe, just maybe, this was the way things were meant to be. And maybe, just maybe, this was what God wanted of her, this was where she could indeed do the most good.

The words from Psalm 119, beloved by her mother, filled her mind. *Sustain me, O God, as you have promised, and I shall live; do not disappoint me in my hope.*

Hope . . . so much hope. But only if she had help. God's help.

Sarah smiled, the certainty she was making the right, the best, decision filling her with peace.

"Where can I accomplish the most good?" she asked, repeating Nick's question. "You know the answer to that as well as I do. First and foremost, it's here, Nick. Here, with Danny, you and Cord, and Emma, Manuela, and Pedro. And even, I think—I hope—with your father.

"But that doesn't mean I won't keep trying my very best

to be there for my father and brothers too. They're God's children as much as the Wainwrights are. And I can't help but always love them and wish the best for them."

"I would never ask you to do otherwise. And neither would Cord."

Cord . . .

The stark reality of why they were sitting here in this cozy, lamp-lit kitchen jerked Sarah back to the present moment. *Please, Lord, keep him safe this night*, she thought, her glance straying into the darkness just outside the kitchen window. *Please, keep him safe and bring him home to me.*

Sunrise of that day came and went, and there was still no news or return of Cord and the rest of the posse who'd gone out after the cattle rustlers. Time passed with maddening slowness. To keep her mind from straying to all sorts of tragic scenarios, Sarah busied herself with as many chores as she could find.

She helped bake bread, pluck chickens for a big meal to feed the men upon their return, and then carted several crocks of apples up from the cellar for pies. She swept and dusted and polished until the rooms sparkled. She ironed sheets, pillowcases, towels, and countless men's shirts.

And still the hours plodded by without Cord's return. Finally, about midafternoon, exhausted from lack of sleep and all the self-imposed work, Sarah could bear the tension no longer. Her basket of eggs clutched in one hand, she finally burst into tears outside the chicken coop.

"Please, oh please, Lord," she prayed in between shuddering sobs. "Nick said it's part of Your plan that Cord and I be together. So I'm going to trust You to keep Cord safe. I love him, Lord. Please don't let anything happen to him. Please!"

After a while, she cried herself out and felt a little better. Wiping away her tears, she made her way to the horse trough near the barn, put down the basket, and splashed some cool water on her swollen eyes and over warm cheeks. Though she felt refreshed, Sarah knew if she ran into Nick or Emma up at the house, they'd easily ascertain she'd been crying.

Deciding a walk was the best way to buy time and allow all signs of her weeping to subside, Sarah left the egg basket in a safe place and headed to the creek. There she climbed onto the large boulder overlooking the rushing waters and lay down on the sun-warmed rock. For a while, she just listened to the sounds of the creek skipping over and around the rocks, while overhead, sparrows chirped gaily as they hopped from branch to branch of the swaying aspens.

Every time a breeze kicked up, the now golden aspen leaves—what few there still were of them—would clatter brightly as they shimmied in the wind. The sun felt warm and comforting on her face. Sarah reveled in the familiar sensations. There wouldn't be many more days left in the high country's Indian summer. Today was the first of November. Winter wouldn't be long in coming.

A winter, this year, spent in a warm, snug house. A house that wouldn't let in every frigid wind that blew down from the mountains. A house that had fireplaces and woodstoves that kept you all nice and toasty for hours on end without constant work to stoke them. A house that had a hand pump in the kitchen where a person could get all the water she needed without having to brave the cold to fetch some from a frozen lake or stream. And a house whose larders were full, with no worry of going hungry no matter how long and hard the storms raged and the snow piled up outside.

Sarah was grateful for all of that, but even more so for Danny's sake. As much as she hated to admit it, those were the same concerns her father should've held first and foremost in his heart. Tending to his wife and children's needs over those of his personal vendetta against the Wainwrights.

Somehow, though, along the way and over the years, what might have first been a need to get back the ranch for the sake of his family had transformed into something far more twisted and unbalanced. In what had eventually become an obsessive pursuit of vengeance, Jacob Caldwell had lost track of what really mattered. Lost track and, in the doing, forfeited first his wife, then his two youngest children. Yet still he persisted in seeing only what it served him to see, what served to feed his insane lust to get even.

Thinking back to their conversation in the kitchen early this morning, Sarah recalled that Nick had reminded her of his intent to join forces in putting an end to the feud. That first day they'd met, however, he'd also spoken of other, equally important matters. Like it being a choice to allow hatred into your heart. A choice *everyone* made whether they recognized it or not.

Though he was yet loath to admit it, her father had chosen to allow hatred into his heart. And, once there, that hatred had stoked the flames of his vengeance until it had consumed him. Until it had distorted everything he thought about and did. Until now he had become incapable of forgiveness, no matter what he lost in the omission, no matter that it was destroying not only him but also those close to him.

But I won't let him destroy me or Danny, Sarah vowed. *I won't! Nothing is worth losing your soul, your humanity, for. And certainly not for some ranch. People matter more than a piece of land, a few cattle, and some buildings. What matters is loving others, caring for them, and even forgiving them if need be. And asking for all of that from them too.*

Her thoughts lifted heavenward. *Loving You and asking*

Your forgiveness is most important of all, Lord. I've turned away from You for far too long in my selfishness and hardness of heart. In my anger and need to blame someone for losing Mama and for how unfairly life had treated my papa. But, in truth, in our blindness we bring so much of our problems on ourselves. Like my poor papa has.

But I won't let myself hate him for his failings. I'll go on loving him, praying for him, and doing my best to help him. I just won't allow him to drag me down with him anymore. And I won't let him hurt Danny either. Or Caleb and Noah, if that opportunity ever presents itself.

With that resolution, the sting of guilt she'd been feeling ever since she'd decided to commit her life to Cord and the Wainwrights eased. Peace filled her. Lulled by the soothing sounds of the chuckling stream, the warm sun, and gentle breezes, Sarah gradually relaxed and grew drowsy. Her lids lowered, closed.

I'll just rest here a few minutes more, she told herself, *before heading back to the house. Just a few minutes more . . .*

"Sarah! Miss Sarah!"

She jerked awake. Levering to one elbow, Sarah glanced groggily around. *Where am I?*

The sensation of hard rock beneath her and the sound of the creek pulled her back to reality. *Oh, my goodness! I fell asleep.*

Looking around, Sarah noted the sun was beginning to slip behind the mountains. The air had also taken on a definite chill. *How long have I been sleeping?*

"Miss Sarah!" Pedro's voice came from the top of a nearby hill. "Come quick. The men are back and Mr. Wainwright's hurt. Hurt bad."

Mr. Wainwright? Sarah shoved to a sitting position then hurriedly climbed to her feet. *Mr. Wainwright's hurt bad? But which one?*

"Who's hurt, Pedro?" she called out to him, her heart pounding now in her chest. "Which Mr. Wainwright? Cord or Edmund?"

There was no answer. No voice to be heard save hers, echoing hollowly off the surrounding rocks and hills. Pedro was gone, already disappearing down the other side of the hill.

11

A crowd of men gathered at the front steps of the ranch house. As Sarah ran toward them, her gaze scanned their faces, desperately seeking out Cord's. He was nowhere to be found.

She did see, however, as she drew closer, several of the men leaned over a makeshift stretcher. Just then Nicholas wheeled his chair out onto the porch, followed by Emma and then Cord. Sarah's heart gave a great leap.

"Thank you, Lord," she whispered, skirting the outside of the group of men. Looking past them, she noted at long last that it was Edmund Wainwright lying on the stretcher.

His eyes were closed, and he appeared to be unconscious. A horrible bruise marred the left side of his face. Blood matted his graying hair and, from beneath the blanket covering him, she could make out a splinted right leg. Sarah hurried around them to join Emma, Nick, and Cord on the porch.

Cord didn't look a whole lot better, with a gashed cheek, bruised jaw, and dried blood on his shirt, but at least he was upright and conscious, and there appeared to be no broken bones. His somber gaze met hers.

"What happened?"

Something hard and enigmatic passed through his eyes. "To us or to your father and brothers?"

His query was like a slap to the face. *Easy*, Sarah cautioned herself. *It's obvious he's been through something terrible, and*

*he's worried sick about his father. He really doesn't mean it
the way it came out.*

"What happened to you and your father, Cord?" she forced
herself to reply, keeping her tone calm and even. "Is Edmund
going to be all right?"

He inhaled a shuddering breath. "I don't know. Doc's on
his way. Suffice it to say, my father met the wrong end of a
cattle stampede."

Cord turned his attention back to the hands at the bottom
of the steps. "The bed's ready. Pick him up as carefully as
you can and carry him into the parlor."

The men grasped the stretcher poles at four ends, gingerly
picked up their human burden, and slowly began to climb
the steps.

"Keep him as level as you can," Cord ordered. He took
Sarah by the arm and pulled her out of the way.

They watched as the litter bearers passed and entered
through the door Emma held open for them.

"What can I do to help?" Sarah glanced up at Cord.

He sighed. "I don't know. See if Emma needs assistance."

She nodded. Following Cord and Nick as they trailed into
the house behind the hands, she halted when she reached
Emma, who was still at the door.

"What can I do?" Sarah's eyes burned with unshed tears.
"Do you need any bandages or a pot of water put on to boil?"

"That's easily taken care of in a bit," the older woman
said. "In the meantime, I'm sure all these men are famished.
Why don't you get a tablecloth onto the dining room table,
then put out a stack of plates and silverware? Manuela's already in the kitchen getting the fried chicken, potato salad,
and bread ready. Once the table's set, you can check with her
and see what other help she needs."

Though she'd have far preferred to remain with Cord and

lend a comforting presence, Sarah did as she was asked. Maybe it was for the best anyway, she decided as she retrieved one of the more sturdy tablecloths from the linen closet and returned to the dining room. Cord appeared to be teetering on the edge of his control. And, from his earlier query, Sarah couldn't help but assume her family had indeed been involved in the cattle rustling. Time enough to return to his side once the other men were fed and Doc got here and had a chance to examine Edmund.

The next half hour sped by as Sarah and the other women served the men a meal. Cord and Nick refused anything to eat, preferring to remain at their father's side. Just about the time the ranch hands finished eating and began to depart, Doc Saunders arrived. Empty serving bowl in hand, Sarah hesitated halfway between the kitchen and the parlor, where Edmund laid, his two sons in attendance.

"Here, child," Emma said, bustling over to take the bowl from her hands. "Doc will want to examine Edmund in private, so why don't you get Cord and Nick to come into the dining room and at least have some coffee. And whatever else you can get into Cord as well," she added.

Grateful for an excuse to see how all the Wainwright men were faring, Sarah nodded. "Thank you, Emma."

The housekeeper paused. "No, thank *you*. Thank you for being here for Cord and Nick. And thank you for not once mentioning your own family, though I know you must be sick with worry over them too."

Sarah managed a wan smile. "It's so hard, Emma. I feel like I'm being torn in two."

"I know, child. Just remember. None of this is your fault."

"It may not be," Sarah said with a sigh, "but I still feel guilty. I just don't want to lose Cord's love over this . . ."

"Now, don't go talking such nonsense. Cord's not mad at you. He's just worried sick about his father."

"He does love him, doesn't he? In spite of all that's passed between them."

Emma nodded. "Yes, he does. And that gives me hope someday those two hard heads will finally mend fences and start being true father and son." She made a shooing motion with her free hand. "Now, get on with you. See to those two young men."

Sarah turned and headed toward the parlor. She met Nick wheeling himself from the room, Cord following in his wake.

"Good." She glanced from one sober-faced Wainwright son to the other. "While Doc's examining Edmund, there's just enough time for you two to grab a cup of coffee and maybe even something to eat."

"I'm not hungry," Cord growled, not meeting her gaze.

"Maybe not, but you're no good to your father if you don't keep up your strength." She cocked her head. "And I'm betting you haven't eaten since all this happened, have you? Which was exactly how many hours ago?"

He shot her a disgruntled look. "The cattle stampeded down the ravine they were hidden in about five this morning."

"So, if the last time you ate was supper yesterday, it's been over twenty-four hours since your last meal. Sounds like yet another reason to get something into your stomach."

"She's right," Nick said, glancing up at him. "I know I could stand a little something to eat."

"Well, maybe a cup of coffee then." Cord grabbed the handlebars of Nick's wheelchair and pushed him into the dining room.

By the time Doc joined them a half hour later, Sarah had managed not only to get two mugs of coffee with cream and sugar into Cord, but also two pieces of fried chicken and one of Emma's famous apple spice oatmeal cookies. At Doc's entrance, both men immediately put down their coffee mugs, and Cord jumped to his feet.

190

The doctor looked to Sarah. "Would you pour me a mug of coffee, my dear? And I like just a splash of cream and no sugar."

As Sarah hurried to comply, Doc Saunders turned to Nick and Cord. "I looked Edmund over. Besides the danger of possible internal injuries, I'm most worried about his head. Cord, can you tell me exactly what happened to him?"

Cord shoved his hand raggedly through his hair. "We suspected the cattle were hidden in that ravine. What we didn't figure on was the Caldwells being holed up behind the herd. When they got wind we were coming, they started firing their pistols and spooked the cattle. Before we knew what was happening, fifty head of cattle were stampeding toward us. At the front of the posse, Gabe, Pa, and I were trapped between the other men and the cattle.

"Gabe and I managed to get our horses turned around in time, but Pa didn't. The first few cattle slammed into him, knocking over Pa and his horse. In the confusion, I don't know what happened to Gabe, but I was pressed against the ravine wall by the cattle racing by. Neither of us could get to Pa until nearly all the herd passed. By then, Pa was wedged beneath his dead horse—which probably saved his life—and he was already unconscious."

Doc Saunders stroked his chin. "Did Edmund wake up at any time after that?"

Cord shook his head. "No. But maybe, considering the extent of his injuries, that was a blessing."

The doctor exhaled a long, slow breath. "Maybe. But maybe not. If Edmund was injured about five this morning, that means he's been unconscious well over twelve hours now. I don't like that. Don't like that at all."

"Is there anything we can do to help, Doc?" Sarah asked, walking up to hand him his coffee.

He smiled, accepted his mug from her, and took a swallow before replying. "Just keep doing what you're doing, child. Keep us sustained with strong coffee and food. We might have a very long night ahead of us."

She glanced at Cord. Besides his torn, dirty clothes and his own injuries, he looked positively worn out and haggard.

"Nick and I could sit with Edmund while you see to Cord. That gash on his forehead looks like it might need some stitching."

Cord scowled. "I don't need any 'seeing to' or stitching. I'm fine."

"Oh, really? Just like you also don't need to go get some sleep, I'd imagine?"

Doc Saunders laughed. "Feisty little thing, isn't she? At least let me patch you up a bit, Cord. That'll take no time at all and, like Sarah said, in the meanwhile she and Nick can keep vigil at Edmund's beside."

"Fine," Cord muttered, sending her a black look. "Best we probably do the doctoring in the kitchen then. After that, though, I'm right back at Pa's side."

"You'll get no argument from me, son," Doc said, gesturing for Cord to head for the kitchen. "I'll need all the company I can get to stay awake tonight."

As Cord turned and walked toward the kitchen, Doc moseyed over to the dining room table and grabbed up a handful of cookies. "Would you fetch my doctor's bag, child?" he then asked before following in Cord's wake.

Sarah hurried to the parlor to retrieve the bag, which she found sitting on the sofa. As she turned, however, Nick blocked her way from the room.

"Leave Cord be for a while, Angel," he said, meeting her inquiring gaze. "Let him work out his jumbled feelings for our father. Those two always did have sort of a love-hate

192

relationship, as much as both of them denied the love part. But I knew differently. I saw what they both refused to see."

She glanced to where Edmund Wainwright lay silent and still on his bed. "Maybe so, Nick. But what will happen to Cord . . . if his father never regains consciousness? If he . . ."

"If he dies before they can finally sort it all out?" Nick softly finished for her. He sighed. "I don't know. I just don't know. One way or another, though, it's in God's hands. All we can do is pray."

All we can do is pray . . .

Yes, I suppose you're right, Sarah thought. *Pray for Edmund. Pray for Cord. And pray for Papa and my brothers. For I greatly fear if Edmund dies, we've only begun to see how bad this feud can be.*

As the night deepened and he, Nick, and Sarah kept their bedside vigil, Cord had plenty of opportunity to relive the last twenty-four hours. This time last night, he was dancing and feuding with Sarah, only to finally stand in the cool evening air and declare his love for her. Yet, now those events seemed like they'd happened years ago.

His glance strayed from his father, lying as still as death on his bed, to where Sarah sat near the parlor window, her head angled toward the flickering lamplight on the nearby table, working on what appeared to be some particularly intricate stitch in her knitting. At the sight of her, a sense of peace and comfort washed over him. She was here in this difficult time, quiet and supportive, thinking only of him when he knew questions must surely burn her lips about what had happened to her father and two brothers. He'd tell her in time. Right now, though, Cord didn't know what he'd do or say if mention was made of those thieving Caldwell men.

No, right now he didn't have the strength or courage to speak of them, but he also wasn't of a mind to keep her hanging for long. Those varmints she called family didn't deserve her or her concern, but Cord knew she still loved and cared about them. And, because he loved her, he didn't wish to add to her suffering.

Somehow, though, he feared there was suffering aplenty still waiting for the both of them, and all because of this cursed feud that refused to play itself out. Even if his father died, Cord wondered if that would be enough to finally satisfy Jacob Caldwell. Indeed, would anything satisfy that man ever again, even in the unlikely event he were to regain control of all Wainwright holdings?

Not that *that* would ever happen as long as *he* lived, Cord silently vowed. After all that had transpired since yesterday evening, something had changed for him. He had Sarah now. He had a responsibility as well to her little brother and to his own brother too. He also had a responsibility to the ranch, to help make it all it could be. And letting Jacob Caldwell get his hands on Castle Mountain Ranch wasn't in any plans he now had for it.

They'd talked a bit last night, he and his father, in the few opportunities they'd had to walk the horses when the terrain got rough. Talked—for what seemed the first time—in a calm, respectful manner like two grown men, rather than as a critical, domineering father to his irresponsible, dim-witted son.

"That Caldwell girl," his father had brought up seemingly out of the blue. "She always loved you, not Nicholas, didn't she? And Nicholas, in his generous if misguided attempts at matchmaking, made you think it was he who wanted Sarah, so you stepped aside for him."

"Did you come up with that all by yourself," Cord asked,

wondering where this conversation was headed, "or did someone tell you?"

Edmund shrugged. "A bit of both. That night at the fall dance, I finally figured out something funny was going on, and Emma just confirmed it for me."

"So then I guess I was the last one to know," Cord replied with a self-deprecating grin. "Kind of confirms your opinion of me as pretty slow and thickheaded, doesn't it?"

His father chuckled. "No more so than most men, when it comes to women. Your mother had to all but wallop me upside the head to get me to admit to loving her."

"Like father, like son, I suppose."

"That girl—Sarah—she's got spunk. Reminds me a lot of your mother." His father sighed. "Too bad she's a Caldwell."

Anger flared and Cord struggled to contain it. "She's the best of them, and you know it."

"Yeah, I reckon she is."

They cleared the top of the ridge then, and there was no time left to talk. Still, though the pace picked up until the posse was galloping along once again, there was plenty to think about. Indeed, Cord couldn't have kept the thoughts out of his mind if he'd tried.

He turned the memory of the earlier conversation over and over in his head, marveling at what had been said . . . and not said. Why his father had decided at this particular moment, after all the years of terse conversations and barely contained hostility, to attempt a civil discussion of any sort with him, Cord didn't know. He sensed his father was expressing approval of Sarah in his own taciturn way. If he tried hard enough, Cord realized he could even read in a grudging acceptance of their engagement.

But such considerations were almost beyond comprehension. His father hated the Caldwells. He had also, all these years, begrudged Cord his birth at the sacrifice of his beloved wife. How could a man like that seemingly change almost overnight?

Maybe it's all just some fluke, Cord thought, returning to the present moment and the sickroom he now sat in. *Give Pa enough time and he'll revert back to his old ways.*

Problem was, if his father died, Cord would never find out. And that, perhaps, was the hardest knot to unravel, the source of the unrelenting uncertainty gnawing at his gut in these long hours of keeping vigil at his father's bedside.

"You don't know whether or not to forgive him, do you?"

Surprise ricocheted through him. Cord jerked around to face his brother. How could Nick so easily have guessed what his thoughts had been leading up to? He hadn't shared with his brother—or anyone else for that matter—what had passed between him and their sire last night.

"What in the Sam Hill are you talking about?" Irritation threaded his voice as he watched his brother wheel his chair across the room to pull up before him.

Nervously, Cord's glance careened off Sarah who, at Nick's words, had lifted her equally startled gaze. At that particular instant, he heartily wished she weren't in the room. *Once Nick senses any weakness in me*, Cord thought, *he's like some broncobuster who sticks like a tick to a horse's back. He hangs on until he breaks you, until you finally give up and spill your guts to him just to shut him up.*

"You know as well as the rest of us that Pa might not make it," Nick softly said, leaning close. "For your own sake, it's time you forgave him. Remember, to err is human but to forgive is divine."

"And you have me confused with someone else." Cord gave a bitter laugh. "Holy isn't anything I do very well."

"Don't do well or don't know how or want to do it?"

He stared down at Nick. *Is that the truth of it then? Do I just don't know how to forgive? Or is there something lacking in me that would make me want to do so? And, even more to the point, would forgiving Pa for all the years of verbal abuse and downright neglect make any difference?*

He sighed and looked down at hands he noticed were clenched before him. "I'm not sure forgiving him would be enough . . . enough to make up for all those years . . ."

"Forgiveness isn't so much about Pa as it is about you, Cord. It's not about feelings but about freedom. It's not about changing the other person—we might not ever succeed in doing that—but in letting go . . . and trusting that God will somehow make it all right."

"I don't have anything to let go," Cord snarled. "And *I'm* not the one who should be asking for forgiveness."

"You're right," Nick said. "You don't have anything to ask forgiveness for. But you're also the only one who *can* do the forgiving. You're the one who can do what it takes to find release from the burden of your anger and bitterness. Before Pa's gone and it's too late." He managed a rueful smile. "Well, before it's too late, anyway, to tell him face-to-face. When there's still a chance he might hear you."

Cord looked up, impaling his brother with a steely gaze. "Yeah, I suppose you're right. But where's the fairness in that? What did I ever do to him to deserve how he treated me?"

"Would you rather be in the right, or be free, little brother? Would you rather risk carrying this the rest of your life and have it taint all your future relationships?" As he asked that final question, Nick angled his head in Sarah's direction. "Wiping the slate clean is a loving thing to do, on so many levels."

As he listened, Cord could feel his defenses crumbling. *Blast Nick anyway,* he thought in a confused mix of frustration and begrudging affection. *Not only does he always have a special way with words, but he can pierce straight through to my heart and see me more clearly than I see myself.*

"You're right as always. It'd be nice to wipe that particular slate clean once and for all," Cord grudgingly admitted. He sighed once again. "I . . . I reckon I'll have to think on that a bit more."

"Yes, you do that." Nick glanced over his shoulder. "Angel, it's almost midnight and I'm starved. Why don't we go see what we can rustle up in the kitchen?" He looked back at Cord. "Want us to bring you something?"

Cord shook his head. "No, I'm fine. I'll just stay here with Pa."

"Take all the time you need." Nick smiled up at Sarah, who had put aside her knitting and joined him. "Let's be on our way then."

No sooner had the two of them departed than Doc Saunders walked in. After a time spent examining Edmund, he sighed, shook his head, and left the room.

No change, Cord thought. *It's not looking good. Not good at all.*

He stood, pulled his chair close to his father's bedside, and sat back down. Doc had forgotten, after his examination, to put his patient's hand back beneath the covers. Cord stared at it for a long time, then, reaching over, took it in his.

His father's hand was cool, the long, strong fingers limp and unmoving. The contrast with his own two warm ones was startling, unnerving even. The man whom he had idolized, as much as he had come to hate, was now weak and helpless, maybe never to be the same even if he somehow did manage to survive. The realization, in Cord's mind, seemed to herald the inevitable change in roles, where the parent became the child, and the child, in many ways, now became the parent and caretaker.

Many were the times Cord had almost wished his father dead—or at least permanently gone from his life—but now, at this moment of nearing the actual possibility, such an event frightened him, filling him with a deep, abiding sorrow. If his father died now, just when hope suddenly loomed on the horizon for a reconciliation, a long-yearned-for meeting of the hearts and minds . . .

Tears blurred his vision. All he had ever wanted was to have his father's love. To be able to feel safe with him, to trust him, to share his doubts and fears and learn from his wisdom. It had always been Cord's secret dream, a dream he'd kept tightly locked away all these years, even as he'd despaired of ever seeing that dream find fruition.

He bowed his head, and the tears trickled down his cheeks. "It's not fair," he gritted through clenched teeth. "Why now, when it almost looked like you might be opening up to me? When you finally seemed to think I'd done something right in wanting to marry Sarah? Why, Pa? Why?"

Forgiveness isn't . . . about feelings but about freedom. As if Nick were in the room right now, his words came back to Cord. *It's not about changing the other person—we might not ever succeed in doing that—but in letting go . . . and trusting that God will somehow make it all right.*

At a time like this, when hope of his father surviving was dwindling by the second, there didn't seem much else to do but let go and trust in God to make it all right. He shook his head. Trust in a God he hadn't given much thought or reverence to for a long while now. Yet, at a time like this, what other option was left for him?

Ever so gently, Cord squeezed his father's hand. "I forgive you, Pa," he said, his voice hoarse with emotion. "I forgive you. And, for whatever I may have done to alienate you, I also ask your forgiveness."

12

"Help me with this boat, will you, son?"

Through the gathering twilight, Cord saw his father standing at the river's edge, shoving at the bow of a small boat that refused to budge. He ambled down to meet him.

"Where are you going, Pa?" Cord gestured to the fading streaks of lavender brushing the sky. "It's getting late. We should be heading back to the house."

"Not me." The older man shook his head. "I've got to get across that river, and I need your help."

Puzzled, Cord eyed him. "But why, Pa? What's across the river?"

His father's smile was enigmatic. "All I've ever needed is across that river." He bent down and began pushing on the boat. "Now, help me with this one last task."

"Well, if that's what you want," Cord replied, moving to the other side of the bow and leaning over to give it a good shove. "All that you need is back home, though."

With their combined strength, the little boat eased down the muddy slope and into the water. Edmund Wainwright nodded in satisfaction.

"Good. Now, hold her steady while I climb in, will you, son?"

Cord gripped the bow, the rough wood biting into his

hands. His father scrambled in, took a seat, and grabbed hold of the two oars.

"Okay, give me a good shove out into the water."

Reluctantly, he did as his father asked. The oars sliced through the gently flowing waters, and gradually Edmund Wainwright pulled farther and farther from shore.

A cool breeze wafted over Cord. Some bird cried out in the darkness. He shivered, wrapping his arms about himself. *Why doesn't this feel right?*

"When will you be home, Pa?" he called. "Emma will want to know if she should keep a plate warm for you."

"Good-bye, son," his father's voice floated back to him, growing ever fainter. "Take care of everyone for me. I know you can do it. I've *always* known that . . ."

An eerie presentiment filled Cord. Fear gripped his heart. He stepped into the water, walking out until the river swirled almost to his knees.

"Pa!" he cried. "Pa, don't go!"

"Good-bye. I love you . . ."

"Cord? Cord?"

The sound of a voice, sharp with concern, accompanied by a firm hand on his shoulder, wrenched Cord from his dreams. He jerked awake.

Sarah, her eyes tear-bright, gazed down at him. "Cord, wake up. Your father . . . He's gone."

He straightened abruptly in the chair. He'd fallen asleep. The first rays of dawn peeked through the parlor window, washing the pine plank floor in faint sunlight. Cord's searching glance met his brother's. Nick, his expression solemn, slowly nodded.

Cord swiveled in his chair, turning to the bed where his

201

father laid. Even then Doc Saunders was lifting the sheet to cover Edmund Wainwright's face.

Shoving back his chair, Cord stood and moved to his father's side. The doctor stepped back.

"Wh-when?" Cord choked out.

"Just a few minutes ago. Sarah noticed he didn't look like he was breathing, and came and got me." Doc laid a hand on his shoulder. "It was for the best, son. His brain was terribly injured. I could see the signs getting worse each time I checked on him."

Numbly, Cord lifted his gaze to the older man. "I figured as much. I'm just glad we got him back home. He loved this ranch. He would've wanted to die here."

Behind him, he could hear Nick wheeling his chair over. Then a hand gripped his arm.

"Jordan should be told. Do you want me to send Sarah to waken her?"

Their stepsister, wife of Robert Travers, and mother of a three-week-old daughter, had arrived only a few hours ago after having ridden all night from their ranch about twenty miles to the southwest of Ashton. She'd been exhausted. After seeing to her infant's needs and spending some time at her stepfather's bedside, Jordan had been all but dragged off to bed by her husband for a few hours' sleep. Not long after her departure, Cord realized, he'd fallen asleep himself.

"No," he said, turning to look at his brother, "I'll go get Jordan. Best she hear the news from me."

"Suit yourself." Nick searched his brother's face. "Are you okay?"

Are you okay?

His father had just died, and the lingering aftereffects of his dream still haunted him. Had the dream been the result of the stress he'd been through of late, or was it something more? Had it, instead, been the medium God had used to allow his dying father's soul to bid farewell? To speak the words he'd never been able to say in life, even if he'd always believed them?

At that moment Cord was glad, thankful deep down to the marrow of his bones, that he'd finally found the courage to offer forgiveness to his father. He was glad for that dream and would cherish it to his dying day, no matter what its source had been. It wasn't the best of deathbed reconciliations, but it was all he'd get. And it was enough.

"Yeah," he said, shooting Nick a wan smile, "I'm okay. More than okay, to tell the truth."

"Good," his brother replied. "Then my prayers have been answered."

Shiloh Wainwright, Cord and Nicholas's other stepsister, arrived from Denver two days later. Sarah took to her right away, just as she had with her older sibling, Jordan. And, when she discovered Shiloh was a teacher at a girl's boarding school in Denver, her interest only deepened.

"I've always thought I'd have liked to be a teacher," she admitted the next morning as they worked together with the other women in the ranch house kitchen. They were set to depart in fifteen minutes for Ashton for Edmund's funeral services at the town's one church and subsequent burial back at the ranch. There were still a few things, however, to finish up for the wake to be held afterward.

Shiloh tossed her dark auburn braid over her shoulder, and nodded. "I had a fight on my hands convincing Papa to let me leave home and go all the way to Nebraska to the Peru State Normal School to get my teacher training. He was rather old-fashioned, you know, and thought a woman's place should be close to home until she got married. Then, if her husband wanted to take her halfway across the world, well, that was how it *should* be."

She paused, her eyes misting. "I barely knew my real father. He died when I was four, and Mama married Edmund just a year later. So, for most of my growing up, Edmund was my papa. He could be crotchety at times, but Jordan and I, well, mostly we could get him to let us do just about anything."

Shiloh shot her sister, working at the other end of the table peeling potatoes, an inquiring glance. "Couldn't we, Jordan?"

Her sister, almost four years senior to the twenty-year-old Shiloh, nodded, then paused to pull a hanky from her pocket and wipe her tear-filled eyes. "Yes, Papa always had a soft spot in his heart for his girls, didn't he?"

Listening to the two sisters, Sarah felt as if they must be talking about some other man entirely. Doting, protective, old-fashioned father? As far as his sons were concerned—or, more specifically, Cord—Edmund had been hard-hearted, critical, and demeaning. It was all Sarah could do to bite her tongue and refrain from setting the sisters straight about a thing or two.

This, however, was neither the time nor place. And why belittle their memories?

Maybe Edmund had indeed possessed other dimensions. He'd warmed up to Danny quickly enough, Caldwell though he was. And, after that night he'd had her sign the document agreeing to leave the ranch to Cord in the event of Nick's death, the Wainwright patriarch had also seemed to soften a bit in his attitude toward her.

What she couldn't forgive him for was how he'd treated Cord. Sarah's mouth quirked sadly. Yet who was she to judge Edmund Wainwright, when her own kin—especially her father—had been largely responsible for the Wainwright patriarch's death, not to mention a robbery and the theft of fifty cattle now?

Sarah exhaled a deep breath.

"It's hard for you too, isn't it?" Shiloh asked, looking up from the cookie dough she was forming into balls then handing to Sarah to place on a cookie sheet. "Papa was going to be your father-in-law."

"Yes, he was." Sarah used the excuse of rearranging the cookies on the now full sheet to avoid meeting the other woman's searching gaze. "Most of all, though, I worry about Cord and the effect all this is having on him. And Nick too, of course."

Shiloh and Jordan exchanged yet another look. *They know about Cord and Edmund's problems*, Sarah thought. *And why wouldn't they? They'd lived in the midst of it all for years.*

At that moment, Cord, dressed in the black suit he'd worn to the fall dance, stuck his head in the room. "Nick's already in the carriage. Are you ladies about ready to load up and head to town for the funeral services?"

Emma immediately covered the loaves of bread with a cloth and removed her apron. "Yes, we're ready. Manuela will be here to tend what's still cooking. And it'll take us no time to get the rest of the food ready for the wake once we return."

Jordan put the last peeled potato into the pot of water and carried it to the cookstove. Sarah followed with the cookies, opened the oven door, and shoved them inside.

She purposely lingered, however, as the other women filed through the kitchen door Cord held open for them. And, as she finally approached him, he moved to block her way, letting the door swing closed behind him.

Sarah halted. "Yes? Did you have something to tell me?"

He eyed her for a long moment, and in that gaze she saw pain, uncertainty, and longing. Her heart went out to him. On impulse, she moved close and hugged him.

For an instant, Cord just stood there. Then, with a shuddering sigh, he wrapped his arms around her and laid his head atop hers.

"Oh, if only you knew how many times in these past days I've wanted to hold you like this!"

Sarah snuggled all the closer. "No more, I'd imagine, than I've wanted to hold you."

"I'm sorry if I seemed to have kept you at a distance," he whispered into her hair. "I've just been so confused . . . so conflicted."

Leaning back, she put a finger to his lips. "Hush, my love. There's a time for everything, and there'll soon be a time again for us. Right now, though, it's time to pray over and bury your father."

Cord stared down at her, his eyes filling with tears. Then he took her hand in his and nodded.

"Thank you for understanding. And thank you, most of all, for standing by me. I love you."

"And I love you."

He squeezed her hand then turned, tugging her along with him. "Come on. Let's go. The others are waiting on us."

Heart so full she thought it couldn't hold any more, she wordlessly followed him from the kitchen.

"Now, you be sure and write," Shiloh said on a chilly November morning three days later as the stagecoach pulled up before the Ashton stage depot. She grabbed Sarah by both arms. "And if you need anything from Denver when you begin your wedding preparations, let me know and I'll send it to you. Or, I can bring it with me when I return for Christmas."

"I will," Sarah replied. "Not that Cord and I have made any definite plans or set a date yet."

Shiloh laughed. "Maybe not, but the way I see my brother looking at you sometimes, I'm thinking a wedding isn't all that far off. Is it, big brother?"

Cord chuckled. "Maybe not. But I'm also not going to let you railroad me or Sarah into picking a date until the both of us are good and ready."

His sister's eyes widened in mock surprise. "Now, why would you think I'd do a thing like that?"

"Because I know you pretty well?" He grinned, then turned to gaze up at the big stagecoach just a few feet from them. "Need any help climbing up into the coach?"

"Trying to get rid of me, are you?" Shiloh asked. "Before I convince you to change your mind and carry Sarah off to the preacher this very day?"

He rolled his eyes. "Hardly."

Shiloh wheeled around and gave Sarah a quick hug. "I'm so glad you're going to be my sister-in-law," she whispered loudly enough for Cord to hear. "And Cord's so blessed to have you, though, with him being a man and all, I'm not certain he'll ever realize how much."

Releasing Sarah, she turned back to her brother. "Well, I guess you *can* lend me a hand in getting into this wooden contraption. Now that I'm a grown woman and professional teacher, I mean."

"Yeah, I've noticed how all that's made such a difference in your dignity and comportment," he said with a smirk as he held out his hand.

"As if *you'd* know," Shiloh said with a disparaging snort, accepting his assistance. "You ran off to New York well before *I* grew up. All you remember is me in pigtails and overalls, trailing around behind you everywhere you went."

"Well, you're not in pigtails and overalls anymore."

"No, I'm most certainly not." His sister paused, her foot

207

on the coach's first step, and gave him a quick kiss on the cheek. "But you'll always be my big brother."

Cord grinned. "That I will. And I wouldn't have it any other way."

With that, Shiloh climbed into the stagecoach and took her seat. Her traveling bag was quickly loaded. In but a few minutes, the driver snapped the reins over the backs of his team of horses, and the coach pulled away from the depot.

Sarah and Cord watched the stagecoach drive off down Main Street, heading east over and through the mountains to Denver. When the vehicle was no longer in sight, Cord turned to her.

"I thought, since we're in town, that we might have lunch at the Wildflower Café before we head back to the ranch. Unless you have other plans?"

She smiled. "No other plans, except to spend this time with you. And lunch would be wonderful."

"Good." He paused. "You know, Shiloh's coming home again for Christmas break and will be staying until after the New Year. Maybe we should get married after Christmas. It's only a short day's ride for Jordan and her family to join us. We can have a small wedding with all the family in attendance." Cord eyed her expectantly. "What do you think?"

Sarah was tempted to mention the fact that *all* of the family actually wouldn't be there for the wedding but decided it was pointless to do so. It wasn't Cord's fault, after all, that her family had refused to meet him even halfway. Indeed, with each passing day, the Wainwrights—all of them—were fast becoming the only real family she and Danny had.

She managed what she fervently hoped was an appropriately happy smile. "The end of December suits me just fine. Should be more than enough time to make all the preparations."

He took her by the arm. "Then we have even more of a

208

reason to have a nice lunch to celebrate our wedding date, wouldn't you say?"

"Yes, indeed," Sarah agreed, nodding.

"On the way, I need to stop by the sheriff's office," Cord said as they started down the boardwalk.

There was only one reason Cord would want to pay Gabe a visit. Sarah halted and turned to him. "Need an update on what's being done to apprehend my father and brothers, do you?"

Her expression told it all. With just a few ill-chosen words, he'd effectively destroyed the formerly happy mood. Cord almost regretted bringing up the subject. Almost.

"I'm not going to keep the truth from you, Sarah," he said. "I thought about it a lot, and we've got to be honest with each other. Your family must be stopped, once and for all, or the trouble will only continue. You know that as well as I."

"Yes, I know that," she replied, looking down. For a long moment, she didn't say anything else. Then, squaring her shoulders, Sarah lifted her glance to his.

"I don't like it, but I know there's no other way. Papa . . . well, he's not all that reasonable anymore. I just keep hoping that once he's had some time to consider things, he'll finally get better."

The man's a raving lunatic, Cord thought, *and so obsessed with revenge he can no longer think straight!* But he also realized how hard it must have been for Sarah to admit what she had. And as much as he could, he wanted to spare her any more pain.

"Well, maybe so." Once again, he offered her his arm, and she looped hers through his. "Let's just get this visit with Gabe over and done with, so we can enjoy the rest of the day."

They strolled down the boardwalk fronting the businesses, Cord dreading the coming visit with Gabe Cooper as much as he imagined Sarah was. What they had, in the first flush of their newfound love, was still so fragile. He didn't want to do anything to threaten it.

Anger at her father welled anew. The man seemed to destroy whatever he got his hands on. Cord feared what his ongoing vendetta against the Wainwrights might ultimately do to his and Sarah's relationship. More than anything he'd ever wanted, he wanted that embittered, vengeful, selfish old man out of their lives. But he also wanted him gone with little or no hurt to Sarah. Realistically, though, that wasn't likely to happen, so the best he could do was try to minimize her pain as much as possible.

The wind kicked up as they walked along, gusting down from the mountains that enclosed the valley. Clouds bunched and collided overhead, growing ever darker. A storm was coming and likely, from the bite in the air, one that would finally bring snow. He only hoped Shiloh would be well on her way to lower elevations before the full brunt of bad weather struck.

"Do you want to be there when I talk with Gabe?" Cord asked as they drew near the sheriff's office. "It's up to you."

She shook her head. "No. You can tell me all about it later."

"Well, it's too cold for you to wait for me outside." An odd relief filled him. "I could be a while."

"The Wildflower Café is just down the street. You can meet me there when you get done." She disentangled her arm from his. "See you soon."

Cord watched her head down the boardwalk and finally cross the street directly opposite the little café. Only when she was safely inside did he turn and enter the sheriff's office. When the blast of cold air heralded Cord's arrival, the lawman and his young deputy looked up from their desks.

210

"I was wondering when you'd be stopping by," Gabe drawled.

"Had a few things to finish up since the funeral." Cord pulled over a chair and sat. "Jordan left for home yesterday, and Sarah and I just saw Shiloh off for Denver on the stage."

Gabe leaned back. "And where's Sarah now?"

"She's waiting for me at the café." Cord smiled grimly. "I reckon she didn't want to hear all the sordid details of our conversation."

"This is sure to be hard on her. Going after her father and brothers, I mean."

"Are you suggesting I just forget and forgive?" Cord found he could barely contain the edge of anger in his voice.

"No." The sheriff adamantly shook his head. "Of course not. A crime's been committed. Even if you didn't want to press charges, I'd still have to bring them in."

Cord glanced toward the open door of the room that held several empty jail cells. "Well, I'm not seeing any of them behind bars yet, so I assume you're still looking."

Gabe sighed. "Those Caldwells know these mountains like the back of their hands. Sooner or later, though, they'll slip up. Then we'll be there to catch them."

"Let's just hope the Wainwrights don't lose many more cattle before that happens. *Or* any more lives."

The blond lawman looked down, hesitated, then met Cord's gaze. "Have you ever asked Sarah where she thinks her family might be holed up? Any leads right about now would surely help."

"No, I haven't and I won't." Once more, Cord's emotions roiled with a mix of frustration and fury. "I'm afraid it might drive a wedge between us that could never be breached. Besides, she's hurting enough as it is."

"That's your choice, I reckon." Gabe shrugged. "But you're also smart enough to realize that decision puts the ranch and all its inhabitants in danger. Leastwise until the Caldwell men are all behind bars. And I'm hoping Sarah realizes that too."

"Maybe she does, and maybe she doesn't." Cord riveted a steely gaze on his friend. "Either way, I don't want you or anyone else bringing that up. Do you understand me?"

Gabe studied him for a long moment, then nodded. "Yeah, I reckon I do."

"And what would you like on such a cold, nasty day?" Ruth Ann Lewis, proprietor, cook, and occasional waitress asked, pencil and pad in hand.

From her seat at a table close to the potbellied stove in the middle of the dining room, Sarah smiled up at her. "I'm waiting on Cord until we order lunch, so a pot of hot tea will do for now."

"With cream and sugar on the side?"

"Yes, that'd be lovely."

As Ruth Ann hurried away, Sarah leisurely surveyed her surroundings. She had passed by this café many times in the years since it had been opened but never once, until today, walked inside. There'd been no reason to do so. It was all she and her family could do to afford the food she cooked at home, much less a meal prepared in such a setting.

But that had all changed now. Though Cord struggled with the ranch finances since the robbery, the Wainwrights still had the means to eat out from time to time. And someday once he had the ranch back on a solid footing, Sarah knew their lives would be quite comfortable. It was a realization that, even now, filled her with wonder and delight.

So today, she allowed herself to bask in the newfound luxury of sitting in the Wildflower Café and feeling for the first time that she belonged here as much as any of the other people in the room. It was a cozy, colorful little place, from its yellow and blue calico café curtains and valances trimmed with a yellow-gingham-checked lower border covering the windows fronting the street, to the white linen tablecloths on each round table with underskirts matching the curtains, to the simple white bud vases with dried flowers decorating the table centers. The walls were painted a soft, soothing, muted blue. The floors were dark stained pine plank. And colorful, framed paintings of springtide fields of mountain wildflowers graced the walls.

Ruth Ann walked up at that moment with a little, flower-painted china teapot and cup and saucer, with matching sugar bowl and creamer, on a tray. "Here you go, sweetie," the older woman said, her chubby cheeks flushed, her smile open and warm. "Would you like a menu to look at while you wait?" she asked as she set the teapot and the other utensils on the table before Sarah.

"Yes, that'd be nice."

A few steps to a nearby long work table against the far wall, and the Wildflower Café's proprietor was back with a small, framed slate on which she'd written the day's offerings. "I change the menu most days," she explained, "depending on what's available and however I feel inspired. That way it keeps things as interesting for me as it does for my customers."

"And also keeps things fun for everyone," Sarah said with a grin.

"So, you like to cook too, do you?"

She considered that question for an instant, then nodded. "Yes, I suppose I do. It was always a challenge trying to make something different with the limited amount and variety of food we had. Still, more often than not, I surprised all of us with how tasty and nourishing most of my meals were."

"Well, I'm always needing extra help in the kitchen, if

213

you're ever looking for a job." Ruth Ann indicated the menu in Sarah's hands. "See what you think of what I came up with today. This time of year, my choice of fresh ingredients gets a bit limited. And there's only so many things you can do with root crops."

"I'm not at all worried. I've heard nothing but praise for your café ever since it opened."

The older woman beamed. "I'm glad to hear it. I—"

The little bell over the front door tinkled, and a blast of chill air swirled in. Both women's glances turned to the newest group of people to enter.

Sarah's heart sank. Allis Findley, accompanied by two women friends, walked in and quickly shut the door behind them. For a moment Allis stood there like some queen, surveying the room and its inhabitants, before finally settling her regal glance on Sarah. Immediately, her expression turned sour. Her mouth puckered in distaste.

"Well, will wonders never cease?" she purred, her eyes glittering with malice. "Some people never know when to keep out of sight or mind, do they?"

13

As she stared back at Allis, several options raced through Sarah's mind. Ignore the woman entirely and continue her conversation with Ruth Ann. Acknowledge the unkind comment with an equally unkind one of her own. Or, last but certainly not least, excuse herself politely, get up, walk over, and punch Allis in the face.

For a fleeting, if most pleasurable instant, Sarah savored the last choice, then regretfully chose the first. Not only was it unladylike, but it was downright disrespectful to Ruth Ann to get in a tussle in her establishment. It was also, as Cord's fiancée, now beneath her to stoop to such childish behavior—no matter how badly the snobbish Allis Findley needed a lesson.

Above all, since she had turned her heart and life back to God, she was trying to live the way He would want her to live. And that, as hard as it was in this particular instance, meant turning the other cheek.

Sarah forced a smile onto her lips. "Good day to you too, Allis," she called, then looked back to Ruth Ann. "Thank you so much for the tea. And the menu," she added, holding up the slate. "Already I'm leaning toward the pork sandwich with coleslaw and fried potatoes, but I'll defer my final decision until Cord arrives."

The older woman glanced uncertainly from her to where

Allis and her two friends had taken a seat across the room. Already, the trio had their heads together whispering.

"The ham and scalloped potato casserole is also particularly tasty, in case you have second thoughts." She paused, managing a tentative smile. "Well, if you don't need anything else right now . . ."

"Believe me, Ruth Ann." Sarah returned her smile with a reassuring one of her own. "I'll be fine. Really, I will."

Ruth Ann nodded and headed off to the kitchen. Just as soon as she was out of earshot, however, the whispering at Allis's table grew loud enough for everyone in the dining room to hear.

"The nerve of her . . . after what happened to poor Edmund Wainwright!"

"Shouldn't surprise you. She's always been a brazen little tart . . ."

"Have you heard the latest rumors about her and the two Wainwright brothers?"

Lord Jesus, help me, Sarah prayed, clenching one hand beneath the tablecloth as she poured a cup of tea, then pretended with all her might to read the menu. *Give me strength. Let me bear this for Your sake, for I surely can't do it for my own.*

The bell over the door tinkled again. Cold air rushed in. Sarah didn't look up, afraid if she did and saw Allis's smirking face, she might lose the last vestiges of her control.

Allis, however, immediately jumped to her feet. "Cord! Darling!"

Sarah's head jerked up. A smile that was as much relief as welcome lifted her lips. Cord's attention, though, was upon Allis, who had rushed over and grabbed his arm.

"Oh, what perfect timing," the brunette cooed, trying to coax him over to her table. "We've just now sat down for luncheon and would *adore* it if you joined us. Wouldn't we, ladies?" she asked, looking to her two friends.

216

Like a pair of puppets on strings, Allis's friends bobbed their heads. Cord, however, refused to budge.

"There was a time when I'd have gladly accepted such a wonderful invitation," he said. "But today—and from here on out—I'm only sharing a table with the woman I'm going to marry. So, if you'll excuse me"—he gently but firmly pulled his arm free of Allis's clasp—"my fiancée is waiting for me over there."

The gazes of all three women followed the direction of his hand, indicating Sarah, and the most comical mix of slack-jawed incredulity and horror filled their eyes. Allis, as always, was the first one to recover her composure.

"But I thought . . . I heard she was engaged to Nicholas, not you."

Cord shrugged, his mouth twisting in amusement. "A slight misunderstanding that was quickly rectified. Sarah is most definitely going to be *my* wife, not my brother's." He took a step back. "Now, if you ladies will excuse me?"

Thank you, Jesus. I couldn't have done this without You.

As she watched Cord turn and walk toward her, it was all Sarah could do to keep a straight face and smile blandly up at Cord when he came to a halt before her. "You were longer than I thought you'd be," she said as he pulled out his chair and sat down. "Did Gabe have any news . . . about my family?"

Cord reached across the table, took her hand, and gave it a squeeze. "We'll talk about that later, okay?" He leaned forward, lifted her hand to his lips, and gave it a kiss. "Whatever Allis and her cronies might eavesdrop of our conversation, I don't want it to be anything they can later gossip about."

Sarah chuckled softly as Cord released her hand and sat back. "Besides the news of our engagement? Because that's going to be all over town in record time now."

He smiled. "Well, now's as good a time as any, don't you

think? I'm very proud and happy that you've agreed to be my wife, and I want everyone to know."

Gladness swelled within her. Allis and her two friends' pettiness a few minutes ago faded, overshadowed by the knowledge that all that truly mattered was sitting here before her. Cord, and his love for her. And her love for him.

"You just want all those men who danced with me at the fall dance to know," she said, her laugh throaty and low. "You just want to eliminate all the competition in one fell swoop."

Cord angled his head to one side and grinned. "Guilty as charged, madam. Guilty as charged."

He picked up the slate menu and glanced at it. "Well, all of this looks very good. Shall we order?"

"Yes, let's." Sarah turned and motioned to Ruth Ann, who had just reentered the dining room. As the woman hurried over, pencil and pad in hand, Sarah looked back to Cord. At that instant, Allis lifted her gaze and it slammed into Sarah's.

A malevolent hatred glowed in her eyes.

Two weeks later, angry and frustrated, Cord stormed into the sheriff's office. When a quick scan of the room and jail cells revealed no one there but Gabe, Cord strode to where the sheriff sat at a long worktable, cleaning his revolver.

"Twice now we set a trap for the Caldwells, and twice they not only didn't show up where we wanted them to, but they hit the herd someplace else!" He slapped the snow off his Stetson, then slammed it down on the worktable and ran a hand roughly through his hair. "If I didn't know better, I'd think someone was tipping them off."

The lawman looked up. "Funny, but I've been thinking the same thing. Who have you told about our plans?"

"The first time, just Nick, Spence, and the hands involved.

The second time, we didn't even tell the hands until it was just about time to ride out."

"So, Sarah never knew?"

Cord shook his head. "No, not unless she overheard something. And I was extra careful the second time around to make sure she wasn't nearby."

"Well, somehow the word's getting to the Caldwells." Gabe took up a cleaning rod and shoved a small piece of cloth into its slotted opening, dipped the cloth end in some cleaning solvent, then slid the apparatus up and down his gun barrel. "And I'd hate to think Sarah was involved in that."

"I don't think it was her. She hasn't been acting any differently of late, and she's never been the sort who skulks around. She's just too open and honest for that sort of thing."

Gabe nodded. "That's always been my impression of her too. Still, what wouldn't one do to protect one's family?"

"Sarah trusts me to do my best to bring in her father and brothers alive. And I trust her not to interfere."

"Still, you don't know all she's thinking and feeling about this matter. And she's always been, up until now anyway, a very loyal, devoted daughter and sister."

Though he knew Gabe was just trying to get him to consider all possibilities, Cord was nonetheless irritated. It was one thing for him to have passing doubts about Sarah. He didn't, however, appreciate having those doubts rubbed in his face.

"I'd like to think, as my future wife," he growled, "Sarah's now transferred that loyalty and devotion to me."

The sheriff looked up from his assiduous cleaning of his gun. "And so would I, Cord. Believe me. I want only the best for her, and don't wish her any ill."

"Well, then I guess we've got to keep a lookout for who else might be spilling the beans, don't we?"

"Have you considered Spencer Womack?"

"In passing. What possible motive could he have for helping the Caldwells?"

"None that I can think of." Gabe swabbed out his gun barrel one last time with a dry piece of cloth, then began scrubbing the outside of the revolver with a brush. "Of course, he could just have motives of his own."

Cord scratched his jaw. "Well, I can't say as how I know Spence all that well. My father hired him about two years ago. We've had better ranch foremen, but he does a decent enough job."

Gage shrugged. "From her reaction to him at the fall dance, I'd wager Sarah doesn't think much of him."

"Why, what was he doing?"

"I didn't hear much, but I'm guessing Spence wasn't talking real nice to her when they were dancing together. Sarah couldn't get away from him fast enough when I walked up and cut in."

"Well, I'll keep an eye on him," Cord said. "If at all possible, this wouldn't be the best time to let him go, though. But later, when things settle down . . ." He shook his head. "Still, none of his behavior toward Sarah explains why Spence might be in cahoots with the Caldwells or rustling our cattle for his own purposes."

"And he might not be. I just think we've got to keep our options open."

"Best thing to do is just find out where Jacob and his sons are holing up. Be a sight easier than posting half my hands to guard the herd every night. That's already getting old, considering the turn the weather's taken these past few weeks."

"I'm working on that angle too." Gabe took an oiled rag and used it to rub the outside of his gun. "In the past few days, I've gotten a few leads that might just pan out."

220

"Good." Cord grabbed his Stetson and shoved it back on his head. "If and when that time comes, let's pick the men we'll take on the posse very carefully, shall we?"

"Oh, don't you worry about that," the lawman said with a dry laugh. "I've already got that part all worked out."

Three days later, Sarah stood on the front porch as Cord rode up late in the morning, dismounted, and handed his horse off to one of the hands. By his grim expression and the fact he couldn't quite meet her gaze, she knew something was decidedly different about last night's posse. Something that didn't bode well for her father and brothers.

Barely had Cord reached the porch when Sarah rushed up to him. "What happened? No one got hurt, did they?"

"Sarah, I've been up all night and I'm cold and hungry." His glance was weary when he finally met hers. "Can't this wait until we get inside and I at least have one cup of coffee?"

She took a step backward. "I'm sorry. I just . . . just need to know if you caught my father and brothers. And that no one got hurt."

He sighed. "No one got seriously hurt, only a little banged up. And yes, we did catch your father and one of your brothers. Your other brother got away."

She swallowed hard, her mouth gone dry. "Which one got away? Caleb or Noah?"

"Caleb." He indicated the front door. "Now, can the rest wait until I get some coffee?"

"Yes, I'm sorry." Fighting back tears, Sarah walked over and opened the door. "I'm sorry. This is just . . . just so hard."

"I know." Cord took hold of the door and motioned her inside. "Let's just take it one day at a time, and we'll get through this. Okay?"

"Okay." Her tears spilled over, and she swiped them away. "I love you very much, you know."

He smiled. "And I love you."

Nick was in the kitchen with Manuela. The woman took one look at Sarah and Cord, pulled two mugs down from the cabinet, filled them with coffee, and put them on the table. Next, after retrieving a covered platter of cinnamon rolls from the top of the warm cookstove, she added them to the table along with three plates and then hurried from the kitchen.

"Leave it to Manuela to always know when to make a strategic exit," Nick said from his spot at one end of the table. "You, little brother, look like something the cat dragged in. And Angel, you've been crying, haven't you? So, I'm guessing something big happened last night."

Cord pulled out a chair for Sarah. She sat down, and he took a seat beside her.

"Yeah, we finally caught Jacob and one of his sons." Cord grabbed his mug and added a spoonful of sugar, stirred his coffee, then looked to his brother. "The other son got away."

"So, what's the plan now?" Nick shot Sarah a concerned look.

"What else? Wait for the circuit judge to show up, and try them in court." He sipped his steaming coffee carefully. "In the meantime, I'm betting the other Caldwell boy won't be rustling any cattle by himself."

"The hands will be glad to hear that. They'd far prefer spending their nights in a warm bunkhouse from here on out, rather than riding the herd . . ."

Gradually, Sarah became aware that the conversation had died. She looked up from the mug of coffee she clasped between her hands and saw two pairs of eyes riveted on her.

"I'm sorry. Did someone ask me a question?"

Nick reached over and laid a hand on her arm. "No, Angel.

We were just making conversation to cover the awkwardness, and finally ran out of things to say."

She glanced from Nick to Cord. "I don't mean to put a damper on your happiness. It's just . . . hard."

"We're not so much happy as relieved that it's over, Sarah," Cord said. "Well, almost over, anyway."

"They'll need a lawyer." She met his gaze, dreading his response but all the same having to ask. "Could . . . could you find someone to defend them?"

"Defend them?" Cord stared back at her, aghast. "What's there to defend? The facts speak for themselves. First, Jacob and his boys robbed us of over two thousand dollars. Then they stole our cattle, most likely several times, and one of those times it resulted in my father's death."

"But there are extenuating circumstances." Her heart pounded in her chest, and every word was wrenched from her, but Sarah had to speak them. "Father's not in his right mind or he'd never have done what he did. And my brothers . . . It's gotten so they no longer know right from wrong. If you at least spoke up for them at the trial, maybe the judge would show a little mercy."

"Mercy?" Cord pushed back his chair and stood, turning to glare down at her. "I think the time's long past for mercy, Sarah. What's needed now is some old-fashioned justice!"

"Easy, Cord," his brother cautioned. "This isn't Sarah's fault."

Cord dragged in a long, slow breath. "No, it's not Sarah's fault."

He looked to her, and she saw something harden in him. Her heart sank.

"This probably isn't the best time to be talking about this," he said. "I'm tired, both mentally and physically, of what your family's put me through these past few months. My father's dead because of them. And we still have yet to recover any of the money your father stole from us, much less our cattle, which seem to have disappeared off the face of the earth. I'm sorry, but I'm just not finding a whole lot of mercy in me right about now. So, no, Sarah. I won't be helping in any way in their defense. Not now or ever!"

With that, Cord wheeled around and stalked from the kitchen, his cup of coffee still steaming on the table.

Fresh tears filled Sarah's eyes. She felt as if he'd slapped her, and slapped her hard. His anger had been a terrible thing to behold, and a sudden realization that she didn't really know him swamped her. Leastwise, not the man who'd just stood before her.

"That probably wasn't the best time to ask for Cord's intervention for your family," Nick offered from his end of the table.

"Would there ever have been a good time?" Sarah heard the bitterness fill her voice. Right about now, though, she didn't really care.

"You're not being fair. In everything he's done regarding your family, Cord's tried to consider your feelings. But the past weeks since Pa's death have worn him down. He hasn't even fully come to terms with losing our father, and then there's been all the long nights going out after your father and brothers, not to mention trying to keep the ranch running on a shoestring."

"And don't you think it's been just as hard on me?" she cried. "I've been agonizing about what to do. About my commitment to Cord and my love for him, over what I still owe my own family. And just because my head tells me one thing doesn't mean my heart isn't trying to convince me of another."

"I know that, Angel, and so does Cord. And don't think he doesn't agonize over that too. He knows you're hurting."

Sarah looked down, her eyes blurred by the tears that just kept coming. "I don't know if this is going to work out between us, Nick. There just seems to be so many things that keep getting in our way."

"Don't think or even say that." He leaned over and took her hand in his. "You're both too worn out and emotional now. This isn't the time to make any decisions about your future— together or otherwise. Let it go for a while. Put it all in the Lord's hands. Hands far more capable than ours can ever be."

She lifted her gaze to his. "Right about now, I'm not seeing the Lord's hand in any of this. Cord refuses to intervene. And with my father's prison record and now the robbery and cattle rustling, not to mention Edmund's death, even if it was an accident, short of a miracle from above my father may well be sentenced to death."

"Most times, the Lord expects *us* to be the miracle workers for each other. But you're right. Miracles might well be in short supply for your father. A man can only keep piling on the evil deeds for so long, and punishment finally catches up with him."

"If he dies . . ." She choked back a sob. "How can God mean for anything good to come out of that?"

"How can any good come out of my father's death either?" He smiled sadly. "We're both still waiting to see about that. But that's where faith comes in. A faith strong and certain that, even in the darkest times, God is closer than ever, holding us up, guiding us toward the light. And there will be light again. There will be answers. The Lord promised us that and, no matter what, you can count on Him to honor His word."

"Now, make sure you keep your face covered with this muffler," Sarah said, leaning down to tug the woolen scarf up over her brother's nose and mouth. "And warm up slowly for fifteen minutes first thing, before you start running about like a crazed mustang. You don't want to set off your asthma out in the cold, you know."

Danny nodded. "Yes, I know. You only remind me every time I go out to play. You'd think I was dumb or something."

She straightened and smiled. "You're right. I do remind you every time, and you're not dumb. So, scoot." She opened the front door, and a gust of snow-laden air whirled in. "And have fun!"

Her brother dashed out the door so fast, Sarah wondered if he'd even heard her last instruction. Only when he hit the bottom of the porch steps did he slow his pace and walk sedately out to where Pedro awaited him. She closed the door with a soft chuckle.

"What's so funny?"

Cord's deep voice, just steps behind her, wrenched Sarah from her happy reverie. Memories of yesterday's unpleasant episode in the kitchen returned. Her smile faded.

"I was chiding Danny not to get too rambunctious outside and set off an asthma attack," she replied, turning to face Cord. "And he chided me in turn, saying I was being too overprotective."

"Well, the boy's had some hard times in the past with his asthma. Although I don't recall any episodes, since that first day he arrived, when he's had an attack as bad as that."

"Nor nearly as many either," Sarah said, mentally counting. "Actually, Danny's done the best ever since he came to live here. And I've got you to thank for that."

His guarded expression softened. "For a long while now, I haven't begrudged either you or Danny a place here. You know that, Sarah."

The same generosity, she well knew, wouldn't be extended

226

to her father and other two brothers. Indeed, Cord seemed intent on never offering any help to them. But why should he? All they'd ever done was try to harm him in some way or another, slapping aside any and all overtures he'd made to ease the tension and hard feelings.

Yet something about his unwillingness to forgive nagged at her . . .

"I know, and I've always appreciated your kindness to us, Cord," Sarah said, forcing the uneasy thoughts back into the recesses of her mind. "Truly, I have."

His gaze warmed. "I'm sorry for yesterday's outburst. It didn't have to come out quite so angry and hard."

"You were tired. I should've waited to speak about it till later."

Cord's hands, lifting to take her by the arms, fell back at his sides. "Maybe so, but waiting would've only spared you my anger. It wouldn't have changed my decision."

Somehow, Sarah had known that. Still, having it confirmed hurt. The sense of pending reconciliation faded. The chasm forming between them widened yet a bit more.

"Well, be that as it may," she forced herself to say, "I do have another favor to ask of you."

"And that favor is?" By the look on his face, Sarah knew he was girding himself for yet another refusal.

"When were you planning on going next to town?"

"This afternoon. It looks like the sun is about to peek through the clouds, and the snow is starting to let up too. Why?"

"I'd like to go with you, if you don't mind." She paused, gathering all her courage for the next part of her request. "I need to see my father and brother."

Cord's expression hardened. She could feel him emotionally withdraw even as he stepped back from her.

"Please, Cord. I can't just turn my back on them, no matter what they've done. Please try and understand."

"And I've no right or desire to keep you from them, if that's what you want. It's always been your choice, Sarah. Just know that you're not the only one stretched pretty thin right about now. Just remember that."

"I know, Cord." Pain twisted in her breast. "I know."

He eyed her intently for a long moment. "Do you?" he softly asked. "Do you really?"

Not awaiting her reply, Cord turned and walked away.

14

Heart pounding, Sarah paused outside Ashton's jail. She shot Cord, standing beside her, a quick, sideways glance. His expression was hard, his jaw set.

He's not looking forward to this visit any more than I am, if for perhaps different reasons.

For a fleeting instant, Sarah considered asking him to take her home. Back to the safe, secure life she'd been building at the ranch. A part of her—a big part—dreaded what was next to come, and the impact it might have on what seemed to be their rapidly shredding relationship.

But another part impelled her to forge ahead. The part of her that still cared for her father and brothers. The part that still clung to the faint hope of reconciliation and, somehow, some way, reparation.

"Nothing good can come of this, Sarah," Cord said just then, turning to look at her. "Your father's beyond saving."

Her gaze narrowed. Anger filled her. "No one's beyond saving. If God wills it—"

"Even God can't save your father from his well-deserved punishment!" he spat out, fury burning now in his eyes. "Leastwise, not while he's still on this earth anyway."

He says that because of what happened to his own father. A father he seemed to hate until just a short while before his death.

An impulse to point out the contradiction in Cord's sudden change of heart swept through Sarah, and she almost uttered the words. But something held her back.

What purpose was served heaping pain upon pain? Someone had to be merciful, to see past all the anger and hatred to what truly mattered. To find Christ and His love somewhere in all of this.

A sense of peace flooded her. She reached out, laid a hand on Cord's arm.

"I just need to do this. Maybe it won't accomplish anything, won't make any difference to my father or Noah. But *I* need to do it. Please, just stand by me."

His dark gaze bored into her, and she saw myriad emotions flash by. Doubt, love, confusion, and fear.

But fear of what? she wondered. *Why is a simple visit to my father and brother a source of fear for him? Does he also sense the rift widening between us? Is he equally as terrified that he might lose me as I am of losing him?*

With all her heart, Sarah wanted to reassure him that nothing would ever come between them and their love. But right now she wasn't so sure anymore. Gazing up at him, she felt like she was almost with a stranger.

"Fine." Cord clipped out the word. "If you're so set on making yourself even more miserable, who am I to get in your way?" He turned from her, gripped the doorknob, and twisted it, shoving open the door. "Ladies first," he said, indicating she should enter before him.

It wasn't the response she'd been hoping for, but Sarah decided this wasn't the time or place to belabor the details. She squared her shoulders and walked inside.

Gabe looked up from the woodstove in the far corner, where, pot in hand, he was pouring himself a mug of coffee. Sam Hayden sat nearby at his desk, reading a book. The warmth of the room felt good after the frigid cold outside. As Cord entered behind her and closed the door, Sarah removed her gloves, wool coat, and hat.

"I figured you'd be paying a visit sooner or later," the lawman said. He lifted his mug. "Want some coffee to warm you up?"

"No, thank you." Sarah glanced to the door that led to the back room and jail cells. "If it's all right with you, I'd rather just see my father and brother."

"Sure." He paused, eyeing her. "I'm assuming you don't have any knives or a gun hidden on you?"

She blushed. She hadn't considered the possibility that her motives for visiting her family might be suspected.

"No, I don't." Sarah firmly shook her head. "Nor any files or dynamite to break them out either."

Gabe gestured in the direction of the cells. "Then have at it."

She nodded in wordless gratitude, then headed across the room.

"How about you, Cord?" she heard Gabe ask as she opened the door and walked inside, taking care to leave the door partially askew so Gabe and Cord would know she had nothing to hide in her visit with her father and brother. "Care for some coffee?"

"Don't mind if I do," was Cord's reply.

Sarah found her father and Noah in the farthest of the four cells in the long, narrow room. At her entrance, both men looked up. Surprise registered on Noah's bruised and battered face. Strangely, though, her father's glance was calm, almost as if he'd fully expected her to come.

A small stool stood in the corner outside their cell, and Sarah pulled it over and sat. For a long moment, she shifted her gaze from her father to her brother, then back again.

Her father looked ill, his skin a pasty color, his lips blue-tinged, his breathing ragged. He had become increasingly short of breath in the past year or so, and suffered at times from swollen feet and ankles, but Sarah had never seen him look this bad. Fear clutched her heart, squeezing it in a painful grip.

"Papa, what's wrong with you? Have you been to see Doc—"

"Is it true?" her father asked of a sudden, cutting her off. "Are you engaged to that tinhorn Wainwright's younger son?"

Of all the things she might have expected her father to say, this was the last question she would've anticipated.

"Yes, I am engaged to Cord," Sarah replied, realizing there was no point served in prevarication. "He's been very kind to Danny and me and, in time, I found myself falling in love with him."

Noah sighed loudly and shook his head. "I never would've thought that of you, Sarah. Selling yourself to the highest bidder, I mean." He looked to his father. "We should've never involved her in that robbery, Pa. We've gone and lost our sweet, innocent little Sarah."

"Now, wait just one minute." This conversation was veering far off course. She wasn't here to defend her actions but to get them to change and repent of theirs. "For one thing, I haven't sold myself to the Wainwrights, and I'm just as innocent as I was that day I came into town with you, Papa, to get that medicine for Danny. The Wainwrights have treated me with respect and kindness"—since it really didn't add to the essential truth of her story, she decided to omit the first few days of her captivity—"and Cord and his brother Nick have always, *always* been the perfect gentlemen.

"But I didn't come here to discuss my choice of a husband," Sarah then continued, "nor is it what really matters right now. You're both in jail and soon to stand trial for robbing the Wainwrights, not to mention cattle rustling. And you're my family and I love you. I came to see how you were, if you need anything."

Jacob Caldwell once more stirred to life. "What do you have of your own, girl, that hasn't been given to you by the Wainwrights? And do you think we'd ever accept anything from those cheating, thieving varmints?"

Exasperation filled her. "It's long past time, Papa, that you stop calling the Wainwrights thieves and cheats. What you and my brothers have been doing of late is far, far more serious. So serious that you, especially, might suffer far worse than just going to prison."

Her father shrugged. "Well, then you'd be well rid of me, wouldn't you? You could forget you ever were a Caldwell, up in that fine house on that fine ranch that was stolen from your papa."

"Don't say that!" Sarah leaned forward and clasped the iron cell bars separating her from them. "I love you, and I always will. But you've got to stop this crazy vendetta before it destroys us all."

"Destroys your chances of marrying into the Wainwrights, you mean," he said with a derisive snort.

"No." She fixed her gaze on him. "Whether Cord and I can get past all this hatred and turmoil isn't what matters here. What matters is what *you're* doing to our family. Rather than return the money you stole, you chose instead to desert Danny and me. If anyone sold anyone out, that's what *you* did to *us*. And look what's become of Caleb and Noah. You've turned them into robbers and cattle rustlers, with Noah now facing prison and Caleb all alone and on the run. Not to mention what this life did to Mama, aging her beyond her years until she finally sickened and died!"

"Don't you ever speak so of your mother!" Jacob screamed, lunging at her.

In her effort to evade her father's hands, curved into claws, stretching toward her through the cell bars, Sarah toppled off her stool. Cord, followed by Gabe, rushed into the room.

His face dark with fury, Cord stalked down the aisle and helped Sarah to her feet. "Are you all right? Did he hurt you?"

"No, he didn't hurt me. I'm fine. Papa just startled me, and I tipped over the stool." She managed a lame little smile. "Guess I wasn't sitting on it as squarely as I should've."

"Yeah, maybe not," Cord replied, not appearing at all convinced. He turned to face Jacob, who was still standing there looking as if he wanted nothing more than to throttle Cord if he could've only reached him. "Just keep the shouting and threats down, Caldwell. There's no cause to treat Sarah that way."

"You're right," the older man snarled. "I should save it for you, corrupter of innocent young women."

Gabe walked over and took Cord by the arm. "Come on. It's best you not be in here right now."

"Or ever," Cord said, his eyes glittering. "Old man or not, I don't know what I'd do if I got my hands on him." He looked to Sarah. "One more outburst like that from your father, and I'm taking you home."

She knew he was only saying that because he was upset with how her father had yelled at her, not to mention all the pent-up anger he must feel toward her father for all the trouble he'd caused. Some part of her, though, didn't like being talked to as if she were some child who needed protecting. Still, Sarah bit back a sharp reply and nodded.

"It was my fault. I said some hurtful things. But it won't happen again. I promise."

Cord gave a curt nod, then wheeled about and followed Gabe from the room. Sarah waited a minute or two, then again faced her father and brother.

"Papa, if there's any of the Wainwrights' money left, telling me where it is might buy you, Noah, and Caleb some goodwill with the judge." She swung her glance from her father to Noah—who was now thoughtfully studying her—before locking gazes with her father. "Please, Papa. It's not too late to try to make amends. Do it for your children, if you won't do it for yourself."

"It won't do any good, girl," her father said, the deranged sheen fading briefly from his eyes. "You saw and heard Wainwright just now. He hates us and means to see Noah and me hang. Even if he got his money back, he's not going to lift a finger to help us. He's as hungry for revenge as his father and I ever were."

Though Sarah wanted to refute his assertions, she couldn't find the conviction to do so. She had seen and heard the fury, the thinly veiled threat in Cord's voice and words just a few minutes ago. It was an aspect of him that she'd never before experienced, even in his times of greatest anger with her when he'd first captured her. This went far, far deeper, and felt ice cold and ruthless.

"It doesn't matter what Cord does or doesn't do on your behalf," she whispered, her voice gone hoarse and raw. "What matters in the end, before God, is that *you* do the right thing. Do it, and then ask forgiveness. Of the Lord, the Wainwrights, and anyone else you may have offended. It's the only way to finally make something good come of this miserable, endless, heart-wrenching feud."

He stared at her for a long, long while. Finally he gave a sharp, strident laugh. The man she had once known disappeared, and the wild, fevered look flared anew in his eyes.

"They've been filling your head with all sorts of crazy notions, haven't they, girl?" he asked, his voice taking on a high, strained pitch. "And turned you, once and for all, against your own kin." He shrugged. "Well, it's your choice, I guess. Whether you believe your own papa or some strangers. One thing's for sure. Save the sermon for the Wainwrights. Not that it'll do you any good. That man you think you want to marry? Well, take another look at him. Take a real good look. For all his fine manners and money, deep down where it matters, he's no better a man than me."

Thanksgiving, two days later, was a far more somber affair than usual. Though the spread of food on the big dining room table was as generous as always, from roasted wild turkey, creamy mashed potatoes, cornbread stuffing, canned green beans from their long-gone summer garden, and, of course, pumpkin pie with real whipped cream, the only people stuffing themselves and exclaiming over the delicious food were Danny and Pedro. The adults tried their best, for the sake of the boys, to smile and make conversation, however stilted it frequently ended up being, but at times the flow of talk around the table faded, and the silence grew strained.

His father's absence was partly to blame, Cord mused as he sat alone in the kitchen, nursing a now tepid mug of coffee that evening after everyone had gone to bed. The rising tension between him and Sarah, however, had only intensified the problem. Since her visit with her father and brother the day before yesterday, she'd been uncharacteristically subdued, avoiding him whenever possible. And, if the truth were told, he hadn't particularly wanted to seek her out either.

Indeed, what could he say to improve the situation? He'd never lift a finger to help Jacob Caldwell. And his two sons needed a good lesson fast, before they permanently sank into that inescapable quagmire their father had dug himself into over the years.

A part of him was also annoyed with Sarah for even putting him into such an unfair and untenable position. How had *he* ever contributed to this insufferable feud, until the Caldwells had finally crossed the line with the robbery and cattle rustling? Then, all he'd done was what any man would do to protect his property—demand that justice be served.

Sarah had most definitely backed him into a corner. Until she gave ground on her demands, they were at a stalemate. It was an unfortunate battle of wills, and one that he intended—

The kitchen door erratically inched open, propelled along by Nick's wheelchair. Cord rose and hurried over to hold the door for his brother.

"Couldn't sleep either, huh?" Cord asked, managing a welcoming smile.

"That, and a case of mild indigestion from that third piece of pumpkin pie, I'm thinking," his brother replied. "Could you get me a glass of milk?"

"Sure thing."

Cord retrieved a glass from the cupboard, then pulled the milk pitcher from the small icebox that, in winter, served as a far more convenient substitute for the springhouse that was a good distance away. He carried the glass and pitcher to the table, poured a full glass for his brother, then put the pitcher back in the icebox. Finally, Cord again took his own seat.

Minutes ticked by without either of them speaking. Nick sipped his milk until it was finally gone. Then, with a contented sigh, he set down the empty glass.

"I feel better already. Still, I think I'll stay sitting up for a while until the indigestion totally subsides."

"That's probably a good idea." Cord shot him an amused glance. "You'd think, after all these years, you'd learn not to overindulge on Thanksgiving."

Nick shrugged. "Well, someone besides the boys needed to show some appreciation for all the work that went into making the meal. You and Sarah, I noted, hardly ate enough to keep a . . . a mouse alive."

Cord stared down at the mug he now clasped between his hands. "I reckon we both had other things on our minds."

"Like who's going to win this battle over what to do about Jacob Caldwell?"

Irritation surged through Cord. He jerked up his head, his glance slamming into his brother's. "Not to sound rude or anything, but this really isn't any of your business."

"Oh, really?" Nick leaned back in his chair. "That might be true, if this little fight of yours wasn't affecting the entire household. In case you didn't notice, it pretty much ruined Thanksgiving for most of us."

"And what do you expect me to do about it?" Cord snarled, his temper fraying by the second. "Are you suggesting I give in, and tell Sarah I'll defend her father and brothers in court? The same people, lest you forget, responsible for *our* father's death."

"As hard as this may be to hear, little brother, that was an unfortunate accident."

"Hogwash!" Cord gave a derisive snort. "Jacob Caldwell has wanted Pa dead for years now, and you know it."

"Maybe so, but I don't think that thought necessarily entered his mind when he started the stampede. I think he was just desperate to escape."

"Well, we'll never know, will we? And Caldwell is just as easily convicted on the robbery and cattle rustling."

"Cattle rustling, yes. He was caught red-handed with our cattle. But the robbery . . ."

"What do you mean?" Cord impaled his brother with a steely glance. "Sarah admitted to . . ."

His voice died away. Sarah admitted to it because she, of all of them, was the only one who hadn't been masked. She was the only one he could identify. And her father had never returned the money. He could claim in court that he didn't have it to return, because he hadn't taken it.

"Sarah's your only suspect, isn't she?" Nick asked softly. "So I guess it comes down to the question of whether you really want to force her to testify against her own family, doesn't it?"

Nick was right. Only Sarah could corroborate his story of the robbery, and Cord knew he couldn't—*wouldn't*—force her to do that. He risked far, far too much in such an attempt, not the least of which was losing Sarah once and for all.

"What does it matter?" he asked. "Cattle rustling is, at best, a prison term. At worst, it's punishable by hanging. And I, for one, am hoping Jacob Caldwell gets sentenced to hang."

"That's pretty bloodthirsty, Cord."

"Yeah, well, this feud isn't going to be over until that crazy old man is dead. And the hold he has on Sarah . . . well, I'm beginning to think we don't have a chance to make it even to a wedding, much less have a successful marriage, unless Caldwell's out of the picture."

"So, now we're finally getting to the heart of the matter," his brother said. "You're afraid you're going to lose Sarah."

"Wouldn't you be, considering what's been going on? I thought she loved me, but I'm beginning to think it'll never hold a candle to her foolish, self-destructive devotion to her family."

Frustration coiled within Cord like some knot twisting on itself, and it hurt. Hurt bad. He fisted his hands so tightly his nails dug into his palms.

"She isn't making a lot of sense of late. I'll give you that." Nick sighed. "But I do see her struggling with it too. Sarah's

239

just not the sort of person to turn her back on those she loves, no matter how badly they've sinned." His mouth quirked. "Kind of like God's unending love for his errant children."

"Yeah, well, God has also been known to mete out punishment where it's due. But just try convincing Sarah her family deserves punishment for what they've done."

"I don't think Sarah would claim what they've done doesn't merit punishment. I just think it goes deeper than that." Nick paused to finger the rim of his glass. "For some reason, Sarah imagines she's responsible for saving her family. And, as unfair a burden as that is, she keeps hoping against hope that she can do it."

"Well, she can't. In the meanwhile, she's ruining her own chances at happiness."

"So, I reckon the dilemma is how to get her to see that and finally step back from this mess her family has created. To accept that what they choose to do of their own accord carries consequences they alone must bear."

"The same also applies to her." Cord shoved back his mug. "These are choices she's making, and though the consequences might not be the best for her, I can't—I *won't*—stop her from making them."

"You're right about that, little brother." Something enigmatic flashed through Nick's eyes. "All anyone can do is learn to make their own choices in the best way they can. Just one word of advice. Before you judge the mote in your brother's eye, be sure the beam in your own eye is gone. It'll make things a whole lot clearer."

Cord scowled. "And exactly what is *that* supposed to mean?"

His brother smiled. "Nothing. Or maybe everything, depending on what you care to make of it."

"No, I don't think it'd be a good idea for you to come with us to church," Sarah said three days later as she buttoned her coat closed and looked down at her brother. "It's frigid today, the winds are blowing pretty badly, and you've still got a slight fever. Next Sunday, maybe. But not today."

Danny stomped his foot. "But I'll miss out on the children's service and the cookies and milk afterward. Plus, I want to see my friends!"

Sarah rolled her eyes. *Children! Why do they all have to be so stubborn?*

She shook her head. "I'm sorry, Danny, but the answer is still no. You've done so well since you've come here, and I'm not going to risk your health. God will understand."

"Well, my friends won't!"

Behind them, Nick chuckled. "Easy there, young fella. How about I make a special point of explaining your absence to them. And, to top it off, I'll also bring back a sample of any of the snacks they serve after services. You have my word on it."

"Really?" Eyes bright, Danny turned to Nick. "That'd be swell, Mr. Wainwright."

Amazing, Sarah thought, *how everything always sounds better if anyone besides family suggests something to a child.* She wasn't about to take any chances of ruining what Nick had orchestrated, and held her tongue. She also held her tongue a few minutes later as Cord arrived to help Nick outside, down the porch steps, and into the carriage.

There wasn't a whole lot to say to him these days at any rate. They'd slammed into a barrier that couldn't easily be gotten around, and this time Sarah wasn't about to budge. Whether Cord liked it or not, if they married, family was part of the bargain. Of course, she thought ruefully, *his* family these days wasn't the problem.

"You've got the rifle, don't you, Nick?" Cord asked as Sarah, followed by Emma, climbed into the carriage beside his brother.

"Yes, it's right under the seat where it always is. As if there's going to be any need for it on the way to town and back. Anyone with any grudge against us is in jail, or have you forgotten that, little brother?"

"Actually, maybe *you've* forgotten that one of Sarah's brothers is still on the loose." Cord assiduously avoided looking at Sarah. "And he might well be getting pretty desperate and willing to try just about anything."

"Like what? Holding us for ransom?"

Cord's jaw went rigid. "Don't make light of this, Nick. Be on the lookout and have a care."

Nick shot Sarah a quick glance, then nodded. "Okay. You're right. I'll keep my eyes open."

"Maybe I should send a few of the hands along as escort."

"Or maybe you could just come along yourself. Some time in the Lord's house might do you a world of good."

"No. It wouldn't." Cord stepped back. "Believe me, it wouldn't."

"Okay. Suit yourself." Nick gathered up the reins and handed them to Sarah. "Want to drive the team today?"

Pleasure filled her. "Yes. I'd love to." She slapped the reins smartly over the two horses' backs. "Let's go!"

With a lurch, the carriage moved out. Nick turned and waved at Cord.

"See you in a few hours."

She was never so glad to be gone from the ranch and Cord's increasingly oppressive presence. The day was bright if cold, but the winds calmed after a time and it didn't seem all that chilly. The heavy throws tucked around their middles and covering their legs and feet, combined with the warm hats, jackets, and scarves helped a lot too.

"You handle the team well," Nick observed from beside her. "You've got a light but authoritative touch."

Sarah beamed at his praise. "Thank you. I've had an excellent teacher. My papa was always so good with horses—"

Her cheeks burned, and she cut off further mention of her father. As kind and tolerant as Nick was, in sharp contrast to his brother of late, Sarah knew he must have mixed feelings about her family. It was just so hard to have to excise her family from her heart and mind. Hard and, in many ways, unfair.

"I'm really looking forward to Pastor Ferguson's Sunday sermon," Emma interjected just then. "He always has such thought-provoking things to say."

"Yes, he certainly does," Nick added. "I'm so glad he's blessed Ashton with his ministry."

As Sarah drove along, she was grateful for Emma and Nick's attempts to keep the conversation going. They had become such good friends and confidants. She appreciated their wisdom and gentle, nonjudgmental insights. If only her relationship with Cord was like the ones she had with Nick and Emma . . .

Sarah sighed. Would they never have peace between them? Would things always be so problematic, so volatile? If so, it didn't bode well for a happy marriage.

Of late, she'd been considering what she would do if things continued so poorly between her and Cord. Going back home wouldn't be good for Danny. But what other options were left them? Maybe she could get a job in town. But doing what?

There weren't many decent jobs for single women in a small but growing town like Ashton. It already had a schoolteacher. And it wasn't as if Sarah had the money to buy some empty house to set up a boardinghouse or start a dining establishment. But Ruth Ann *had* made mention, that day at the Wildflower Café, that she needed to hire an extra cook to help her in the kitchen. Maybe *that* might be the answer to her growing concerns over her and Cord.

Sarah spent the next half hour considering all the ramifications of possibly leaving the Wainwright ranch, and they were soon pulling up before Ashton's whitewashed, clapboard church. Some of the church elders came out and assisted Nick in getting into the building, and the next hour was spent in prayer, song, and hearing God's Word.

In the meanwhile, the weather had taken a decided turn for the worse. One look at the dark clouds churning overhead, and Nick made the decision to depart immediately after the services. Danny, he said, would just have to understand. Halfway home, a rider suddenly appeared from some trees near the creek and headed their way, racing toward the road before them as if to cut them off. Nick leaned over and pulled the rifle up from beneath the seat.

"I don't like the looks of him," he muttered. "He doesn't resemble anyone I—"

Sarah pulled back hard on the reins. The horses came to a jerky halt.

"It's okay, Nick. I know him."

He gripped the rifle on his lap. "Who is it, Sarah?"

Her heart thudding in her chest, she swallowed hard. "It's my brother."

"Land sakes," Emma whispered beside them. "Land sakes . . ."

"The one who's still free?" Nick asked. "Caleb?"

"No." Sarah shook her head, not quite certain she should believe what she was seeing or what it meant. "It's not Caleb. It's my other brother. Noah."

15

"Sarah!" Noah's voice echoed off the mountains looming behind him. "I need to talk with you. It's important!"

He nudged his horse forward. "I just want to talk. That's all."

"Angel, I don't think it's a good idea to let him get too close," Nick said beside her, warily eyeing Noah's approach. "Best we just send him on his way with a little warning."

She laid a firm hand on his rifle's barrel as he began to lift it higher. "I've got a better idea. You cover me while I go and see what he wants. He won't try anything foolish with you holding that rifle."

"Child, I agree with Nicholas." On her other side, Emma gripped her arm. "This could be some sort of setup, or even a trap. You don't know if your brother came alone or if there are others hiding in the trees."

"You're right." Sarah shot the older woman a quick smile. "I don't know anything about why Noah's here. But it's obvious he's escaped from jail. And with Gabe and a posse likely hot on his trail, Noah wouldn't risk this if it wasn't of the utmost importance. Besides, he won't hurt me. You know that as well as I."

Nick sighed and shook his head. "I don't like it, Sarah. And if Cord finds out . . ."

"Well, I'm not asking you to keep secrets from him."

She wrapped the reins around the brake handle, stood, and climbed down from the carriage. "And it's not as if either of you can stop me. So, let me bear the brunt of Cord's ire. In fact, I'll be the first to tell him what I did."

"Make it fast then." Nick raised his rifle and made a great show of cocking it before lowering it back to his lap. "Nothing good is served, for any of us, lingering out in the open."

"I'll be quick. I promise."

With that, she set out at a slow run across the snowy ground, heading straight for her brother. As she neared, she scanned the trees at the base of the mountain, searching for sign of others. There was no one there.

Relief filled her. If her father or Caleb had been hiding, just waiting until she was safely away to ambush Nick . . .

Even the consideration of such a possibility sent a shudder through her. Out here in the open, they were all sitting ducks. And if anything should happen to Nick, she'd never forgive herself.

"Well, what is it, Noah?" Sarah demanded, finally drawing up before him. "What have you gone and done to get out of jail and end up here?"

Her brother's mouth quirked sadly. "A fine way to greet me. I thought you of all people would be happiest to see us free again. Considering what sort of fate awaited us at trial."

"Oh, Noah! I'm sorry." She expelled an exasperated breath. "Everything's becoming more and more dangerous and complicated by the moment." She paused to once again study the trees. "Where's Papa and Caleb? Are they here too?"

"No, they're not here." Noah's expression grew serious, worried. "Caleb was shot helping us break out. He's with Pa at our hideout. Caleb's shot bad, Sarah. Real bad. And though Pa's not hearing any of it, I don't think Caleb's going to make it."

246

"What?" For an instant, the world spun wildly and Sarah had to grab hold of Noah's stirrup to steady herself. "Caleb's d-dying?"

He nodded. "I'm no doctor, but he's gut shot. And the blood . . ." Noah swallowed hard. "No matter what we try, we can't stop it for long."

"Then you shouldn't have wasted your time on me. You should've gone straight for Doc Saunders!"

"As if Pa or I could've gotten close to Doc." He laughed unsteadily. "That new deputy of Gabe Cooper's a crack shot. We left a trail of blood behind us, until Pa finally packed enough snow in Caleb's wound to stop the bleeding for a while. Even then, we had to back track a lot, and ride down a couple of streams before we finally lost them."

"So, why are you here? What can I possibly do?"

"Caleb keeps calling for you, Sarah. I think he knows he's not going to make it, and he wants you." He paused, gazing down at her with imploring eyes. "Will you come?"

It took only the space of an inhaled breath for Sarah to decide. Her brother might be dying, and he needed her. What else *could* she do?

"Of course, I'll come." She lifted her hand to him. "Help me up on your horse, will you?"

Noah bent down, took Sarah by the hand, and pulled her up behind him. He then glanced back at her.

"Ready?"

"Just one minute more. Ride closer to Nick, will you, so I can tell them what I'm doing and why."

"I'm not so sure that's a good idea," her brother said. "How good is he with that rifle?"

"Very good. But Nick's not the sort to back shoot a man, so you're safe."

"Guess I'll have to trust you on that."

247

"Just get closer, will you?" Sarah wrapped her arms about his waist. "Time's short, if we're to make it to Papa and Caleb before dark and"—she lifted her gaze to the ever-darkening clouds—"before this storm comes in."

"You're right about that, little sister." As he talked, Noah urged his horse toward the carriage. "We've got a new hide-out, and it's even farther away than the old one."

"I figured as much."

His gaze narrowed, Nick watched them approach. Finally, he motioned with his rifle.

"That's close enough." He locked glances with Sarah. "What's going on?"

"My brother Caleb's been shot and is in a bad way. He's asking for me, Nick, and I've got to go to him. Tell Danny . . . well, tell him that his brother's sick and I'll be home soon."

"And what do I tell Cord?"

What indeed, Sarah thought. *Will he even care what my reasons are, once he hears what I've done? Likely, he'll imagine I'm relieved that Noah and Papa made good their escape. And a part of me is relieved, even if the other part dreads that now it's going to start all over again, the feuding, the thieving, and the killing. Especially if Caleb dies. Oh, dear Lord, especially if Caleb dies!*

"Tell him I've got to do this, Nick," she finally replied. "Tell him, and ask him to please, please try to understand."

A pounding at the front door interrupted Cord's calculations of December's budget. With an irritated snarl, he shoved back his chair and headed to the entry foyer. With Nick, Sarah, and Emma gone, Manuela and Pedro on their day off, and Danny napping in his room, there was no one left to answer the door but him. Not that he didn't have his hands full enough right now, trying to squeeze every penny he could from the already skeletal ranch funds.

With a less-than-welcoming attitude, he wrenched open the door. Gabe Cooper, accompanied by his deputy, stood there. Neither man wore a very happy expression.

For an instant, Cord's heart did a flip-flop. Had something happened to Nick or the women? But that was ridiculous. Nick was armed and an excellent marksman.

Remembering his manners, he swung the door wide. "Come in. No sense standing in the cold, since I know you must have had a chilly ride out here."

The two men stomped the snow off their boots and walked inside. Cord shut the door behind them.

"Care for a cup of coffee?"

Gabe and Sam exchanged a glance.

"Well, maybe a quick one," the lawman said. "Then, we'll need to be on our way."

"So, what brings you to Castle Mountain Ranch on a Sunday, no less?" Cord asked a few moments later as he poured two steaming mugs of coffee and handed one to each man. "Just in the neighborhood and decided to stop by to warm up a bit?"

"Not exactly." Gabe finished stirring sugar and cream into his coffee, then met Cord's inquiring gaze. "We had a jail-break last night. Though I find it hard to believe that younger Caldwell boy could've managed it all by himself, right now it appears that he did. He dynamited the back wall of the cell holding his father and brother."

The sheriff looked to his deputy. "Sam was on duty that night, and did me proud. The Caldwells got away, but Sam thinks he wounded one of the sons pretty badly."

The Caldwells . . . free once again . . .

For a long moment, Cord stood there slowly digesting the

information and its implications. A sense of déjà vu engulfed him. The Caldwells free again . . . The cattle rustling likely to resume . . . And the ranch and its inhabitants once more in danger of their lives . . .

To add to it all, if the one Caldwell son who was wounded was to die . . . Well, there was no telling to what lengths Jacob Caldwell might go to avenge his death.

"Nick's gone to town with Sarah and Emma for Sunday services," Cord said of a sudden. "Usually I send several armed hands along with them, but I thought Jacob was locked up and it was safe . . ."

He shot Gabe and Sam a hard glance. "Finish up your coffee and meet me down at the barn. I'm going to saddle up."

"I think we can escort Nick and the women home without—"

"No." Cord shook his head. "You've got enough on your hands. I'll take care of my family. In the meantime, you see to getting the Caldwells back behind bars—just as fast as you can!"

As soon as they were out of sight of Nick and Emma, Noah reined in his horse. He dug in his pocket and extracted a long piece of cloth.

"Here." He handed it back to Sarah. "Cover your eyes with this. Pa made me promise to make sure you didn't figure out the way to our hideout. Didn't want to take any chances you'd tell the Wainwrights where we're at, I reckon."

Sarah took the cloth, wrapped it around her head several times, then knotted it firmly. "That suits me fine too. I don't want to be put in the middle of having to lie or have my loyalty to Cord questioned. You've got to promise me one thing, though."

"What's that, little sister?"

"That you'll bring me back when I ask you, no matter what Papa wants." She slid her hands tightly around his waist again. "My primary concern has to be for Danny now, and I won't leave him."

"You could always find some way to sneak him back home," her brother said as he urged his horse forward again. "You'd just have to say the word, and I'd be there to get both of you."

She hesitated, wondering how to word what she was next to say without angering him. Whether things ultimately worked out between her and Cord, Sarah was determined never to return to her old life. To remain near her father a minute longer than necessary these days was to risk being sickened by the poison of his vengefulness. Maybe she'd already absorbed more of that venom than was healthy, but she'd at least not expose her little brother to any more of it.

"If it was just you and Caleb . . ." She sighed. "Well, it doesn't matter. What matters is I don't see eye to eye with Papa anymore. And I won't have Danny near him."

"That's pretty harsh, Sarah. Speaking of Pa that way."

"I know." She sighed and laid her head against her brother's back. "I know, but look what he's done, Noah. And now . . . now Caleb may be dying because of Papa's all-consuming need for revenge. He frightens me. Scares me down to the depths of my soul."

"Then why are you coming back with me?"

"It's for Caleb." Sarah shivered. "That day I visited you and Papa in jail . . . well, it was like I didn't know Papa anymore. I felt like I was looking into the eyes of a stranger, and that stranger wasn't any friend of mine."

"So, now you hate him, do you?"

"No." She shook her head. "I know he's still my papa, and I'll always love him. I pray for him all the time too, and keep hoping that somehow, some day, he'll finally open his eyes to the terrible things he has wrought. Yet even now that Edmund Wainwright's dead, has he changed or lessened his need to continue on until he's destroyed everything? Has he, Noah?"

"He's our father, Sarah. It's not our place to judge him."

"Maybe not, but I'm not following in his footsteps anymore either. The Lord gave me the ability to see right and wrong, and to choose which path to take. And I don't think He wants me to follow Papa's lead."

"So where does that leave me and Caleb?" her brother snarled. Beneath her hands, she could feel his body go taut. "Are we just as blind and foolish as you now seem to think Pa is? Or maybe the Wainwrights have filled your head with all sorts of highfalutin ideas, and now you're too good for us?"

Frustration filled her. "It's not that at all. What's changed is that I started thinking again about what Mama taught us of God, and the right and wrong of things. And God doesn't take kindly to holding grudges or not letting go of anger. You know that as well as I, Noah. Mama didn't just read the Bible to me. She read it to *all* of her children."

"Well, I'm glad you've got the luxury of turning the other cheek and forgiving the Wainwrights," Noah muttered, bitterness now threading his voice. "But someone's got to stay with Pa. He's getting real sick, and I don't think he's got a lot of time left. It's his heart, you know."

"He looked really bad, that day at the jail." Tears stung Sarah's eyes. "And I'm glad you're with him. Just don't let him do anything else, Noah. Let it finally stop, so whatever time he has left can be lived in peace. I just want him to die in peace, not still mired in all that anger and hatred."

"I'll try, Sarah. But I'm not making any promises."

With that, he kicked his horse into a lope. Sarah hung on, knowing the time for talk was over. From the change in the angle of the horse's body, she could tell they had reached level ground. For about the next fifteen minutes, they traveled at a rapid pace before Noah slowed the animal again and they once more began to climb.

As time passed, the periodic change in elevation happened over and over until Sarah gave up trying to figure out where they were. The snow finally began to fall, and the wind picked up. She was grateful she'd dressed warmly. Her fingers grew numb and her feet started to tingle. More and more often, she had to flex her limbs to keep the blood flowing.

"How much longer?" she finally asked. "If we're not going to make it before dark, maybe we need to find a place to stay for the night and get a fire going."

"We're almost there," her brother replied. "I can see the firelight from the cabin now. Hang on, little sister. Just a few more minutes."

Blessedly, it was indeed just another ten minutes, and Noah halted his horse. He helped her slide down, then dismounted himself.

"Here," he then said, his hands going to the knot of the cloth still covering her eyes. "You can take that off now."

Sarah blinked in the dimming light, allowing a moment for her eyes to adjust. Then she turned toward the rickety old miner's cabin and hurried up the steps.

At the sound of the door opening, her father glanced up from his chair set beside the only bed in the room. Momentarily, his gaze warmed, then he quickly shuttered his joy beneath a mask of indifference.

"So, you came, girl. You surprised me. I didn't think you would."

"I came because Caleb asked for me." She shed her gloves and unbuttoned her coat as she hurried over to the bed. As she did, her father rose and pulled back his chair.

Caleb lay there, so white and still Sarah feared she had arrived too late. She knelt beside him, took a pale hand in hers.

"Caleb? It's Sarah," she whispered, her throat going tight. "Noah said you wanted to see me."

Sandy lashes fluttered against his cheeks. Ever so slowly her brother opened his eyes. They had a faraway look, and it appeared to require a great effort for him to focus. When he did, however, a tired smile lifted one corner of his mouth.

"S-Sarah? You came . . ."

He tried to lever himself to one elbow, and failed. It was all he could do just to weakly squeeze her hand.

"I'm . . . I'm done for, Sarah," he said, his voice barely audible. "But you came . . . in time."

"Hush. Save your strength." She laid a finger to his lips. "Time enough later to talk."

"No time left." Caleb shook his head. "Forgive."

She frowned. "Forgive? Forgive what, Caleb?"

"That day . . . I called you . . . a tramp." He sighed, closed his eyes for a long moment, then finally opened them. "I didn't . . . mean it. I was just . . . just mad. And confused."

"Oh, Caleb!" She took his hand and lifted it to her lips. "I knew that. We've all been mad and confused for a long while now. But I never, ever doubted that you still loved me. As I've always loved you."

"G-good. Didn't want that . . . on my conscience . . . when I face my Maker."

"Have no fear, big brother. When that time comes, the Lord is going to welcome you with open arms."

He frowned. "I . . . don't know about that. I've done some bad things . . ."

"Then tell Jesus how sorry you are for them," she urged, her eyes filling with tears. "That's all He asks."

His lips curved in a soft, beatific smile. "It's that . . . easy . . . is it?"

"He has already paid the full price for our sins, Caleb. You just need to repent of them. Repent of them with all your heart."

Caleb closed his eyes, and Sarah could see his lips silently moving. She lowered her head, offering up her own prayers, entreating the Lord to spare her brother's life if it was His will, and if not, to carry him gently and painlessly up to heaven. Prayed with all her heart and felt, after a time, a great peace fill her.

A great peace and overflowing joy the like of which she'd never felt before flowed over her. Yet, as much as it filled and uplifted her, Sarah knew that it was a vicarious experience. That it was really her brother's emotions touching her. Emotions he was feeling as his soul was lifted from his now lifeless body to rise heavenward.

"Caleb!" her father wailed at that very instant. "Caleb!"

Sarah opened her eyes and looked up. All the pain and suffering that had twisted her brother's features had vanished. In its place was a look of ineffable peace.

Sadness swamped her. She would miss her childhood friend and sibling. Miss him deeply and for a long, long time to come.

But she was also relieved, and even a tiny bit envious. Caleb at least was finally free of all the pain and worry. All the unpleasant tension of living with and trying to please a parent who refused ever to be happy or satisfied. There was no more unrequited hunger for vengeance and destruction in Caleb's life anymore. His way was clear now, his goal obvious.

Not so for her, though. And maybe never.

Sarah covered her face and wept.

Two days later, once darkness had settled over the land, Noah halted his horse behind the Wainwright ranch barn. From her vantage behind her brother, Sarah could see the main house, its windows glowing warmly in the blackness. Gazing at the big, wood frame dwelling, she felt a bittersweet emotion fill her.

It was now the only real home she had. Still, though it held the people she'd committed her life and love to, Sarah wasn't sure she belonged there anymore. But then, she wasn't sure *where* she belonged anymore.

"Time to get down and head on over to the house," her brother said. "Even as dark and cold as it is tonight, I can't risk someone venturing from the bunkhouse or barn and catching me here. If the Wainwrights had anything to say about it, I'm likely wanted dead or alive by now."

Sarah sighed and laid her head against him, clinging tightly to his waist. *Just one more minute. Just one more minute with you, because it might have to last me a lifetime.*

"Where will you go for the night?" she asked finally. "It's too late to make it back to the hideout, and I don't want you riding up into those mountains in the dark."

Noah chuckled. "Don't worry about me. I've still got a few friends who'll put me up. And some live closer than you might think."

"Good."

She loosened her grip about his waist and slid from the horse. She didn't, however, step away.

"Take care of yourself, and Pa, will you? And no more rustling, okay?"

"We've still got enough money left for a while. But after that, a man's got to live. Once Pa goes, though . . . well, I'm thinking I'll head west and see if I can start over."

"If you do, will you let me know somehow?"

There was no point in asking Noah to come for her when

their father was dying. He couldn't be in two places at once, and it was best he be there for their father in his final hours. Whenever that time came . . .

"I'll try to get word to you somehow." A sad smile on his lips, Noah leaned down to tug at a lock of her hair. It had always been his way of showing affection. At the memory, Sarah's eyes filled with tears. "No promises, though. It just might not be safe to do so."

"Oh, N-Noah," she whispered. "I just . . . I just don't want to part like this. Like we might never see each other again!"

"Neither do I, but it's the way things have turned out. And you're a woman now, soon to be a wife. Things would've changed between us when that happened anyway. Your own family would have to take precedence—your husband and, eventually, your children. You know that as well as I."

"Yes, I know, but I also thought we'd live near each other and would be able to visit, share holiday celebrations, special times . . ."

"At least you've got Danny. He'll be with you for a long while to come."

And you'll soon have no one, Sarah thought, then quickly shoved that painful realization from her mind. She and Noah had both made their choices and must now abide by them.

"I'll take good care of Danny. I promise."

Her brother straightened in his saddle and gathered his reins. "I know you will. Just like you've tried to take care of all of us."

She gave an unsteady laugh. "And a whole lot of good I was at it too."

"You can't live our lives for us, Sarah. You can only live your own. And that, I think, is more than enough for anyone."

With that, Noah turned his horse, whispered an "I love you, little sister," then headed off into the night.

Sarah watched him until he disappeared from view, a dark, solitary figure against the frozen backdrop of snow. Tears streamed down her cheeks. In but the span of a few days, she had lost two brothers, if in entirely different ways. And her father, well, as hard an admission as it was, she had lost him a long, long time ago.

"You can't live our lives for us, Sarah . . ."

When had she taken on that task, and why? Had she imagined it was what her dying mother had been asking when she'd requested that Sarah take care of her father and brothers? Or had it, instead, been nothing more than an excuse not to follow her own dreams and risk them failing? Whatever the motives, they'd all made choices—many of them poor ones, and many for the wrong reasons.

Turning, Sarah strode out around the barn and toward the house. It was past time to begin anew, to choose differently and more wisely. For her sake. For the sake of her brother.

She just wasn't sure anymore what those choices should be.

16

Cord both yearned for and dreaded Sarah's return. Yearned for it because he loved her and, as time passed, realized evermore how much he needed her. But also dreaded that she might return only to retrieve Danny, then make her way back to her father and brothers. *If* her one brother still even lived.

And if he didn't . . .

What would Sarah's response to that death be? What would her response to *him* be?

Maybe, though, she should be just as concerned about how *he* felt over her little outing into the mountains. There was no telling what her crazy father would do to her, especially if his son died. Cord's greatest fear was Jacob Caldwell taking out his pain-clouded revenge on his daughter, a daughter he was now convinced had betrayed him.

Fear, however, was but one of the chaotic emotions that assaulted him whenever he thought of Sarah's departure. He was equally as angry at her. How could she do something so rash, so ill-advised, at a time like this? If word got out, she could be put up on charges of aiding and abetting outlaws. Why was she so determined to risk everything, when nothing she could do would alter the tragic, downward spiral the Caldwell men had put themselves in?

He sighed, laid aside the book he was reading by the light

of the room's single oil lamp, and glanced at the clock sitting on the mantel of the library fireplace. Ten past ten.

Another day over and done, and Sarah still wasn't back. But it *had* only been two days since she'd ridden off with her brother Noah. And if her brother Caleb was lingering on, or was even recovering from his gunshot wound, there was no telling how much longer she might be.

Time I head to bed, Cord thought, pushing to his feet. *Plenty of ranch work awaits tomorrow, and I'll need a good—*

Footsteps sounded on the porch. Then, as if ridding shoes of excess snow, someone stomped right outside the front door before turning the handle and entering.

Cord tensed. *Who'd be visiting at this hour?*

Taking up the oil lamp, he headed for the entry and almost slammed into Sarah. For a long moment, they just stared at each other. Then Cord cleared his throat.

"You're home," he observed lamely, his mouth gone dry, his heart pounding at the sight of her.

"Yes." She took a step back, pulled off her mittens, and stuffed them into her coat pocket. "I'm sorry I couldn't get word to you. I'd imagine you were worried . . ."

"Only that something would happen to you, or you'd decide you'd had enough of me and come back only to fetch Danny and then be on your way."

Irritated at himself, Cord clamped down on further utterances. He could've bitten off his tongue for all the babbling he was doing. At a time like this, what mattered most was Sarah and what she'd been through, not his own fears.

"Here"—he reached for her coat as she removed it—"let me take that. You must be chilled to the bone. Go in and sit by the fire. I'll fetch you a mug of hot coffee."

She smiled wanly. "That would be wonderful. Two spoonfuls of sugar and a—"

"A splash of cream. I know."

Cord hung her coat on one of the pegs beside the front door, and headed for the kitchen. He quickly poured a steaming mug of coffee and added the sugar before finally noting that his hands were shaking. Laying aside the spoon, he paused to inhale a steadying breath, then took the cream from the icebox and splashed a bit into the coffee.

Easy there, son, he cautioned himself. *This is no time to get yourself all riled. And this certainly isn't the time to berate her for her crazy, impulsive actions or smother her with questions. Just stand back and let Sarah tell you what she wants, when she's ready. By the look of her, things didn't go well.*

He found her sitting on a stool she'd pulled close to the hearth, hunched toward the fire with hands extended. Her long, pale hair tumbled down about her shoulders like some gossamer veil. Cord swallowed hard against an intense swell of longing. It seemed like forever since he'd held her in his arms, kissed her, fingered that gloriously silken hair.

Sarah glanced up just then. Their gazes locked, and Cord was swamped by an impression of intense sorrow. Then Sarah shuttered her emotions behind a stoic façade. She rose, walked over to him, and extended a hand.

Though he wished it were him she was reaching out to, he knew it was really just for the coffee. He handed her the mug.

"Be careful. It's hot, and I filled it too full."

Gingerly, she accepted his offering. "Thank you." Sarah took a careful sip.

A faint smile teased the corner of her mouth when she finally glanced back up. "It tastes so good. I really missed Emma's coffee. No one makes it like she does."

"No, no one does." He gestured to the hearth, bright with leaping flames and fragrant with the bracing scent of burning pine. "Want to sit and talk for a while? Or would you prefer some time to yourself, with the coffee and a warm fire?"

She hesitated, then gestured to the fireplace. "If you're not too tired, I wouldn't mind some company. Especially yours."

Her response heartened him. "I'm not at all tired, now that you're back home." It was his turn to hesitate. "I've missed you, Sarah. Missed you more than you might imagine."

Briefly, humor flared in her eyes. "Oh, I don't know about that. I've got a *very* good imagination."

Cord chuckled. "Then imagine away, just as long as I'm the center of it all."

Sarah took another sip of her coffee, then used it to gesture to the fire. "Let's go sit. I've got a lot to tell you."

He followed her. When they were both seated, he leaned forward, clasping his hands between his knees. "How did things go with your brother? The one that was shot."

"He died." She looked down. "In the end, it was a peaceful death, and I think he reconciled with the Lord."

"I'm sorry, Sarah. For your loss. I know you loved him very much."

"Yes, I loved Caleb." She lifted a tear-sheened gaze. "He was so young, had so much life ahead of him. It shouldn't have happened the way it did."

What could he say to that, save to agree? "No, it shouldn't have happened the way it did."

"I'm so tired, Cord. So tired of all of this. The hatred. The fighting. The deaths."

"So am I. So am I."

A tear trickled down her cheek. Angrily, she brushed it away.

"Why won't it stop? We try so hard, you and I, and it just won't stop!"

"It's almost over. We've just got to hang on for a little while longer. And not do anything ourselves to drag it out or make it any worse." He locked gazes with her. "You and I, we've got to stay strong and not give up on each other."

When she didn't reply, an uneasy premonition washed over him. "Can you do that?" Cord reached out, took her hand. "And, more importantly, do you still even want to?"

In his own inimitable way, Cord had cut to the very heart of the matter. Even if she should—for Danny's sake at the very least—did she still want to keep on fighting and stand with Cord? Did she still wish to marry him?

Sarah had thought she had. But seeing him, being with him again, had thrown all her emotions into renewed turmoil. Her earlier doubts resurfaced. What did she really know of him? Their courtship had been brief and filled with a wild mix of happiness and pain.

How committed to her was he really? How deep did his anger and need for revenge go? Cord's unresolved feelings for his father had reemerged in a flash of fury when she'd asked him for help defending Noah and her father. He was still so torn between anger and grief over his own father's death . . .

Yet wasn't she equally torn over *her* father? And how could she be fair or judge Cord when she couldn't even make up her mind—at least not for long anyway—over what to do about family loyalties? She owed the man she'd agreed to marry better than that. Oh, if only they could both turn their backs on their fathers and all the unhappiness they'd wrought, and start their lives anew!

She wanted to do that—be strong, stand by Cord, marry him—but was it the right thing to do? Even more importantly, was it the right time? Maybe it was better to slow things down a bit, to work through all the crazy emotions and see where it took them, rather than going ahead with their wedding plans. Plans that, if not put to a halt soon, would culminate in a marriage on December 31, just another four weeks from today.

"Best you *do* marry him, girl," her father had urged just this afternoon as she was preparing to depart with Noah for the ranch. "From here on out, we'll need someone on the inside. Someone to warn us of Wainwright's plans and feed us information. Once you're his wife, after all, he'll think it's safe to tell you everything."

Jacob Caldwell chuckled grimly. "I had my doubts at first, but it's the perfect solution. We can continue to work in our own ways to destroy him, while you undermine him at home. And then, when it's all over and done with, you can deliver the final and worst blow when you leave him."

Sarah knew her father was raving mad even to consider such a plan, but it still angered her. "So, once again, you're willing to prostitute me to Cord Wainwright, just to avenge yourself against him and his family. There's not anything or anyone you'll spare in order to win, is there?"

He gave her a blank look. "But you said you wanted to marry him."

"Yes, I did. But not to betray him."

"So Caleb's death doesn't change anything for you? He just died in vain?"

"He died in vain because of *you*, Papa! Because you drove both him and Noah to commit crimes, and those crimes finally caught up with them." Sarah threw up her hands in exasperation. "Oh, what's the point of trying to reason with you anymore?"

Fury reddened her father's face. He reached out, grabbing her by the arm.

"Don't you *ever* talk to me that way again, do you hear me, girl? You just do as you're told." He released her with a jerk, causing Sarah almost to lose her balance and fall. "Now, get on with you. Noah needs to sneak you back under cover of darkness, and you've a long ride ahead. No more sassing me, do you hear?"

More than anything she'd ever wanted, Sarah wanted to tell her father that she was done obeying him. That she wasn't about to do what he asked, not now or ever again.

But Sarah also feared if she pushed her father any further, he might change his mind and not allow her to leave. And, no matter what, she didn't intend to remain with him a moment longer. So Sarah just nodded and mumbled a "Yes, Papa," and she and Noah were soon mounted up and heading back down the mountain.

Not that Cord needs to know about any of what transpired between me and Papa, she thought, recalling her attention back to the present. *Right about now, there are probably as many doubts about me in his mind as there are about him in mine.*

Help me, Lord, she thought, lifting a prayer heavenward. *Help me to know what's best for the both of us. And help me to say the right things, things that'll help him understand.*

Sarah swallowed hard, then nodded. "Yes, I still want to stand by you, Cord. I don't want to give up on what I think—I hope—we have. But the things that have happened of late . . . well, I'm not so sure we should rush into marriage. At least not in another four weeks."

His gaze narrowed. His jaw clenched.

"And why's that, Sarah?"

Blast him, she thought. *He's not going to make this easy. But then, why should I be surprised? He's always been as prickly as some pinecone.*

"Do you want me to be honest, or would you rather I dance around things and pretend all's well with us?" Though Sarah

265

tried to keep the irritation from her voice, she feared she was far from successful. "Because it *isn't* right now. We've got a lot to sort through before we can focus on a life together."

"The only thing that needs sorting through is your inability to separate yourself, once and for all, from your crazy father!"

The first tendrils of anger licked at Sarah. It took all her willpower to smother the flames.

"Yes, I'll admit to that," she replied, struggling to speak calmly. "But you've also got a lot of unresolved feelings about *your* father, and it makes you defensive and ready to fly off the handle at the least provocation."

Cord expelled a weary breath. "So, it always comes back to my refusal to defend your father and brother, doesn't it? You just won't let it go, will you?"

"On the contrary. I'll let the part go about defending my family. At the time, I was desperate and not thinking straight. I was unfair to you." Sarah paused, considering how best to word what she was next to say. "The part I won't let go is your unwillingness—or maybe even your inability—to forgive. Because it eats at you, Cord, and makes you so unhappy. And I'm afraid, so afraid, that if you don't find some way to forgive, you'll end up like . . . l-like my f-father."

As if she were speaking gibberish, he stared uncomprehendingly at her. Despair filled her. He didn't understand or, worse, didn't want to understand.

Tears welled, trickled down her cheeks. Sarah clasped her arms about her.

"I-I don't think this was such a good idea," she whispered, her voice clogging. "It's late and we're both tired. I-I think I'll head up to bed."

Just as she stood and turned to go, Cord groaned out her name. He climbed to his feet and swiftly covered the space separating them. Taking her into his arms, he pulled her close.

"No," he said, "this *is* a good idea. We've got to start talking to each other. No matter what, we can't keep tiptoeing around each other and the things that are bothering us. It's no way to begin a life together."

Despite the harsh words they'd so recently shared, it felt so good to be held, to feel Cord's strong arms about her. Sarah clung to him like one drowning. The tears came in earnest then, and she wept long and hard.

Wept for Caleb. Wept for the shattered dreams of a happy family and a father she could trust and depend upon. Wept for the sense of isolation from and tension between her and Cord that had been going on for much too long. And wept in relief, that though there were still unresolved issues between them, he finally seemed willing to meet her halfway, to try and work things out.

"Y-yes," she croaked out the word. "We've got to k-keep talking. It's the honest and loving thing to do."

Ever so tenderly, Cord kissed her on the forehead. "I love you, Sarah. No matter what, I don't want to lose you. And certainly not because of my father or your father. We can't let them destroy what we have. We just can't!"

A fierce resolve filled her. Maybe she didn't know everything about him. But what she did know was enough. Cord had the courage to face what needed to be done to heal the breach between them, and that gave her renewed hope for a life together.

"No, we can't let them—or anyone—destroy what we have." She leaned back and looked into his eyes. "Do you still want to marry me on New Year's Eve?"

Joy warmed his eyes and made him smile. "Yes. But I don't want to rush you into anything."

She chuckled softly. "Oh, maybe we are still rushing things a bit. But being held in your arms also reminded me how much I want—I need—to be married to you. And I think, if we just keep talking things out, we'll be fine."

Sarah smiled softly. "Indeed, more than fine."

The following day, and with great trepidation, Sarah took Danny aside to tell him about Caleb. Understandably, the little boy was very upset when he learned of his brother's death, and wept long and hard. Unfortunately, it also set off an asthma attack.

For the next hour, the entire household labored to bring Danny back under control, having him breathe in copious amounts of steam and take the remaining medicine Doc Saunders had given them at the last attack, now almost three months ago. Blessedly, this time the symptoms abated far more quickly than before, even though Danny continued to sniffle off and on about his brother for the rest of the day.

Once again, Sarah was grateful for all the support, both physical and emotional, that Cord, Nick, and the others provided. It only reconfirmed the rightness of her decision to go ahead and marry Cord as originally planned. This was where she and Danny both belonged. This was now home.

In the ensuing days the wedding plans that, in the past two weeks had noticeably slowed, picked up with a vengeance. Invitations were penned and delivered. The wedding reception to be held at Ashton's church after the ceremony was planned, and food stores checked for available ingredients, before a shopping list was made. Finally, just four days before Christmas in the last flurry of holiday baking, decorating, and gift wrapping, the time came for Sarah's final fitting of her wedding dress.

A storm had blown in the night before, dropping several inches of fresh snow, but the morning of that next day dawned sunny, calm, and clear. As Sarah and Emma pulled on their coats and mittens in preparation for a visit to town and the dressmaker, Danny ran up.

"Can I come? Can I come?" her brother asked, hopping from one foot to the other, his blue eyes bright with hope. "With all the storms and cold, I haven't been able to go to town in a month of Sundays!"

At Danny's rather gross exaggeration, it was all Sarah could do not to roll her eyes. "In actuality, little brother, it's only been—"

"I need to do some Christmas shopping!" he said, cutting her off in midsentence. "And this might be my only chance before Christmas."

"Christmas shopping?" She eyed him suspiciously. "And exactly when did you come into any money to buy anything?"

"Golly, I didn't steal nothing." Danny heaved an injured sigh. "Mr. Nick gave me some money and asked me to buy some presents for everyone." He dug in his pocket, pulling out several bills, which he showed to her. "See?"

Remorse instantly filled Sarah. She was overreacting just because stealing seemed to run in her family these days. She squatted before her brother and took him by both arms.

"I'm sorry. I guess I jumped the gun a bit, didn't I?"

"Yeah, I guess you did," he agreed solemnly. "So, can I go with you and Emma?"

After a moment's hesitation, she nodded. "You have to be patient, though, while I try on my wedding dress. It could get a little boring. And you have to dress warm and wear a muffler over your nose and mouth whenever we're outside, okay?"

"Sure." Danny's grin was wide and joyous. "I don't care how much time it takes for you to try on your dress, just as long as I can go shopping afterward."

"I guess that can be arranged." Sarah shot the housekeeper

a questioning glance. "Would that work out all right for you, Emma?"

"Sure it would. And maybe, if there's time, we can even stop by the Wildflower Café for a piece of pie before heading home."

"Oh, that'd be swell." Her brother shoved the money back in his pocket and grabbed his own coat from the lower row of pegs near the front door. "I can't wait!"

An hour later, they pulled up in front of Edith Wolfe's dress shop. The trip to town had gone well, the ranch sleigh gliding smoothly over the fresh snow. While Emma tied the horse to the hitching post in front of the dress shop, Sarah helped Danny down from the front seat.

"Now, whatever you do," she cautioned him as they climbed onto the boardwalk, "you're not to say a word to Cord about my dress. The groom isn't supposed to see it or know what it looks like until he sees the bride in it on the wedding day. So, can you keep a secret?"

"Of course I can. I'm not some baby, you know!"

She had to smile at his show of righteous indignation, Sarah thought as she opened the door and ushered her brother inside. He was going to be eight years old next month, and was growing up. He indeed wasn't her baby brother anymore, but getting to be a big boy.

A big boy who resembled his two older brothers more and more with each passing day. Well, one living and one dead brother anyway, she corrected herself with a fleeting stab of pain, then quickly brushed that thought aside. The memory of Caleb's recent demise was still very, very tender, and tears frequently hovered on the brink of falling.

Today, however, was to be a day of fun and happiness. For her sake but, even more, for Danny's sake. He too mourned his brother. Though she tried to shield him from the worst of the news about his father and brothers, he had always been a very sensitive, perceptive child. Probably came with the territory, Sarah mused, when so much of one's life had to be spent as a semi-invalid, with not much else to do but listen and observe.

That was going to change, and indeed had already begun to do so, since Danny had come to the ranch. His asthma attacks had dramatically lessened, and the few he'd had were far less severe. He played outside a lot more, weather permitting, and had even made some friends at church. In time, Sarah hoped he'd be healthy enough to attend regular school. More than anything, she wanted for Danny to live as normal a life as possible.

As they entered the little dress shop, the bell over the door tinkled. Edith Wolfe immediately hurried out from the back fitting room. At the sight of Sarah, Emma, and Danny, she broke into a smile.

"Oh, I'm so glad you were able to come today," the tall, thin spinster exclaimed. "I wasn't sure how the roads to town were, and after last night's snow . . ."

"We took the sleigh and hadn't any problems getting here," Sarah said as she removed her mittens, coat, and hat, then proceeded to help Danny with his. She laid the coats and other paraphernalia on a nearby bench.

"Are you excited to see your dress, now that it's finished?"

Edith's question sent a shiver of happy anticipation through Sarah. "Yes, indeed. Will you help me get it on?"

The seamstress motioned her in the direction of the back room. "It'll be my pleasure." She glanced at Emma and Danny. "Why don't you both wait out here? Once Sarah's dressed, she can come out and show off her gown. In the meanwhile, there's a pot of hot water in that kettle over yonder"—she pointed toward the potbellied stove in the corner—"and there

271

are mugs and tea, plus some fresh sugar cookies I made this morning on the counter."

Danny didn't need a second invitation. He immediately made a beeline for the plate of cookies.

Emma smiled and shook her head. "You two go and get on that dress. I'll make sure Danny doesn't eat all of the cookies. At least not in the next few minutes anyway."

Chuckling, the two women headed to the fitting room and, less than ten minutes later, Sarah was garbed in her wedding dress. The dress had originally been Mary Wainwright's, but she was a much taller, larger-boned woman than Sarah. Edith had finally decided it best to open all the seams and essentially use the ivory silk and lace fabric to craft an entirely new dress to fit Sarah.

A row of tiny, silk-covered buttons fastened the cuffs of the tight, long sleeves of a gown of alternating silk and lace panels that ran full length from shoulder to the long hem, ending in a train of ribbon and lace. The waist was fitted, the neckline off the shoulder, and the matching veil of lace and silk flowed from a pretty coronet of silk roses.

Gazing at herself in the tall dressing mirror, Sarah thought she must be dreaming. The dress and veil were exquisite. Never had she imagined she'd be wearing something as fine as this to her wedding. But then, she'd never imagined ever marrying. Her life was to be dedicated to taking care of her brothers and father.

But no more. No more.

Her gaze met Edith's in the mirror. Both women smiled.

"Guess we shouldn't keep Emma and Danny in suspense, should we?" Sarah asked.

"No, you shouldn't."

At the sight of her, Emma's eyes grew wide then immediately filled with tears. Danny's mouth dropped open.

"Wow, Sarah!" her brother said. "You look beautiful."

"Do you think so?" She bent down, picked up her train, then whirled around.

Danny laughed and clapped his hands.

"I can't wait to see the expression on Cord's face when he first sees you, child," Emma said, hastily swiping at her tears. "He's going to near swoon from joy."

"Now that's a picture," Sarah said with a chuckle. "Cord swooning, I mean."

For several minutes more, she basked in the attention and admiration, then turned to Edith. "Thank you so much for all your work. The dress is lovely. You're a true artist."

The seamstress beamed. "Only a woman as beautiful as you could do the dress justice. But I thank you for your kind words. It does my heart good to have my work so appreciated."

"We have a bit of shopping to do, then would like to stop at the Wildflower Café for a short while." Sarah began unbuttoning the cuffs of her sleeves. "Could you hold the gown until our return?"

"Of course." Edith stepped aside so Sarah could make her way back to the fitting room. "It'll be wrapped and waiting for you."

Fifteen minutes later, dressed and bundled back in her coat, mittens, and hat, Sarah followed Danny and Emma from the dress shop. Just as she closed the door behind them, a man and woman walked from the Wildflower Café. Their voices, angry and strident, carried across and down the street.

Sarah's head jerked up, and she turned in the direction of the arguing couple. At that moment, the woman slapped the man's face, then wheeled around and stalked away. Emma shot a startled glance over her shoulder at Sarah.

The cause of the housekeeper's shock wasn't hard to fathom. They both knew the man and woman. They were none other than Allis Findley and Spencer Womack.

273

17

New Year's Day, the morning after their wedding, Sarah awoke to sunshine spilling through Cord's bedroom window. *Rather*, she quickly corrected herself as she yawned and stretched, *Cord's and* my *bedroom window. But that'll take some getting used to, I suppose. In fact, married life in general will take some getting used to.*

She glanced tenderly at the man sleeping beside her. One arm flung up over his head, Cord slumbered on, apparently dreaming deep and peacefully. Not that she could blame him. They *had* spent a goodly part of the night, after all had finally retired to their beds, enjoying each other's company in a variety of delightful ways.

Cord was a surprisingly gentle and considerate lover. But then, she had equally surprised herself. Almost from the start, Sarah hadn't felt any shyness or hesitation around him. And her unabashed ardor, she soon discovered, had immensely pleased her new husband.

Then, of course, Sarah mused, as she perused Cord's bare chest and arms, she *did* have the most handsome and fit of husbands. All that boxing, which he still practiced almost daily with a leather punching bag hung in one corner of the barn, kept him in prime physical condition. A prime physical condition, she thought as she reached out and languidly traced a line from his collarbone down his chest to his muscled abdomen, that she was more than happy to admire.

Her touch must have finally woken him. Cord stirred and, as she continued her tactile exploration, smiled. He laid a hand over hers.

"Best you not start something you don't want to finish," he growled, his voice still husky with sleep.

Sarah giggled. She lay down beside him and snuggled close. "What makes you think I don't want to finish what I started?"

A chuckle rumbled from deep within his chest. "I read you right the very first time I met you. You're nothing but a little flirt."

"Only with my husband." She smiled. "Only with you."

"Well, I don't know about that. You seemed like you knew exactly what you were doing that day at the barn."

"And that knowledge amounted to exactly everything I'd observed or heard the crib girls say to passing cowboys, whenever we happened to ride through that part of town. The rest"—she shrugged—"I just made up as I went."

Cord shot her a teasing grin. "Well, wife, you just keep making up things to your heart's content. I'll be more than happy to be the recipient of any and everything you care to try."

Sarah laughed, shoved to one elbow, and stared down at him. "Oh, I'll just bet you will. You're not the only one who read the other right, that day—"

A tentative knock sounded at their bedroom door.

Cord scowled. "Who is it?"

"I'm sorry, Cord," Emma's voice came from the other side. "I wouldn't bother you and Sarah unless it was important. But Spencer Womack's waiting downstairs and needs to talk to you pronto. He said more of the cattle have gone missing."

For an instant, Cord went still. Then, with a low curse, he

pushed up, flung aside the covers, and climbed out of bed. With an angry, jerky motion, he grabbed his trousers from a nearby chair.

"Thank you, Emma," he called to the housekeeper. "Tell Spence I'll be down in five minutes."

As the sound of the older woman's footsteps retreated down the hallway, Sarah sat up and drew the comforter close, fighting back a swell of nausea. She watched Cord pull on his denims, socks, boots, and then fling on a flannel shirt he'd retrieved from the wardrobe.

Not now, Lord. Please, not now. Can't we have just a little bit of peace and happiness together, before all the trouble starts again? Just a little bit of time to strengthen our relationship, to learn how to stand firm together as man and wife?

"Because some cattle are missing doesn't mean Papa and Noah are back to rustling," she finally managed to choke out. "I already told you how sick my father is these days. And Noah said they still had plenty of money, and he didn't aim to start thieving anytime soon, if ever again."

His fingers rapidly fastening his shirt buttons, Cord wheeled around to face her. "Maybe it *isn't* them this time. I hope and pray that's the case. Not that we can afford to keep losing cattle, no matter who's stealing them."

He unbuttoned his pants and shoved his shirttails inside, then refastened them, threaded a belt through the loops, and finished by quickly brushing his hair. Halfheartedly, he ran his hand over his beard-shadowed jaw, then shook his head. With a sigh, Cord turned to face her.

"I'll return as soon as I can, but likely Spence and I will have to head out with some hands to reconnoiter the situation. So, I don't know exactly when I'll be home."

"Do what needs to be done." Sarah forced a brave smile for his benefit as he headed to the door then paused to glance back at her. "One way or another, I'll be here, waiting for you, when you get home."

A fleeting expression of sadness mixed with regret flashed across his face. "That's the best thing you could say, Mrs. Wainwright. And just thinking of you waiting for me will make me ride back as fast as I can. Nothing's going to keep me away from you for long. That much I can promise."

"The signs are exactly the same as before," Cord informed Sarah, Nick, and their two sisters later that evening when he and the other men finally returned. "Two unshod horses heading west into the mountains. And, like all the other times, we tracked the cattle into the high country before their prints finally disappeared on the rocky terrain."

Nick fingered his mug of hot cocoa, then met his brother's glance down the length of the kitchen table where everyone was seated. "Well, unshod horses don't tell us much. Indians aren't the only ones who don't shoe their animals. Plenty of locals have unshod horses too."

"Yeah," Cord muttered, clamping down hard on his growing frustration. "The Caldwells being one of them."

At the mention of her family, Sarah's head shot up. She opened her mouth as if to say something, then quickly shut it. Cord would've bitten off his tongue if the action could've taken back his rancorous words, but he couldn't. So he instead mumbled an apologetic "Sorry" and shook his head.

"So, what's the plan this time?" his brother asked before taking a sip of his cocoa. "Same as before?"

Cord expelled a weary breath. "Pretty much. The hands will have to resume taking shifts to guard the herd. There's just too many cattle to bring them in close to the ranch. Or, leastwise," he added with a grim smile, "there are so far. In time, if the rustlers keep whittling away at the herd, we'll only have to lock what little we have left in the barns."

"If I knew where they were," Sarah piped up just then, "I'd bring you to them. But I don't know. I swear to you, Cord. I don't know."

"Angel, he never said anything about you keeping secrets from us," Nick began, looking to Sarah. "We know you'd help us any way you could."

"Yes, I would." Sarah glanced beseechingly at Cord, and the anguish burning in her eyes tore at his heart. "I'm just so tired of all this. So fed up. And if I was certain Papa and Noah were at it again—"

She threw up her hands, then jumped to her feet. "I-I'm sorry. I just can't . . . I just can't deal with this right now." She bolted from the kitchen.

Shiloh and Jordan impaled him with angry glares, then rose and hurried after her.

Cord watched Sarah and his sisters leave, not knowing what to say to calm his wife or convince her to stay. *If* he even wanted her there just now. He was in a foul mood, and had been so since the moment Emma informed him of Spence's arrival and the reason for his visit. He wasn't good company for anyone right now, but most especially not for his brand-new wife.

"This is lousy timing," his brother softly interjected just then. "One could almost imagine someone isn't very happy about your and Sarah's marriage."

"Well, it's not hard to figure out who that would be, is it?" Cord demanded with a sharp laugh.

"Might be harder than you'd think. Holed up in the mountains like they are, I wonder how much news gets to the Caldwells very often."

"Meaning what?" Cord eyed him narrowly.

Nick shrugged. "Meaning, who else might hold a grudge against us, or against you and Sarah for marrying?"

"Can't think of anyone offhand who'd be mad enough at us to do something as lamebrained as stealing our cattle. Aside from the Caldwells, of course." Puzzlement furrowed Cord's brow. "And, as far as anyone mad at Sarah and me for getting married, Allis is likely the only one who might've taken it badly. Can't see her rustling our cattle, though." He chuckled wryly. "Leastwise, not unless she's got some talents she's keeping well hidden from everyone."

His brother paused to take another swallow from his mug. "Well, all I know is this isn't a one-man operation, and from what Sarah's told us of her father's worsening heart condition, I'm inclined to doubt he's able to do anything as strenuous as cattle rustling anymore. Which leaves us with—"

"With discovering who else might be picking up where the Caldwells left off?" Cord finished for him. "I suppose we've got to be open to other suspects. According to Sarah, though, the Caldwells have plenty of our money left. But her brother could just as easily have hired a few malcontents or men down on their luck to help him, now that his father likely can't. There are plenty of failed prospectors out there these days with barely two pennies to scrape together."

Nick sighed and rubbed his jaw. "Yes, there are. Still, though the Caldwells are the ones who got caught red-handed, I hope it's not them this time. I want all this feuding and strife with them over and done with. For our sakes, their sakes, but most importantly, for your and Sarah's sake."

Cord gave a grunt of agreement. "It'd be nice to have some peace and quiet to work on our marriage." He laughed, the sound harsh. "And maybe enjoy a honeymoon of sorts, even if we can only afford to have it here at the ranch."

"Don't worry, little brother. Once things settle down a bit, you and Sarah can have a real honeymoon." He paused. "Just as long as it's not in New York City, of course."

"And why's that? Afraid we might decide to stay there, and I'd go back to my law practice?"

"Something like that." Nick finished his cocoa and set down the mug. "Seriously, what *are* your plans, now that you've finally gone and taken a wife? Assuming you've even spoken with Sarah about the possibility of returning to New York City."

"Actually, the subject hasn't come up yet."

"Why's that?"

Cord shrugged. "Probably a combination of things. The ongoing upheaval in both of our lives, courtesy of our fathers. Our rather tumultuous and whirlwind romance. And, I secretly suspect, Sarah's assumed now that Pa's died that I'll stay on to help you run the ranch."

"Can't say as how I'd mind that. I could use a little of your brawn to complement my brains."

"Oh, so that's how it is?" Cord chuckled. "Even after all these years, I'm still just the youngest with nothing of value to contribute save the sweat of my brow."

Nick smiled. "Hardly, but for old time's sake if for nothing else, I thought that fiddle was worth playing one last time." He leaned forward, his expression growing serious. "Let's be honest here, Cord. To make a success of this ranch, not only do I need that sharp, analytical mind of yours, but I need your eyes, ears, and legs. Someone has to be out there with the hands, go on the roundups, and be a presence to be reckoned with. And you possess all that and more."

"Not to mention you'd like to keep Sarah around."

"Well, I'll admit that thought also crossed my mind." Nick straightened in his wheelchair. "What can I say? I like having my family nearby, and you and Sarah—and Danny now too—are the only family I've got."

"Family . . ." Cord chewed on that for a moment, then glanced up. "Never thought I'd say this, but I kind of like the idea of family myself. It was never the ranch, you know, that I hated. It was just Pa, plain and simple."

"And maybe it wasn't really Pa you hated, but more the pain and rejection he liked to throw your way," his brother offered gently.

"Yeah. Maybe that was more what it was."

Nick cocked his head and studied Cord. "You're beginning to get over it, aren't you? The pain and anger you felt toward Pa."

Cord shrugged. "Maybe. Is it that apparent?"

"In a lot of little ways. The tone of your voice right now. And the fact that you didn't heap all the blame on Pa." He smiled. "Just your whole manner has changed, and I noticed it beginning the day Pa died."

"Actually, it began that night we rode out after the cattle, that first time the Caldwells rustled them. Pa and I finally started talking a bit, and it was like something hard and impenetrable came crashing down between us."

"So, you're beginning to forgive and let it go."

Am I? The question that sounded in his mind gave Cord pause. He'd never thought he'd ever forgive his father for all those years of misery and recrimination. But the effort required to maintain those unpleasant emotions now seemed more trouble than it was worth. He had more important, more happy things to address. Like Sarah, their marriage, and the anticipation of a new life here at the ranch.

Cord scratched his jaw. "Yeah, I reckon so. It doesn't mean I'm ready to march off to church every Sunday, though. God and I still have some things to work through."

"Take all the time you need. God's not like Pa. He's not aloof and judgmental. Far, far from it. And He's quite patient, especially when it comes to a prodigal child."

"A prodigal child, am I?" Cord's mouth quirked. "Well, maybe I am. Maybe I am."

"In the meantime, while you're busy working out things with the Lord," Nick said, "use the opportunity to build the kind of family and life you've always wanted. Always deserved."

At the kind, encouraging words, gratitude filled Cord. He was so blessed to have Nick for his brother. Nick had always been there for him. Nick had tried, as best he could, to play the peacemaker between him and their father. And, without thought to the gaping hole it would create in his own life, Nick had always supported Cord's dream to seek a better existence far from the ranch and their sire's disapproving presence.

It was time—no, past time—to pay his brother back, to support *him*. And, because the ranch was all Nick knew and had ever wanted, Cord would give up his old life back East and remain here. Remain in Colorado, in the land the Indians had long ago named the Shining Mountains, and rebuild his life.

Rebuild it with his family around him. And maybe, just maybe, even rebuild it with the Lord God Himself. Stranger things had happened, he thought, surprisingly at peace with the idea. The turn his life had taken of late was proof enough.

Somehow, though, there was hope where none had existed before. And he had all the time in the world to wait now, to let life be, to allow things to unfold. For he wasn't alone anymore. He had family. He had the Lord. He was loved.

And that certainty, more than anything he'd ever known, filled Cord with a sweet, soul-searing joy.

"Emma, what would you recommend for an upset stomach?" Sarah asked one morning over a month and a half later.

"I don't know what I ate, but the last few mornings I've felt so queasy and out of sorts."

The housekeeper smiled, finished kneading the mound of dough that would soon be baking into a crusty loaf of bread, and covered it with a cloth before turning to Sarah. "Queasy, out of sorts, and sleeping far later these days than usual," she said by way of agreement as she wiped her floured hands on her apron. "Doesn't surprise me a bit. Just didn't expect it quite so soon, is all."

Sarah frowned and stepped farther into the kitchen. "What doesn't surprise you? You're not making any sense."

"Aren't I?" Emma ambled to the sink with the bowl she'd used to mix the bread dough, and began filling it with water. "Well, before I say more, why don't you shut that door so the news isn't common knowledge long before you're ready to share it?"

Not at all certain what the other woman was getting at, Sarah walked back and closed the kitchen door. "Fine. It's now our little secret," she said as she returned to stand at the sink beside the housekeeper. "Whatever the secret really is."

As she continued to scrub out the bowl, Emma sent her a slanting glance. "You're with child, of course. It's quite evident."

A quick glance down at her belly did little to confirm Emma's pronouncement. Her midsection was washboard flat. Sarah looked up.

"No, that's not possible. How could I be . . . ?"

She blushed. Of course it was possible. She was now a married woman.

Though there were still times when things were strained between her and Cord—primarily when a few more cattle were noted to be missing and the subject of her father and Noah inevitably came up—there seemed to be nothing strained about their relationship in the marital bed. There, above all else, they were happy and fulfilled, not to mention completely relaxed with each other.

"But it hasn't been that long since my . . ."

Sarah's voice faded. *Actually, it has been almost six weeks since I last had my woman's courses,* she thought as she did a swift calculation. *But I've been late before, if only by a few days at the very most. Surely, though, there hasn't been enough time to know for certain.*

"I'm sure in just another day or so . . ."

Once more the words died as she saw the knowing look in the other woman's eyes. Sarah swallowed hard. There were other signs, signs that her body was changing. Signs she'd tried to ignore, thinking they were of little import and would soon disappear.

Her hand slipped to her belly. "Do you think . . . do you think it *could* be possible?"

Emma nodded. "Oh yes indeed, honey. In fact, I'd wager it's nigh on to a certainty."

Tears filled Sarah's eyes. "A baby. I'm going to have a baby!"

"Yes, you are," the housekeeper softly agreed. She wiped her hands on a towel, hurried over, and engulfed Sarah in a hug. "Oh yes, you are!"

After a moment, Emma leaned back. "So, when are you going to tell Cord the good news?"

Her question took Sarah by surprise. Cord. The discussion of children hadn't actually come up yet. Neither of them, she supposed, had imagined she would become pregnant so quickly. And there was still so much to resolve between them. She'd thought they had plenty of time to get to know each other, to settle into their marriage a bit more . . .

Not for the first time, Sarah wondered if they hadn't rushed into getting married. Yet, whenever she caught a passing glimpse of him throughout the day, her mouth always went dry and her pulse quickened. And when they retired each night into the cozy privacy of their bedroom and she snuggled against the comforting warmth of his big, strong body, her misgivings were soon replaced with far more pleasurable concerns.

No, there wasn't any doubt Cord loved her and she loved him. That much, at the very least, she knew deep down to the depths of her soul.

And he was good with children. Sarah had repeatedly seen that in his interactions with Danny. Her husband possessed surprising patience coupled with a gentle attentiveness that warmed her heart. And he wasn't above a good snowball fight or allowing her little brother to tag along with him when he went riding out to check the cattle or do most chores. No, it wasn't Cord's ability to be a good father that gave Sarah pause.

"I'm not sure," she said, finally meeting the older woman's gaze. "I think I'll give it a few more weeks, just to be certain. Cord's got a lot on his mind these days. There's no sense adding to it prematurely."

For a long moment, Emma didn't say a word. Then she nodded.

"Well, I'm not thinking the news that he's going to be a father would add to his burdens or upset him. More the opposite, instead. Still, it's your prerogative to share the news when you see fit. In the meanwhile, your secret's safe with me."

Sarah managed a grateful smile. "Thank you, Emma." She sighed. "Maybe it's just me. Maybe I just need time to mull it all over. To carry it close and get a little more used to the fact that I'm going to be a mother."

"To keep all these things, and ponder them in your heart . . ."
The quote from the Gospel of Luke, making mention of

how Mary, the mother of God, had savored the wonders of her Son's birth, seemed apropos just then. Sarah felt a deepened kinship with Mary, a bond that many women must feel when they first discover they are to bear a child.

Keep all these things, and ponder them in your heart . . .

"Yes," she replied as, yet again, she laid a hand gently, tenderly over her belly. "This is a special time, isn't it? A special, sacred time."

Once more, Emma nodded. "It is indeed, child. It is indeed."

✌︎﹏✌︎ **18** ✌︎﹏✌︎

Cord slammed the letter down on his desk. *Why, when it seems things can't get any worse*, he asked himself, *does yet another calamity raise its ugly head?*

He stared at the sheet of fine stationery with its embossed header of Stengel, Matthews, and Joslin, Attorneys-at-Law. It was dated the seventeenth of January, exactly one month ago. Considering the winter weather and slowed delivery up in the mountains, the letter had made it in reasonably good time.

The Denver legal firm claimed to represent the rancher from whom his father had purchased the second bull, after the first one's untimely death. Not only the ill-fated bull that had soon upped and died but his replacement as well. Two bulls now that his father had failed to pay for. Two bulls about which his father had also failed to consult with his sons before buying.

Fleetingly, renewed anger at Edmund Wainwright surged through Cord. With an effort, he quashed it. Nothing was served blaming a dead man.

His father had always tried to do what he deemed best for the ranch. And improving the bloodlines of their herd was long overdue. If only his sire had been a better manager of his money . . .

As he refolded the letter and shoved it back into its envelope, Cord considered his options. So far, he'd managed to successfully hold off the bank on the first bull. He might also be able to buy a bit more time with the second animal, in attempting to draw things out by a back and forth correspondence. But that could just as easily irritate both the lawyers and their client to the point they might go through with their threatened lien on the ranch.

The odds of winning an agreement to spread out payments would be better served in a face-to-face meeting. A meeting that, of necessity, would entail his traveling to Denver as soon as possible.

Not that the middle of a Colorado winter, especially considering that the ongoing cattle rustling had yet to be resolved, was the best time to leave the ranch. But then, Cord thought as he pushed back his chair, rose, and headed off to find Nick and Sarah, when had anything lately gone his way? Well, gone his way at least when it came to the ranch, he added, his mood brightening as he left the study and caught sight of his beautiful young wife on her way to the kitchen.

In all the ways that *really* mattered, things had most definitely gone his way the day he'd first met Sarah.

"I could help, you know," Sarah offered the next day as she watched Cord finish packing his satchel with the clothes he'd need in Denver.

Her husband glanced up, a quizzical expression on his face. "With my packing, you mean?"

"No." From her perch on the side of the bed, she shook her head. "With helping pay back the money for the bulls. It's not like I don't bear some responsibility for your current financial situation, after all."

"I don't blame you, Sarah." He managed a smile, then

looked down and snapped his satchel shut. "You at least were willing to pay it back."

She slid off the bed and walked over to stand before him. "I know, but I still feel badly about the robbery. And, right now with money so tight, I thought I could maybe take Ruth Ann at the Wildflower Café up on her offer to work there. Any and every bit of extra money can only help, at least until things settle down."

Cord sighed, set aside his satchel, and took her by both arms. "First, it wouldn't make sense to get a job in town unless you lived there. And I'm sure hoping *that* isn't in your plans. Second, it wouldn't instill a lot of confidence right now in any of our other creditors to see my wife working. And third, maybe I'm a bit too big and proud for my britches, but I really don't like the idea of my wife having to take an outside job to help support the ranch."

Sarah gazed up at him in frustration. Though she hated to admit it, for the most part, Cord was right. It'd be difficult and sometimes even impossible to make it to town during the winter. And they most certainly didn't need any other creditors calling in their loans just now. But the part about him not wanting her to help out in trying to save the ranch . . .

"I won't argue with you about the first two reasons," she said, trying to choose her words carefully, "and for the time being, I'll respect your pride. But I am now your wife. This ranch is my home, its people are now my family, and I'm not one to stand by and not pitch in when and where help is needed. So just take that under advisement, Mr. Cord Wainwright. If things get much worse, I mean."

Tenderness flared in his dark eyes. Cord leaned down, kissed her, then pulled back.

"If things get much worse, not only will I be sending you out to tend tables at the Café," he said with a grin, "but I'll be getting Nick to hawk apples on the boardwalk and Danny to sing songs with his little tin cup held out for donations. But not just yet, okay? I'm not at the end of my rope just yet. I have a few more ideas up my sleeve."

Relief filled her. Though it was quite apparent Cord had a proudly stubborn streak, she hadn't had much opportunity to feel him out about it. It was good to know he could be made to see reason if need be.

"Okay. Just don't leave me out. I deserve to know what's going on and be valued for what I can contribute."

He released her arms and paused to gently stroke her cheek. "Oh, you're very much valued, sweetheart. Very, very much.

"Now"—he leaned down, picked up his satchel, and straightened—"the sooner I set out and get this unpleasant business settled in Denver, the sooner I can head home. So, if you don't mind, Mrs. Wainwright . . ."

Sarah stepped aside. "Yes, please do. Head back home just as soon as you can. It's not like we've been married all that long, you know. And we still have a lot of 'getting to know each other' left to do."

Her husband chuckled as he paused at their bedroom door. "You sure know what to say to motivate a man, don't you, wife?"

"I suppose I do," she said with a giggle. "But then, who wouldn't when they've got such a good teacher?"

Ten days later, with a weary sigh, Sarah paused yet again in her dusting of the parlor and headed out into the foyer. Danny and Pedro, full of high spirits and pent-up energy after the past two days of frigid weather that had kept both man and beast inside, were at it again. The first time, she had broken up their racing pell-mell down the hall, which had rattled not only the floors but nearly the whole house as well.

This time, they were playing checkers in the library, which of itself was a benign enough game. Every time one boy apparently jumped the other's piece, however, it was accompanied by shouts of victory and loud stomping of feet. Innocent and understandable noise which under most circumstances, considering their housebound situation, Sarah could've tolerated.

But Nick was having a bout of the severe leg and lower back pain he experienced from time to time, and she and Emma had only recently gotten him comfortable with a combination of massage and a dose of laudanum. He desperately needed sleep. The two boys, though, weren't aiding that sleep in any shape, form, or fashion.

"Okay," Sarah announced as she walked into the library. "Time for a break for some sugar cookies and milk."

Her brother slammed down his checker piece and leaped to his feet. "Swell! Let's go, Pedro."

Sarah grabbed Danny as he raced by. "Hold on there, young man." She managed a stern look. "Walk quietly. No running. How many times do I have to remind you that Nick's trying to sleep?"

"Oh, I forgot. Sorry."

She released him. "I know. Luckily, the sun's starting to shine and the wind's dying down. I'm thinking you two can head outside pretty soon. Just hang on a bit longer, will you?"

Pedro and Danny both nodded solemnly. "Yes, ma'am."

They made their way to the kitchen with admirable decorum, save for Danny only once jabbing Pedro in the ribs, and the older boy returning the favor. It seemed, with her brother's much more stable good health these days, all the vigor of a boy his age had returned with a vengeance. A two-edged sword, it was, but one she welcomed more times than not. With a roll of her eyes, Sarah started back to the parlor when she heard the bell tingle in Nick's room.

"Great," she muttered. "They managed to wake Nick anyway."

She hurried down the hall and gently rapped at his door. "Nick?"

"C-come in."

His reply, sounding almost like a moan, didn't bode well. Sarah opened the door and walked in.

Nick lay on his bed near the window, his hands fisted knuckle white, clutching his blanket, his face contorted in pain. Concern swelled within. She rushed to his side.

"Has it started up again? The pain, I mean?"

"Y-yes," he all but gasped out. "I tried to relax and th-think of other things, pray even, but n-nothing seemed to work for long."

Sarah glanced at the nickel-plated alarm clock on the bedside table. They'd given Nick a dose of laudanum about two hours ago. Technically, it was a bit too soon to give him any more. Doc Saunders, however, had also instructed them that the usual dose could, if necessary, be doubled. Taking another look at Nick's contorted, sweat-dampened features, Sarah decided this was one of those times.

She grabbed the laudanum sitting on the bedside table and poured a second dose into the spoon. After setting the bottle aside, she bent over him and slid a hand beneath his head to lift it.

"Here, take this." Sarah offered him the reddish brown colored liquid. "Maybe this is just one of those times when you need a larger dose to help the pain."

He took it almost eagerly, which was confirmation in itself that Nick was hurting badly. Most times, he was the last one to ask for something to ease his pain, and would only accept the smallest dose necessary. Her heart went out to him. He was always so strong, so brave in the face of his horrible, life-altering injury.

"Is there something I could do to help?" she asked as she laid the spoon back beside the laudanum. "Would you like me to read to you or rub your back and—"

A loud crash sounded somewhere in the house. Sarah jumped, bumping the bedside table. She reached out to right it as the bottle of laudanum teetered and fell. With a gasp, Sarah grabbed for the medicine and missed. The little container hit the hard plank floor and shattered.

"Oh no!" she wailed, gazing down as the remainder of the liquid opium drained onto the floor. "That was our last bottle. I'm so sorry, Nick!"

"It's okay," he replied, shooting her a wan, pain-wracked smile. "We can g-get more. Maybe you should go see what broke, though. Since it's Emma's d-day off, and Manuela's sick . . ."

His reminder of the cause for the ruined bottle of laudanum jerked Sarah's thoughts back to two boys who were now in *very* big trouble. "I can well imagine *who* broke something, even if I've yet to find out what," she ground out in irritation.

A weak smile tipped one corner of Nick's mouth. "Well, don't go too h-hard on the boys. Cord and I sure br-broke our fair share of things in our youth too."

"Yes, boys will be boys," she said, "but I've been after them all morning to calm down. I'm about ready to dump them both outside in the snow, I am." She glanced down at the broken bottle. "I'll be back in a few minutes with something to clean up the mess. Once I've again settled down some wild young men, of course."

"I'll be here. Got no place else to go today."

She smiled at him tenderly. Already, the extra dose of medication was beginning to work, if the relaxation of the taut lines about Nick's mouth were any indication. If she was lucky, she'd be able to get to Ashton and back in a couple of hours with a new prescription of laudanum from Doc Saunders. More than enough time, she hoped, before Nick might need another dose.

But to do so she'd need to hurry on her way, and very soon. Just as soon as, she thought in irritation, she got *two* messes cleaned up and two boys settled down once and for all.

An hour later, she and Danny set out for town. After careful consideration, Sarah decided it was better to divide and conquer than hope the two boys would settle down if left alone in the big ranch house. Plus, Pedro was old enough to keep an eye on Nick. If any problems arose, he was to fetch Emma from her little cabin that was the original ranch house and only a five minute walk away.

Sarah fervently hoped, however, that all would go smoothly while she and Danny were gone. That Nick would finally get some pain relief and rest. That Emma wouldn't have to be disturbed on her one day off a week. And that she'd be fortunate enough to find Doc Saunders in his office so they wouldn't have to wait until he returned from a house call.

The drive to Ashton was uneventful. They bundled up in thick bear robes, besides their usual winter garb, and Sarah took along a rifle for protection. The cold weather of late had, providentially, not brought additional snow, so the carriage with its covered top and sides provided decent protection from the wind. It was also, on the rutted, windswept dirt road, much easier to handle than the sleigh.

Doc was in his office, so the refill of additional bottles of laudanum went quickly. A quick stop at McPherson's Mercantile to pick up a stick of penny candy for Danny and one for Pedro as well, a few minutes talking with Dougal, and they were once more headed back to the ranch. Driving along, Sarah reveled in the view of majestic peaks surrounding the long, wide valley. With heights craggy and imposing, and snow looking so very fresh and pristine, the mountains glinted like shining silver.

The air was crisp. The sense of power and purpose as she went along her important task filled her with joy. Nick needed her. Cord depended on her. And she felt so very capable and—

The carriage lurched violently, then swayed to one side at a precarious angle. As Sarah struggled to control the now panicky horses, from the corner of her eye she saw one of the carriage wheels bounce down a steep hill and out of sight. With great difficulty, Sarah finally pulled the spooked animals to a halt, set the hand brake, then looked to her brother sitting beside her.

"Are you all right?"

He grinned up at her. "Yep. I thought we were going to tip over."

She'd thought the same thing but decided not to belabor the very real danger they had been in. "Well, let's get down, shall we? You can hold the horses while I start looking for that wheel. At the rate it was going, it might take me quite a hike to retrieve it."

Ever so carefully, they climbed from the now lopsided carriage. Luckily for the both of them, the two mares they'd hooked in the harness today were usually calm and gentle. Now that the carriage wasn't going anywhere or likely to do anything else to frighten the animals, she felt quite safe leaving Danny to hold them. She did retrieve the rifle, however. The terrain she'd have to traverse in search of the wheel looked a bit rough and full of hills and ravines.

"You whistle if anyone or anything shows up, you hear?" she told her brother. "And if you have to, you can always climb back into the carriage for protection."

"I'll be okay." Danny gestured in the direction the wheel had taken. "You'd better hurry. It'll take us a while to put on the wheel. If we can."

That was exactly her worry, Sarah thought as she nodded and set out, the rifle clasped firmly in her hand. She knew she'd find the wheel, sooner or later. Depending on what had caused it to come loose, however, might well determine if the wheel would be useable or not. She'd probably have to hold up the carriage and have Danny try to slide it back on its axle. *If* they even could.

If worst came to worst, they had the horses and could always unfasten them from the carriage and ride them home. There was no reason to fear they'd be trapped out here for the night. Things weren't really that bad, she reassured herself as she trudged down a steep hillside and across a snow-filled gully. Things could've turned out far, far worse.

The wheel, though, had apparently possessed enough momentum to cover a surprising amount of ground. Sarah was soon out of sight of the road and carriage and trekking up a small hill then down into another ravine that was so steeply inclined she soon realized it had served as a natural course for the wheel to careen down. Twenty minutes later, she caught sight of the errant carriage wheel lying on its side in the middle of the very long and now narrow ravine.

She trudged up to it and groaned in dismay. Not only had two of the spokes apparently broken in the wheel's bouncing, furious flight, but now, on closer inspection, she found the hub had cracked through, which was what had caused the wheel to loosen and fall off. There was nothing to be done now but leave the disabled carriage on the road and ride the horses home. Some of the hands could return tomorrow to repair the wheel or bring a good one in its place.

Sarah looked up. Already, the sun was veering toward the west. It would be dusk in another few hours. She didn't care to still be out on the road in the dark. Briefly, she considered trying to drag the wheel back to the carriage, then decided it would just slow her down. Better to return tomorrow with the hands to show them its location.

As she began her trudge back, the wind whipped up. On the chill breeze, Sarah thought she caught the sound of bawling cattle. She halted, listening intently. Then, as the wind died, the sound disappeared.

She shook her head. "Must be starting to hear things."

As she resumed her trek, however, the bawling came again. She whirled around, trying to make out where the sounds were coming from. There weren't any ranches nearby. Indeed, another half mile or so, and they'd arrive at the outskirts of Castle Mountain land. There was no reason to be hearing cattle out here. No reason, unless . . .

Unless someone had cattle hidden in one of the dry ravines common in this area. And the only reason to hide cattle was if you'd stolen them.

Excitement vibrating through her, Sarah headed in the direction she'd heard the cattle bawling. They couldn't be very far away. She'd just take a quick peek around, if it seemed like there was enough cover to hide in. She wouldn't do anything foolish. She couldn't afford to, not with Danny still awaiting her on the road.

She climbed to a tree-covered hill, then down the other side, before she began to notice tracks in the snow. Cattle tracks and also those of unshod horses. Could they possibly be the same unshod horses used to rustle their cattle? But those tracks had led up into the mountains far west of here.

"They could've always backtracked," she said aloud, trying to talk through the dilemma, "once they'd made sure their trail was gone. And who'd think to look this close to the road? It wouldn't make sense."

The sounds of the cattle were louder now. Sarah paused, scanning the area for sign of any possible lookouts. When she saw none, she trudged across the next ravine and up another hill. As she neared the top, this time she crouched low and carefully peered down the other side.

There, in yet another ravine, about thirty head of cattle milled about in a makeshift pen. Though it looked as if no one was about, signs of a gutted campfire and a pine-bough-covered lean-to gave ample evidence that people had been here. She sucked in a breath. Even from this distance, she could make out the distinctive Castle Mountain brand.

Scuttling back down the hill until there was no chance she could be seen from the ravine below, Sarah stood and made her way to the road as fast as the snow drifts would allow. All the while, her mind raced with possible actions she could take.

In the end, she decided to return to the ranch with Danny. After informing Nick of what she'd found, Sarah would next round up Spence and several hands and lead them back to the hidden Wainwright cattle. Even if they didn't catch up with any of the rustlers today, a sizeable amount of their stolen cattle would be safely back home. Besides, there was always the chance they might find evidence around the campsite of who the perpetrators were.

"Am I glad to see you," her brother exclaimed when she finally rejoined him on the road. "I was afraid a bear had eaten you."

She gave a derisive snort. "Well, if there'd been bears you would've at least heard me fire the rifle before the beast ate me."

With no time to waste, Sarah leaned the rifle against the carriage and began unfastening the harnesses from the carriage poles. Eventually, after lifting up Danny onto one horse, she was able to mount the other. She briefly considered retrieving the rifle, then thought better of it. It was going to be awkward enough riding bareback and keeping her brother on his horse without trying to hold onto a rifle in the bargain. She could just get it when she returned with the men.

They made it back to the ranch in good time. After helping Danny down, she followed him into the house. It felt wonderful to be inside where it was so nice and warm, Sarah thought as she pulled off her hat, coat, and mittens.

"Want something warm to drink?" she asked as she guided her brother down the hall to the kitchen. "How about hot cocoa?"

"That sounds great," Danny replied, smacking his lips.

To her surprise, Emma was in the kitchen. "Oh, good, you're back safe and sound. I was beginning to worry about you two."

"The carriage lost a wheel, so we rode the horses back." Sarah glanced around. "Where's Pedro? And why are you here on your day off?"

"Pedro's in the barn milking the cow. And I happened to look out my window as you drove by. Figured something was up. So I moseyed on over."

"How's Nick?" Sarah dug the two bottles of laudanum from her pocket. "Guess Pedro told you about us needing more medicine?"

The older woman nodded. "Yes, he did. And Nick's finally asleep. Has been for a good hour or so, but it was touch-and-go for a while."

"Oh, then I guess it's best I don't bother him. He was so exhausted from the pain . . ."

Emma cocked her head. "And exactly what were you planning on bothering him about?"

Excitement tightened Sarah's voice. "I found some of our cattle. Some of the stolen ones, I mean. They're hidden in a ravine near where our carriage broke down." She paused. "I promised Danny some hot cocoa to warm him. It's pretty chilly outside. Could you make him some while I go find Spence?"

"Whoa, hold on there!" Emma said, grabbing her arm as Sarah turned to leave. "And exactly what do you plan to do? About those stolen cattle, and with Spence?"

"What else?" Sarah glanced over her shoulder at the housekeeper. "I've got to lead him and some of the hands to where the cattle are. I'm the only one who can, after all." She laughed, suddenly overjoyed. "Just think, Emma. I've finally got an opportunity to do something really important for Cord and the ranch. Something to finally make up for all the trouble I've caused!"

"So, you're certain this is where you first heard the cattle?" Spencer Womack asked an hour later as he reined in his mount and looked to Sarah. "Seems a mighty strange spot to try to hide stolen cattle. Don't you think so, boys?"

Stan Bevins and Roy Taylor grinned and nodded. "Sure seems so to us, boss," Roy, the older and more scruffy of the pair, replied.

She decided to ignore their shared smirks and patronizing manner. They'd eat their words, she told herself grimly, just as soon as they reached the top of the next hill. Not that she cared, really, what any of them thought.

Spence she'd never cared much for, though Cord and Nick seemed to think he was a good enough worker. The other two hands had been recent hires, former prospectors who'd never struck it rich or even found enough to make a living until they'd been taken on two months ago at Spence's recommendation. She supposed, though, not everyone would be pleased just because she was now Cord's wife. It was certainly evident Spence wasn't impressed. And his attitude was likely rubbing off on some of the hands as well.

"I couldn't agree more that it's a mighty strange spot to hide cattle," she said, meeting the foreman's skeptical gaze with a steady one of her own. "But I know what I saw. So why don't we just head on out again? The cattle are penned just over the next hill."

The going was steep and slippery, but they finally made it to the top of the hill. For a long moment, the three men were silent. Then Roy, the more loquacious of the two hands, sighed, rubbed his jaw, and looked to Spence.

"What do you want to do now, boss? Now that she knows where the cattle are?"

"Oh, I'm not too worried about her knowing," the foreman replied as he leaned over and quickly pulled Sarah's rifle free of its scabbard. He then cocked it and pointed it at her. "She's a Caldwell, after all. It won't be hard to pin the stolen cattle on her."

Her gaze riveted on the rifle barrel now aimed at her, Sarah struggled to make sense of the sudden turn of events. Could it be? Had Spence been involved with the cattle rustling all this time? But, if so, why?

"So, what are you going to do, Womack?" she asked, forcing the words past a dry throat even as she willed her mind to clear and find some way out of this rapidly worsening mess. "Shoot me and pin the blame on me and my family? The blame that has been yours all along?"

He chuckled, the sound so malicious it sent a premonitory

shiver down Sarah's spine. "Well, maybe in the beginning it was all my doing. By myself, though, I didn't dare take too many cattle. But once the real ringleader took over . . ."

"Yeah, I know," she said with a sharp laugh. "My father's been in charge of everything for a while now, hasn't he?"

"No, not at all." Ever so slowly, he gave a shake of his head. "He's just been a scapegoat to pin it all on, and divert attention from the real culprit. It's always been someone else. Someone a whole lot smarter and with just as much to gain, if for an entirely different reason. Someone who I've finally decided isn't worth any more of my time and effort."

His gaze darkened, turning flinty and hard. "Seems she's been leading me on all the while, and never meant to marry me. Seems all she's ever wanted was revenge against Cord and, even more especially, revenge against you."

As Sarah stared at him, the implications of Spence's words took on a form, person, and finally a scene outside the Wildflower Café. A scene of Spence and Allis, arguing, then her slapping him and stomping off. She couldn't help a small gasp.

"Allis? You're talking about Allis Findley, aren't you?"

Anger sparked in his eyes. "You really aren't all that surprised, are you? After all, when has Allis ever thought of anyone but herself?"

19

The stagecoach came to a shuddering halt before Ashton's stage station. Only Cord's innate good manners prevented him from being the first out of the nine person coach. As it was, the other passengers seemed to take forever in unloading. At long last, though, he climbed from the large conveyance.

He inhaled a deep breath of fresh mountain air, so glad to be home. The meeting with the other rancher and his lawyers had gone well. Indeed, far better than he'd expected.

The rancher had agreed to quarterly payments. While in Denver, Cord had also taken the opportunity to telegraph his two partners in New York City, offering them a very reasonable price to buy him out of their joint legal practice. His partners had needed a day or two to talk things over, necessitating Cord remaining in Denver a bit longer than he'd originally planned, but they'd finally wired him, accepting his offer. The use of the extra money from his share of the practice would easily cover the payments for the two bulls through the next year, plus begin whittling down some of the ranch's other debts.

Before then, Cord hoped to have the issue with the rustlers solved once and for all, and the ranch back in the black. Things were finally starting to look up. He couldn't wait to tell Nick and Sarah the news. He couldn't wait, as well, just to reunite with his new bride.

Humming a little tune, Cord retrieved his satchel and headed for McPherson's. He wanted to share the good news with his old friend and pick up a gift for Sarah before heading to the livery stable to rent a horse. He had another couple hours of daylight left. An hour, no more, and he'd be on his way home.

"She's sure to like that," Dougal observed a half hour later as he rang up Cord's purchase of a matching set of shell side combs with sterling silver ornamentations for Sarah's hair. He carefully wrapped each comb in paper, then placed them in a bag.

"Come into a bit of money, have ye?" The old man handed Cord the bag.

"Not just yet, but soon, Dougal. Soon." Cord grinned. "And my debts to you will be the first I'll pay off."

"Och, I wasn't hinting at aught, lad. I know ye're good for the money ye owe me."

"And I appreciate that, old friend. Even so—"

The bell over the mercantile's front door tinkled as a blast of cold air heralded the entrance of another customer. Both men's heads turned. One look, and Cord's heart sank. He barely contained a groan.

It was Allis Findley.

As soon as she caught sight of him, her frowning expression immediately brightened. "Oh, Cord, darling!" she cried, hurrying over. "Just the person I've been *desperately* needing to see. How fortuitous to find you in town."

Now that he was a married man, Cord didn't see any reason for Allis desperately needing to see him about anything, much less continuing to call him "darling." But he was too much a gentleman to voice such thoughts. He did, however, take a step back when she reached out to link his arm with hers.

"Nice to see you too, Allis." He paused, held up the bag Dougal had just given him, and smiled at the older man. "Thanks for the good company and service, my friend. I'll be sure to stop by next time I'm in town."

"Oh, are you already on your way out, darling?" Allis's lips puckered in a carefully practiced pout. "But I *so* need to speak with you about a *most* disturbing matter."

For the life of him, he couldn't imagine what Allis would think disturbing enough to concern him, but he indicated the front door. "I'm on my way to the livery. I intend to head home just as soon as I rent a horse, but you're welcome to talk with me on the way."

"Wouldn't it be a *far* more comfortable and enjoyable time if we visited over tea and pastries at the Wildflower Café?"

"More comfortable, to be sure, than braving the cold," Cord said, "but I've been gone ten days and I want to get home. So, this little talk can either wait until some other time, or you can walk with me to the livery. Take your pick."

A look of annoyance crossed Allis's face. She quickly covered it with a brittle smile.

"Suit yourself, then, darling." She smoothly fell into place beside him, this time managing to capture his arm with hers.

"Er, Allis," he said, immediately pulling free, "I'm a married man now. I don't think it's appropriate to be seen walking arm in arm down Main Street with another woman."

"Well, you might just change your mind," she softly muttered, "once you hear what I have to say. But, for now, I'll respect your wishes."

Behind him, Cord heard Dougal softly chuckle. "Good-bye and good luck, lad. I'm thinking ye'll be needing it."

From over his shoulder, Cord shot his friend a jaundiced look, then opened the front door. Once they were outside, he turned to Allis.

"Okay, spit it out. What's the news you absolutely can't wait to tell me?"

She hesitated, glancing around to make sure no one was headed their way. Then she stepped close and laid a gloved hand on his arm.

"It's about Spencer Womack. He's been courting me, you know?"

He sighed. He wasn't in the mood for any of Allis's games.

"That's been the rumor. What about it?"

"I've always had my doubts about him, but for a time I encouraged his suit of me." She glanced down, then up at him through her long lashes. "I'd hoped it would make you jealous."

"Allis . . ." Cord said warningly.

"Well, it doesn't matter anymore, does it?" She patted his arm, then pulled her hand away. "I finally decided he wasn't the man for me and told him I'd no longer favor his continued intentions."

Relief filled him. If that was Allis's big news, then they were done.

"I'm sorry to hear that. I'm sure Spence will be devastated. And that said, I really need to get to the livery—"

He turned to go when Allis sharply halted him. "Cord. Wait. There's more. A *lot* more."

Cord rolled his eyes, then slowly looked back at her. "What, Allis? What more is there to tell?"

"He's been involved with the Caldwells all this time. In the rustling of your cattle."

For a long moment, all he could do was stand there, staring at her. His thoughts raced. *Spence, involved in the rustling? But why? And if Allis is lying, what are her motives for implicating an innocent man?*

"Why would Spence steal from us?" Cord finally asked.

306

"He has a decent paying job and seems content with the work. Even more to the point, if he was rustling cattle, why would he tell you?"

"Spencer thought to win my heart and hand by getting more money. And he figured you'd blame the Caldwells for any cattle stolen, and never suspect him." She shrugged. "I suppose it just seemed the easiest and quickest way for him."

Cord's gaze narrowed. "And how exactly did you find all this out, Allis? Why would Spence share such incriminating information with you?"

"He's not the smartest man around, darling." She gave a tinkling little laugh. "*Surely* you've noticed that?"

"I'd think he was smart enough not to tell the woman he was courting that the money he was lavishing on her was ill-gotten gains."

"Oh, he wouldn't admit it at first, darling, but I finally wheedled the truth out of him." Allis paused, eyeing him with the avid intensity of a mountain lion getting ready to pounce on its next victim. "There's more. Not only did Spencer implicate the Caldwell men, but he swore to me that, from the start, Sarah has also been involved."

"Sarah?" Cord gave a derisive laugh. "Come on, Allis. Considering your feelings for my wife, do you seriously think I'd believe that?"

"Believe what you want." Head held high in what he suspected was a great show of affront, she took a step back from him. "Just consider this. How is it that, save for that one time, no one was ever able to catch any of the rustlers? Or even figure out why the thieves always seemed to know how to avoid all the traps set for them?"

Anger flared in him, and Cord didn't know if it was at Allis for daring to say what she'd just said, or at himself, for the immediate ripple of doubt and dismay her accusations stirred.

He had thought he'd excised the last, lingering misgivings he'd had about Sarah, but apparently he hadn't.

The admission shamed him. His wife deserved better than that.

"Maybe because Spence knew and was able to warn the other rustlers?" Cord managed to choke out. "After all, most times, Spence was involved in the planning."

"Yes, most times. But not all, I'd be willing to wager." She cocked her head, challenge in her eyes. "Am I right?"

She was indeed right. There had been a few, a very few, times when Nick and he hadn't included anyone else in their plans until the very last minute. But he wasn't about to admit that to Allis. Besides, there were other ways to get information to the rustlers, even at the last minute.

"It doesn't matter, Allis," Cord replied, the conviction growing with each word that left his lips. "I love and trust Sarah. Nothing you can tell me will make me doubt her."

"Then be a fool!" She gave a toss of her head. "It's your life and your ranch. Just mark my words—the words of a good and true friend—the day Sarah Caldwell turns her back on you, once and for all, and goes home to her real family. Just mark my words, and don't come crawling back to me when you've lost everything!"

With that parting salvo, Allis pivoted about and flounced off in high dudgeon, leaving Cord to stand there, staring after her.

"I don't have a good feeling about this," Gabe Cooper said twenty minutes later as he, Cord, and his deputy headed toward the ranch. "Even taking what Allis says with a grain of salt, I don't think she's crazy enough to make everything up."

"Crazy?" Cord glanced over at his friend. "I've never thought Allis was crazy, just rather calculating and self-absorbed."

"Oh, I meant driven crazy with heartbreak over losing you, of course."

Cord scowled at the good-natured ribbing. "And you seriously think Allis was in love with me? Come on, Gabe."

The sheriff shrugged. "Oh, I don't know. Reckon she was as much in love with you as with the idea of being the wife of a successful Eastern lawyer. I wouldn't be surprised if she didn't harbor dreams of attending fancy New York City balls on your arm."

"Well, her dreams would've been cruelly dashed. I've sold my share of the law practice. I'm staying put on the ranch."

Gabe chuckled. "Why doesn't that surprise me? I always knew you loved that ranch. And the life here in the Rockies."

"Then you knew a lot more than I did, and for a long time before I finally figured it out."

"Yes, I am pretty astute about those kinds of things."

"Before you dislocate that arm patting yourself on the back," Cord said, shooting his friend an amused look, "just remember you weren't any more quick about tying Spence to the cattle rustling than I was."

"Guess the Caldwells were just so easy to blame it all on."

"Yeah." Frustration warred a bitter battle with shame, and Cord didn't know which of the two to claim. "An enterprising person could very easily manipulate the situation, couldn't he? I just never thought Spence clever enough to see all the possibilities."

"Me neither. The pieces are starting to come together, but something still doesn't fit just right." He paused. "I'm thinking that once we've got Spence in custody, maybe we should look a little closer at Allis."

Cord smiled grimly. "I was thinking the very same thing."

The ranch house came into view. Apprehension rippled through Cord. Would things go easy for a change, and they would find Spence still there? And would Sarah somehow sense he'd once again had doubts about her?

He had such mixed emotions about so many things. The only saving grace in this confused muddle was the fact that, at long last, the issue of the cattle rustling and who all the participants actually were seemed to be fast coming to an end. Life might finally get back to normal. He was more than ready for that. Indeed, he dearly yearned for it.

As the three men drew up before the big house, Nick, accompanied by Emma, Pedro, and Danny, wheeled himself out onto the front porch. An air of weariness dogged him, but his brother's eyes were clear and calm as he met Cord's gaze. Cord dismounted, tied his horse to the hitching post, and climbed the steps.

"If this is a welcome home party, my wife seems to be missing," he said with a prickle of unease. "Where's Sarah?"

Nick and Emma exchanged a troubled glance. "You just missed her by an hour or so. She found some of our stolen cattle and headed out to get them with Spence and a couple of hands."

Cord looked at Gabe. "This isn't good."

"No, it isn't."

"What's going on?" Nick demanded. "Is Sarah in danger? I was asleep when she got home after going to town to get me some more laudanum, but she assured Emma she'd be all right. And Spence told Emma he'd be sure to take good care of Sarah."

"I just bet he will," Cord growled. "Seems Spence might be involved in the cattle rustling, likely from the start. Or so Allis claims."

"Allis?" Confusion lit Nick's eyes. "What does Allis have to do with all that? And when did you have time, since just getting home, to come up with this?"

"It's a long story," Cord said, waving aside further explanation. "Do you have any idea where they went?"

"I do." Danny stepped forward. "On the way home, a wheel came off the carriage. Sarah went to find it. Maybe that's where you should start looking."

Cord nodded. "We saw the carriage. I recognized it as ours and was wondering what had happened to it." He turned to Gabe. "We need to get back there pronto. Will you do me a favor and put away the livery horse, then saddle up my gelding? While you're doing that, I'll go roust out the rest of the hands from the bunkhouse."

"Will do." Gabe tied up his horse, then grabbed Cord's rented mount and signaled his deputy to join him.

"You might be outside for a while," Emma said. "After you get the hands going, I suggest you come back and get dressed in warmer clothes. In the meanwhile, I'll start making sandwiches and such for you men to take with you."

Cord smiled in gratitude. "Thanks, Emma." He started down the steps.

"What can *I* do, Mr. Cord?"

Halting in midstride, Cord swung back to where Danny stood, his blue eyes dark with worry. He supposed he could've sent both the boys away before they discussed the issue at hand, but Danny had been involved from the start. He would've figured out something was wrong pretty quickly.

Climbing back up the steps, Cord crouched down before his little brother-in-law and took him by the arms. "I'm glad you asked, because I'm going to need someone back here to help Nick keep things running. Can you do that for me?"

Danny solemnly nodded. "Sure can."

"Okay, then. First thing, can you wheel Mr. Nick back inside, then get him to help you and Emma make those sandwiches? And will you and Pedro make sure all the chores get done tonight and maybe even tomorrow, if we're not back by then? I know none of that is as exciting as going after the stolen cattle and finding Sarah, but I've got to know someone's back here while we're gone, making sure the ranch is still running. And it's a big responsibility."

The boy's chest visibly swelled with pride. "I can do that, Mr. Cord. I'll do my part."

"Good. I really appreciate that, Danny." Cord stood. "Now, I need to get the hands going."

"And I need to get everyone making those sandwiches." Danny walked to where Nick still sat and began to guide the wheelchair toward the front door.

Nick met Cord's gaze and grinned. Cord returned the gesture, then spun about and headed down the steps and toward the bunkhouse. As he strode along, his smile faded. Time was of the essence, if they were to pick up the trail before it got too dark. If Spence had shown his hand once Sarah had led him to the cattle, there was no telling what might happen.

He didn't know Spencer Womack as well as he'd once thought. And that made the man—and what he might do to Sarah—very frightening indeed.

"So, what are you planning on doing with the cattle?" Sarah asked, hands tied, seated in front of Spencer Womack on his horse.

It was starting to get dark. Luckily, tonight was a full moon. With all the snow, the mountainous terrain would be reasonably illuminated. Just in case she could manage to slip away sometime tonight, she thought it wise to find out as much as she could about his plans.

"Don't you think it might be better to wonder what I'm planning on doing with you, little lady?" he replied with a cynical chuckle. "Aren't you afraid I just might dump you over some cliff and be done with you?"

"Only if you want to be charged with murder, rather than just an accessory to murder in the death of Edmund Wainwright."

"You've been listening to that fancy lawyer husband a bit too much." Spence gave a derisive snort. "'Accessory to murder' now, am I? Well, only if Cord catches me, which he won't."

"Well, we'll have to see about that, won't we?"

"Oh, you won't be seeing anything. You're not going to be with us much longer."

Fear stabbed at her. *What's Spence planning now?*

"So you've reconsidered letting me go, have you?" Sarah inquired coolly, though her heart was pounding in her chest. "Probably one of the smarter things you've done lately."

He laughed, and the sound wasn't friendly or warm. "We'll see if Cord thinks so, when he finds out I'm dumping you off at your father's."

"My father?" She twisted in the saddle to look back at him. "You know where my father's hiding?"

"Sure I do. How do you think I got messages to him about the best time to hit Wainwright's herd?"

"But it's so far away from here . . ."

"You think so? But then, backtracking for several hours could lead anyone to think that, couldn't it?"

Yes, it could, Sarah thought. *And considering how protective Noah has become of Papa, quite understandable too.*

"So, how soon will we be there?"

Though she had mixed feelings about reuniting with her father and, considering she was now Cord's wife, wondered what kind of reception she'd receive, odds were it was still a safer place to be than remaining with Spence and his two shiftless partners. When the time came, she'd just have to find some way to convince Noah to take her back home.

He grimaced. "At the rate we're going in this dad-blasted snow, probably another half hour before we reach the turn-off to their hideout. And then maybe another half hour before we reach their shack."

The snow Spence was so bitterly complaining about, Sarah thought, would likely be his undoing. It wouldn't be long before Nick figured out something was up. Then he'd either send for Gabe Cooper or set the rest of the hands out to search for them. And men on horseback, with no cattle to herd, could cover ground a lot faster than the rate they were currently going.

Spence would be wiser, now that his treachery would soon be discovered, to hightail it out of the area just as fast as he could. His greed, in the form of thirty head of cattle, however, was going to be his downfall.

"Your father especially isn't going to be very happy with you, is he?" the foreman asked slyly. "Once he finds out you married a Wainwright, I mean."

"He knew I was going to marry Cord. Or didn't he tell you that?"

"We don't talk much these days, Jacob and I. Not since he took sick, and your yellow-bellied brother decided he didn't want any more of helping me rustle Wainwright cattle."

Sarah shrugged. "Sounds like Noah finally found the sense you still seem to be lacking."

Spence snickered nastily. "Well, we'll see. You'd just better hope your brother's on your side."

Unease fluttered through her. "Why's that?"

"Last time I talked with your father, he sure seemed like he was falling deeper and deeper into that madness of his. And he swore to me, if he ever got hold of you again, he was going to kill you rather than allow you to further shame the family by consorting with the Wainwrights."

20

They caught up with Spence and his two men about mid-morning. With ten rifles aiming at them from an overlook, the three rustlers, trapped in a small bowl with the cattle, surrendered without a fight. And, as Cord and Gabe then headed down to disarm the three men, Cord's anger grew apace with the closing distance.

Sarah was nowhere to be seen. That terrified him. Though he'd never imagined Spencer Womack to be a cold-blooded killer, he'd never thought the man would steal his cattle either. If the lowlife had harmed one hair of Sarah's head . . .

No sooner had they pulled in their mounts than Cord leaped off his horse and stalked over to Spence, who stood with his two partners, hands in the air, their guns on the ground several feet from them. He reached out and grabbed the other man by the front of his coat.

"Where's Sarah?" he snarled. "You'd better tell me some good news, or I swear I'll beat your face to a pulp and not spare a moment's regret!"

Abject fear flared in Spence's eyes. "I didn't hurt her. She's safe enough."

"Cord . . ." From behind him, he heard the warning note in Gabe's voice. He dragged in a deep breath.

"What do you mean, 'safe enough'?"

Spence shrugged. "First, let go of me. Give a man some breathing room."

His former foreman was in no position to make any demands, and Cord almost pointed that out to him. Instead, he fought a mighty battle with his temper, finally getting it back under control. What mattered now was finding Sarah, safe and sound, not teaching Spencer Womack a much-needed lesson. That could wait until later.

He released his stranglehold on the other man and took a step back. "Spit it out, Womack. Answer my question."

Spence took a moment to rearrange his jacket. "She's with her father and brother," he replied at last, not meeting Cord's icy stare. "I didn't see the point of taking her with us. Had enough on my hands with the cattle."

Disbelief, mixed with a fair amount of horror, filled Cord. "You took her back to that crazy old man? There's no telling what he might do to Sarah, now that we're . . ."

The faintest glimmer of a smile curled one corner of Spence's mouth. Cord saw red. He lunged at the man, slamming a fist into his jaw.

Spence dropped like a rock, knocked unconscious. The other two ranch hands, arms still in the air, jumped away in fright. Gabe grabbed Cord's arm and yanked him backward.

"Okay, Spence deserved that and more," the sheriff said, his voice dropped low for Cord's ears only, "but he's out cold now, and I'm not going to let you beat up on a helpless man. So cool down, Cord, and do it fast!"

His chest heaving with fury, Cord managed to back away of his own accord. Shame filling him, he rubbed his abraded fist with his other hand. *Forgive me, Lord.*

"Sorry," he said, shooting Gabe an apologetic look. "Old habits die hard. And I lost it when I realized Spence knew exactly what the consequences to Sarah might be, and still took her to her father."

"Yeah, I figured as much." His friend glanced dispassionately at the man now lying prone in the snow. "Still, if you kill him, you might have a very hard time finding out where Jacob Caldwell's holed up. In case that thought didn't enter your mind a minute or so ago."

"No, I'm afraid it didn't."

Cord knelt beside Spence, turned him over, and began to rub snow on the man's face in an attempt to waken him. After a time, Spence groaned, and his lids fluttered open.

"Wh . . . what happened?" He groaned again, one hand rising to his rapidly reddening jaw.

"I hit you." Cord grasped him by the arm and pulled him to a sitting position. "I didn't much like your evident malicious intent in taking Sarah to her father. I'm going to give you a chance to make up for that, though."

Spence eyed him warily. "How's that?"

"You're going to take me there. Now." He jerked the man to his feet, then immediately had to grab him by both arms to steady him.

"I don't . . . don't think that's such a good idea," Spence mumbled "Once I show you the hideout, who's to say you might not finish me off?"

"It's a definite consideration." Cord's mouth quirked wryly. "But, since I'm not currently inclined to kill you, and I won't want you around to complicate things, the deputy will accompany us. When I'm done with you, he can bring you back to town." He turned to Gabe. "Does that meet with your approval?"

"All but the part of you going in to face the Caldwells on your own. That could be tricky."

"I think I can handle a sick, crazy old man and his son."

"Normally, I'd agree, but you don't know what Jacob might try."

Cord sighed and shook his head. "No, I don't. But it's my

wife he's got, and it's time to end this feud once and for all. And that, Sheriff Cooper, is exactly what I intend to do."

Later that afternoon, Sarah gazed past the tattered remnants of the flour sacks that served as a curtain and out the window of the miner's shack. She hadn't slept much since Spence had unceremoniously deposited her on her father's doorstep around midnight, then rode off. At first, her father hadn't even been inclined to take her in. Thankfully, her older brother had finally prevailed on him to give her shelter, promising they'd deal with everything in the morning.

She'd spent the rest of the night on the hard floor before the hearth fire, her hands and feet tied so she wouldn't escape. But at least she'd been warm, Sarah consoled herself later that day as she'd sat by the window, watching for signs of rescue she knew would surely be forthcoming. And, despite Spencer Womack's dire predictions to the contrary, her father had yet to kill her for her transgressions.

All that matters is staying alive. Staying alive until help comes. Staying alive for Cord. Her gaze slid protectively to her belly. *And staying alive for our baby.*

The consideration of telling her father of his grandchild-to-be had briefly crossed her mind. For a fleeting moment, the hope that his knowing the Caldwells, through her and Cord's child, might someday inherit the ranch had lured her into imagining he might find comfort—and acceptance—in her marriage. But only for a fleeting moment.

No sooner had he awoken and set eyes on her than Jacob had commenced ranting at Sarah about her betrayal and slatternly ways. And, the more he talked, the angrier he became, until a murderous light glowed in his eyes. Sarah soon gave up trying to reason with him and backed as far away from him as she could get in the close confines of the little cabin.

Only Noah's intervention finally saved her from her father attacking her. Noah's intervention and her father's failing health. His strength soon dissipated, and he had to lie down or literally collapse where he stood.

So now Sarah sat across the room from where he lay on his bed, watching him sleep, his face ashen, his chest struggling for each breath. For a fleeting moment, she wondered who might survive the other. Her heart clenched with pain and pity. Pain for the man whom she'd once cherished with all her being. Pity for the empty, angry, bitter shell that was now left of him.

Help me, dear Lord, she prayed, her eyes filling with tears, *to forgive him. To love him for Your sake, if no longer for his own. And, if it's Your will, help me to find a way to make him see, to understand, to let go of his unhappy vendetta and find some peace before he dies.*

"You hurt him, and deeply so, you know."

She whirled around in her chair, unaware that Noah, his arms laden with a load of wood, had walked in the front door. She must be more tired than she thought, not to have heard her brother's approach. Sarah sighed.

"I never meant to. Whether you believe that or not, I never meant to."

"Oh, I believe you." As he spoke, Noah strode to the hearth and, as quietly as he could, deposited the wood. "I've never thought it was all your fault, this estrangement between you and Pa. Far from it."

Sarah shot a quick glance back at their father before once more meeting her brother's gaze. Jacob slept on.

"Then let me go, Noah," she said, her voice cast low. "I don't feel safe with Papa anymore. And if he should go into another one of his rages while you happen to be gone . . ."

Her brother held up a silencing hand. "He won't hurt you, Sarah. No matter how he rants, how bad his madness gets at times, he still knows you're his daughter. And, deep down, he still loves you."

"Do you really think so?" She sighed again and slowly shook her head. "I'm not so sure. Not anymore. These days, I don't think anything's more important to him than—"

From outside, high up on the trail leading down to the cabin, a voice hailed them. Sarah's heart skipped a beat. The voice . . . it sounded like—

She turned in her chair to look back out the window. A form, tall, broad-shouldered, and oh, so very familiar, was walking his horse toward them.

With a foul curse, Jacob Caldwell stirred, shoved to his elbows, then motioned for Noah to help him from the bed. Together, the two men made their way to the window.

The old man's gaze narrowed. As he appeared finally to recognize their visitor, his face mottled in rage. "Get my rifle, son," he rasped, leaning forward to grip the windowsill for support. "My prayers have been answered. Today, I get to kill another Wainwright. And, once he's gone, the only one left between me and the ranch will be his useless, crippled brother."

Just as soon as Noah and her father exited the house, Sarah glanced frantically around the room, searching for anything to use to cut herself free. Unfortunately, no one had conveniently left a sharp knife around, and there was no glass object she could break to use as a shard to saw through her ropes. With a sigh, she hobbled to the hearth. Fire seemed her only option.

She picked up a long stick from the pile of wood Noah had

dumped nearby and stuck it into the flames. It took what seemed an eternity to heat up enough, but she was finally able to use its glowing tip to set both her wrist and then her ankle bonds afire. Her high, leather riding boots, she well knew, would protect her from much of the heat of the burning ropes about her ankles. Her wrists, however, wouldn't be so well protected.

The searing flames built rapidly to a painful intensity. Sarah had to grit her teeth as the ropes began to smolder then burn. She pulled hard against the wrist bonds, hoping to aid the fire. Tears welled in her eyes.

"Hold on. Hold on," she told herself, grinding her teeth against the pain. *And please, Lord*, she silently added, *please, don't let Papa or Noah do anything foolish before I can get to them.*

Not that she had any idea what she was going to do to prevent them from harming Cord, she thought, finally snapping the last few rope fibers on her now singed wrists and then applying the burning brand to her ankle bonds. That, however, was just what she intended on doing. Outside, Sarah could hear her father's voice raised in anger, but he was now far enough from the cabin that she couldn't make out what was being said. Not that it mattered what he thought or said anymore. All that mattered was her husband.

She finally kicked free of the burnt ropes about her feet, stood, and hurried to the door, flinging it wide. The scene that greeted her, as she had feared, filled her with horror. Cord stood there, unarmed, his hands at his sides, looking at her father, who had his rifle aimed at Cord's heart. Beside her father, Noah eyed his sire uncertainly.

"Jesus, help me. Please, help me." She whispered a frantic, fervent prayer, then headed resolutely toward the men.

Facing toward the shack, Cord was the first to see her. His eyes widened. He gave a quick, firm shake of his head.

He doesn't want me in the middle of this, Sarah realized. *He's warning me to stay out of it.*

The possible consequences to him, however, if she stayed out of it were life-threatening. She ignored him. Skirting her father and brother, Sarah made a beeline straight for her husband.

Too late, Noah and her father realized she'd gotten free. By the time they did, Sarah had already broken into a run to cover the last few yards. Once she reached Cord, she stepped in front of him, then wheeled around to face her father, who had just lowered his rifle.

"Get away from him, girl," Jacob Caldwell snarled. "You're not going to save him from what he's got coming to him."

"And exactly what does Cord have coming to him, Papa?" she demanded as she felt Cord's hands settle on her arms. "He wasn't even born when you lost the ranch. How is he to blame for any of this?"

"Sarah," her husband softly said, leaning close, "it's long past time anyone can reason with him. Let me handle this."

She turned slightly to gaze up at him, and saw his intent burning hot and resolute in his eyes. Realization flashed through her. He wasn't as unarmed and helpless as he made himself out to be. And he intended, if need be, to kill her father before her father killed him.

Is this how You intend for it to end, Lord? she silently asked. *For either my father to kill my husband or for my husband to kill my father?*

Mind-numbing despair swamped her. For a fleeting instant, Sarah was paralyzed with the sheer futility of it all. As if in a dream, she watched her father's gaze narrow. Watched him lift his rifle again. *Does he mean to kill me then*, she wondered, *if I don't move from in front of my husband?*

"I'm not going to tell you again, girl," he said, his voice rife with menace. "Get out of the way or—"

Cord pulled her forcibly back behind him. Suddenly, all Sarah wanted to do was hide her face and close her eyes against what she feared would come next.

"No more," she moaned, cowering for a brief, blessed moment behind him. "Please . . . No more . . ."

"Or what, Caldwell?" Cord demanded as he shielded Sarah with his own body. "Are you so intent on murder these days that you'll kill your own child?"

"Sh-she's no child of mine if she chooses to betray her own father." Jacob's hold on the rifle wavered a bit. His breathing turned shallow and fast.

"You're wrong if you think Sarah's ever betrayed you. She's always loved you. Always."

As he spoke, Cord cast about for how to get her out of harm's way. If Jacob fired on him, and he was forced to draw and discharge the pistol he had shoved in the back of his belt, Sarah could get caught in the crossfire. And if anything should happen to her . . .

With a fierce effort, he shoved that consideration aside. This wasn't the time to get bogged down in emotion. He had to keep a clear head. He had to remain alert to any signal Caldwell might give indicating he was about to shoot him.

The way the old man was shaking now, Cord thought, eyeing him closely, it'd be a wonder if he could even manage to pull the trigger. He was so sick and weak, he could barely remain upright. But Jacob stood there nonetheless, struggling with all his remaining strength to salvage some shred of his pride, of his long-held, if futile and self-destructive dream.

A surprising compassion filled Cord. As wrong and

misguided as Sarah's father had always been, he wasn't much different from any other man who'd lost what he'd deemed most important. True, Jacob had chosen poorly and, in the doing, had forfeited everything that really mattered in life. But hadn't he himself almost done the very same thing? And hadn't his own father, as well?

He exhaled a long, weary breath. *Help me, Lord. For Sarah's sake, if not for my own, help me find some honorable way out of this. Help me finally bring some good from all these years of pain and suffering.*

"She's always loved you," he softly reiterated. "Always wanted the best for you. And for her sake, and the sake of your two remaining sons, it's time we end this feud. You're my father-in-law now, and I love my wife. I won't press charges against you or Noah if you just give this up. Now and forever."

Caldwell's face had gone ashen. He could barely hold up his rifle. "And give up the ranch. No, never!"

"Then don't give it up." Inspiration struck Cord. "Come back with us, you and Noah, and live on the ranch with us. In peace. As family."

Behind him, he heard Sarah gasp. Her arms encircled his waist and she hugged him.

For a long moment, Jacob Caldwell stared at him in disbelief. Then he savagely shook his head.

"No. It's a trick. A lie." He lifted his rifle and pointed it at Cord. "You're a liar and cheat, just like your father. And now you're going to die, just like—"

With an agonized cry, Noah leaped toward his father, deflecting the rifle upward just as it fired. Sarah screamed. Cord lunged forward and reached Jacob just as he was leveling his rifle for another shot.

Cord grabbed the weapon and wrenched it away. Jacob charged at him. Noah recovered and grabbed his father by the arm, jerking him back. Jacob turned on his son, flailing wildly. Then, of a sudden, the old man sagged. His knees buckled and he plummeted to the snow-covered ground.

"Papa!" Sarah cried and ran toward him, joining her brother, who had immediately sunk down beside their father to gather him into his arms. "Papa, what's wrong?"

Jacob turned his head toward her, his mouth opening and closing soundlessly.

She leaned forward, straining to hear what he was saying, but couldn't. Was it possible? Was her father finally asking for forgiveness?

"Forgiveness isn't so much about Pa as it is about you, Cord." Sarah suddenly heard Nick's words to his brother in her mind. *"It's not about feelings, but about freedom. It's not about changing the other person—we might not ever succeed in doing that—but in letting go . . . and trusting that God will somehow make it all right."*

The words, spoken as Edmund Wainwright lay slowly dying, had been as appropriately uttered for her sake as for her husband's. Whether or not her father truly *was* asking for forgiveness in the last few moments of his life wasn't as important as her forgiveness of him. Wasn't as important as her letting go and trusting that God would somehow make it all right.

"I love you, Papa," she whispered, bending close until her lips hovered next to his ear. "Tell Mama hello when you get to heaven. Tell her I tried my best always to be there for you, to never give up hope that you'd finally find a new heart and turn back to God. Tell her that for me, will you, Papa?"

His eyes fluttered shut. He gave a long, deep sigh and went still.

"Papa!"

Cord knelt beside her and probed for a pulse in the man's neck. There was none. He met her tear-bright, searching gaze.

"He's gone, Sarah."

Her head, like some flower wilting on its stem, sagged. She picked up her father's now lifeless hand and gently kissed it.

"Oh, Papa. Papa . . ."

Two days later, they buried Jacob Caldwell in the little family cemetery high on a tree-shaded bluff overlooking the ranch. Buried him beside Caleb and his mother—whose remains they had exhumed from their separate burial spots—and not far from Edmund and Mary Wainwright's graves. It was fitting, Cord had told her. Just as the Wainwrights and Caldwells had joined bloodlines when they had married, so the two families should now also share a common resting place. Just as the two families, in so many ways, now also finally shared the ranch.

Sarah's love for her husband swelled as he'd spoken those words. Long after the others had left, preferring a warm house and tasty victuals to remaining in the chill, overcast winter weather, she and Cord had stood there gazing down at the graves. Finally, she turned to him, giving his hand a squeeze.

"We should be getting back to the house. Before everyone starts worrying about us."

"Yes, I suppose we should." He looked down at her, and she could tell he had been far away.

"A penny for your thoughts," she said, patting his cheek with a mitten-clad hand.

He shrugged. "Oh, I was marveling at the fact it's all over. The feud . . . the anger . . . the hatred and retribution. Reckon it'll take some time to get used to it."

"Reckon it will," Sarah replied with a little smile. "But I think it'll also become more and more pleasant—the realization, I mean—as time goes on. I think I'll very much enjoy all the peace and lack of strife."

She paused, her thoughts flitting to her older brother who, at Cord's urging, had reluctantly accompanied them back to the ranch. "Noah. I've been meaning to ask you. What do you want to do about Noah?"

Cord reached up and tenderly brushed an errant strand of hair from her face. "I meant what I said. I won't press charges against him. Besides, he gave us back what was left of the money. If he wants, he's free to stay on here and help us with the ranch." He grinned. "Who knows? Maybe I can train him up to be the new foreman. What with Spence now in jail, we can certainly use one."

Sarah frowned in sudden remembrance. "Oh yes. Spence. In all the confusion after Papa died, and then the preparations for the funeral, I forgot to pass on what he'd told me about the plot to rustle the cattle. And, believe it or not, it was never my father behind it all. At first it was Spence, and then later Allis once she got wind of what he was doing. It was her idea to involve my family in order to get back at me. Seems she just couldn't let you go."

His gaze darkened. "That doesn't come as much of a surprise. Gabe and I were starting to have our suspicions about her. According to what he told me just before the funeral services for your father today, first thing when Gabe got to town after helping deliver the cattle back to the ranch and depositing Spence and his men in jail, he went calling on Allis. She's now under house arrest. Just as soon as the circuit judge can get here, Miss Allis Findley will be standing trial with Spence and his cronies."

Relief—and a certain satisfaction—flooded Sarah. Though she knew she shouldn't wish the wretched woman ill, it was only fair that Allis Findley face the consequences of her self-serving and ultimately tragic schemes. She was as responsible for what had happened as the men—including her father and brothers—who had so willingly gone along with her plans. Complete forgiveness might be a time in coming for the unhappy woman, but Sarah knew she would do it for the Lord's sake if not quite as soon for Allis's.

"She caused a lot of heartache and pain. For the both of us."

Cord nodded solemnly. "Yes, she did. But I think, she did the most damage to herself. And she'll have the most to answer for, when and where it counts the most." His mouth quirked. "That realization, I hate to admit, is about the only thing that has kept me from riding into town and wringing her arrogant little neck. Just to get back at her for all she did."

"Well, *that* puts my worries to rest," Sarah said, stifling a giggle. "The thought of you wringing anyone's neck, I mean. Still, I'm glad you already suspected Allis. Otherwise, I didn't know how you'd take me accusing her of such a horrible crime."

"And why would that be a concern, sweetheart? I never pegged you for the jealous type." He cocked his head. "Is there something you've been hiding from me?"

"Hardly." Sarah gave a disgusted snort, then hesitated as a certain omission *did* occur to her. "Well, not about Allis anyway . . ."

He crooked her gently beneath her chin, lifting her gaze to his. "Then what? If the end to the feud's going to hold, we really shouldn't be keeping any secrets from each other."

She giggled. "Well, I suppose you're right. If the end to the feud's going to hold, I mean." Sarah glanced away briefly, then looked back, slowly wetting her lips. "We don't have a lot of time left, you and I. Time just for the two of us."

Unease narrowed his eyes. "What are you talking about, Sarah? Is there something wrong? Are you sick?"

"Well, no . . . and yes. Sort of." She laughed. "I'm pregnant, Cord. We're going to have a baby."

His gaze widened. For a moment, he just stared down at her. Then with a shout, he gathered her up into his arms and whirled around and around.

"A baby? I'm going to be a father?"

"Cord, stop!" Sarah cried. "You're making me dizzy. And I'm most definitely not past having morning sickness, even if it's no longer morning."

"Oh." Immediately, he came to a halt. "I'm sorry. I wasn't thinking about your delicate condition." Ever so carefully, he lowered her back to her feet. A lopsided grin on his face, he met her gaze. "Family. Suddenly my family is growing by leaps and bounds."

She heard the wonderment in his voice and marveled at it. "That makes you happy, does it?"

"Yes, it does," her handsome cowboy husband replied, his smile openhearted and joyous. "It does indeed."

Kathleen Morgan is the author of the bestselling Brides of Culdee Creek series and *As High as the Heavens*, as well as the These Highland Hills series. She lives in Colorado.

"If you're looking for an awesome writer and a story charged with romance, you don't want to miss *A Hope Undaunted*."

—Judith Miller, author of *Somewhere to Belong*, Daughters of Amana series

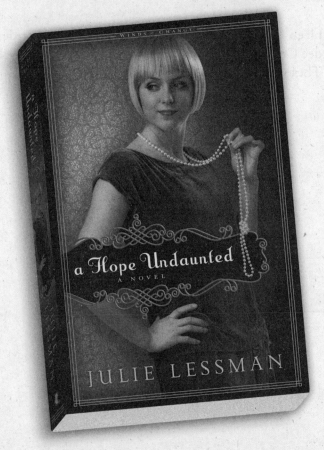

Kate O'Connor is a smart and sassy woman who has her goals laid out for the future—including the perfect husband and career. Will she follow her plans or her heart?

Revell
a division of Baker Publishing Group
www.RevellBooks.com

Find yourself immersed in this powerful story of love, faith and forgiveness.

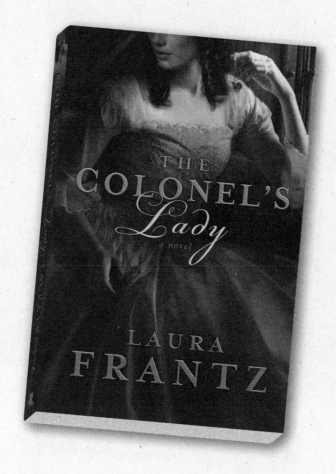

In 1779, a search for her father brings Roxanna to the Kentucky frontier—but instead she discovers a young colonel, a dark secret. . . and a compelling reason to stay.

Journey into the
Heart of the West

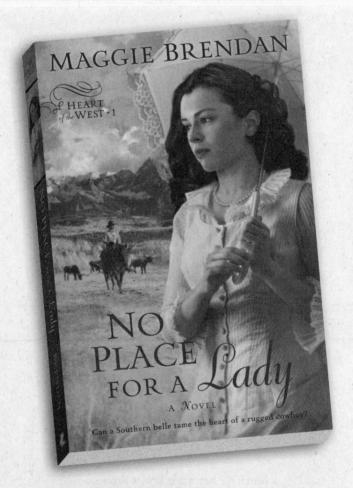

Can a southern belle tame the heart of
a rugged cowboy?

Revell
a division of Baker Publishing Group
www.RevellBooks.com

Sweet Romances
That Capture the Heart

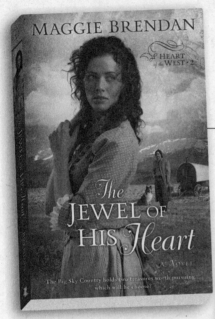

The Big Sky Country holds two treasures worth pursuing. . . which will he choose?

Her father's money could buy her anything except true love.